THE
WILDEST RIDE

For a full list of books by Marcella Bell,
visit her website at www.marcellabell.com.

THE
WILDEST RIDE

MARCELLA BELL

HQN®

Recycling programs
for this product may
not exist in your area.

ISBN-13: 978-1-335-77322-7

The Wildest Ride

This edition published by arrangement with Harlequin Books S.A.

For questions and comments about the quality of this book, please contact us
at CustomerService@Harlequin.com.

HQN
22 Adelaide St. West, 40th Floor
Toronto, Ontario M5H 4E3, Canada
www.Harlequin.com

Printed in U.S.A.

To Josh.

For late nights on swings and walking along the Seine.
Thank you for never letting me give up.
You are the seed of everything wonderful in my life.

THE
WILDEST RIDE

1

On their own, the sheep weren't that bad. It was the goats that were the problem. They gave the sheep ideas.

And what the hell sheep needed with ideas, Lilian Island did not know.

The dogs, Oreo and Carrot, had gone in opposite directions, each pulling wide to flank the scattered sheep on the left and right while Lil and her horse harried them from behind. As they picked up speed, her heart caught the rhythm of her horse's hooves thundering against the ground as they chased the lead ewe together, two beings becoming one in motion.

The wind whipped across the shaved sides of her head, drowning out all other sounds beneath its gusty whoosh. It deposited traces of prairie dust in the loosely braided column of black hair that trailed back along the center of her head to hang down the midpoint of her spine.

Lil transferred the reins to her left hand in order to wrap

them around the pommel of her saddle, steadying herself with her thighs as she did.

With her right hand, she reached for the rope coiled at her hip.

Her tornado-gray eyes, both narrowed beneath two thick black eyebrows, locked on the sheep like a missile on target.

Woman and horse flanked the sheep. Lil uncoiled the rope with a snap of her wrist while releasing the pommel with her other hand, letting her body tilt down the side of the horse until she was level with their quarry.

This close, she recognized the sheep as BB, or Bossy Betty, the herd's matriarch.

It just went to show: a fierce woman could be counted on to keep everybody in line, but watch out when they got wild.

Lil surprised herself by laughing out loud as she leaped from the side of her horse to tackle the sheep. Catching three of its legs in her left hand, she quickly roped them off with her right.

She might not be quite as fast as she once was, but there was no denying she still had it.

After a few half-hearted attempts at resistance, BB heaved a huge sigh and slumped against the ground. To the tune of the occasional disgruntled bleat, Lil freed the defeated but unharmed animal.

She made the rope into a makeshift lead and tied the wayward leader to her saddle, giving her a consolation pat along the way, making a mental note to tell Piper that the herd was coming due for shearing.

Still smiling, Lil said to the sheep, "Inconvenient, BB, but it's been a long time since I did any mutton bustin'." With a final pat and chuckle, she added, "A damn long time."

The lingering rush of the chase was familiar—once it got you, the thrill of the ride never really let go—but the wish to do it again, that was unexpected.

She was a grown woman, well past her rodeo days.

Sharp barking approaching from her right signaled that Carrot and Oreo were on their way back with the rest of the flock.

Soon they would have the whole herd of them back in the yard, and then Lil could start her actual workday.

Feeding the barn stock was supposed to be her meditative morning ritual.

One that might need reconsideration, she thought as she hooked a foot into her stirrup and swung onto her horse.

The horse was the same stormy gray color as Lil's eyes, with a black mane and tail matched to the inky midnight tone of Lil's hair. Fanciful, Lil had named her Aurora, the most beautiful thing she could think of at the time, but everybody called her Rory.

Rory had been Lil's twenty-fifth birthday present from her granddad. The last one he ever gave her.

Leaning forward, she pressed the side of her face against Rory's warm neck, breathing deep that unique-in-all-the-world scent that was horse.

Oreo and Carrot brought in the remaining six sheep, and Lil led the group back toward the yard.

The coyotes could have the goats for all she cared. They had been the ones to open the fence.

She turned to Oreo, on her left. "With my luck, they would just eat the coyotes, and then we'd still have the stupid things, plus an enormous vet bill, to boot."

Oreo gave a cheerful whuff, and Lil tried not to wonder what it meant that the response satisfied her.

Lil led the sheep and dogs back into the barnyard and tied the gate shut with the backup rope. The broken lock needed replacing—another task she added to her mental list. Once a goat figured out the mechanism, you had to get a whole new style lock.

Shaking her head, she unsaddled Rory, brushed the horse down, gave her a pat of hay, and tossed her a handful of oats.

Wrapping up her morning routine, Lil spread feed out in the yard for the chickens. They'd eat bugs and other bits around the farmhouse throughout the day, but it was always a good idea to start the day with a hearty breakfast. Besides, there was comfort in the action of spreading feed, especially after the chaotic morning.

The familiar action finally brought her heart some of the calm she typically found in doing the morning chores. She might spend her days chained to a desk running the business end of things, but she was still a hands-on rancher at heart.

The chickens settled into contented clucking and rooting just in time for Lil to hear her grandmother shriek from the kitchen.

Lil was across the yard in four seconds, up the stairs, and into the kitchen in another two.

Her eyes and muscles worked faster than her mind. Before she knew what she was doing, her rope was out, its tail end lashing out to snake around the delicate wrist of the arm raised against the woman who had raised her.

A flick of Lil's wrist and the stranger—a woman, after a second more processing—flipped into the air before landing hard on her back on the kitchen floor.

"Lil." Gran's voice was cross.

Lil crossed the kitchen in three strides, crouched at the stranger's side, and rolled her over.

The woman's face had gone pale and sweaty, all the more unfortunate for being paired with a green three-piece skirt suit with a little too much square in the shoulders. She was probably in her midforties and had a tight perm shorn close to her head. Based on the faint traces of grow-out, the woman was a natural sensible brown that she had dyed an even more sensible brown.

Lil considered the woman for a second longer before saying casually, "I could shoot you, you know." Granddad had always said calm was scarier. "You're in my home, uninvited, and this is Oklahoma."

"Lil." Gran's voice turned up a notch, breaking through the cold rage in her mind. "Apologize."

Lil's chin angled up, and her heels dug down. "I'm not saying sorry to this stranger. She was about to hit you."

Gran's face cracked with a smile that had a hint of bite in it. She patted the front pocket of her apron before pulling out her mace key chain. It was the color of a purple highlighter. "I might have said a few provoking words about her mother… But that's beside the point. I had the situation under control. I've got my mace. Carry it everywhere since Granddad passed."

Lil groaned, her mind filled with images of Gran spraying innocent fools in the face, all of which were more comfortable than knowing that carrying mace around was just another sign that Gran felt a little less safe in the world without Granddad around.

"Gran. You know that doesn't make you any safer. And were you planning to wait until after she hit you to use it?"

The woman cleared her throat, the disapproving sound instantly transporting Lil back in time to her second grade teacher's class, Mrs. Donkin. Students in Mrs. Donkin's class were guests in her realm and were expected to act accordingly.

Lil hadn't liked the sound coming from her teacher, and she certainly didn't like it coming from a stranger in her own kitchen.

"I'm with the Bank of—"

Lil cut her off with a raised hand. "We all know you're from the bank—" There were certain professions a person couldn't hide, no matter how hard they tried—cops, bankers, lawyers, teachers, pastors, and cowboys—each one was obvious a mile away. "As modern bankers aren't known for door-to-door recruitment, it then seems pretty safe to assume you're from the bank we do business with, the Bank of Muskogee. Now, we don't have much in our accounts, so we wouldn't be the kind of clientele they'd send a representative out all this way to for a friendly check-in. That means you're here about our larger investment, this ranch. I run the books here, so I can think of a whole host of reasons you might be interested in paying us a visit regarding the ranch. What I can't think of, though, is a single damn reason you would be in my kitchen, in my home, lifting a hand to my grandmother. I find that so stupefying that it seems only natural to assume you're capable of anything, moving me toward my only recourse—*the use of force to protect myself from attempted injury.*"

The woman huffed at Lil's words but refrained from commenting until she'd risen to her feet, straightened her skirt, dusted off her suit jacket, and patted her hair.

Then she said, "I *am* with the Bank of Muskogee, and Miss Lilian—I assume you are the Miss Lilian described in my file—I would be happy to explain myself to the authorities, including how you assaulted me, so go ahead and call them." She had patted her file when referencing it and now stood tapping her foot on the tile flooring. Lil and Granddad had spent weeks one achingly hot summer installing the incredible discontinued turquoise tile. Gran had gotten them for a steal, importing them direct from a Jamaica-based tile maker she'd met in an online forum about beading. The labor had been hard, the result worth it. No one else in Muscogee had a kitchen floor like Gran's, which was just how she liked it.

The woman's tapping was becoming irritating, so Lil smiled

her mean smile and said, "Nobody said anything about calling anybody. I rather think I'd drive leisurely down to the
station to let everyone know what happened after-the-fact if
you understand what I'm saying."

The woman's mouth made a little O of outrage, and she
clutched her file in front of her. "I assure you, I will make a
note of this hostility in my file."

Lil rolled her eyes before crossing her arms in front of her
chest. "What're you here for?"

The woman lifted her nose in the air. "As I was getting to
before your grandmother verbally attacked me—"

Lil let out a low growling noise, and the woman stopped
talking to take an audible gulp.

"As. I. Was. Saying. The Bank of Muscogee sent me to deliver the news that your bereavement grace period has ended.
I am also to remind you that, as per the terms of the agreement, you, the heirs of Herman Island, may, without a down
payment, begin making adjusted mortgage payments beginning November of this year. Alternatively, with a new down
payment, an adjusted payment set at a rate equal to that of the
average final six payments of the previous mortgage is available to you. If none of those options are feasible, you are free
to leave the ranch and all of its associated troubles—my file
indicates difficulties securing improvement permit approv-
als and equipment rentals, as well as challenges with making
timely mortgage payments—to the bank."

"Now, what nonsense are you talking about?" Lil asked,
eyebrows and nose screwed up in genuine bewilderment.
"That file of yours might paint a part of the picture true, but
without a doubt, this ranch has one thing going for it, and
that's the fact that it's paid for."

The woman shook her head, the movement mechanical like
a clock, her expression a blend of smug and pleased that Lil's

mind immediately coined *smleased*. "Not for the last six and a half years since your grandfather walked through the doors of the central street branch and applied for a reverse mortgage."

"What?" Lil's mouth dropped open this time. "You mean those things sleazy banks use to prey on lonely old folk without kin?"

The woman had the gall to look affronted. "Reverse mortgages are an important mode of financial freedom for seniors without traditional options!"

Lil shook her head, amazed. The woman moved like a clock and spoke with all the heart of a robot. "You're telling me that the Bank of Muscogee somehow fooled my granddad into signing his land away?" Heat built in her chest, making its way upward toward her neck and face.

"The Bank of Muscogee was merely the facilitator. Your grandfather walked in, submitted the appropriate paperwork, and walked out with 1.2 million dollars."

Lil laughed. "$1.2 million? Lady, you had me going. You truly did. But you lost me at 1.2 million dollars. I spent nearly every day of the last two years of his life with my granddad. If he'd have had a million dollars, I would have known about it."

Gran, having been quietly observing the exchange, chose the moment to reenter the conversation. "She's telling the truth, Lil."

Lil's head whipped around to face her gran. "That's crazy, Gran. Where'd the money go if he did it?"

"I found the money."

All the heat building inside abandoned Lil as swiftly as it'd arrived, leaving her shivering in the morning warmth of the kitchen.

"He set up a separate account. Most of it's gone. Spent on the ranch before you go worrying," Gran said, looking severe and firm. "Your granddad was a good man. I haven't worked it all out yet, but the secret was his only sin."

Some of the tightness left Lil's chest at her gran's words, but she mumbled, "It's a big enough sin."

"Lilian Island, I'll not have you speaking ill of the dead."

"How could he have done this?"

For a moment, it was as if the bank representative had disappeared, and it was just the two of them, a bewildered granddaughter trying to understand the world from her weary widowed grandmother.

Gran shook her head, the motion small for all the volumes it spoke. "He must have had a good reason."

The woman from the bank cleared her throat. "Yes. Well. Your grandfather's motivations notwithstanding, it is my task to get your signature on this paper, which states I've informed you of the terms of the reverse mortgage." She held up a mul-tipage form, the top few pages folded back to reveal a signature line at the base of a long page, which she jabbed with a finger Lil knew had done more than its fair share of pointing.

Gran's eyebrow ticked up, and Lil's stomach tightened on reflex—years spent under the woman's watchful eye had taught her to be wary of that look.

Gran was irritated and through with the woman's presence in her kitchen.

Without speaking a word, with barely even a glance in the woman's direction, Gran's arm flashed out and signed the paper, the whole motion eerily like the one she had so often reached back and used to smack some sense into her old fool cowboy of a husband.

Lil wondered if the millions of tiny memories she stumbled into each day on the ranch would always hurt. This deep into them with no sign of abating, she'd nearly reconciled herself to the fact that chances were they would.

On a groan, Lil said, "Gran, you can't just sign like that. You didn't even look at the document."

The bank woman virtually salivated. "Thank you, Mrs. Island. I'm sure the bank will be pleased with your response."

Gran scoffed, still not looking at the woman. "I'm sure they will be SherriDawn Daniels, but, as I was saying before you so rudely lost your temper after I invited you into my home, it won't get you any closer to knowing who your real daddy is."

Lil grimaced, and SherriDawn—old enough to be Lil's mother and who had, according to Gran, been one of the wild girls Lil's mother had palled around with as a teen—actually growled.

Lil's hand tensed at her side, ready to repeat the scene from earlier if need be.

But this time SherriDawn held her temper, instead, plastering a broad smile on her face, saying through clenched teeth, "I'll just be on my way, now, Mrs. Island. It was nice seeing you again."

Gran cackled. "Don't you lie to me, SherriDawn. I've seen right through you since you were fifteen years old, and don't pretend like it isn't true."

The growling sound moved lower down into her throat, but this time SherriDawn took the wise course: she shut her mouth, clasped her briefcase, and swiveled narrowly to the door.

Watching her walk away, so prim and proper that it seemed anally uncomfortable, it was hard to imagine SherriDawn might have been wild enough to ride with her mother. In Lil's mind, her mother represented all that was wild and dangerous, as well as what happened when you chased after it. She'd been wild enough to run around and have herself a baby by a mystery man she refused to name at sixteen. Wild enough to run off and never come back, leaving that baby to be raised by her grandparents.

SherriDawn didn't seem like she had the balls for all of that.

After the door slammed shut, the old screen let to fall without care by SherriDawn on her way out, Gran gathered herself with a shuddering breath, which she then let out on a long theatrical sigh.

Lil's Spidey senses tingled.

Given what Gran already seemed to know about things, the whole scene with SherriDawn now seemed put on. And Gran's long sigh was telling. That meant that all of it—goading the bank woman, the dramatic reveal, perhaps even the sheep and the goats, now that Lil was thinking about it—was part of one of Gran's plots then.

If she knew her gran, and she did like the back of her hand, this one would be related to the reverse mortgage but would be no less outrageous for being grounded in their real problems.

Gran put on a sober look before sighing. "Everyone ought to be here—I only want to say this once." Then she opened her mouth and hollered at the top of her considerable lungs, "PIPER! TOMMY!"

Piper, their petite red-haired farmhand, came running in first, clearly having grabbed the closest thing at hand to use as a weapon if needed—a horseshoe.

Tommy, Lil's live-in cousin from Granddad's side, had a rifle.

Steady, dependable, Tommy.

"What's going on?" they asked in unison.

"You're all going to want to sit down for this," Gran said with an arm toward the kitchen table and more weariness in her voice than the unveiling of a scheme usually allowed.

Following her grandmother's gesture, Lil noticed for the

first time the plaid thermos of coffee that sat in the center of the round table.

It wasn't the new stainless steel one.

Gran had taken out the plaid one. She reserved the plaid thermos for tough conversations.

Four chairs sat around the table, each with an empty coffee mug in front of it.

Lil's seat, where she sat now that she knew what was going on, was the east point of the compass of their table.

Gran sat in the north, Tommy the south, and Piper the west.

Granddad had always been in the northeast, a steady anchor between Gran and Lil.

Without him, they held each other as best they could, but both had become more prone to drifting.

Gran waited for everyone to pour a cup before she spoke. "I'll start with the good news. We have each other. We have our stock, and, for the moment, we have the land."

"Not a promising start, Gran," Lil observed.

"It is when it might be all we've got," Gran said simply. "Unbeknownst to me, Granddad took a reverse mortgage on the ranch in the years before he died. I received a letter informing me of this in the mail last week."

Lil frowned. That Gran had sat on information this critical for a week settled about as well as lemon juice in cream.

Gran continued, "After some digging, what I can piece together is this: about five years ago, Granddad lost the Wilson drive contract."

Lil shook her head. "That's impossible. He went right up until he died. That's half the reason he got sick in the first place."

Gran placed a hand on Lil's wrist, just below where the hand attached to it had clenched into a fist.

Gran, never one to pull her punches, said, "He didn't go. He kept a separate bank account for the money, and he tracked his expenses. He spent the time in Tulsa at a hotel renting movies and ordering room service." A half smile broke through the frustration. "Greedy old cuss."

But it wasn't an endearing foible to Lil's frame of mind. He had lied to them, and, in his own words, like all lies, it had spiraled into an avalanche of deceit.

"In the agreement, he included a provision to give us extra time before we had to make a decision, but that time is up. We have sixty days to come up with a down payment for the ranch, following which the bank will establish monthly mortgage payments. Every way I've looked at it, it's our only option. We would never be able to afford the payment the bank offered without the down payment. But nobody is going to evict us from land my husband's family has held on to, hardscrabble as it's been, through hell on earth." The last she directed specifically to Lil and Tommy. Through their granddad's line, Tommy and Lil were Muscogee Creek Freedmen, the descendants of enslaved people under the double burden of being property during the relocation and later forced removal of the Muscogee from their homelands in the southeast. And after the tribe disenrolled the freedmen in the seventies, their citizenship revoked in a blow her granddad had never quite recovered from, this land, this dry patch of Oklahoma allotted to their family after the Civil War—insignificant dust mote of a ranch that it was—was the only proof they had left, the only hint as to how their family had ended up in Oklahoma in the first place. Tearing folks from their history was one of the ways to break them, so Lil's family had held on to theirs through their land—through cultural hostility, the dust bowl, outright deception, attempts to steal, and everything else that time and life had thrown their way.

They had refused to sell even when their neighbors, cousins, and relatives packed up and left, seeking the green of other pastures and the heat of other suns. The Islands had stuck it out, and the reward was being able to say they'd held on to the first and only thing they'd ever been given.

Until now.

Lil was glad she had taken Gran's advice to sit down. The floor had become somewhat less substantial beneath her boots.

It occurred to her that they were nice boots. She could probably sell them for some quick cash. It wouldn't be anywhere near enough if what she thought might be true was true.

Sixty days wasn't enough time at all. Lil frowned. They had a cash reserve of five thousand to keep them and the stock fed through a pinch, and they had the value of their stock itself, which could bring in another eighty thousand in a quick sale at auction, but as far as she knew, they didn't have any other assets.

Her 1980s Toyota was too beat-up to be worth anything, and she didn't own any personal items of value.

Finally, she found her voice. "But why would Granddad do something like that?"

Gran sighed. "I don't think that he could admit he was too old to do it all himself anymore. Looking at his paperwork, in addition to withdrawing the amounts it took to look like he'd still been going on the drives, it looks like he'd been dipping in those funds rather liberally."

"Rory…" Lil grimaced. She had wondered where he'd scrounged up the money for a papered Arabian filly.

Now she knew.

Gran nodded. "And Gorgeous," she said, referring to the brand-new Subaru station wagon that sat in her driveway, souped-up with every safety and luxury feature available.

Lil brought her fingers to her temples and rubbed. "So how much is left in his secret pot, then?" she asked.

Gran shook her head. "Just ten thousand."

"What?" Lil gasped.

Whining wasn't her usual way, but, as the woman from the bank had gone, and there was no one left to throttle, it was the only option available.

"Don't be theatrical." Gran's comment was automatic, so much so that Lil wasn't even sure the woman noticed she'd made it, nor that, as far as statements went, it was the pot calling the kettle. "They want twenty percent for the down payment. We don't have that."

Lil groaned. "Nor enough for the mortgage payments after that. We're barely making it by as is." Lil couldn't tell the truth: they weren't making it. She had been contemplating selling equipment to stretch the final distance to make ends meet. Every month it was a struggle, but Lil had been somehow managing, just eking it out of the red. A mortgage payment, any mortgage payment, would break them.

Gran waited a beat after Lil's interruption, punctuating the unspoken admonishment with a lifted eyebrow and communicating clearly without words: *Are you done yet?*

Lil blushed.

"But—" Gran continued. "We have each other. And we have Lil."

The way her gran said her name made the hair stand up on the back of her neck, but when she opened her mouth to question, her grandmother lifted her palm to her, a signal to Lil to hold her tongue.

Out of respect, she did.

"Lil. You're on temporary reassignment."

"What are you talking about?" Lil asked.

"I'm the owner, aren't I?" she asked.

"Yes, but we agreed that I was in charge of daily operations."

"I've changed my mind."

"Gran."

"I can do your job. Nobody but you can do what we need you for now."

Here was the plot, then. Lil's skin crawled with a warning, but she asked anyway, "And what is that?"

Gran handed her a glossy quarter sheet flyer in response. Lil read the largest print and then set it facedown on the table and brought her fingers to her temples.

Gran's voice was soft when she next spoke. "We need the money, Lil. I don't see any other way."

Lil groaned.

Gran added, "You're the best there's ever been."

The old woman wasn't pulling any punches.

Lil's voice flirted with the edge of hysteria. "Says a nobody's grandma with a stopwatch and pasture."

"'Nobody's grandma?' Excuse you." She pointed to the third line of the flyer. "Did you see the prize? There are no points required, just a qualifier. It's part of the whole thing. Like *American Idol*."

Lil went ahead and dove fully into hysteria. When she spoke, her voice squeaked high to low like a pubescent boy. *"American Idol?"*

Gran's next words had the same effect as being hit by a bucket of cold water: "You could ride a bull."

Lil's body froze and tingled at the same time.

She hadn't stepped foot in an arena in years and had never competed in a PBRA-sponsored rodeo.

She had walked away a junior champion and ridden pro a few times in the Indian National Rodeo rodeos. Still, the world of rodeo mostly had forgotten about her—except for the few administrators who would always remember her as the girl who had tried and failed, over and over, to get women into the

PBRA's, the Professional Bull Riders Association, rough stock events. Because in Lil's mind, what did it matter if she won every other event if she couldn't win on the back of a bull?

She was skilled enough to have made a good living between women's events in the PBRA and the Indian rodeos, but if she couldn't ride a bull under the banner of PBRA, she didn't want any of it.

So she rode for a college scholarship and then quit when she graduated instead. And then she'd come back to the ranch. End of story. And that was good enough for her.

Since her retirement, rodeo had opened up a lot, and she was happy for the younger generation. A handful of girls had even been allowed on top of bulls. None had made it far, but Lil knew it was only a matter of time.

She shook her head with a sigh. "I can't, Gran. I'm rusty as an old nail, and there's just too much to do around here. Besides, the ranch is too much for Tommy and Piper to run on their own."

Gran snorted. "You work in the office most of the day, anyway."

"Gran, you don't have the energy for it," Lil insisted.

"Energy? Hell, after more years of doing it than you've been alive, I could do the ranch's books half asleep—and have! I just let you take over because it's a snoozefest."

"Snoozefest? Gran, do you hear yourself?" Lil turned to Piper and Tommy for help. "You don't support this, do you?"

Both shrugged.

Piper said, "We trust Gran."

Gran crossed her arms in front of her chest and lifted a brow. "*They* trust me."

"It's a lot more work," Lil tried.

Tommy said, "We've been doing more and more of it while you've been up there pinching pennies."

Lil's cheeks heated, but she didn't contradict him. He and Piper had been pulling more and more of her weight as she tried to do the impossible.

The impossible that she wasn't very good at. The impossible that Gran could do in her sleep—which was true. Gran ran a tight ship, whatever ship she came to, and she had been far more organized in running Swallowtail Ranch than Lil could ever hope to be.

They had supported her through the last sad and stumbling years. Participating in this crazy scheme was what they were asking of her in return.

Mentally sweating, Lil pushed her chair back, its legs screeching across the floor, and stood up. Turning around, she headed to the door without saying another word.

"Where are you going, Lilian?" Gran only used her full name when she got stern.

Lil stopped midstep. "I'm going to clear out my desk," she said.

Behind her back, Gran smiled. Lil didn't have to see it to know it was true. Gran always smiled when she got what she wanted, and she always got what she wanted.

"Don't worry about that now. You've got training to do. Gotten a bit out of shape, if you ask me."

Piper erupted in a fit of witchy cackles as Lil stormed out of the kitchen. Ignoring them all, Lil went to her office.

On the second floor of the farmhouse, the room used to be her gran and granddad's bedroom, but she and Gran had turned it into the office after he passed. Gran said she couldn't bear to sleep in there alone.

It made a lovely office—wide and bright, with delicately framed French doors that led to a weight-bearing balcony. Weight-bearing because Lil's summer project last year had been to reinforce the support beams, replace the decking, and weather coat the whole thing.

She figured that should get her five years' worth of good use of Muskogee's extreme annual mood swings before she'd need to do any repairs. That is if she kept up on refinishing it every year, which she had planned to, since walking out on the balcony had preserved her sanity after a long stint of pushing paper many a time.

She walked through the doors and stood there now, enjoying it while she could still call it hers. There were bills to pay, orders to fulfill, and emails to respond to, but that wasn't her job now. Now her job was to enter a rodeo contest and try to win some money to save the ranch.

And to think she'd thought the goats were bad.

2

"Read it again." AJ Garza ground the words out between gritted teeth, his shoulder burning like it did every time he gripped his riggin' these days.

Claudio sighed but read aloud from the glossy quarter sheet ad he held. "'The PBRA Closed Circuit Tour, a rough stock rodeo unlike any other, kicks off this June. This is a tournament-style traveling rodeo with a one-million-dollar cash prize. The PBRA Closed Circuit is a testament to God's greatest battle: man versus nature—or in this case, man versus the rankest bulls on earth! The final three cowboys will compete for the million-dollar prize. For the grand finale, each cowboy goes up against a never-been-beaten man killer. But don't worry, folks, to show that these cowboys are a match for any set of horns, each rodeo on tour features a different set of special challenges—including unpredictable untried bulls, fresh-caught mustangs, and more! You've heard of reality TV. Well, this is *Rodeo TV*, folks. Fans will get to know every cowboy through in-depth interviews, candid videos, and special VIP events! Follow along from start to finish and get a chance to get up close and personal with your favorite. The PBRA Closed Circuit, where reality TV meets the rodeo.'"

"How long?" he grunted.

"Twenty-five seconds, on the highest setting," he said. "You can probably get off now."

Judging from the way the younger man drummed his fingers against his thigh, Claudio Ramiro, CityBoyz's under-the-table, on-again, off-again office manager, was getting tired of counting seconds. He was supposed to be stuffing the emergency closure notice letters at his desk—the job for which he was on-again.

"Nope. Keep going. This old thing is at least five times slower, dumber, and weaker than every dick of a bull I've ever been on," AJ grunted while thrashing and jerking wildly atop the aging mechanical bull.

"So The Old Man's got you riding dick again, AJ? I heard you guys needed money, but that's extreme..." A sardonic voice sliced through the noise of the robotic bull.

The unexpected arrival of Diablo Jones, the best friend he had ever had, didn't throw AJ off the bull.

That he stood next to The Old Man did.

It'd been three years since he'd seen either man in the flesh.

AJ tucked and rolled as he flew off the bull, landing flat-assed on the mat, winded, his ears full of the music of a machine that needed oil.

The Old Man was not due in the office for a few more hours. But here he was, which meant AJ was caught.

"Hello, Alonso." Henry Bowman had a baritone rumble that had only deepened with age, like expensive whiskey. The sound of it in person, instead of a thin and distant thing over a weak signal across an ocean, hooked into the center of AJ's chest.

Lying on a wrestling mat looking up at The Old Man's shadowed face against the backdrop of a ceiling was as familiar to him as the smell of leather.

A grin spread across AJ's face, revealing a set of dimples and two rows of relatively straight pearly whites with what he liked to think was a charming chip in his front tooth. Even though the smile was for The Old Man, he spoke to Diablo when he said, "The stubborn old coot left me no choice. He wouldn't take my money."

Henry ignored the two younger men, instead pointing out the painfully obvious: "You're too old for this."

The Old Man had a reputation for telling it like it was. Why would that be any different today than it had been fifteen years before when he'd stood over AJ after he'd been thrown the first time?

Back then, he'd said: *You let the bull win.*

Henry offered a hand.

Today, AJ accepted it.

It was damn good to see the man. His bald head gleamed from a fresh razor and oil, his rich dark brown skin betraying only about fifty of his sixty-four years—even with a salt-and-pepper beard.

Like all riders, Henry had received his share of unintended cosmetic surgery over the years: a bit of eyebrow lost forever, a nose with a few additional curves, a slight droop to the left eye. Time had lightened the charcoal gray of his eyes, but AJ doubted that even death would dim their lightning.

Henry Bowman was an old-school cowboy, a man who had run cattle when there was still a use for it, learning the tricks of the trade on the range rather than in a rusty Houston gym like AJ and Diablo. Henry had been the second Black cowboy to win the PBRA world championship and the first to bring in over a million in prize money. In his heyday, no one had called him The Old Man. They called him Black Butter.

The name, thankfully, didn't last.

His reputation as the smoothest ride in the history of the PBRA did. Not even AJ could match him there.

AJ tilted his head toward Diablo before asking The Old Man, "Devil drag you in?"

Henry shook his head with a smile. "Nope. Claudio called me this morning," he said, tipping his hat in Claudio's direction.

Claudio held up the stopwatch. "30.09 seconds."

The time wasn't good enough, but AJ held back his grimace. Henry was right—he was old. Six years ago, he'd have clocked twice that, distractions and all, and with a lot less pain. Returning The Old Man's smile and adding a shrug, AJ said, "I'll fire him later."

"You can't fire him," Henry said. "He doesn't work for you."

"Can too. He's here on my dime this morning."

Henry started, "Now, AJ…"

AJ raised his hands. "I know, I know, I know. You don't want me 'wasting any money in this sinking ship,' but seeing as he's here timing me, it made sense he's working for me. Besides, this was the only place I could think to go."

"Something wrong with the equipment at your ma's?" The knowing warmth in Henry's eyes took any bite out of the words.

AJ smiled. "She might catch me…" It wasn't a lie.

Henry shuddered. He had gone his own rounds with Meredith Garza, and he wasn't inclined to repeat. He said, "Diablo tells me there's a bit of nonsense at play."

AJ shrugged. "Well, I don't know about all that."

"You're coming out of retirement?"

AJ didn't miss the way both men's eyes latched onto him

like hawks eyeing a mouse. Each would scrutinize every element of his response, so he hedged.

"Temporarily."

"AJ. Anything you win is still your money. I won't take it."

"Not technically."

Lawyer's ears piquing, Diablo said, "What do you mean, 'not technically'?"

"Technically, CityBoyz is the entrant…"

Henry sighed. "And how did an after-school boys program enter a rodeo as a contestant?"

"Email. And we're not in yet," he said, his dimple flashing again. "We've got to qualify first."

The corner of Diablo's wide mouth lifted. "I take it the PBRA Closed Circuit 'rodeo-like-no-other' was open to the idea of the great AJ Garza coming out of retirement to sponsor an imploding charity?"

The Old Man flinched. The move was minuscule. AJ only saw it because he was looking so closely.

He might try to hide it, but Henry was ashamed of what was happening to CityBoyz.

A frown drifted across AJ's eyes, though he kept it from his face, answering Diablo's question with a slight smirk. "They've included it in their newest ad…"

Henry muttered, "I'll just bet. Now, you know this isn't necessary, AJ. You've only just got back. I talked to Diablo in the hallway. What we'll do is shut down and regroup, go through and do it proper. Got our Devil out here all the way from Phoenix. He's going to get us proper nonprofit status so we can apply for real grants. There's no need for all this foolishness." Henry gestured toward the bull and Claudio and the stopwatch. "You're closer to forty than twenty."

AJ brought a hand to his heart. "You're shooting to kill there."

"A bull's going to end up killing you. I'm trying to make you see some sense."

AJ gestured toward Diablo with his thumb. "This guy charges an arm and a leg, and it will take you a good year to get enough funding from grants. If I win, CityBoyz will have enough to get through this year and make it through until the donations start coming in—without sending out those letters."

"You know I'd never charge The Old Man… I have a required amount of pro bono work to do after all," Diablo said, pretending to be dry and uninterested when he would gladly lay down his life for The Old Man.

Henry sighed, closed his eyes, and rubbed his temples. The bull whirred.

No one spoke until he said, "Did you tell your ma?"

AJ's grin faltered, and he looked away. "Not yet."

Henry's voice steeled. "No."

AJ's grin returned. "It's a good idea. We might even get some donations coming in faster just by putting the story out. That means money coming in before they even start handing out buckles."

Henry closed his eyes and sucked in a heavy breath.

AJ held his breath, hoping The Old Man would let him take over some of the weight.

When Henry opened his gray eyes again, they were clear and calm. To Claudio, he said, "Claudio, there's better things for you to be doing with your time here than this. We haven't even opened those accounts since your last shift."

Claudio smiled at The Old Man's change of heart and tossed the stopwatch to AJ with a look of approval before turning back to Henry. "I'll be in the office," he said.

"I'll walk with you. Looks like we'll need to pay the web hosting after all…" The two of them left the echoing tin chamber that was the practice gym, and AJ and Diablo were alone.

Once they were out of sight, Diablo nodded toward the bull. "You going to turn that thing off?"

AJ hopped over the rope that pretended to be a fence around a pretend bull, and pressed the big red button. Then he said, "How you been?"

"Good. Phoenix is good. Practicing is good. Making money is really good."

AJ chuckled, "Sure is. Almost as good as beating a bull."

Diablo grinned. "Or burying yourself in a woman."

They clasped hands and pulled each other in for a hug before releasing with a pat on the back. It'd been too long.

"How was South America?"

"Phenomenal."

"Europe and Asia?"

"I went riding with a duchess in Yorkshire and was proposed to by a breeder in Japan."

Diablo tipped his black Stetson. "To the buckle bunnies all over the world."

"Amen, and thank the good Lord." Warmth spread through AJ's chest. He had forgotten how good it felt to be in the company of people who knew you back when.

"So when are you going to quit for real?" Diablo asked.

AJ's eyebrows came together though the smile remained. "What do you mean?"

"Well, if I recall correctly, you've spent the first three years of your retirement on a farewell world tour. Now, being back less than four days, you're finding reasons to sign up for another rodeo. Makes a man wonder how retired you want to be."

AJ looked away and pushed his hands into his pockets. He balanced his bulk on the cordon rope, adjusting his position against the low tension of the rope.

He wore a backward baseball cap—a PBRA promo hat from seven years ago—and a few days' worth of stubble.

At six feet five inches, with a broad, muscled body, a cleft chin, square jaw, creamy brown skin, deep brown half-moon eyes, and stupidly white teeth, he looked more like an underwear model than a "retired" rodeo champion.

When he turned back to Diablo, his smile was in place. "I'm retired—just doing this to help The Old Man out. I'd planned to come back and coach for him anyway. This is just a onetime thing. Then I'm out of the arena for good and on this side of the gate." He gestured with raised palms toward the space around him.

"Between the two of us, we could have guilted The Old Man into taking the money."

AJ chuckled, "You tell yourself that…"

Diablo cracked a smile. "Well, not that. But we could have hosted a fundraiser. We could have talked him around to that, at least."

Smile fading, AJ caught Diablo's black eyes. "He's too proud. Told me on the phone after one too many whiskeys that he thought it might be time just to let it lay to rest. Said he was too old. Claudio said he's got diabetes now. Said he's been doing less and less. Each year, fewer and fewer kids, things a little more run-down. He needs help—and for more than just paperwork."

Diablo held his gaze for a silent moment before saying, "He's entitled to his rest."

The other man had kept his voice low, forcing AJ to listen close. It was a courtroom trick.

They knew all of each other's tricks.

"No one denies that," AJ said.

"But?"

"I don't think this is the way he wants it to end."

A pause, then, "He wants…or you?"

AJ let out a laugh that was really a groan. What was family for if not to push you through uncomfortable truths? And Diablo was family, by heart, if not by blood.

They'd been brothers since their first day at CityBoyz.

AJ had been there because his dad had just died, and his mom needed a safe place for an angry boy. If Meredith Garza needed something, she got it, and in this case, it was an after-school rodeo program for inner-city youth. But even missing his dad and looking to hurt things outside as much as he hurt inside, AJ was no match for Diablo.

And neither of them was a match for Henry.

Diablo was at CityBoyz by court order. His nana had pleaded with the judge and promised to take him in hand. She'd been at a loss as to how to do that until she'd met Henry at the grocery store. Fortunately, the judge, an old white hair with deep Texas roots, thought rodeo was just the thing to straighten out the boy. It turned out even the most challenging kid was no match for an angry bull.

Diablo was good but hadn't taken the sport past undergrad. Back then, he said it was because he didn't want to risk his pretty face anymore. In actuality, he had found his passion in the law. But it was rodeo that had calmed him down enough to hear its siren call, then helped him pay for college, and prepared his mind and body for the rigors of law school.

It was different for AJ. He had gone pro straight out of high school. It was only after fourteen years, three world championships, and twelve million dollars that he retired. Then there was the world tour. And now, likely, two months with the Closed Circuit—barely enough time to consider it an extension.

Finally, he answered Diablo's question. "I know he doesn't want to be forced out like this. This is his life's work. What else has he got? I think he'd like to pass it on to someone."

Diablo stared at him for a moment before speaking. "Do you think you can win?"

The question brought AJ's smile back. "You doubt me?"

Diablo shrugged. "You're old."

AJ laughed, "I'm still the best there's ever been."

"Might have the biggest head there's ever been."

"Only at the tip of my dick."

Diablo's stare was as dry as a desert. "Real adult."

AJ laughed, "Go ahead and pretend you're not a filthy teenager inside. I won't tell."

Diablo ignored him. "Supporting your theory, The Old Man wants to register as an official nonprofit organization. That's why I'm out here. Told him I'd come take care of it for him."

AJ's eyebrow lifted. "Had to come out here to do it?"

It was Diablo's turn to shrug and look away. "Figured I'd see Nana while I was out."

And the rest of us, AJ realized with a start. Diablo missed them. Just like AJ had, no matter where he'd gone.

Another one of those things about family.

He asked, "How's she doing?"

"She's alright. Old. But that's no different."

"Bet she'd still slap you if she heard you say that."

Diablo nodded with rare openness in his eyes. "Oh, for sure. She might do that even after she's dead."

Their laughter echoed in the cavernous space like memories of childhood. But things were different now. Now The Old Man needed their help.

Shaking his head to himself, AJ asked, "Did you have any idea?"

"No. Everything seemed so smooth as a participant. I never wondered where the money was coming from."

"What I don't get is how this guy funded the program year after year but didn't mention it at all in his will."

Diablo gave him the side-eye. "Bet you have no idea how entitled that sounds."

AJ punched him. "Shut up. My dad's dead."

"You can't play that card anymore."

"Get back, Devil. I can play that card forever."

"Har-har. Anyway, I'm here for two weeks. Whittling away my vacation time back home working pro bono."

"You've gone noble on us."

Diablo lifted an eyebrow. "Too bad noble doesn't come with quite the luxury of the Caribbean all-inclusive I was going to take."

"You know you'll do both." A wicked glint lit AJ's eye. "Come to the qualifier. How long's it been?"

"Not long enough to get the music out of my head yet."

"You know you love it."

"I don't."

"So, you going to come?" AJ pressed.

Diablo hesitated. "Absolutely not."

"Come on. It'll be fun. The three of us together again."

"Three of us? What makes you think The Old Man will come?"

"You know he'll be there. When has he ever missed?"

"No."

AJ's grin stretched from ear to ear. "Everyone says Caribbean girls ain't got nothing on rodeo girls…"

"No one says that. I am not going to a rodeo on my vacation. Next thing, you'll want to drag me to a high school football game. There's no way in hell."

"No way in hell? Even for the Devil?"

Diablo responded in a droll voice. "My favorite thing about that joke is how it never gets old. *Evergreen*, you might say. Don't you have something to do? Something a regular adult human would be doing?"

AJ shook his head. "I'm free as a bird outside of practice.

Retirement is great." He winked, knowing it'd infuriate Diablo even more.

"Great. I'll let your mom know you have so much time on your hands."

AJ's smile disappeared. "You wouldn't."

Diablo took his phone out of his pocket and unlocked it.

"Do it, and I give Nana your regular email address."

Diablo's phone went back into the pocket. He opened his arms wide, and AJ went in for the hug. After three years on the road, it was good to be home. Even if "home" was just the house he'd bought for his mom, a rusty old gym, and a short visit from a friend.

When he'd heard CityBoyz was about to close, he hadn't thought, just acted. The old rodeo mailing lists hadn't let him down. Neither had PBRA. Why would they? His little stunt was precisely the kind of thing they were looking for for the Closed Circuit: drama—a way for the rodeo to snag the interest of those tech-addicted kids.

He didn't doubt they would arrange for it to happen that way if he couldn't make it on his own merit. The story was just too good: *AJ Garza puts off retirement to compete in the PBRA's first-ever Closed Circuit rodeo tour—for a youth rodeo charity!*

But he'd qualify. There still wasn't anybody out there who could beat him. He wasn't retiring because he was slipping. Even now, he was in a class all his own. He was just getting tired of beating himself up. He'd broken his collarbone three times, had six concussions, had his forearm crushed by a bull, dislocated his right shoulder countless times, and nearly had his head stepped on by a bronco. And he'd done it not in the name of competition but just to beat his own records.

There was no challenge in it anymore, and nobody liked a show-off, especially one that didn't know when to quit. He should be grateful he got to go out on top. Rodeo chewed most cowboys up only to spit them out broken with nothing to show.

Diablo cleared his throat. "Earth to AJ."

AJ started. "Sorry, just thinking. It's good to be back. Strange."

Diablo gave the room another three-sixty. "I know what you mean. You going to get your own place?"

"Eventually. After the circuit, now. Probably someplace nearby."

"Here? You could afford to live in Piney Point."

"What for? I'm going to be here all the time anyway."

"Why bother, then? Just stay at your mom's."

AJ laughed, "And endure the long line of friends' daughters…"

"How's that any different than the long line of bunnies and club rats?"

"Can't sleep with friends' daughters."

"Can't sleep with anybody under Meredith Garza's roof."

"More to the point."

Diablo laughed. "Like anybody wants a rodeo cowboy who lives with his mama and doesn't know how to quit anyway."

"Better that than a slick-talking Devil in a black suit."

"As always, your humor reaches the height of sophistication."

"That's your gig, man." AJ winked. "I'm just a yokel."

"Right…"

"Let's grab breakfast. You can tell me your plan, and we can talk how best CityBoyz can spend the prize money."

"You haven't won it yet, but I'll let you buy me breakfast."

"It's as good as done, and you know it. I'm the greatest bull rider there's ever been."

3

Lil stood one footed on top of a large rubber exercise ball in the center of the corral. She had been in the position for two minutes and counting. Piper, perched on the top bar of the corral, was doing the counting. She was also playing Cupcake Crush on her phone.

That was fine with Lil. Sweat beaded along her hairline and dripped down her face and nose.

Conversation was the last thing she needed.

She had drawn her focus inward, resting it in the quiet center that even a thousand pounds of raging animal couldn't shake. Her breathing was slow and even, her heartbeat steady. She was fluid and still at the same time, her standing leg faintly rolling along with the movements of the ball in order to remain centered on its top.

Piper's alarm went off, nearly startling the woman off her seat on the fence.

Lil didn't budge.

"Time to switch legs!" Piper called out once she had found her own balance.

Lil had returned from her morning training run before the sun had come up. She'd fed the farmyard animals, exercised Rory, and headed straight to the barn. It was past noon now, and she planned to stay in the barn, painstakingly scraping the rodeo rust off until well after sunset—just like she had every day for the past two weeks.

It was the training program of a champion. She knew because it was what her granddad had taught her—the same training methods and wisdom he'd applied for years himself— and he had been a rodeo wunderkind in the arena. They only had a couple of grainy and short videos of it, but no one rode like her granddad. He'd been the best of the best—a king of the rodeo world—at least in the sliver of it where he'd been free to compete.

Her granddad had been old-timer enough that trying to ride in the white rodeos as a Black and Native cowboy from Indian country would have been asking for trouble. And while he probably could have made a place for himself there, he'd never felt like he fit in at the Black rodeos. While he shared a skin tone and the experience of racism with the cowboys there, they didn't share a recent lived history and Muscogee values.

Gran walked into the stables as Lil began the slow transition from one foot to the other.

Lowering her lifted leg, mostly relying on the unshakeable balance she had been born with—"a gift," her granddad had called it—before she raised the other.

She would stand there, moving only with the gentle sway of the ball, for another three minutes, same as always—just like her granddad taught her.

Gran smiled. "Glad to see you're not sittin' on your laurels. Just got word that AJ Garza is delaying his retirement to try out."

Lil's ankle wobbled on the ball. On a deep inhale, she steadied herself to remain on the ball and opened her eyes.

"Where'd you hear that?" she asked, surefooted again. Or close. Her voice and leg were steady, but her pulse jumped.

"I read it in a headline this morning."

Lil sighed, and Piper's timer went off, once again startling the woman from her perch on the fence.

Lil hopped down from the ball and wiped her brow with the back of her hand. "Gran, this is crazy."

Task completed, Piper climbed down from the fence, her khaki shorts and green khaki steel-toed calf boots looking more appropriate for a wildlife safari than the day on the ranch she was due to start. Lil mentally rolled her eyes. Like she did with everything else, Piper would do things her way, or no way at all.

Brushing bits of fence and dust off her shorts, Piper asked, "Who's AJ Garza?"

Lil answered, "Undefeated rodeo champion. He retired three years ago and has been on a farewell world tour in Europe ever since."

Piper eyed her from the corners of her huge grass-green eyes. "You sure know a lot about him…"

Lil snorted. "He's the greatest bull rider alive." She added, "And he's half-Black, too." Lil couldn't help the glow of pride that crept into her voice.

AJ Garza had inspired a whole generation of riders like her, proving without a shadow of a doubt that grit could rule in the arena. He was a six-time Triple Crown winner, plus took top prizes at three additional PBRA world championships and had set a high score for a bull ride that had yet to be beat.

Lil sighed to Gran, "This isn't going to work. We've got to

come up with something else. If AJ Garza's involved, there's no way I'm winning."

Gran shook her head. "Nonsense. You've beaten him tons of times."

"That's at home, with you as my judge, on baby bulls they were paying us to break. Completely different. Nobody beats Garza in competition. That's the whole reason he's *AJ Garza*."

Gran tsked. "That's not true—you regularly got higher scores in the Indian rodeos you rode in. Besides, you've got no choice. We're going to lose Swallowtail otherwise."

Lil frowned. "That's exactly why we need to stop this and come up with a real plan."

Gran gave her an arch look. "*My* plan is plenty real, young lady. You don't have to win the buckle. You just have to get enough money for a down payment and a cushion to make those monthly payments. Remember how I used to tell you that there was always going to be another rodeo?"

Lil mostly recalled that Gran had seen right through her adolescent attempts to use rodeo as an excuse to get out of doing homework, but she nodded.

"Well, that's not true anymore. Not for you, and not for the ranch."

"Gran. I'm not even going to make it in. Spending money on the entry fee and travel is wasteful when money's as important as it is now."

Gran crossed her arms in front of her chest and cocked her head to the side. "If you thought you could change my mind, then why have you been practicing all this time?"

Piper chimed in, "Up and at it pretty early, too."

Gran smiled. "'Run to beat the sun and the day is yours.'"

Lil's answering smile was a small one, but enough to crack through the concrete of her face.

The phrase had been one of her granddad's favorites.

Shaking the smile off, though, she said, "Change your mind? Never. Might've been hoping you'd come to your senses." And because she couldn't help herself, she added, "It was a better idea before AJ Garza."

"I never knew you to be afraid of riding with the boys before…"

Lil's eyes narrowed. "That's low and obvious, Gran."

"Sure is."

They glared at one another until Tommy, entering the barn with a folded black bundle, coughed. "Hate to interrupt cousin Lilian making an ass of herself," he said, "but I've got the thing, Gran."

Gran's entire demeanor changed. Her attention zeroed in on the bundle and her shoulders lifted, chest filling with air, eyes crinkling. She stretched her arms toward it. "Well, bring it over!"

Tommy and the bundle made their way to stand at Gran's right hand, a smug smile plastered on his face.

Gran took the bundle and held it up.

Then Lil's breath caught in her throat as the bundle was revealed. "Gran…" she whispered.

Gran raised an eyebrow. "Not bad if I do so say myself."

Lil's expression didn't falter though tears sprang up in her eyes. She cleared her throat before she asked, "When?"

"Took it out the same day I showed you the flyer. You missed the commotion, holed up in the office as you were. Had Tommy get up in the attic and the damn fool fell while he was up there."

Tears threatening to turn her into a soup sandwich, Lil brought a hand up to cover her mouth. "I love it."

Gran went on, ignoring the sheen of tears as she knew her granddaughter would want, "I did the beading, replaced the ribbons, and took it in a bit for you."

Lil swiped escaping tears from her cheeks with the back of a dusty hand. "It's perfect."

"You always cared about how you looked for competition."

Lil grinned and pulled her grandmother into a hug, and whispered a quiet "thanks" into the top of her short gray hair.

Gran smiled. "You're welcome, caterpillar. Time to go show off your colors."

Lil gave a sly grin. "And win some money."

Gran chuckled along with her nod, "And win some money."

Lil reached for the vest.

Eyeballing her granddaughter's hands, Gran kept hold of it, opting instead to turn it slowly so Lil could see the whole thing.

The design was simple: a black leather vest with fresh darts sewn into the back so she could wear it without looking like a child in an adult-sized costume.

Dusty and grayed, permanently, she knew from the experience of having tried to buff and polish it for her granddad, it was thick and tough, intended to protect, but soft, ever willing to bend in for a hug, just like her granddad.

The back, though, that had become a thing of magnificent beauty, born again and anew through the addition of thousands of microbeads, sewn by hand to create the iridescent black, cream, blue, and rust-colored spots of a black swallowtail butterfly—Oklahoma's state butterfly, and the source of the nickname her granddad had given her and their ranch—*Swallowtail*.

He said she rode like a little butterfly landing on a flower, unconcerned and lovely.

Gran had replaced her granddad's old ribbons with new ones in colors that matched her incredible beadwork. The ribbons were sewn across the breasts on either side of the vest, as well as let to dangle freely.

The vest had been her granddad's favorite one to wear to gatherings and rodeos. The beading, a skill she learned early in her marriage to make her new husband proud, was all Gran.

By offering it to her, her grandmother was giving her something of him to take along, a way for him to ride with her. By adding the beading and new ribbons, though, Gran had given herself, as well. As always, they would be with her.

"Thank you." She sighed.

"You're welcome, dear girl. I've got one more nearly done for you—the old brown one. Did a bison theme on that one—to remind you that you're too stubborn to lose." She cackled at her own joke before slapping a hand on Lil's back. "Now get back to practice, girl. You got a whole lot more to be doing than just standing on top of a ball."

4

Two more weeks of "a lot more," and an eight-hour drive later, Lil stood outside the main gate of Houston's Blue Ribbon Arena.

She was battered and bruised—her wrists and right shoulder taped, her stomach churning.

She felt better than she had in years.

Cameras, people, and cowboys flowed in a sea all around her in varied currents, pulling in every direction.

Tailgaters filled the parking lot with grills, folding chairs, and dueling country music stations. Reporters had stationed themselves everywhere, territorial, wearing logos from ESPN, ESPN2, Fox Sports, as well as all the local stations.

Lil had never been to a rodeo with so much television coverage.

Reporters with microphones roped likely-looking cowboys wearing safety-pinned contestant numbers into interviews, as if the place wasn't crawling with hundreds more just like them.

When released, the cowboys went back to prowling around like wild dogs with nothing to do. The reporters went back to roping.

The qualifier kicked off in two hours. That gave her two hours to sign in and pick up her competitor number, before heading back to her car to gear up. She'd left the ranch with enough time to spare but not with so much that she would have a lot to kill. Less time for nerves to build.

For the qualifier, she wore her granddad's black vest, a pair of black jeans, her faded old black boots, and her junior champion buckle, the first one she ever won.

The buckle was at Gran's insistence—*for luck*.

Lil wondered if that made the T-shirt something old, then?

Now that she was out of Gran's sight, she could roll her eyes. The other kids were going to make fun of her—no buckle at all was better than wearing a youth buckle.

She had freshened the shaved sides of her head before the sun was up that morning, giving herself lightning fade lines on either side of her head for flair. The long curly hair in the middle was tightly braided into a fishtail braid that started at her hairline and ended in the middle of her back. Without a single strand out of place, the braid was a perfect replica of the fish bones it was named after. It'd only taken three tries.

Lil skipped on wearing a hat until it was required. Cowboy hats made her look like a fifteen-year-old boy playing dress-up.

It was bad enough she was compact and muscular everywhere a woman ought to be soft and round—she didn't need a hat to make her look any more like an underage male.

She didn't wear jewelry or makeup for practical reasons: makeup could drip into your eyes, and jewelry could get ripped out. Her only accessory was her rope, but that was fine. The vest was loud enough.

She left her riding gear in the car. Even at a "rodeo like no other" one typically didn't need to be in costume at the registration table.

The noise level increased the closer to the entrance she got, but she became a part of it. Rodeo was like riding a bike, something you never forgot—a symphony made up of the unintelligible stream of intercom announcements, the staccato bursts of words you wouldn't want your grandma to hear you say, clinking spurs, spit hitting solid ground, and bravado—and all of it punctuated by the muffled stampede of a thousand cowboy boots pounding dirt and pavement.

It could have been the sound of her own heartbeat.

Lil closed her eyes, a feral grin spreading across her face. She breathed deep. It was good to be home.

A reporter tapped her shoulder, killing the moment.

"You're a contestant?" the woman shouted to be heard over the blare. She had a Houston 5 badge on, salon blond hair, and shrewd brown eyes. "You look young. What's your story? Why are you competing tonight? You think you'll make it?" The woman fired questions faster than Lil could blink while her cameraman filmed.

The woman was at least a head taller than Lil, but as Lil was five-foot-two, most adults were.

Lil opened her mouth to reply. "I—"

"You getting this, Don? The kid's eighteen if he's a day."

Don grunted his confirmation as Lil started to correct the woman. Before any sound came out, though, the woman returned to the camera with, "We're outside the arena at the PBRA Closed Circuit rodeo. Dubbed the first-ever *reality rodeo show,* it's poised to change the way the world rodeos! Tonight, hundreds of young hopefuls try out for their opportunity to travel with the Closed Circuit for the next month in a tournament-style rough stock rodeo—as well as their shot at winning one million dollars! We've got one such hopeful with us now. Tell us, young man, what's your name, and how do you think you'll do out there tonight?"

The woman shoved the mic in front of Lil's mouth, and Lil found herself replying without thinking, "Lil, and I'm just looking to get a good ride out there tonight."

The mic zipped back to the reporter's very red lips, and Lil was instantly forgotten as the woman wrapped her segment.

Free once more to make her way to registration, Lil gave a nod to the cameraman and headed off. She could worry about correcting people if she made it into the competition. If not, it wouldn't matter if people thought she was a young man.

She made it another six feet before another woman with a camera caught her. This one was shorter, her brown hair cut into a sharp chin-length bob. She wore thick black-framed glasses and a bright green PBRA Closed Circuit Staff T-shirt. Holding her own camera, she had the aura of an intern.

Lil spotted a WTF bracelet, and her eyes narrowed. *A social media intern.*

"Hi there," the girl chirped brightly. "You look like you're trying out? I'm getting quick bios and shots of the cowboys trying out tonight. Mind if I take a few minutes?" she asked.

Lil shook her head. "No…"

The young woman smiled. "Great! First off, where're ya coming from?"

Lil answered, "Muskogee."

The intern smiled an icebreaker kind of smile and said, "A real live Okie from Muskogee!"

Lil returned the smile like she hadn't heard that line at every rodeo she'd ever been to in her life and said, "That's right."

"One of the unique features of the Closed Circuit is its open qualifier. That means even complete novices can try out." The young woman eyed her. "Have you ever competed in a major PBRA event before?"

Lil heaved a mental sigh at the girl's odd specificity, but her smile didn't waver. "I have not. I was a junior champion and competed professionally in the Indian rodeo circuit..." She regretted the words before they were out but couldn't take them back. It was the worst thing she could have said. She looked like she was trying to prove something. Her granddad had always said silence was the best response. Your words couldn't make a fool of you if you didn't say them.

The interviewer narrowed her eyes but retained her cheerful expression. "How old are you?"

So much for not looking like a kid trying to sit at the grown-up table.

Face carefully open, Lil said, "Twenty-seven."

As she spoke, however, a commotion erupted in the parking lot when a lifted white-and-chrome F450 pulled up and parked alongside the red curb blaring Hank Williams Jr. loud enough to drown out both the country coming from the stadium speakers and the tailgaters in the parking lot.

The vanity plates read RDO PRO1 and the windows were tinted.

Gran always said showing what you really thought on your face was inviting enemies, so Lil held back her disdain, but it was hard.

Beside Lil, the intern whispered, "That's got to be AJ."

Unimpressed as she was, Lil still leaned forward when the door cracked open, just like the girl next to her.

Everyone else did too, a strange hush settling over the crowd that had only moments before been as restless as a yard filled with horny cats.

The passenger-side door opened farther and a gleaming boot stepped down. It was chocolate-brown leather, supple, and obviously expensive. The door swung open and a sigh of disappointment rippled across the crowd.

Hank's volume lost some of its potency as people returned to what they had been doing before the truck pulled up. Lil used the intern's lingering distraction as an opportunity to slide around and get back on her way.

Hank DeRoy—the cowboy from the truck—might be a three-time second-place PBRA world champion and rodeo legend in his own right, but he was no AJ Garza.

Lil arrived at the registration table without any further interruptions, but by the time she got there, the lines that waited for her looked like they were in a competition to rival the Great Wall.

Brow creasing, Lil gauged the line's progress. It had taken her about fifteen minutes just to make it through the crowd to get to the table. It'd take at least twice that to get through the line. The amount of contestants was almost as absurd as the whole scene.

She closed her eyes, breathed deep, and focused instead on the old familiar sensations woven in among this *first of its kind* rodeo.

The smell was the same. Dirt, leather, beer, hot dogs, metal, livestock.

The cowboys were the same. Cowboys were always the same: Work hard. Play hard. Rise hard. Fall hard. Whatever you do, do it hard.

The wildness in the air was a remembered friend, as well. It was as if the energy of the stock permeated the atmosphere, bringing out a little bit of the untamed in everyone.

Even with her eyes closed, all around her, she knew that people laughed louder, drank too much, flirted, envied, dug in, grabbed on, and held on with more force and passion than they allowed themselves in their daily lives.

A thread of that wild lived in her, too—it was the part that wanted to hoot and holler and dance with a raging bull.

"Move!"

Lil's eyes shot open. The command belied the frustration of having said something more than once. She had been totally zoned out.

Ahead of her, there was a foot-and-a-half gap in the line. She whipped around and dipped her head in apology toward the disgruntled voice behind her, then hurried to close the gap.

Back in place, she laughed at herself for her beating heart. Getting spooked served her right for daydreaming on other people's time.

"You laughing at me?" The voice from behind was less commanding this time, but no less disgruntled.

Lil turned around, this time getting a better look at the speaker. He was short, for a man, but still taller than her, and at least three times as wide, a solid brick wall of muscle.

Lil held her palms up. "No, sir."

Beady black eyes glared at her from below a weathered and bushy brow, but, judging from the huff and shrug of his response, he seemed satisfied with the explanation.

She got to the table without further incident and pulled out her ID. The curly-haired blond teenager had silver tinsel and green yarn braided into her pigtails and a bright green T-shirt on. She looked up at Lil, panicked, and blurted, "You have to be at least eighteen years old to take part in the Closed Circuit qualifier."

Lil shoved the grimace deep inside and smiled instead. "Yes, miss. I've got ID to verify my age."

The girl's face transformed into a bright welcome. "Oh perfect. Thanks."

Lil handed over her driver's license and stood back.

The young woman glanced at the date and started to hand it back, but pulled it back to look again a second time.

Lil took a deep breath, heart picking up. *Here it comes…*

She and Gran had poured over the fine print. Nothing excluded women from entering, but she couldn't shake the feeling that that was a far cry from it being allowed.

Tickled surprise filled the girl's voice when she finally spoke. "So crazy! That's really your name. We thought it was some kind of stage name or something." She handed the license back without another glance at it and twisted around in her seat to pull a stapled stack of paper out of a box behind her. She trailed her finger down the list of names and, after a few pages, found Lil's name and put a checkmark by it.

That done, the girl returned to rummaging through the box until she pulled out an envelope. On top of it was a crisp set of contestant numbers.

A thrill ran up Lil's spine.

At sixteen it had been her greatest dream to be the first woman to win a PBRA championship buckle. She had given up on that dream, but the feeling that rose in her on seeing those large black numbers printed on the thick wax-coated paper made her realize it hadn't really ever died.

The registration girl leaned forward with a clipboard. "I need you to sign here, here, here, on this page, this page, and this one. Then please initial each of these statements before signing here."

Lil got to work with the pen, but stopped when someone slammed their palm against the table to her left.

A few feet away, Hank DeRoy stood in front of a trembling teenager, his palm flat and white-knuckled against the table.

"It's ridiculous that I even have to put up with this like some kind of nobody. This place is more circus than circuit." The arrogance in his tone was topped only by the angle of his nose in the air. Three shorter men made a ring around his back. They all laughed, which was the whole reason they were there.

Lil ground her teeth. This kind of nonsense was all too familiar, as well.

The rodeo veteran towered over the redheaded green-shirted teenager who huddled in her chair, her long ponytail shaking.

The girl held her ground, though, saying, "I'm sorry, Mr. DeRoy, but you have to wait in line like everyone else. That mob would kill me if I let you cut." Keeping her arms close to her body, she pointed to the line of scowling cowboys.

Her braces caught the glint of the stadium lights. She had light green rubber bands.

DeRoy smirked. "You think I'm afraid of a few no-name cowboys?"

A low growl slipped out of Lil's lips. It was too quiet for anyone else to hear, a private sign of her temper breaking its dam.

When she spoke, her voice was as low and raspy as it always was. "The young lady said *she* was scared of them—the gentlemanly thing to do is respect that."

A hush took root in the space between Lil and Hank, quickly spreading to a ten-foot radius around them.

Hank's smile twisted into a sneer as he turned to fully face Lil. "Well, what have we here?"

What Lil had was the complete focus of DeRoy, his three amigos, the girls at the registration table, and the cowboys behind them in line.

So much for keeping a low profile, she thought.

After a pretend pause for thought, one of his cronies lifted his knee to slap his thigh. "I got it, boss!"

Here we go, Lil thought. Insults that needed physical punctuation tended to blow their load early…

"We got ourselves an honest-to-God prairie n*****."

The hush around them became the quiet of the grave. Then it turned into a rippled murmur. Like a skipping stone, all around Lil whispers of the insult spread through the gathered crowd, hopping from one group to the next, travelling far and fast before sinking hard in the ears of a burly pair whose green Closed Circuit T-shirts had the word SECURITY emblazoned on them. Making their way to where the three of them stood, they stopped next to a kid and the bigger of the two crouched down beside them. After a quiet consultation, the child pointed to Hank's lackey and then the guard rose to join their partner. Both of them walked with long calm strides toward the lackey, who, of course, attempted to run. The crowd didn't let him, though, and after a brief struggle in which the lackey ridiculously tried to crawl between a security guard's legs to escape, losing his hat in the process, they gathered him up and carried him away while the crowd watched.

When they were out of sight, Hank laughed, shaking his head and tipping his hat in the direction of his fallen crony. "And that, my friends, is what I call affirmative action in action."

The blood drained from Lil's face. A strange, foamy, roar filled her ears and the storm clouds of her eyes glinted like hard flint.

Oddly, her granddad's wisdom went strangely silent in the moment. Instead, it was Piper's voice that filled her mind, an image of the redhead standing in her safari boots, hands on her hips, saying, *Oh, it's on now!*

Lil's hand inched closer to the rope at her hip. DeRoy missed the motion. He was wiping tears of laughter from his eyes. He thought he was real funny…

Her fingertips grazed rope and the corded smoothness of its surface brought with it a different voice, her granddad's.

Whatever it is, Lilian, save it for the ride.

The caution wasn't enough to stop her, not after he'd mocked the first time she'd seen that kind of justice served in an event like this, but it was enough to change her plans: instead of taking his feet out from under him like she wanted to, she merely knocked his hat off his head.

The whole thing was done in an instant. It just took a wrist-flick rope trick with just enough force to punch the hat off a damn fool's head, plus another flick for the recoil.

Again, the crowd stopped breathing.

And then everything happened at once.

DeRoy yanked a beer can from one of his cronies and hurled it at Lil's head. Lil ducked and the can crashed into the face of another baby-faced cowboy—this one wearing brand-new boots.

The young man stumbled back then stepped forward, wiped the beer off his face, lowered his head, and charged.

Lil leaped clear of his path while one of Hank's cronies pushed Hank out of the way to take the hit for him. The two men crashed into Hank's other two cronies, sending the whole bunch of them tumbling into a heap on the ground.

The cowboy that Hank had knocked into came back swinging, but Hank ducked, so the man made contact with a different bystander, who responded by throwing his own punches.

Cameras rushed toward the commotion from all directions, reminding Lil of the images she'd seen in high school of spermatozoa surrounding an egg.

The thought would have made her laugh if she weren't right in the middle of it with a brick fist barreling toward her face.

She ducked, evading it, but decided it was time to break free from the fight.

She slipped around two other brawlers unnoticed, weaving her way toward the edge of the crowd. She had nearly made it out when somebody got the bright idea to pick up somebody else and throw them at the registration tables.

By dumb luck, he crashed into the one table that didn't have high school volunteers sitting at it.

The thrown man jumped up immediately and climbed back over the table to take his turn to hit while the registration girls scattered. They fled like a panicked deer, so, of course, one of them ran straight into the fray.

Lil groaned and turned around, locking her eyes on the girl's bright green shirt.

Lil had heard that fools had special angels, and it must have been right because the girl wandered deeper and deeper into the melee without becoming a casualty to any of the wild swinging and kicking going on all around her.

Until, as if the devil had heard Lil's thoughts, the girl startled suddenly and swung right, placing herself in the path of an active fistfight.

Lil sped up, skimming under swings and over bodies to get to the girl before she ended up taking one right in the kisser.

About three feet away, Lil realized she wasn't going to make it to the girl in time. So, leaping with a running start, she knocked the girl out of the way, bracing to take the hit herself.

But it never came.

Instead, a strong hand caught the fist zeroing in on her head and pushed it aside before catching her with the force of an iron bar in the gut, knocking the wind out of her, but stopping her from hitting the ground. The thought flashed across her mind that it might have been gentler to fall.

She gasped a quick "thanks" as the stranger helped her back to her feet, where she pulled her vest straight, giving it a quick scan for torn ribbons before registering the absolute silence around her.

In fact, nobody even moved.

What had only moments before been an active brawl suddenly looked like a group of grown men caught playing dress-up freeze tag for an audience of reporters and interns in green T-shirts.

And every single eye, camera, and mic was aimed at her.

Or, not at her, but at whoever was behind her.

Turning around slowly, she found herself staring at a broad expanse of white cotton. She took a step back.

The man in front of her wore a plain white T-shirt. Crisp and clean, it stretched tight across a set of pecs that had seen the gym at least as much as the pasture. Thick arms framed his chest, obviously grown and honed from a similar combination of effort and vanity.

His hands, though, his hands were all bull rider.

Huge, rough, layered, and callused, they were the hands of a man who let go of something only when he was ready to.

Her eyes trailed lower, taking in and lingering at the narrow tapering of his waist and the low sling of his jeans before she remembered her manners and shot her gaze back up toward his face.

There, a cleft chin jutted out from a large sharply square jaw.

His lips were wide and full and looked like they had been made for midnight in a dark room.

And they were frowning. At her.

An answering frown wrinkled her own brow.

His eyebrows, drawn together, were thick, straight, and jet-black, standing out in strong contrast against the warm golden brown of his skin. His eyes, almost black, were narrowed down at her. He wore a backward baseball hat.

A part of her mind broke off to wonder how it was possible for someone to pull off *Stern Disapproval* while wearing a backward baseball hat.

He managed it.

The lower half of his face was covered with something between a five-o'clock shadow and beard, which should have made him look lazy but instead accentuated the sculpted lines of his face.

He was the word *masculine* brought to life, and she couldn't take her eyes off him.

He was the one who broke their stare, opening and closing his right hand. His other hand was hooked into the front pocket of his jeans, tugging them tantalizingly lower on one side.

Lil's eyes and brain fought over which hand to pay attention to. They compromised by darting away.

To his left stood an older Black man with a neatly groomed salt-and-pepper beard, his face shadowed by a well-worn cowboy hat, the scent of former champion all over him.

At his right was a man with Photoshop-perfect deep black skin and equally thick black eyebrows. He'd come to the rodeo dressed in a three-piece suit and casually held back the other half of the fight Lil had crashed as if that other half weren't two hundred and fifty pounds of angry cattleman. In fact, the man in the suit looked bored with his job, like her brawl had underperformed.

Lil's eyebrow and lip quirked up. She was so sorry to disappoint.

Behind and around the trio, the sea of people had parted like Moses was in the vicinity.

It wasn't Moses, though.

It was AJ Garza.

Their gazes returned to each other like magnets, hers rolling like a dark storm coming in on the horizon. His deep, steady, and, upon closer inspection, rich brown rather than black, like a freshly turned field right after the rain.

She wanted to dig in and plant.

He broke the connection again, his eyes quickly darting to the rise and fall of her chest before jumping back to her face. His frown deepened to a scowl, carving deep grooves around his downturned mouth.

"Glad to see I finally have your attention." His drawl screamed *Texas!*—like just about everything did about Texas.

"Now that I do," he continued, "I would suggest that you refrain from starting fights outside rodeos. It's not a good look." He gestured to the cameras ringing them, as well as the security guards huffing in their direction. Then he nodded toward the suit that still held a brawler. "Not safe, either. Be a shame to get your head bashed in before you even get the opportunity to ride in your first rodeo…"

Nobody said it out loud, but a collective "Oooooooooo…" swept across the crowd. As far as rodeo insults went, AJ's was palpable.

Heat darkened Lil's cheeks. *First rodeo, my ass.* She gritted her teeth and held her tongue. It might be her first *PBRA* rodeo, but it wasn't even her first *professional* rodeo, let alone her first rodeo.

They'd built the south barn with the prize money she'd won!

The hand that had been in his pocket slid out, and with it, a business card. He offered it to her.

"Good luck out there tonight, kid. Come and see us when you're ready to get to the next level." He sized her up once more before adding, "A piece of advice—don't bite at bait like Hank's. That kind of guy wins if he gets to you. Save the angry for the bull." He tossed the last over his shoulder as he turned away, not bothering to see how his generous advice had been received.

The suit released the brawler and joined the old-timer in following AJ back along the way they came.

Lil steamed.

More like pressure-cooked.

She had nearly been punched in the face, mistaken for a man by every single person she had encountered, mistaken for a child by a few, insulted by Hank DeRoy, and lectured by AJ Garza—and the competition hadn't even started.

The fact that he had used her own granddad's words against her was merely the salt in the wound.

And then the stadium horns sounded, startling her.

The twenty-minute warning.

Fantastic.

It was time to get ready to ride.

5

AJ's mind should have been on riding a bareback bronc. Instead, it was on the kid whose head he'd saved from getting smashed in.

All of AJ's instincts said something was off there, and not *off* in the sense of a skinny Black kid with a dramatically long double undercut and a Native-style vest competing at a PBRA rodeo. As a former skinny Black kid who had sported a mini fro and a vaquero shirt and had gone on to become one of the PBRA's most decorated winners, he didn't see any *off* in that whatsoever. But his instincts were telling him that something was definitely off—and one didn't become a champion bull rider without listening to their instincts.

He, Diablo, and The Old Man had arrived at the line just in time to catch Hank's big words and see the kid knock his hat off.

The rope skills were impressive.

The kid's ability to weave in and out of the melee had been even more so.

AJ had almost laughed, watching as the kid nearly broke

out, scot-free, from the rumble he'd created. He had been surprised when the kid had then gone back in. Following his line of sight made the reason obvious, though.

One of the registration girls had gotten stuck in the middle of the fight.

At that point, AJ didn't think. He moved.

As if his change in energy broke through his cloak of invisibility, people simultaneously recognized him and got out of his way.

Diablo and Henry kept pace behind him, backing him up without needing to know why.

He made it just in time to stop the kid from taking a brick fist in the temple.

Using the attacking cowboy's momentum against him, AJ knocked him on the ground at the same time as he reached out his other arm to catch the kid.

The kid couldn't have weighed more than a hundred and twenty pounds soaking wet, but he bounced back from the tumble quick, jumping to his feet with a thank-you and a scan of the area before he turned back to face AJ.

AJ read it all as the signs of someone hungry and used to fighting to eat.

Whether the hunger was for glory or something else was hard to tell. Cowboys the kid's age tended to confuse the two.

If it was the former, CityBoyz had no place for him.

If it was the latter, there might be something there. But only if AJ could figure out why his instincts were shouting that something wasn't quite what it seemed.

A little hotshotting could be forgiven—it was part of the game, after all. Based on the exaggerated once-over he had given AJ, the kid had that part down pat. That kind of arrogance could eventually be molded into a strength.

In its rough form, the posturing had just given AJ time to

take his own measurements. Enough time to note the kid's narrow, almost delicate frame, as well as the neon-yellow athlete's tape peeking out from under his sleeves. His lack of height was unfortunate but could be worked with. There were plenty of short cowboys.

AJ frowned. *Delicate* was not usually a characteristic of the next great rodeo star. Combine delicate with hot-tempered, and it wasn't a great recipe for a successful Black cowboy, either. One needed broad, steady shoulders to bear the yoke of being an example. And a target.

But there were plenty of skinny Black cowboys who could still get the job done. The hall of greats was peppered with the tough, rangy little bastards.

It wasn't size or color that mattered in the arena. It was the try—the spark that signaled an unbreakable will.

A man had it, or he didn't. The kid had it.

That had been clear from the moment their gazes had locked. It was a moment AJ couldn't get out of his mind.

First off, no man had the right to eyes the color of the sky during a summer thunderstorm, especially not when they were framed by thick black curling eyelashes and sat beneath full, straight eyebrows.

Women would kill for eyes like that.

Behind the pretty-boy eyes, though, there was a spark that AJ had seen only twice before in his life—in the eyes of Henry Bowman, and in his own mirror.

It was the kind of spark that spoke of champions. AJ didn't need to see him ride to know the kid had the makings of a champion, even if he was skinny and green.

The question now was whether or not the kid could master his temper.

CityBoyz had seen plenty of great potentials come and go over the years, but no amount of talent could make up for control—or lack of it. It'd taken a while, but Henry had taught him that.

Diablo's voice trickled through his thoughts like water through the growing cracks in a dam. "No way. He's just getting into the game."

The Old Man's words broke the dam down: "You ask me, he's as far away from the game as it gets…"

As usual, The Old Man was right.

Coming back to the present, AJ looked at the leaderboard and asked, "Am I up?"

Diablo burst out laughing, and Henry gave him a searching look before answering, "Not yet. Just thought you might be interested in watching the kid from earlier."

He didn't add, *since that's where your mind is anyway*, even though AJ knew he knew. The Old Man was psychic.

AJ pushed off the wall he was leaning against.

It was a move that took effort. At six-five and two hundred fifty pounds, he was a large man—and that was before adding the vest, leather chaps, brace, and spurs.

The chaps were molded perfectly to his legs, broken in from frequent use. His jeans were belted and buckled, and his riggin' hung lightly in his left hand. He'd tossed a plain, fitted navy blue button-up on over his T-shirt and wore his Stetson low on his brow.

All of it was as familiar as a wife of forty years—as ardently adored.

And his mother worried he was afraid of commitment.

Wasn't he here, the same place he'd been a million times before, eager as if it were brand-new? What was that, if not commitment?

Probably something different.

After all, each rodeo offered a little something different—something brand-new.

He felt a thrill of excitement at the prospect of watching the kid ride. It was the first time he could remember feeling that way in a long time. But the kid had the scent of the next generation all over him. A generation AJ intended to shape.

If the kid was good enough, he would have him under his wing in no time—of that he had no doubt.

He just needed to know if the kid was good enough.

"Awfully quiet over there, AJ. Getting scared?" Diablo asked it dryly, his lack of effort in delivery the real insult.

"He's thinking about the kid," Henry observed.

Diablo mock considered, "Oh yeah? Well, I would say there was definite interest on the little guy's side, just didn't think AJ swung that way..."

AJ ignored him. "There's something about him."

Henry snorted. "He reminds you of you."

"Maybe." AJ grinned. "Probably."

That had to be what was screaming *off* at him, too. Like recognizing like or matching poles of a magnet repelling each other.

AJ shrugged. "Doesn't matter if he's shit on the horse, though."

Henry said, "You don't think he will be."

AJ agreed, "I don't."

Diablo said, "Well, he's definitely not afraid. He went right back in there for the girl."

Henry chuckled, "Not sure that's a lack of fear. Not much a boy his age won't do for a girl..."

Grinning, AJ added, "And what's a little brawl when you're about to get your ass handed to you on a bareback bronco?"

All three knew the answer to that intimately: not a whole lot.

The Closed Circuit qualifier consisted of just a single ride on a bareback bronc. Disqualify, and you were out—no re-rides. Score below 80, and you were out. It was straightforward and brutal, but an effective way to sift through two-hundred cowboys in a single night.

The circuit had chosen bareback bronc riding as the kick-off to cull out the weak. No other event beat you to shit quite like it. And if you wanted to score over 80, you better be ready to feel the pain.

Even with the protective gear and neck brace, the experience was like taking on an NFL defensive line all on your own.

The contest organizers said their goal was to pit man against nature, and the bareback bronc was the perfect kickoff to do just that. In this event, nature was smarter, stronger, and had more hooves.

AJ, Diablo, and Henry walked up the stairs to the stand on the platform at the top of the bucking chute. The area was usually reserved for staff and coaches, but rules didn't apply when you were AJ Garza at a rodeo.

From where they stood, they had a clear view of the arena and the chutes. But, although they were just feet away, they might as well have been in a different world.

The kid was in position on the horse in the chute, left hand resting on the top bar of the gate.

AJ frowned. The hand was tiny—not promising as far as grip potential went.

The kid's right hand was in place in his itty bitty riggin'. His back was to them, so while AJ couldn't see his face, he did get a closer look at the kid's vest.

Thousands of tiny beads glinted in the fluorescent lighting of the arena. Iridescent black beads covered most of the upper portion of the vest, which was edged with three rows of circular forms made from cream, blue, and orange. The ribbons that lined and dangled from the vest's front matched the shades of blue, cream, and orange in the beads.

There didn't seem to be anyone on the platform there with the kid. No coach, no family, nobody nervous and expectant on the sidelines, rooting him on. Nobody wringing their hands and praying he didn't get hurt.

That was bad luck.

The CityBoyz always made sure their crew had support, from each other, and from family, which was often one and the same.

His own mother had watched all of his early competitions, and Henry hadn't missed a single one during his professional career.

The previous rider cleared the arena, and the kid was up.

The announcer rang out: "From Muskogee, Oklahoma, rider one-thirty-seven, Lil Sorrow!"

AJ grimaced. They would have to talk him out of that name.

They always did. Every kid who came through CityBoyz wanted some kind of stage name like it made them scary, or hard, or whatever image it was those young boys cared about presenting to the world.

In reality, it just made them harder to separate from the clowns—real and figurative.

The horn sounded, the chute flew open, and kid and bronc came roaring out. The young man marked out perfectly, keeping his spurs in constant contact with the horse as he exited, his left arm raised high overhead with a slight bend in the elbow.

Good.

A stiff arm didn't disperse energy as well.

The kid was off to a great start.

Centered on the bronc, grip firm, heels down, toes out, and spurs pressed continuously against the flanks of the horse. The kid looked like an instructional video for the event. His upper body slammed against the horse's back in time to its wild bucking like a paddle ball with perfect rhythm. His legs bent and extended with each seesaw as the horse reared and descended.

The kid was excellent, giving the impression of a perfectly balanced, if manic, teeter-totter, even as the horse jumped and twisted.

He had drawn a particularly wild bronc, too. Extra points.

The seconds came and went, and the kid showed no sign of losing his grip or alignment. When the buzzer rang out at eight, the pickup men rode out to rein in the bronc.

The kid dismounted with a flourish, and the crowd went wild.

"Ay, Dios mío, folks! Have you seen a ride like that?" The Closed Circuit hostess, none other than world-famous rodeo queen and eternal mild itch in AJ's boots, Sierra Quintanilla, shouted, her voice and the mic more than a match for the thunderous crowd. "Give it up for Lil Sorrow and that absolutely pristine ride! Who would have expected such a display from a PBRA newcomer! We promised you drama, folks, and we delivered!"

As she finished her announcement, Lil Sorrow tore off his hat, black braid shining in the arena lights, and threw it in the air, letting out the loudest whistle AJ'd ever heard—and he'd once spent the holidays with his cousins in Oaxaca.

"You look about as pleased as if that was your ride out there," The Old Man observed.

AJ started. He hadn't felt the Cheshire cat grin spreading across his face, but it'd appeared sometime in the last eight seconds.

Diablo grinned. "Isn't often AJ sees someone as good as he is."

Henry shook his head. "That kid's better."

AJ laughed as Sierra shouted, "Unbelievable! We have a

score to beat for the night, and it's a doozy! At 97 points—it's a near-perfect ride!"

The kid's scream at the announcement was high-pitched and girlish enough to make AJ wonder if he'd lied about his age in order to qualify. No grown man could hit those notes.

"We'll be seeing a lot more of Lil Sorrow in the Closed Circuit future, folks! And you can take that to the bank!" Sierra squealed, her voice dripping with homespun sweetness about as deep as cotton candy.

Even from the safe distance of the chute, AJ shivered. As far as he'd traveled, rodeo was a small world, and his and Sierra's paths had crossed many a time. Every time he walked away, grateful the encounter was over. It was just his luck, then, that as the hostess of the Closed Circuit, she was going to be along for the long haul.

She and the full host of cameras rushed the kid as he left the arena.

AJ's eyebrows drew together.

Reporters were sharks, but that was something the kid was going to have to figure out for himself, probably the hard way, which was why he was surprised to find himself turning in that direction.

"Where are you going?" Diablo asked after him.

"Checking on the kid. He doesn't have anybody with him."

"And you think adding yourself to the herd of strangers about to stampede him is going to help with that?" The Old Man lifted a brow, his arms crossed in front of his chest. He'd been to many a rodeo with AJ and had never seen him pull this stunt before—the expression on his face said as much.

AJ grinned, turned around, and did what he was going to do anyway—just like he always did.

He arrived just in time to hear the reporter from ESPN2 ask the kid, "Are you single?"

He heaved a mental sigh.

The ESPN2 field team was the worst. Each and every one of their reporters was new to the business and hungry to climb the cable sports ladder. They went for blood.

But in truth, they merely had the balls to ask what all of the other reporters wanted to know and were too repressed to ask for—whether by network, class, respect for journalism, shame, or some combination thereof.

With the question out, each and every one of them leaned in closer to catch the kid's response.

The kid blushed, opened his mouth, closed it, and opened it again.

They were going to eat him alive.

Smiling his TV smile, AJ stepped in before the kid could say something he'd regret, "He's married to rodeo, of course."

Every camera and outstretched mic spun around to face him.

"AJ Garza! How long have you known Lil Sorrow?"

"Do you train together?"

"Are you his coach?"

AJ's easy smile never faltered. "No. We've only just met tonight, in fact. I'm just coming over to offer my congratulations on a great ride."

The kid snorted, likely remembering exactly how they met, and the cameras flipped back around to him.

AJ sent the kid an almost imperceptible shake of his head, but it was too late. Scenting the potential for drama, the sharks were back to circling the kid, and the kid had no idea.

"Lil Sorrow, do you know AJ Garza?" The reporters had become a pack, united in their scent for a story. This was another question they all wanted to know the answer to.

Finally becoming alert to a trap, even if he still didn't quite get it, the kid quickly shot a glance at AJ, uncertainty churning in his storm-cloud eyes, before saying cautiously, "Everybody knows AJ Garza."

AJ barely held back a scowl. The kid's hedging was obvious enough to imply bad blood. Had his tone been just a shade warmer, it would have put an end to any rumors before they started. At this rate, though, they'd have a manufactured rivalry on their hands by the end of the night.

AJ drew the attention back to himself, saying, "I'm trying to recruit him to CityBoyz, the nonprofit I'm riding for tonight. We partner young cowboys from underserved backgrounds with more experienced pro rodeo mentors. With the help of an old-timer, our boys go from wild, raw talent to the top of the rodeo game. I went through the program myself."

It was a solid redirect to a good cause. AJ could feed them a few more lines about CityBoyz, they'd get bored and move on, and Lil Sorrow wouldn't be starting his career off with a scandal—though maybe that was his intent? If it were, AJ would be disappointed. Many young cowboys these days thought they could make a name for themselves with the drama they got into outside of the arena over their performance inside of it. He hadn't read Lil Sorrow as that kind of competitor, though.

Lil Sorrow cleared his throat, drawing the attention back to himself, the sound eerily reminiscent of the sound AJ's mother used to make when she had just about had it with him.

When the shorter man opened his mouth to speak, eyebrows lifted, his voice was raspy, low, and steady—if tinged with irritation. "The 'wild raw talent' in question here is, in fact, twenty-seven years old, by no means a newcomer, and, perhaps most importantly—a woman. I manage a ranch, sixteen horses, a herd of cattle, and have been riding—on my own—since before I could talk. But don't worry. If you're so dead set on recruitment, I'd love to come work for City-

Boyz—as a coach. All you've got to do is get a higher score than me tonight. Ladies and gentlemen." The kid—or rather, the *adult woman*—tipped her hat to the crowd of reporters before spinning on her heels to walk away.

But if she thought she could drop a bomb like that and simply walk away, she was sorely mistaken.

However, for an instant, the entire group of them watched her go in silence, mouths open, an island of frozen time amidst the sea of chaos and noise outside of the arena.

Her hips swayed as she walked away from them and a part of him observed that he should have realized the truth of things immediately.

No cowboy he'd ever met walked like that.

And the hands, and the timbre of voice that he'd mistaken for youth trying to put on age—hell, even the way she rode a bronc screamed, *"Woman!"*

Taking her in in this new light, she transformed. Her thick black braid swung over her astounding vest, all the way down to the center of her back in perfect time with her hips, and he couldn't look away.

Compact she may be, tiny really, he realized she was nonetheless perfectly adult proportioned with long, lean limbs and a gorgeous round ass he was only just now observing.

She was a woman, alright.

But she wasn't just a woman.

She was the first woman he had ever heard of, in all of PBRA history, to score a 97 bareback on a bronc. The first woman to score on a bareback bronc at all. She was history-making, living, breathing, right in front of all of them—and all wrapped up in a sexy little package.

And just like the explosive ride she'd debuted with, she'd just detonated before his eyes.

AJ, as well versed in playing with fire as he was in getting burned, recovered first.

Giving a laugh that sounded relaxed and casual though it was entirely manufactured and controlled, and lacing his voice with a smile, he said, "Well, you heard her folks! Looks like I've got to show up on the bronc if I want to get Lil Sorrow, the PBRA's first female rough stock rider, if I'm not mistaken, on the CityBoyz roster." He winked, adding, "Good thing I'm coming up in the queue. Now you've got even more reason to watch me ride."

He knew he wasn't mistaken—a man didn't dominate his field without knowing everything there was to know about it, and the PBRA had never seen anything like Lil Sorrow.

He'd known the Closed Circuit would be a rodeo unlike any other. He hadn't expected it to change the very future of the sport—but that was just what would happen because there was no way Lil Sorrow wasn't making it into the competition, and there was no way her presence wouldn't rock the rodeo world to its core.

And he'd thought he'd seen all that rodeo had to offer, that there were no more secrets to be uncovered.

The school of reporters jolted back into the present, joining him in the laugh even as they readied themselves to race after the most important person in the entire arena.

Lil Sorrow was everything they could have wanted and more—brand-new content with the added benefit of a combination of dramatic packaging and the prospect of an exciting new rodeo rivalry. Any remaining tension evaporated. Everyone left knew the score.

With a wide, bright grin, AJ asked, "Well, friends, DeRoy is up next, and you know what that means."

AJ's and Hank's was the longest-standing established rivalry in modern professional rodeo history. On par with the

Yankees and Red Sox, in the world of rodeo, it had become such a popular feature that the PBRA had turned it into a tradition to place their rides back-to-back, Hank first, then AJ.

And, conveniently, it gave the reporters and AJ a reason to part ways without it looking like what it was: abandonment in favor of bigger news.

With a last dimpled smile and wink, AJ waved to the reporters, who had already begun to run in the direction that Lil Sorrow had sauntered off in, and made his way back to Diablo and The Old Man. The kid—and grown woman or not, she was brand new to the PBRA, so that made her a kid, dammit—was no longer a wet-behind-the-ears lone Black cowboy at a rodeo in his mind, and she didn't want his help. Whether she needed his help or not was another story. Based on the events of the night thus far, he wasn't so sure she didn't.

But he wasn't one to force himself where he wasn't welcome, and she'd made it abundantly clear that she didn't want him playing knight.

She'd made many things abundantly clear, in fact.

None more so than the fact that she wasn't just the first woman to ride rough stock for the PBRA, she was the first woman—first person even—to give him a real run for his money in over a decade, and he was hungry for more.

6

Lil's temper had stirred when AJ'd said the word *young* and had risen with his every word thereafter. She shouldn't have let it get to her. She could have even taken it as a compliment.

AJ Garza, her childhood hero, and, if she were honest with herself, her biggest crush, thought she was talented.

But she was a fourth-generation rancher and prize-winning rider, not some newbie on the block.

And even without the lineage, being born and raised on a ranch made her more experienced than AJ Garza—certainly not some kind of wet-behind-the-ears kid in need of mentorship from an arrogant gym rat from the city.

She steamed as she stormed back to her car until the growing stiffness in her neck and back demanded she slow down. Rubbing the place where her skull met her neck, she took a deep breath. Amidst all the nonsense with AJ and the reporters, she'd neglected the fact that a wild bronco had just throttled her.

And that she had just had the best bronc ride of her life.

She sent a little prayer of thanks up for her draw as the ride replayed in her mind. Three perfect twist-and-spins were more than a girl could ask for from any wild creature. Lil'd held her line as strongly as the bronc had tried to shake her off, their wills and rhythms perfectly matched. She hadn't needed or wanted to break him, but she was sure enough going to show him she wouldn't be broken, either.

A shiver traveled down her spine. That was the kind of perfect tension that held the universe together. She sucked in a breath of exhilarating night air.

And then the reporters caught up with her.

"Lil Sorrow!"

"Lil Sorrow!"

"Excuse me, Lil Sorrow!"

"Ms. Sorrow!"

Mics were thrust in her face from all directions, while questions rang out, seemingly heedless of being answered.

"Did you always know you would be the first female rodeo star?"

"When did you know you were destined for the rodeo?"

"When did you start riding rough stock events?"

"When did you know you were a woman?"

Questions kept coming, faster than Lil could comprehend, let alone answer.

"Where were you before the Closed Circuit?"

"Who was your coach?"

"How long have you been riding?"

"Aren't you scared of the bulls?"

"What kind of jeans are you wearing?"

"Who made your vest?"

The reporters and their associated cameramen pushed in closer, and, seeing the growing group, others began to drift in her direction. Soon she was surrounded by a rather large crowd of media, the buzz of real news electric amongst the crowd.

"Lil Sorrow is a woman!"

"A woman! Lil Sorrow is a woman!"

"She scored a 97!"

"A woman that rides like a man!"

Lil scoffed and, suddenly, like a creature with a hive mind or a school of fish, the crowd of reporters turned, their collective attention focused on her, and, though she wouldn't have ever been able to say what came over her, she cracked a smile and said, "So far it looks like I ride better than a man."

If they were focused on her before, they were absolutely riveted now, and, to their benefit, though she wasn't sure where they were coming from, words continued to flow from Lil's mouth. "Been riding my whole life and learned everything I know from my granddad. Of course I'm scared of a bull—only a fool wouldn't be. My jeans are Levi's, and I've been riding rough stock since I could prove my head was hard enough to take a fall. Wanted to be rodeo's first female rough stock champion since I was six years old. Been here and there, but mostly in my own pasture since nobody in the PBRA would let me try until tonight. Known I was a woman as long as I've been old enough to know such a thing, and my gran made my vest."

As a unit, the reporters scribbled furiously.

As if she'd been possessed, the words had flowed out of her mouth with smooth charm, the only proof they were her own the unique combination of gravel and Muskogee that was all her voice.

And then, the same voice from earlier called out once more, "So, are you single?"

As they had before, Lil's cheeks heated, darkening to a beet red color obvious to anyone familiar with her.

Lil wasn't the type to talk about her private life. With anyone—least of all a gaggle of journalists.

But she'd watched AJ earlier, and even through temper and resentment, she'd learned.

The reporters were like sheep, or goats, or middle schoolers, or any other creature that traveled in packs and dealt in intimidation. If she didn't master them—establish early and quick that she wasn't to be trifled with—then there would be no end to their torment.

And so, hot cheeked, she angled her chin upward, cast her mind for an appropriate facial expression, settled on the only image her mind seemed willing to provide—AJ's cocky, one-sided grin—and said, "I've been chasing one man my whole life—he weighs three thousand pounds, is sponsored by the PBRA, and if you can ride him for a full eight seconds you get a shiny buckle and a pot of gold." Once again, rodeo's first-ever female rough stock star tipped her hat to them, and once again, she turned on her boot heel and walked away.

This time, no one followed, for which she was grateful. She would hate to have disappointed them with her destination: her beat-up old white Camry, parked at the far end of the lot. It was a '99, but it might as well have been a tank—nothing could hurt it or stop it. It certainly wasn't anything flashy, and Lil had no intention of ever replacing it. Even pushing 350,000 miles, it purred like a kitten and drove like a dream.

Unlocking the car, she slid into the front seat, set her hat beside her where a passenger might have sat, and pulled the sunshade down, flicking open the mirror panel at the same time in one smooth motion.

She hadn't planned on changing after her ride, but she also hadn't planned on being mistaken for a man by everyone who saw her. Her eyebrows were thick, that was true, and she did have a squarish jaw. Her eyelashes were long and curled, her mouth and nose were feminine in their fullness.

She didn't think it was the clothes. Women all over the rodeo wore the same outfit without confusion, from dusty cowgirls who competed as barrel racers to the full glitz and glam of the rodeo queens.

Taking in her appearance, barefaced and serious, she wondered if it was her hair, then. The undercut sides, her tight braid—looser now, but still pulled back flat to her head for the ride—was more severe and dramatic than most women were willing to dare.

When she'd come into her gran's kitchen, two-thirds of her "Crown of Glory" as her gran called it shorn clean off to the skin, her gran had had to sit down for a moment. Maybe that, coupled with her being a competitor, was just enough to throw the entire arena off.

She wondered if anyone in the whole place had realized she was a woman while she rode. AJ certainly hadn't.

But who could blame him? If it looked like a duck and quacked like a duck, why would you even bother checking if it was a duck?

Shaking her head at both her thoughts and her reflections, she winced. After the brawl, the ride, the argument, and storming off, her neck and back were beginning to scream, protesting their long string of abuse, and—between the ride, the jeans, and the chaps—her legs were well on their way to rigid and stiff.

And to make matters worse, after all of it, her complexion had gone shiny and red—more like an angry toddler than an adult. Disgusted with it all, she nearly flipped the shade back up when her grandmother's voice echoed in her mind. *It doesn't matter what happens to you. It matters what you do about it.*

Her grandmother dealt truisms like white on rice. But it

applied. She couldn't control what people assumed, but she could do a little to help them out.

She kept a bare-bones makeup bag in her glove box, and, while there were good reasons not to have started the night all dolled up—when it came to riding, it wasn't so much a question of waterproof enough as not even an option—she was done riding now. And she was done being taken for anything other than what she was, which was the highest-scoring rider of the night.

Dabbing a layer of foundation and adding a quick lining of black and mascara to her eyes, and a dusky rose-tinted cream to her lips was her first step.

As always, she was startled by the effect after pulling back to examine her handiwork. She knew no special techniques, did nothing out of the ordinary, but somehow the little bit of accentuation transformed her from the kind of woman men's eyes skipped over to the kind that stopped men in their tracks.

The simple lining set off her half-moon-shaped eyes, the gray of them jumping out of her face so much, it demanded attention. The smooth, creamy rose of the lip tint emphasized the rich fullness of her lips.

She looked seductive but dangerous—like a tempest.

But most importantly, she looked like a woman.

Makeup complete, she unbraided her hair, parting it down the middle and shaking the long curls loose from the crown of her head as she did. Massaging her scalp, she let out a low moan. Her hair was thick enough and curly enough that even with the undercuts, she still had enough to fake a full head of coverage. Her long full curls settled around her shoulders and down her back as she massaged her head, the black of them shimmering like a crow's wing in the low light of the parking lot. She could never be described as girly, but she was admittedly vain about her hair. It was her beauty failing, and she channeled any desire to adorn herself into its care, spending hundreds of dollars in creams, masques, specialized shampoos, microfiber towels, silk pillowcases, and protective braids every year. Since there'd never been enough extra money for fancy things like salon relaxers or paying someone outside of the ranch to braid her hair—and Gran'd had no time to spare for installing hairstyles which required a greater time investment than a half an hour or so—Lil'd had to master the management of her uniquely blended hair herself—and at a young age. But right now, released in its glory and ready to do the apparently heavy lifting of convincing the world she was a woman, she had no doubt it was all worth it.

Hair and makeup in place, she retrieved the slender gold hoops her gran had given her for her twenty-first birthday from her wallet and slid them in each ear. Then she wiggled her finger around in the coin pocket until she found the diamond nose stud she wore when she wasn't riding rodeo, wiped it with the alcohol wipe she carried—also in her coin purse—for just that purpose, and angled it back into her right nostril.

Now, even with the hat on—as was required at the podium—there would be no mistaking her for anything but an adult woman. She flicked the mirror closed and pushed the shade flap up. Zipping the makeup bag and tossing it back into the glove box, she grabbed her keys and hopped out of the car.

In the parking lot, she heard the distant murmur of the PA system blare a name whose ride she couldn't care less about but whose position in the queue meant she needed to get back to the stadium fast. If Hank DeRoy was riding now, that meant that AJ was up next, and while he might be an arrogant gym rat from the city, AJ Garza was still the best rodeo cowboy on the planet.

There was no way she was going to miss a chance to be chute side for his ride. She jogged back to the stadium.

All she'd done was take down her hair and put a little makeup on, but she might as well have had a complete transformation for the difference in her journey back to the chutes. Incognito as she was—now looking more like a low-rung rodeo queen or maybe a contestant's wife—she didn't warrant the attention of reporters, and, overdressed for the average buckle bunny, she didn't warrant the attention of cowboys. Rodeo-goers, even the ones looking for snags, weren't in the market for chasing down lone wolves either, so she didn't get stopped by anyone while making her way to the contestants' entrance.

Security let her through to the chute without any questions, and she momentarily marveled at the absurdity of the world she loved so dearly. The way a rodeo behaved, you'd think her ability in the saddle, or bareback for that matter, disappeared when she took her braid out.

Weaving her way through the crowd of cowboys bunched up at the chute, she arrived just in time to watch it pop open.

For a stomach-sinkingly long time, nothing happened. Then the bronc, with AJ on top, stumbled out and staggered to a standstill.

Lil's heart thudded.

This was bad.

AJ would never make score with a dud of a draw.

Something was wrong with his horse, which simply stood, almost meditative, even as AJ's spurs dug into its haunches, and a stadium of people shouted at it.

In any other sport, they'd stop the clock, but AJ's seconds ticked away. Lil's heart beat fast in her chest, and her breath came short.

The horse wasn't doing anything, and in what was about to become the biggest upset in recent history, AJ Garza, rodeo's greatest champion, was about to be disqualified.

7

The blood thundering in AJ's ears was louder than all the sounds of the arena combined. Staring at failure in the face for the first time in over a decade, time as inert as the beast below him, a part of him was dumbfounded.

There had been no question that he would qualify.

Before it was announced he was coming on board, all of the current top rodeo pros had snubbed their noses at the Closed Circuit, calling it a publicity stunt for novices. The announcement of his participation lent the whole thing credibility. Yes, he had retired, but there had never been any question as to whether or not he'd make it.

So there was an extra sting to the fact that while the seconds bled away, it was becoming apparent, in front of seventy thousand people and his first time riding for something other than himself, that he would not qualify.

He hated to be the man who blamed his tools, but something was wrong with his horse—something beyond bad luck and a poor draw. It had been obvious as soon as they'd come out of the gate.

And the horse was half the score.

He'd be lucky if he earned over 40 points at this rate. Silence began to creep its slow way through the crowd as the time ticked away.

And then a high-pitched whistle, as screeching and terrible as nails on a chalkboard, tore through the air like a missile targeted at his horse's ears. The horse twitched, taking a few staggering steps to the side.

But if the horse was only mildly impacted, AJ saw the light, the sound ripping down his spine and setting off a storm of neurons firing.

Time was short, but he had a bull bell in his front vest pocket. He would have to let go of the riggin' entirely in order to get it because he wasn't allowed to touch anything on his person with his left hand, but considering what a dud his bronc had turned out to be, it wasn't like he was betting it all.

He went for it, his motions quick and practiced as if he'd trained for just this occurrence.

He hadn't.

Then, bringing the bell so close to the horse's ear that it was nearly inside the thing, he rang it hard.

His bronc came roaring to life. The bell flew out of AJ's hand. He swung his right hand back for his riggin' but couldn't catch it before his upper body snapped backward toward the horse's haunches. By sheer force of will, coupled with iron muscle memory and years of practice, his left arm remained curved upward, touching nothing, while he gripped the horse with his legs, praying they didn't give out.

Head and back whipping toward the horse's rear, his focus zeroed in on what came next: catching the riggin' the next time he flew forward or flying off and getting stomped.

Easy.

All of it took less than a second—thankfully, as he didn't have many of those left. When his body lurched forward, he grabbed the loop, fingers sticking like a slap, and that was that.

His right hand once again in place, cemented into his custom riggin', he held on tight while his horse made up for its slow start by bucking and twisting like a maniac now.

His right shoulder screamed, angrier than it always was at having had no time to brace for the force of his body's momentum against the horse's power before the storm of bucking began.

But AJ's grip held.

The crowd went wild.

For the rest of the ride, the horse fought for its life, and AJ held on for his.

The judges let the seconds tick past eight, extending the spectacle to allow a full eight seconds of thrashing before sounding the buzzer.

The drama was up there with the debut of rodeo's first female rodeo pro in terms of the perfect reality TV kickoff for the PBRA Closed Circuit.

Pickup men appeared at his side, flanking him in order to take control of the still-wild bronc. AJ slid free of the saddle, his own roar of triumph drowned out beneath the stadium's avalanche of sound.

Opening his arms to the onslaught, he circled the arena once, letting out wild whoops and whistles in response before he threw his hat to the crowd and made his way back to the gate, blood thundering in his veins.

This was it, the greatest feeling in the world—a reason to live.

He couldn't remember a ride like that since his first time riding in a pro rodeo at eighteen.

The thrill of it singing in his blood stoked the hunger for more. There wasn't a feeling like it in the world—the reason men were willing to die for it—as addictive as heroin.

He was still hollering as he swung the gate open, nearly knocking off the petite woman who stood on it, her boots hooked on the bottom bar, before he caught it.

She wore all black, long curls cascading down from under her hat, too conservatively dressed to be a buckle bunny, but too alternative to be a rodeo queen.

She had a nose ring, warm brown skin, and smoky-gray irises that swirled like a hurricane, dangerous and mesmerizing, twin eyes of the storm, lit up with stars, which were ringed by thick pitch-black lashes. Her lips were full and stubborn looking, begging to be tamed, or at the very least ridden hard. They parted as he stared, and the triumphant rush in his blood abruptly reversed course, thundering powerfully in other directions.

Somewhere in the distance, his score was being announced over the PA system, but as their eyes remained locked, her mouth took on the shape of a silent *Oh*, and that breathless syllable suddenly became the most important thing AJ had ever witnessed.

Almost imperceptibly, she leaned forward. It was as if the cord that connected their gazes compelled her. As if the draw was about more than bright lights and the thrill of the ride. As if she was trying to hold back but losing out.

And though The Old Man's frown flashed through his mind, the small motion was an encouragement he couldn't ignore.

He drew the gate to him, closing the distance until only the metal gate separated them. With his free hand, he tilted her chin up before sliding around to cradle the back of her skull. Her hands came to his shoulders with a firm grip as she lifted up to her toes on the gate, offering exactly the angle he needed to capture her mouth with his own.

She tasted like late springtime: warm, sweet, and a little naughty.

Sighing into his kiss like she'd been waiting for this moment her whole life, she stoked the fire that had driven him to kiss her in the first place, thickening into something more possessive, urging him to take more. He pressed closer, and she leaned in.

"AJ Garza!" The Old Man's slightly raised, slightly outraged voice somehow cut through both the single-minded haze of his focus and the astronomical noise of the arena.

Reluctantly, he pulled back from the kiss without taking his eyes off her.

Around them, he realized the arena's applause had morphed into playground whistles. Vague recollections of strict rules about keeping his personal life outside of the arena pestered the back of his mind, but he ignored them.

"I trust you realize you're fraternizing with the enemy?" Diablo asked, voice dry as ever and lazy, even as he stepped into the spontaneous combustion of age-old arguments.

And then Diablo's words sank in.

He was staring into the same stormy eyes he'd clashed with not once, but twice, already—even if at the moment the swirling cloudiness in her tempest gaze had nothing to do with temper.

Still kiss drunk, her full lips even fuller, emphasized by her lipstick and the swollen plumpness that he'd kissed into existence, she had no idea of the unheard-of effect she was having on his behavior. Was it any surprise that rodeo's first female star would inspire unprecedented behavior in him? Either way, he'd answered a question he hadn't even realized he'd been dying to know the answer to.

Lil Sorrow could kiss as well as she could ride.

He wondered what else she was good at.

She shined up well—not that he'd thought she wasn't fine-looking before, he realized recalling his earlier images of her, he just hadn't been looking at her as a woman. He'd been looking at her as a cowboy, he realized.

She was a damn fine cowboy. As a woman, she was mesmerizing.

Enough so, that, like Clark Kent, all it'd taken to fool him was a slight change in hair and accessories—a fall of curls and a nose stud—and he'd completely missed the things that were unmistakable about her: her clothes, the way she carried herself, and those one-in-a-million eyes. Eyes which even now threatened to yank him back into their private world—circumstances be damned.

Dawning awareness of their situation, however, rolled over her like a deadly wave of molasses. He watched it happen. A part of him was glad to know that getting all dolled up didn't make her face any less transparent, though why that would make him happy, he didn't know.

First came shock. Shock which he was honor bound to avenge, as it appeared that she had not considered the fact that she had been fraternizing with the enemy until Diablo had said so, and, more importantly, might have gone on doing so.

Next came shame. Heat radiated off her body that had nothing to do with him, and she came spurring to squirming life, jumping off the gate like it was lava. She landed as if the dismount were a routine they'd been working on, and his heart beamed a little in pride at her balance.

Finally, came horror, as she turned to realize that the entire enterprise had unfolded on the jumbotron, broadcast on the big screen to the delight of the audience.

Angling to shield her face with his body from both the

camera and The Old Man and Diablo, he was the only one to see the sheen of tears glistening in her eyes as she tucked her face down, hiding it in the shadow of her hat, and dashed around him, trying to get lost in the crowd.

He watched her go, knowing she wouldn't make it far. Not now, and probably never again at a rodeo. She was a star now, whether she knew it or not.

The Old Man didn't approve of cowboys "taking up with strange women," as he was famous for saying. He had drilled it into his boys as youths and demanded it from his pros as an example for those coming up.

AJ was respectful enough to be circumspect. Usually.

And so, though he wanted to go after her, even though it would only add fuel to the fire their very public kiss had undoubtedly just stirred up, he didn't.

Instead, when The Old Man clapped a hand down on his shoulder and said, "You know the drill. Check-up time. Especially after a stunt like that." AJ let himself be led away.

Respect for The Old Man might have him willing to let Lil Sorrow go without chasing her down to at least say something about their kiss, but respect wasn't enough to keep the grit of irritation out of his voice when he replied, "Had no choice. You saw what I was working with."

On The Old Man's other side, Diablo nodded. "Looked like you were out of it for sure this time."

The comment brought the cowboy in him to the surface, and he gave a lazy grin. "I always have a trick up my sleeve."

The Old Man frowned. "That was a damn fool thing to do. You're too old for those kinds of tricks."

"Still around to get older."

"Don't make me be the one to deliver bad news to your mama."

AJ frowned. It wasn't the first time he'd heard the line.

Henry Bowman had no qualms about hitting below the belt. But there was a new weight to it. A truth to the statement that demanded he take his mentor seriously. He could get hurt out there.

"Honestly, I didn't think it'd even work." AJ nodded toward Diablo as he echoed his words. "*I* thought I was out of this one. There was something wrong with that horse. More than just a bad draw."

The Old Man shrugged. "They'll find it, if so. Let's get back to the hotel." He was never one for wasting time in speculation.

AJ raised an eyebrow. "Maybe I got plans with Lil Sorrow."

Henry snorted. "Not while you're riding for CityBoyz, you don't."

Diablo laughed, "Uh-oh, AJ. Under The Old Man's rules again."

Henry shot Diablo a sharp look out of the corner of his eye. "You're too old for that nonsense, too. A couple of geezers acting like little boys, if you ask me…"

AJ laughed this time. "You would deny me my shot at true love?"

Henry's slap stung AJ's back, reminding him that The Old Man wasn't too old to lay him on his ass. "Don't see any evidence of *true love* anymore, do you? Besides, you'll see her again soon. She's going to be right above you on that podium in the next half an hour or so. In case you missed it."

AJ started. In all that had happened since the chute had opened, he had missed his score.

He couldn't recall that ever happening before.

Implied, along with a mild cackle, in The Old Man's words was the fact that he hadn't beat Lil's score. AJ's ride had been the finale of the night. He had time for a quick post-ride physical and to spruce up before it was time for announcements and closing up.

If what The Old Man said was true, it would be the first time he wasn't at the top in over ten years. The knowledge had a familiar thrill surging through his blood, even as the pathway was rusty. For the first time in a long time, he had some real competition.

With an unrepentant grin, AJ asked, "So what did it all come down to?"

The Old Man sounded amused, a joke hiding in his smooth baritone: "Ninety-six points."

One point less than Lil Sorrow.

CityBoyz was out rodeo's one and only Lil Sorrow as a coach. For now.

Because, just like her place in the number one spot, things at the rodeo had a way of changing quick, and AJ wasn't known for giving up.

8

Lil tried to push through the crowd since crying and self-immolation were neither in her nature nor scope of abilities, but as she navigated toward the exit, the crowd pressed her back, coagulating from an amorphous blob into a sea of people pointing mics and cameras at her.

Each and every one of them wanted to know one thing: "What's the story with you and AJ Garza?"

She could ask the same thing and, in fact, had been on a manic loop since running away, which made her both a fool and a coward. That she had no more idea of the answer than the reporters surrounding her didn't make things any better. What in the hell had she been thinking, kissing AJ Garza in front of God and everyone?

That she'd been caught up in the moment—thrilling and thunderous after the unexpected agony of watching his near miss—that it had swept her up in a whirlwind of the sounds of the rodeo swirling around them and the thrill of the ride still high in both their veins, each of them keenly invested in the other's rush, in the other's utter union with everything that was rodeo, their bodies pulsing as they met, crashing into one another head-on like two raging bulls, *that* was unconscionable. Completely unacceptable.

"Are you friends?"

"Lovers?"

"Enemies?"

Shaking her head, Lil tried to sift through the battering of questions, grasping for something she could hold on to, anything, so she didn't blurt out something disastrous like, *No, I've just idolized him since I was fourteen.*

Anything other than that, because it couldn't be that. That was worse than wearing a junior champion buckle to a pro rodeo.

It was the intensity of the night—the brawl, her own ride, her wildest dreams coming true, AJ's dramatic ride—all of it had carried her away in the moment, swept aside her steady clear sight and common sense. It could not have been the fact that, as impossible as it seemed, when their eyes had connected, her blood still singing with his incredible turnaround, the entire arena had melted away, leaving them in a world of just two.

It couldn't be that because that was absurd. Almost as absurd as the questions still flying at her.

"Are you his protégée?"

Thankfully there were journalists in the crowd more interested in her skills than her personal life.

"You're the first female rough stock rider in a PBRA rodeo to score higher than 67. Do you see yourself as a pioneer?"

A voice in her head snorted at the question. To her way of thinking, *pioneers* were the feckless sorts who left their homes and families to heed the siren call of the sea. Same as the folks that got scared away by a little dust.

She came from steadier stock than that.

The tide of questions had shifted, though.

"Where have you been hiding?"

"How long have you been riding rough stock events?"

"How tall are you?"

"How old are you?"

"How much do you weigh?"

"Now, y'all know you can't ask a woman questions like that!" Sierra Quintanilla's voice was citrus and vanilla, pure, unadulterated, orange Creamsicle, as she sidled up beside Lil, one jean jacket–clad arm coming to wrap around Lil's shoulders, while the other drew her own mic into the intimate circle she'd created between the two of them. Smoothly, she steered Lil away from the crowd of reporters and greenies toward her hostess's lounge that was set up between the arena exit and the stage.

Speaking to the cameraman that walked backward in front of them, his camera trained on rodeo's number one queen and its fresh new female star.

"I've got high-scoring contestant Lil Sorrow with me now," Sierra said, "just moments before the final ceremony of the night. Lil Sorrow—" she turned to Lil "—it'd be an understatement to call you the surprise star of the evening. Your story is straight out of the movies: a mysterious cowboy from the north blows everyone away on a bronc, only to turn out not to be a cowboy at all, but a cowgirl! What an upset! But now, we must know! Who are you? Where did you come from, and why haven't we seen you around the circuit until now, because— and I don't think it's a lie to say this—there're a lot of little girls out there who've been waiting for the likes of you!"

The women of the audience, watching the exchange on the jumbotron overhead with rapt attention, cheered at Sierra's words, the sound a wave of high-pitched "*hell yeah!*"'s that felt a little bit like a sugar rush in Lil's veins.

Sierra's energy was captivating—the sparkle she gave off nothing short of impressive. Her beauty was undeniable, her blunt bangs falling in a charming, eternally youthful fringe across her forehead beneath her hat. Thick, expertly dyed and curled hair tumbled out from beneath her hat around her shoulders and down her back. Her makeup was full and flawless, much like her figure—the opposite of Lil's tiny muscular frame, in fact.

Sierra was tall with curves that eating all the sandwiches in the world wouldn't have been able to give Lil. The rodeo queen wore jeans and cowboy boots, and a matching jean jacket. Beneath the jacket, her Western-style button-up boasted a classic red gingham pattern, mother-of-pearl snaps, and red piping.

She looked wholesome, all-American, and pretty. A hometown girl, sweet as apple pie, with a killer grin—everything a rodeo queen should be.

Lil had always admired women like Sierra, perfectly put together with their impenetrable smiles and ability to carry it all off without coming across as too matchy-matchy or kitschy.

There was a reason Sierra was the country's top rodeo queen, and it wasn't just that she looked beautiful in a Stetson. Her sharp gaze and smooth manner were those of a professional woman who knew her business at least as well as Lil knew hers in the arena. Maybe even better, since Sierra hadn't taken any time off.

Unlike some of her peers growing up—those rider girls who saw themselves as somehow better than the queens—Lil had never underestimated or written off the work of the rodeo queens. They were responsible for managing the crowd, wooing and welcoming them when they started to turn ornery or feel left out and bored. Rodeo queens were the bright hostesses that personified the magic of the rodeo, sparking dreams just as much as the cowboys in the arena, with their rhinestones and big hair and bright white teeth.

Lil was better at riding bulls than wooing and welcoming, but that didn't mean she didn't see that each was necessary at the rodeo.

Perhaps that was why, where others had failed, for Sierra, Lil opened up.

"I can't say I was thinking much about being a role model on the way out here—having been out of the game for the past few years, I was mostly just worried about putting in a good ride—but if I have inspired any other young women tonight, I am honored."

The response set off another wave of high-pitched cheering through the arena.

Sierra slapped her knee. "You did that and more! You walked away with the high score of the night. Did you have any idea you would do so well?"

Lil shook her head. "Absolutely not. As I said, I came into this pretty rusty. I just hoped to qualify."

"Well, if this is rusty, we can't wait to see you warmed up!" Sierra waited for the crowd to quiet down before leaning in closer. "Now you said you've been 'out of the game.' That's another understatement. We haven't seen you anywhere around the PBRA, so tell us, where have you been all these years?"

Lil almost frowned at the question, getting the odd feeling that her age was being pointed out as a negative when she was barely twenty-seven years old, but shrugged it off as being overly sensitive. Smiling, she answered, "My rodeo days mostly ended in college, but I was fortunate to compete for the Indian National Finals Rodeo."

"Hmmmmm." Sierra's lips pressed together, and the sound was filled with meaning. It was unspoken there was no stiffer competition than at the INFR, but it didn't offer the opportunity for stardom and riches that the PBRA did. Smaller pots, lack of press, and a history of outright racism and discrimination had kept many world-class INFR cowboys from getting their due in the PBRA—and both the groups knew it.

Her granddad had been one of them.

But her granddad would have said moaning about the loss did less toward avenging it than getting out there and getting on a bronc, which she had done tonight.

The truth of it sank in right there, in Sierra's kingdom, with a strange start.

She'd spent so much time bemoaning Gran's scheming that she hadn't noticed that, in the process, the nagging voice inside that insisted she show the world what its ignorance had robbed it of all these years had gone quiet for the first time in decades.

"My granddad, a ten-time INFR champion with more buckles than you can count on your fingers and toes, taught me everything I know—starting when I was five years old."

Making a noise of approval in her throat, Sierra smiled at the camera. "Well, there's our answer, folks! A child prodigy with lineage! Did I hear right? You're a rancher, as well? It seems our unconventional star of the evening is traditional, through and through."

Lil smiled, always happy to talk about the ranch, even if the rodeo queen's words carried a familiar edge of derision to them. She didn't mind if her peers saw her as old-fashioned. She looked at time on a longer scale than a single lifespan, no matter that modernity offered more shortcuts than ever. In other words, it didn't matter which direction you swiped if you didn't have solid ground to stand on when you met in real life. Doing things the tried-and-true way, without shortcuts, might take longer, but the results were stronger. That was true in everything, from rodeo to family.

"I am," she said, a smile warming the whiskey scratch in her voice. "Everything I learned about rodeo I learned the old-fashioned way—doing it on the ranch. My granddad said, and I believe him, that there isn't an artificial training environment in the world that can replicate the experience of doing it where the stakes are high and the consequences real."

Sierra chuckled, the sound cultured and light, as charming and sparkling as a Disney princess. "Your granddad sounds like someone we all need in our life!" Pausing with a mischievous smile and sideways glance, letting the previous subject naturally die down, Sierra leaned in, her entire demeanor turning conspiratorial. "We're just minutes away from making PBRA history, crowning the first-ever female rough stock buckle winner, but I can't let you get away without addressing everyone's biggest question. What's the story with you and PBRA's golden boy, AJ Garza?"

Lil's mind went blank.

She should have expected the question, of course—or something like it. But she had forgotten, lulled by the other woman's smooth warmth, that Sierra wasn't simply a regular cast member in the drama that was rodeo. She was a monstrous Chimera, part rodeo queen, part reality TV show hostess. Her job went beyond inspiring the future boys and girls of rodeo. No, like the packs of reporters Lil had been encountering all night long, it was Sierra's job to ferret out the juiciest drama and amplify it for the delight of the audience.

Inside, Lil vowed not to make the mistake again.

Outside, grinning as if the question hadn't sent her stomach plummeting to the floor at the same time as it set her cheeks to boiling, Lil leaned back, posture full of casual ease, and said with a wicked sideways glance, "If by that you mean, 'how did a nobody come out of the shadows to beat the PBRA's greatest champion?' I think that's just your classic tale of girl *beats* boy."

A spark of respect sharpened the glint in the hostess's eye, though her expression didn't change. "Now you know that's not what I meant!" she teased. "We want to know about that whopper of a kiss, don't we, folks?"

The response was a thunderous affirmative. It seemed there was nothing anybody wanted to know about more, in fact.

Lil continued to grin, looking for all the world as if she was unbothered, when, in fact, she was mortified that the truth would be obvious: she had no more knowledge about why it had happened than anyone else.

She had no idea why she'd let him kiss her like that.

She had never let anyone kiss her like that in the whole of her existence.

She wasn't the kind of girl who kissed people. Hell, she'd made her college boyfriend—the only one she'd ever had— wait months before she would even let him think of kissing her.

And here she'd kissed not just a stranger, but *the enemy*, as his companion had so kindly pointed out.

But the crowd was waiting, and if Lil took any longer, they'd start taking her silence for talking.

"Oh, that? Just taking care of a little bet. I'm as honest a loser as I am a winner," Lil added with a wink, the lie rolling off her tongue as smoothly as the TV-cowboy personality. "And if I'm not mistaken, they're calling us back to the stage, now—both of us, I'd think. Shall we make like girls and go together?"

The audience laughed on their cue while a flicker of irritation darted across Sierra's face, but she let out a giggle as if she thought it was funny, too.

"Why, certainly! And on that note, isn't it a wonder what a little makeup and hair will do to a woman? Why you practically transformed before our eyes without even changing clothes!"

Lil held her temper, blaming her raised hackles on AJ and the bronco and the fact that she was up past her usual bedtime without dinner—anything besides the fact that she was finding it awfully hard not to hear insults hidden in Sierra's chatter.

And why the hell was the woman talking to her about hair and makeup as they walked up for Lil to claim her qualifier's champion buckle? If this was what it meant to be the PBRA's first female champion, she wasn't sure she was better off with the world knowing she was a woman after all.

Voice as light as gravel could be, Lil replied with a false chuckle, "Family always said I cleaned up well—but we all know family is the first to lie."

Again, the audience laughed at her joke, warming away some of her stiff and cranky as the two women walked up the stairs, fully mic'd, with what looked like friendship blossoming between them for all the world to see.

Reality TV was wild.

Sierra opened her mouth again, but Lil beat her to speaking. "But you're so right—you know. It was so nice to get a chance to freshen up after the ride. I may be the high score of the night, but I'm still just a girl." Her words landed in time with their boots hitting the stage, and the combination of timing, and lighting, and the perfect kismet of Gretchen Wilson coming on over the PA system, had the women of the audience leaping to their feet roaring.

Despite all the fierce feminine energy of a rodeo—from the barrel racers to the ultracompetitive queens, and all the girl dreamers in between—Lil would have said the Houston Blue Ribbon Arena was the last place she'd expect a girl power riot to erupt, but faced with these women tonight, she wouldn't be surprised to stand corrected.

Swept up in it in a way she would have never expected of herself—would likely be ashamed of later, even—she gave in to the urge to stomp her foot and clap her hands in time to the music, moving in unison with the arena full of women who were going to go home tonight and show their men who was boss.

The camera crew zoomed in on her, her image, long curls falling in front of her shoulders to blend with her black vest, eyes laughing, diamond-nose stud catching the arena lights and sparkling, in a Stetson but still pretty and adult about all of it with the help of makeup, with, at least for the moment, the attention of each and every person in the audience. She had shown them all tonight.

The only thing that could have made it perfect was if her granddad had been there to witness it. Instead, she had a crowd of twenty thousand and her teen idol, AJ Garza.

He wasn't her granddad by any stretch of the imagination, but it was a different kind of dream come true. She'd had the chance to watch her hero, the greatest living rodeo cowboy, ride up close and personal.

And that was after she'd beat him.

And then he'd kissed her.

It almost made up for the missing.

At the very least, it was proof that even impossible dreams could come true.

As the song died down, Lil's moment with the audience drew to its natural conclusion, and she turned to Sierra, who stood smiling out at the crowd. Blinding lights prevented anyone on stage from really seeing the people there, but, in this case, Lil wasn't sure it mattered.

Sierra's face might wear a smile, but she was anything but happy.

Whether it was due to the fact that Lil had momentarily stolen her stage or simply because she'd successfully maneuvered around her questions, Lil would never know. And quickly, it was out of her mind to even wonder.

Sierra swept her arm grandly, drawing the cameras back to

her before shouting brightly, "And here she is folks, the one, the only—and I mean that quite literally—Lil Sorrow! PBRA's first female rough stock champion! Give it up for Lil Sorrow! The mysterious little cowgirl that swept in out of nowhere and reminded us all how to ride a bronc!"

Following her gesture, Lil stepped onto the top step of the small riser, and the arena thundered, filling Lil's bones with a tingle of restless power she didn't know what to do with.

"And here *he* is, folks!" Sierra called, voice curling around the *he* like a cat in a lap. "The one, the only, AJ Garza, our undisputed king of rodeo!"

If the crowd had thundered before, its roar now threatened to tear down the stadium, rattling the stage and risers.

AJ stepped onto the step below her and still stood taller.

Next to him, Lil shivered.

This close, she caught his scent: desert pine, with a hint of tantalizing wildness, like riding off into a sunset—with the top down in a convertible.

For the fourth time of the night, their eyes locked, and it occurred to her that standing on the top step of a tiered podium while he stood in second place was likely the closest to eye to eye they were ever going to see.

AJ reached out a hand with a friendly smile, completely nonchalant for the fact that he'd held her far more intimately with that hand less than an hour before. "From where I'm standing," he said, "it looks like CityBoyz won't be getting a new coach after all."

It was a peace offering.

Lil opened her mouth to respond, but as the crowd finally settled down, Sierra announced the third-place contestant. "And in third place, nipping at AJ's heels like always, that old dirty dog, the unshakeable, Hank DeRoy!"

As the noise settled back to a normal rodeo level, Sierra

went on, "With the awarding of these buckles, the PBRA Closed Circuit goes live! Stay tuned folks, we're coming to a town near you, and if you want to get an even closer, electrifying look, don't forget to follow the show on all your favorite social media channels!"

And quicker than seemed fair, given how long Lil'd waited for this moment, Sierra pressed a buckle in her hand and moved on to AJ.

The buckle was cold and heavy in Lil's palm, as alive as it was dead, and more precious than gold. Lil held it to her heart and closed her eyes. AJ caught the move and smiled at her, no trace of mockery in his warm brown eyes.

The same couldn't be said for Hank.

"Now, sugar, you didn't have to risk your life on a bronco to find a good ride. All you had to do was let Ol' Hankey here know, and I could've taken care of you."

Lil replied between her teeth, speaking through her picture smile as she said, "You didn't even recognize I had the equipment. I doubt you'd know how to handle it."

On her other side, AJ snorted, adding, "Watch out, *Hankey*, this one might be out of your league."

DeRoy shifted his attention entirely to AJ as a girl in a green shirt came to usher Lil off the stage.

She didn't look back, not exiting the arena, not making her way through the crowd, stopping for pictures and autographs as she went, and not along the final stretch through the long parking lot on the way back to her car.

The two of them could have at it.

She might be the PBRA's first female rough stock champion, but she was sleeping in her own bed tonight, and that meant she had a long drive back to Muscogee.

9

AJ stared at the second-place tour RV with a bemused grin on his face. The vehicle was a first. So was the second place—at least in a long time. The RV would be his home for the next month—or at least as long as he held the second-place spot.

He didn't plan on getting comfortable.

Relax-o-wagon was sponsoring the tour in the form of thirteen tour vehicles—enough to house and transport the fifty contestants for the road trip portion of the eight-week tour—at least until they were eliminated.

The first-place contestant got the top-of-the-line model. Second place got a super deluxe, and third, merely deluxe. But they each got their own. The remaining forty-seven cowboys were split amongst the ten remaining standard models at a rate of about five men per bus. That meant a lot of cowboy musk in a small space.

In the Closed Circuit, there were more reasons than money to run ahead of the pack.

Above the fleet, the sky was the kind of dark that only five thirty in the morning could achieve, and AJ was the first contestant on site.

He stood ten feet from the vehicle that would be his for the first leg of the tour, an oversized duffel bag hanging over one shoulder. Around him, greenies hauled black tubs with yellow lids from truck beds to storage compartments beneath the RVs while the green-shirted folks on the media-team side scuttled around taking photos and shooting video.

AJ hadn't always been an early riser—it was something that Henry had drilled into him over their twenty-four-year relationship—but now he considered it one of the things that gave him an edge.

Taking in the pristine RV in front of him, luxury in every way, though slightly smaller than the one parked in front of it, he realized he wasn't quite ready to give up that edge yet.

In fact, he was going to drop his bag off and go on a quick run.

Contestants weren't expected to check in until eight, and the caravan wouldn't be hitting the road until nine—plenty of time.

As he reached into his pocket for the keys they'd mailed him, a light switched on in the first-place RV. Lil Sorrow walked out of what AJ guessed was the bathroom, head tilted to the side, drying her long hair with the towel in her hands. The thin white tank top she wore emphasized her slender, toned frame.

After taking what seemed like too long to dry her hair, she shook the towel out and did a quick hotel-style three-fold like she was going to hang it up all nice and pretty.

Obviously uptight, AJ thought, shaking his head with a smirk. That, or she was keeping the place nice because she knew she wouldn't be there long. Maybe bareback bronc just happened to be her one event.

As if she sensed she was being watched, Lil Sorrow's head whipped in AJ's direction. Their eyes met, and something like genuine horror flashed across her face before her arm shot out to flip the blinds closed on a glare.

For a second, AJ didn't move, feeling almost guilty, like he'd been caught peeping or something. He shook himself to clear the sensation. She had been fully clothed.

AJ ran a hand down his face, once again thrown off by Lil Sorrow. Who was she? She came out of nowhere but rode like a seasoned pro—and had an attitude to go along with it.

As AJ's thoughts settled, his mind began processing other details of the scene. She had come out of the shower in her trailer. That meant she had beaten him to the site.

Hell, a shower this early probably meant she had beaten him to a morning run, too.

AJ made a noise of disgust in the back of his throat, unlocked the door to the second-place RV, and stepped inside. The woman was really starting to become a thorn in his side.

10

The drive from Houston to Dallas had been one of the smoothest rides AJ had ever taken. He'd never have thought it, but RVing wasn't a bad way to travel.

Yet another thing the old folks were right about.

Thoughts like that wove through his consciousness the same way stray gray hairs showed up in his stubble.

The signs he wasn't getting any younger.

Fortunately, with age came good sense. He was past both the age and income bracket where he should have to tolerate discomfort.

And Winnie, as he'd begun calling the RV, was damn comfortable to drive.

The driver's seat sat high and plush with the kind of view that made you feel like the king of the road. Adjustable armrests and an ideally positioned steering wheel meant long stretches of driving remained gentle on the shoulders, elbows, and wrists. He appreciated that on a day when he had

an event, particularly as tonight's rodeo was dedicated to roping and wrestling.

The Closed Circuit officially kicked off with a demonstra-
tion of the basic ranch skills that were the seeds of rodeo: steer
wrestling and tie-down roping. But to make sure the folks of
Dallas didn't go home feeling like they'd been cheated out of
a real show, the Closed Circuit was upping the ante.

Every cowboy was going to do both events in the classic
rodeo style. For wrestling, that meant cowboy in the box, calf
behind the rope, hazer helping out. For roping, it would be
just cowboy and calf.

After that, things got creative. For the second round of
wrestling, each cowboy would have to do it without a hazer.
For the second round of roping, the Closed Circuit had created
a ranch simulation with one cowboy, seven calves, and one
goal: rope your mark just like you'd have to out on the range.

Contestants would be given two hours for practice in the
arena before the space was cleared out to prepare for the show,
but there would be no time to practice with multiple calves.

The exercise was a first, like just about everything else
about the Closed Circuit, so nobody had an advantage on
that front—but any cowboy that had ever worked a real ranch
damn sure had a leg up.

AJ hadn't worked on a ranch a single day in his life.

Although he'd finally shed his gym rat label after his third
championship, the rub hadn't become any less applicable. AJ
might be the greatest rodeo cowboy in a generation, but he'd
learned everything he knew in a downtown Houston gym.

As the son of two teachers, rodeo wasn't exactly in his
blood.

Well, that wasn't quite true. His father came from multiple
proud Tejano lines—all of them Texans longer than Texas.

There'd been more than a few cowboys in that ancestry.

But his mom had been born and raised in Houston's third ward, as her parents had been before her. There hadn't been a cowboy or a farmer in that family line since 1865.

And if things hadn't gone so wrong with his dad, he'd never have discovered rodeo himself. Blessings disguised as tragedies.

Ahead of him in the caravan—the driving order of which reflected the Closed Circuit standings—Lil Sorrow's RV signaled and turned left onto the off-ramp. They'd arrive at the arena in another fifteen minutes.

Two and a half hours later, AJ lay in the soft dirt of the arena grounds, grinning like a fool. The calf he'd been practicing with gave a moo, and he quickly untied her. The greenie timing him called out three-point-nine seconds, and his grin stretched wider. Six attempts, and all of them under four seconds—that meant a certain shorty's days in that first-place RV were numbered…

Around him, other contestants practiced to a symphony of shouted advice. As usual, a few coaches had approached AJ, but, as usual, he'd declined their assistance.

He worked with The Old Man, or alone.

It wasn't just because he was loyal, though that was true, as well. He'd just learned a long time ago not to trust every helping hand that came his way, and he'd learned it just like he learned everything else: the hard way, at the rodeo.

Whether it was cowboys trying to sabotage the competition or sweet little bunnies that wanted to get a little closer to his money, jackals had been sniffing around him since back in the days when he'd still been called an up-and-comer.

It was hard to keep your money a secret when you made it in front of audiences of thousands. He wouldn't have it any other way, though. Rodeo had saved his life.

After his dad moved out, he'd been a wreck. Literally. He'd wanted to wreck everything, and he had.

He started with his bike. Red, with chrome accents, it had thick, high-tread tires and straight handlebars. It was a grown-up bike, not just a kid's neighborhood bike, but also a bike he could take with him when they went camping in the desert. In his head, he'd named it Stallion, though at twelve, he'd never have in a million years admitted that out loud. He and his dad had spent his whole birthday putting it together, and he hadn't resented a second of the time. He took it with them camping two years in a row. The second time, at thirteen and with no idea what was coming, he'd ridden the bike out farther than he'd ever gone from camp.

He'd brought a flashlight and a telescope. He'd used only the telescope. The moonlight had been enough to ride by. He made it back to camp to find his mom and dad sitting at opposite sides of the fire, looking up at the stars. They'd smiled and asked what he'd seen. He'd told them the constellations he'd seen, and when they got home, they told him they were getting a divorce.

A week after that, he found the tallest hill in Houston that also had railroad tracks at its base. The requirements were oddly specific, but so was his intent. He waited for two hours and then let go. The train's horn had been shrill and urgent, but not enough to save the bike.

A light tap on his shoulder shook him from the memory. A young man in a green shirt stood above him, shifting his weight from side to side.

"I'm sorry, Mr. Garza. Practice time is over. We've got to clear the arena now."

AJ rose to his feet, head swiveling around. The arena had cleared out to just him and a handful of staff while he'd been lost in thought.

He shook his head to clear it, but it didn't bring an accounting of the lollygagged time back—more signs of age.

As he followed the staffer out of the arena, it occurred to him that he hadn't seen Lil Sorrow come in at all during the practice window. AJ had been the first in and, unintentionally this time, the last out.

Lil Sorrow was probably one of those who thought pre-practice was bad luck.

AJ hoped not. That type was common but usually didn't have stamina. AJ was surprised by the disappointment he felt at the thought. He hadn't realized how much he was looking forward to the competition.

But anybody who thought they could do two months straight of intense rodeo and beat AJ Garza doing it was going to need a whole lot of stamina.

Rubbing his shoulder, he walked back to the RVs thinking through the rest of his afternoon: a shave, a shower, and a hot meal. The shower might be cramped, and the meal might be something microwaved, but the whole setup was still cushy compared to what most cowboys were used to on the real rodeo circuit.

He and The Old Man had slept in the truck and eaten microwaved Chef Boyardee in mini-marts many a night in his early days.

That'd been a long time ago, though—back when D was still in college and before AJ'd won his first big prize. A lifetime ago now.

These days he could afford hotels and restaurants. Or, rather, he could during his last days as a pro.

These days he was retired. Closed Circuit or not, he had to remember that.

And when he wrapped this up, he was going to go back to Houston and settle down.

The lie fell flat even to his own mind. No wonder it didn't work on anyone he considered family.

He didn't even have a home to stay in.

Houston might be where his mother was, where her life and her students were, her school, her house—everything in her life besides him—but he was just a passerby there, a visitor whose real life was spent on the road.

And while she'd always have a place for him at her house, at thirty-six years old, he sure as hell wasn't going to move back in with his mama.

No matter how much she badgered him.

He'd meant it when he'd said he'd probably find a place near the gym. It didn't need to be fancy, just a place to crash after coaching. That was the only thing about his future he was sure about. If he wasn't going to ride anymore, he was going to have a hand in shaping the next generation of champions.

And if that happened to be in his image, then so much the better. Was that very different from any other man?

If he'd been more inclined to think ahead, he might have found a steadier career, as Diablo had, but rodeo had hooked AJ young, leaving no room for anything else. Like any other professional calling, a man wanted to leave his mark.

As far as callings went, rodeo hadn't done him wrong.

He'd made good money—enough to buy his mom a house and enough to retire comfortably at thirty-six—and, unlike most, his body was still in good shape. The only crutch it'd left him with, in his eyes, was a long stretch of life ahead of him with nothing much to do with it. What else was there to do when rodeo had been all he'd ever wanted to do?

Arriving at his RV, he decided to eat first, tossing one of the frozen dinners the competition provided in the microwave. It was fresher than he'd expected but hit the spot only because it was food.

In the bathroom, the RV's mirror and sink were fine for shaving, but the shower was too small for a man his size. The water hitting the top of his shoulders and sliding down his back, however, was still a hot, slick massage he appreciated.

AJ took longer in the shower than he should have, but the water stayed warm.

He was really starting to fall in love with the RV. He could just get one of these and live in the gym's parking lot.

The thought had a certain amount of rich-guy-next-door appeal. Whether parents would be real keen on leaving their children at a facility that boasted the desirable amenity of a single man living in a trailer in the parking lot was, however, questionable.

A knock on his door drew him out of his thoughts. He turned off the water and hollered, "Just a minute," before wrapping a towel around his waist.

Lil Sorrow stood on the other side, arms crossed in front of her chest. The mulish cast of her face widened to alarm as her gray eyes swept down from AJ's face to take in his bare chest and towel-clad body. Cheeks reddening, she looked away, and AJ fought the urge to let the towel slip a little lower, just to see what she'd do. Nothing too prurient, of course, this was still rodeo after all, but enough to throw her off balance. His need to throw her off balance seemed to grow every time he tried and failed.

Standing this close, her skin looked more baby soft and creamy than it had before, her cheeks silky brown and perfectly smooth—and blushing. He was staring at her, he realized with a start.

Straightening abruptly as he cleared his throat, AJ asked, "What's up?"

Looking at his feet, she mumbled, "Saw DeRoy messing around over here earlier. Thought I'd let you know."

AJ laughed, startling them both. "Don't worry about him. Hank's always up to something. He's been up to something for eighteen years. It's always harmless and always within the rules."

She gave a curt nod and then turned and left without another word, and AJ found he was a little disappointed to realize that, despite the blush, there'd been no pretense or ulterior motive to her visit. She'd said her piece and left.

Without so much as a goodbye.

He shook his head, clicking his tongue at her back. Some people just didn't prioritize manners.

And AJ had always heard how friendly people from Oklahoma were—just went to show you couldn't believe everything you heard.

Alone again, he unwrapped the towel and slid on a pair of boxer briefs. Over those, a pair of dark wash blue jeans and a fitted bright red Western-style button up. He wore fancy shirts for promos and photoshoots but stuck to solid colors for events. He was the flash. His clothes merely accentuated it.

His belt was dark brown, as were his boots because his mama taught him right. His hat was plain brown leather and also simple. Again, he saved the artistry for the performance.

Finally, he chapped up and grabbed his rope.

It was time to go make some money for CityBoyz.

The RVs were parked in the employee parking lot of the arena, a key card–accessible section at the farthest edge of the farthest corner of the lot. They were also assigned a security guard. It was a funny thing to have an out-of-shape guy with a badge guarding fifty honed and grown men, but AJ figured that was the whole reality TV thing.

All the contestants were scheduled for a media day tomorrow, and the following day, the first skills challenge of the competition would take place. Each of the skills challenges was broadcast live as well as recorded for the internet audience, but otherwise performed in front of skeleton crews of media, site stage, greenies, and contestants. The goal of the skills challenges was to show that the Closed Circuit cowboys, unlike other rodeos, were made of more than just showing off in the arena. Closed Circuit challenges were meant to prove that the winning cowboy had the try: in the arena and out on the range, too.

The first set of challenges each took place in a rural town located somewhere along the tour route. When they were down to the final three, the Closed Circuit would announce the final surprise challenges, each based on the final three cowboys that were going through to the finale.

For this first challenge, though, they'd be roping wild mustangs in Ardmore, Oklahoma.

But that was for another day. Before that, and before tomorrow's media day, was the wrestling and roping he was headed to.

The volume of the noise grew as AJ neared the arena. So did the size of the crowd.

There were more buckle bunnies around tonight than there had been in Houston, which was a surprise. Only the most serious buckle bunnies actually followed the rodeo. Most just made sure to be in attendance wearing their best when the rodeo came to town—a fact that AJ had greatly appreciated, coming of age as a rising rodeo star.

He'd appreciated it traveling around the world, too.

The Old Man had always been clear about how he felt about things, though, so he wouldn't be sampling while he rode for CityBoyz. It was a commitment he would have made without The Old Man even having to ask, but because he had, AJ was doubly honor bound.

AJ pulled his hat lower as he made his way through the

crowd. It was easier to navigate when his face wasn't so obvious. Face obscured, men noticed him only enough to get out of the way. Women still noticed him for more than that, but they didn't recognize him, and that made all the difference.

Near the gates, Lil Sorrow had somehow found three feet of space outside the box within which to pace, nerves written all over her. She wore another beaded ribbon vest. This one dark brown with three different shades of brown ribbon. Rather than an abstract pattern, the beading of this one created a picture of a buffalo standing against a sunset silhouette.

Once again, the thousands of beads caught the light—yellows, oranges, and reds making up the sun while different shades of brown and gold brought the buffalo to almost three-dimensional life. Every time Lil Sorrow turned in her pacing, the beads caught the light and flashed, possibly accounting for some of the space around her. If being the only woman on deck wasn't enough, her vests set her apart.

Outside of her bubble, cowboys, VIPs, coaches, and fans pressed to be as close to the action as they could.

AJ stepped into her space.

She stopped midpace and looked up, her thick eyebrows drawn straight over her eyes.

"Scared?" he asked.

Her frown deepened, but there was a kick in her low voice when she spoke. "Just scared I might embarrass you. My folks taught me to respect my elders, and I just don't know what to do when I beat you."

AJ grinned lazily. "Nice comeback, but you've got to look less serious about it all."

The corner of her lips lifted, just a little, and AJ was satisfied.

"Stop showing your feelings on your face, though," AJ

added, unable to help himself from giving advice. "They'll use it against you."

A single eyebrow lifted. "They?"

"Your competition."

"You mean you," she reminded him.

AJ raised his palms. "I'm just trying to help you. You might not be a kid, but you're sure as hell new around here."

"Why do you want to help me?"

AJ wondered that himself. The woman in front of him was cranky, small, and hotheaded, and it'd be a damn sight easier to give her a wide berth than it was to offer her a hand.

But she also smelled like the future of rodeo. And vanilla.

"You've got something special," he said.

Her mouth dropped open, eyes going wide with shock.

AJ laughed. "Don't let it get to your head. You've still got to ride tonight."

Her eyes narrowed again. Suspicion written all over her face, she said, "This is you trying to get in my head."

AJ shrugged with a grin. "Maybe. Or maybe I'm just an old man feeling sentimental on the brink of retirement." Then he stepped out of her pacing space.

But she was intrigued. "What's that supposed to mean?"

He shrugged. "I got nothing to lose."

Lil Sorrow shot back, "Except this competition." But a smile stretched across her face.

It was exactly what he'd come over for, though he hadn't realized it had been his intention until now.

And then she was up.

AJ watched from above the chute. As usual, she looked even smaller on a horse. AJ frowned. If she was going to ride rough stock, she needed some protein shakes or something.

The steer shot out of the barrier.

The hazer and Lil Sorrow flew out after it as soon as her

rope dropped. Lil Sorrow slid down the right side of her horse and leaped at the steer, kicking her heels as they cleared the stirrups. She hooked the steer around the neck with her right elbow and grabbed the horns lightly with her left hand.

AJ frowned, watching even as he saddled up for his turn. Lil Sorrow's grip wasn't strong enough to force the steer down, momentum or not.

But then she twisted her body again at the same time as she pushed the steer's horns upward with her left hand.

The steer's entire body gave another spin.

Beast and cowboy slid to stop in the dirt, steer on its side, all four feet pointing in the same direction. Three-point-one seconds had passed. Once again, the arena erupted with cheers for Lil Sorrow.

AJ had never seen the little twist move before, and he'd been to a lot of rodeos. The kid had opened the night with flair.

As the second-place contestant, AJ was up next. He didn't have any fancy new moves to showcase. He was fortunate enough to rely on the old-fashioned way—brute strength.

Once Lil Sorrow had cleared the arena, everything reset to do it all over again—this time with him at center stage.

His steer shot out. He and his hazer followed when the barrier dropped. He took his steer down in classic fashion: right hook and left push. And he didn't know if it was the adrenaline of having real competition for the first time in years, or simply the thrill of watching her in action, but he got it done in three seconds.

11

AJ left the arena momentarily deaf and headed straight for the green room. Lil Sorrow was already in the room when he got there, of course, sitting at the end of the table by herself.

AJ grabbed a water out of the fridge and then walked over to lean against the counter near where she sat.

"Weird move out there."

She grunted.

"Made up for your size alright."

Dry and raspy, she replied, "It's almost like I planned it."

AJ tipped his water to her with a chuckle. "Ready for the next round?"

She nodded once. "You don't usually get a hazer on a ranch."

Touchy. The short ones always were. "I almost bought a ranch once," he said wistfully.

She stiffened, but forced a smile. "What stopped you?"

He grinned. "No hazers on a ranch."

She snorted at the same time as the door slammed open and

Hank DeRoy stalked in. Without taking note of the room's occupants, he tossed his hat on a table, ran a hand through his hair, and went straight to the fridge, from which he pulled out a beer and shotgunned it.

Only then, wiping his mouth with the back of his hand, did he finally look around the room. AJ and Lil Sorrow were stationed at one end of the counter. Both looked at him—AJ leaning back and grinning, amused at the fool's constant obviousness, Lil Sorrow, upright and inscrutable. Neither said a word.

Hank looked from him to Lil Sorrow, then back to him, a frown coming to mar his sweaty blond brow. Slowly, he straightened and retrieved his hat before putting his can in the recycling bin. Hat in place, he strolled over with an exaggerated cowboy swagger.

"Didn't mean to interrupt your make-out session," he said cheerfully to both of them before angling his body toward Lil Sorrow's. "If you ever feel like graduating to a real man, cowgirl, you can always give me a try."

AJ's voice was warm when he responded, like he was talking to an old friend, despite the fact that Hank's crude words had his hackles rising: "Bad run, DeRoy?"

In a way they were old friends.

They'd known each other long enough for AJ to realize the sharp tang in Hank's voice meant he had been beat.

"Never heard of such a thing, Garza. And I believe the lady and I were chatting."

Lil Sorrow pushed between the two, moving away from both.

AJ frowned. Hank turned his attention to Lil Sorrow.

"*The lady* was just on her way," she said as she passed.

"Now hold on, we're just getting to know each other. It isn't often you meet a woman who makes you envious of livestock."

Based on his experience with her, AJ expected Lil Sorrow to lose her temper with the man's forwardness. He was closer to it, himself, than he'd like to admit. But, to AJ's surprise, Lil Sorrow didn't rise to the bait. If anything, she looked bored.

Shrugging lightly, she said, "Nor is it often that you meet men who make you envious of feedlot stock, but as they say, 'there are more things in heaven and earth…'" She turned to AJ. "Trust your horse and focus on the steer, Garza."

AJ laughed, the reaction more genuine than his typical show of laid-backness. Lil Sorrow tipped her hat to punctuate the insult and walked out without looking back, beaded vest twinkling in the light.

Hank whistled as he watched her leave, hollering after her, "You can throw a punch as well as you rope a steer, princess. But I'll keep coming back for more—I just love beating a man killer."

"As always, DeRoy. You're out of your league." AJ finished his water and tossed it in the plastic bin.

"Watch it, Garza… We might be peers in the arena, but outside, you're not just outmanned, you're outclassed." It was a well-known fact that Hank came from Kentucky horse royalty, the cowboy with the silver spoon to go with all his shiny silver buckles. Rodeo traditionally didn't have much room for rich boys, but Hank fancied himself a Southern gentleman and apparently that was a kind of fancy rodeo folk *would* accept. But only because, lagging behind AJ aside, Hank knew his way around a bull.

Sighing dramatically, AJ said, "A man can only watch the same old thing—be it my name climbing higher and higher than yours in the standings or your terrible game—for so long, DeRoy."

But instead of another threat, Hank smiled, instantly putting AJ's senses on alert.

"But not quite number one, this time. How's that feel?"

The words struck closer than Hank usually managed, but AJ wasn't about to let it show, or answer the other man's question. Instead, he brought his finger and thumb to his face, an imitation of *The Thinker*, saying, "And, since you're always behind me, that makes you third, right?"

Hank flipped him off and AJ grinned.

The intercom in the room crackled and a young voice gave the twenty-minute warning, followed by the jangle of a phone hanging up.

"There's our call." AJ grinned. "Better get your head in the game, DeRoy. Time's running out."

"Eat a dick, Garza."

Taking the old-timey cowboy cue from Lil Sorrow, AJ tipped his hat with a wide grin on his face and headed back to the arena, leaving Hank in the room.

The grin didn't last.

It took AJ twice as long to wrestle his steer without a hazer.

Each and every other cowboy took three times their average—except Lil Sorrow. She'd lost only a second and a half on her time, and that looked like it had more to do with her steer reacting to the crowd than the lack of a hazer.

Either way, he was feeling a lot less chatty when he entered the contestant's room after the second round. Fortunately, he didn't need to worry. The only people in the room were a couple greenies and one of the bottom twenty-fivers. The bottom twenty-five cowboys would be cut in the first elimination round, after the challenge.

Barring some dramatic turn of luck, the young man wasn't going much farther than Ardmore.

Which meant there was no need to make conversation, a fact that suited AJ's mood just fine.

Instead, he replayed the scene from the arena in his mind.

Steers, it turned out, were smarter than folks gave them credit for. More than he'd given them credit for, at least.

It had been Lil Sorrow's voice in his head that'd finally sorted him out enough to get the thing done.

After trying everything else, AJ had focused on the steer and let his body naturally follow it. The horse followed the natural lean of his body and suddenly he was where he needed to be. The steer was where it needed to be an instant later.

He'd thank her later, though, after he secured a win. There were two more rounds to go before he had it for tonight, though.

Tie-down roping followed the intermission. One round with a single calf and one picking out a single marked calf out of a panicked group of ten.

He didn't expect to set any new world records in classic tie-down roping, but he knew he'd give Lil Sorrow a run for her money.

Catching a calf in a bunch was going to take longer, but it was essentially the same skill set.

However, an hour and a half later, AJ was back in the contestant's lounge, no closer to beating Lil Sorrow out of the number one spot.

Watching the woman in action with a rope was like an evening at the symphony. When you tossed in a horse and calf, it was a goddamn Vegas show.

She was like a centaur, or at the very least an ancient steppe warrior on top of a horse before she leaped off for her prey.

Thus far, AJ was one for three, and the final event of the night wasn't one that inspired confidence.

His odds weren't great, considering the last event was another ranch simulation and the woman's day job was ranching. His shoulder burned at the thought, but AJ refused to give the sensation space. The night wasn't over yet and neither was the challenge.

As if summoned by his thoughts, Lil Sorrow entered the room and AJ sat up straighter.

Both of them seemed surprised when she said, "Nice job out there."

AJ recovered first with an easy smile. "Feeling friendly, now that your lead is secure?" he teased.

She laughed. "No. Must be all the excitement going to my head." She tossed AJ a water bottle and watched him open it. After AJ took a swig, she said, "Focus on your mark and push out farther left than you think you need to. It'll keep the other calves out of the way and give you more space."

AJ took another swig of water before he asked, "And why would you help me?"

Lil Sorrow shrugged. "Don't want to see an old man embarrassed."

AJ's laugh lifted some of the tightness in his shoulders. It'd already been a long night. "With how quick you are to make me look like a fool? What's the real reason? I know you want to win."

A light dusky rose blossomed on her cheeks, and she looked away before grumbling, "I sure do, but when I beat the world's greatest rodeo cowboy, I want to be sure that it's because of skill and not ignorance. It doesn't mean anything if it only happened 'cause you didn't know."

He snorted. He should have known she'd say something like that. Ms. Solitary Cowboy would never admit to helping the enemy for the simple fact that they were becoming friends.

"Fair enough, Lil Sorrow. Thanks for the tip."

She turned back to him with a smile, her gray eyes warming to sparkling crescent moons above her grinning cheeks, and AJ's heart stopped. It was like a mini sun had risen in the room, bright and fully capable of energizing the cosmos.

"No problem," she said, adding, "and call me Lil."

But she was wrong. It was a problem, a series of them, in fact, and not insignificant. It was an unforgettable kiss, an incredible talent, and a galaxy-charging smile.

After AJ didn't say anything, Lil shrugged, and on her way out, smile wavering, said, "Anyway. Good luck out there," on her way out.

AJ stayed where he was. The final event of the night was less than thirty minutes away. He didn't have the time to be laid to waste by a smile.

But there he was.

12

AJ's first moments in the arena with the calves were chaos—but, once again, Lil had been right.

AJ's calf had been marked with a strip of blue paint on its flank, a color that turned out to be far harder to track amongst the panicked calves than he would have guessed. Creating the extra space on the left kept the others away and made it a whole lot easier to rope his mark.

But not easy enough to beat Lil's time.

The next day, the novelty of waking up in second place was starting to wear off.

Unfortunately, his next opportunity to change things involved catching wild mustangs.

Having never encountered a wild mustang in real life, AJ was at a disadvantage. He knew how to rope, and at its core, the whole thing was just more rope work, but AJ knew better than to think that was how it would go.

As always, a small pod of greenies bustled around the RVs,

running errands, taking pictures, and stocking mini fridges. AJ felt bad for those on snack duty. They had to go inside the bullpens, as the multibunk vehicles had started to be called. Just being downwind was enough to knock you over.

It was just too small a space for that many grown men...

Once again, AJ appreciated the spacious, pleasant-smelling accommodations of the top tier. He tilted back in one of his plush leather seats and stretched out his legs. He wore a white T-shirt, gray sweats, and a backward baseball hat. The ensemble had been his basic at-home attire since he was ten years old.

Why change what worked?

He was tempted to look out the window to see if Lil's blinds were open. He bet the woman probably relaxed in full rodeo gear—if she even knew how to relax. He honestly wasn't sure.

But, knowing Lil, she probably skipped the usual routine of coffee and instead wrestled with mustangs for breakfast.

AJ snorted. She was a real cowboy, that one.

Jokes aside, though, it was never a good idea to ignore a resource when one had one, and he was going to need more help.

He slipped on a pair of shoes and headed next door.

Lil opened after the first knock, but not all the way.

Just as AJ'd imagined, the woman was dressed full cowboy: Wranglers, black button-up, black hat, black books, big buckle.

AJ smirked.

Lil's eyes narrowed. "What?"

AJ said, "Now what kind of welcome is that?" He laid the Texas on thick, enjoying the way it brought a frown to Lil's face. AJ felt an almost moral obligation to break her of her habit of taking everything too seriously.

Lil muttered, "Better than you deserve. What do you want?"

AJ wouldn't have been surprised to hear a humph at the end. She reminded him of his grandmother—old, and cranky about it. So, just like he did with granny, he smiled sweetly.

"Had a few questions about mustangs," he said. Smiles always worked on his granny.

They worked on Lil, too. Her shoulders relaxed and she opened the door all the way, even if she didn't stop frowning. "Don't have much time, but sure."

AJ waited a beat until it was clear Lil wasn't going to invite him in. Then he said, "Any suggestions? Never dealt with wild horses."

Lil thought for a moment. "Wear them out first and start with the ones that group together."

AJ asked, "Wear them out?"

Lil turned her back to AJ while speaking. "Make noise, walk at them, get them running around. They're prey animals, you're not." Then she turned around to finish. "That's all I got. Sorry, I've got to get to my interview." She turned around with a jacket in her hand and stepped out of the RV around AJ.

AJ nodded and backed down the steps. "Thanks."

Lil sent him a quick nod in acknowledgment before locking her door and hustling off toward a black sedan that idled near the RVs. She slipped inside the car and was lost behind tinted glass.

AJ watched after them for a moment before heading back to his own RV. His car wasn't due for another hour.

The top ten contestants were being featured in one-on-one videos that "told their story." It wasn't really their story, though. It was the reality TV version of their story—the parts that made good entertainment.

The videos would be aired as filler during broadcasts as well as go up on the Closed Circuit website and social media.

AJ planned to use every sound bite to spread the word about CityBoyz. The Old Man was going to need a full staff to coach all the new sign-ups after he was done. He hoped

Lil had something in mind for hers, because if she didn't give them a strong lead, the media was going to continue running her as ragged as a herd of wild horses.

The first challenge started at high noon.

Mounted in full gear and positioned beneath a hot and angry sun, AJ wondered if it was possible for a rodeo to go overboard with Western references. Based on the number of viewers that tuned in and the sold-out arenas, he didn't think so.

Lil stood in the center of a large fenced ring, a miniature pillar of black in a cowboy hat with a rope coiled at her hip.

The five mustangs were scattered around the ring, each one standing alone.

The go sign was a bell, and when it rang, Lil took off. On foot, she ran in circles inside the ring, hazing the horses with whistles and claps. The horses panicked, bunching together as they ran along the fence and away from Lil. Lil kept the hullabaloo up for a full two minutes, while AJ watched her time tick away. She hadn't even reached for her rope yet. Hadn't even tried to catch a single horse.

After far too much time wasted, both Lil and the horses slowed. The horses were slick with sweat and breathing heavy. Lil hadn't lost any energy, though, not even as she slowed. Instead, she reached for the rope at her side and advanced slowly on the horse closest to her. The horse's ears flicked, signaling awareness, but the creature didn't move.

AJ willed Lil to loose the rope quickly, before the horse bolted, but instead, she took another step closer. The horse shuffled uneasily, but his reflexes were poor after the hard run. Then Lil's lasso flew out, catching the creature around the neck before it could spook.

She trotted the horse to the gate quickly, then grabbed the

rest of the ropes before going back for the rest of the horses. She caught two more close together as they'd paired up, before rounding up the final two. Each one was easier than the last, with the final horse joining her without fuss.

All said and done, the five horses took her six-point-eight minutes to round up.

She had followed her own advice, which was a good sign.

Now it was AJ's turn.

The crew cleared and raked the ring, and AJ walked to its center. The horses scattered away from him in four directions with one pairing amongst the lot of them.

Lucky him.

The bell rang, and AJ did what Lil had done, but, like always, he did it with the added support of superior musculature.

When he was done, his horses stopped circling, standing panting in three bunches, a group of two, a group of three, and a singleton.

He started with the group of three. They were already the most docile. The group of two were more standoffish but got in line with the rest soon enough. Brute strength brought in the last one, shaving off valuable extra time to come in at six-point-five minutes.

When the challenge was over, he went looking for Lil.

He found her sitting in the shade of an old barn, possibly the only shade to be had on the flat farm.

AJ said, "Great work out there. And thanks again for the advice. It worked."

Lil jumped at the sound of his voice, gray eyes going a little too wide before she replied, "Oh yeah. No problem."

"How'd the interview go?"

Lil frowned. "It was fine. Didn't seem like many of the questions had anything to do with rodeo."

"It's not supposed to be about rodeo. They want to know

about you. Your backstory. The things that tug the heart-strings."

"Oh. Well I don't have much of that."

AJ laughed, "Everybody's got that."

Digging in, Lil shook her head. "Not me. I just ranch and that's it."

AJ said dryly, "You're the first female rough stock rider to win a PBRA buckle. Lead with that."

Lil sighed, the sound weighted with real emotion. "I'm not the first the female to love rodeo, though, and that's really what it all comes down to—the same as every other cowboy out there."

"With one important difference—" he began.

"My anatomy?" she cut in with disgust.

He lifted an eyebrow. "It's about more than that and you can't pretend otherwise. You represent something. Every time you go out there, you don't just show them what you can do. You show them how foolish and artificial the barriers ever were to begin with."

For a moment she was quiet, just staring at him gray-eyed and serious, as beautiful in thought and open to setting down a little bit of her stubborn as she was in the arena and on the winner's podium.

Then she smiled, and he felt it like a warm snake uncoiling in his belly.

Humor brought honey to the whiskey of her voice when she said, "You should have done the interview for me. That was better than what I said."

Laughing, AJ turned away, if only to give his system a break from mainlining Lil. The effect she had on him was something else. Keeping his voice casual, he replied, "What can I say? I've been in the game a long time."

This time it was Lil who got a faraway look in her eye,

letting out a dry scoff. "It sure seems like everywhere I turn someone is quick to remind me that I haven't been—no matter that I've been riding my whole life and this isn't my first rodeo."

He gave her shoulder a light nudge. "Everybody loves a mystery. It's an advantage."

When she laughed, the sound was lukewarm and limp, not the lively thing he was coming to know and love. "In the hands of someone more skilled, maybe." She held up her palms and looked at them. "Not as much in these ones. No sir, indeed. These hands really have no business being this far from the ranch."

She joked, but it would be impossible to miss the thread of real weariness that wove through her words. She was out of her depth. The idea was laughable, she was doing so well, but her fear was real.

"I tell you what. How about I help you out on that front. It's the least I could do after all your help. As long as you're willing to take some tips and hints from an old-timer, that is." He flashed his cheering-up grumpy women grin again and tried to ignore the feeling of triumph when a little lightning spark came back to her eyes.

Crossing her arms in front of her chest, the corner of her mouth lifting, she said, "I don't know. Depends on how yours went."

As he wasn't lying, the cockiness in AJ's tone came backed by confidence. "Exactly how I planned it. Talked about City-Boyz the whole time. 'The organization that birthed the great AJ Garza threatened with closing its doors.'"

Lil rolled her eyes but nodded. "That's good. I'll consider your offer. So why rodeo?"

AJ frowned. "What?"

"Why rodeo to save it? Why don't you just make a donation? Did you lose all your money?"

AJ held a hand up to stop the barrage of questions. "One at a time," he laughed. "First: it's never *why* rodeo. Rodeo is always the answer. The question is, *how* rodeo? Plus Henry wouldn't take money from me directly. This way he'll be taking it from PBRA—and he loves to do that."

"Assuming you win…"

AJ loved it when Lil's voice dropped like that, its general dryness taking on an intriguing depth, like a whisper with a kick—aged bourbon, or a Santa Ana wind.

A corner of AJ's lips lifted absently. "I always win," he said.

"That hasn't been my experience." She delivered the line stoically, while squinting off into the horizon, as if she were commenting on an upcoming storm.

AJ laughed out loud, if only because she was right. Having some real competition again felt great, though. It'd been a long time since he'd been given a run for his money.

Now he just needed to catch up.

Changing the subject, he asked, "So back to this interview."

Lil frowned. "Past is past. There's no use dwelling on what's done."

He loved it when she went full cowboy on him. Almost as much as he loved it when he knew more than she did, rare as that had shown to be. "Ah, ah, ah, young Padawan. There is always something to be learned from past rides. You have to have analyzed videos of your rides in training."

Lil snorted. "Videos? Who's got time—or money—for videos? Granddad gave me all the feedback I needed, most of it 'needs improvement.'"

AJ smacked his palm on his forehead. "Unbelievable. Nothing is a better teacher than seeing how embarrassing your form is for yourself. I'm recording your next ride. That's it."

Lil laughed. "You go ahead and do that, but there won't be anything embarrassing about my form."

For a moment, her words hung between them, hot and heavy, until her lips parted and her pulse beat fast in her neck, and he gave them both the break they needed before things went somewhere they might not be able to control.

Clearing his throat, he chuckled, "You're probably right about that. But that kind of talk is best saved for the locker room. I hope you went more hopeful and inspiring for your interview."

Lil stiffened, an expression of discomfort coming to her face. "What do you mean?"

"Ranch girl with big dreams to change the world of rodeo?" he asked, lifting his eyebrows. It was the obvious angle.

Her shoulders relaxed. "Something like that."

He eyed her suspiciously. "Did you tell them where you're from?"

Once again she squirmed. "You mean, Muskogee?"

"No. I mean where you've been to get to be so good? Where you learned moves I've never seen or heard of."

"And you've been everywhere?" Lil asked.

"Just got back." He grinned.

Lil smiled and AJ's gaze caught on her lips.

What was going on with him? She'd proven time and again he couldn't afford any distractions. And he knew from personal experience just how distracting her lips could be.

"Obviously not everywhere," she said.

"Where'd I miss?"

"The middle of nowhere." She lifted an eyebrow at him. "Your *advice* is starting to sound a lot like spying."

His answering grin was as unrepentant as it was bold. "I need every advantage I can get when it comes to you." The sad thing was, it was true.

"We didn't get into the nitty-gritty of my technique, no. And we didn't really talk about my ranch or Oklahoma, or what I did in my time off. Nothing like that."

"It's pretty clear by now that all you do is cowboy. Sunup to sundown, 24/7." Though cowboys didn't typically have "time off" from rodeo. They gave it everything it wanted from them until it didn't want them anymore, or they walked away on top. There wasn't usually an in-between.

Lil didn't argue, saying with a smile, "As I was saying—boring."

"How long?"

"Five years."

AJ whistled. "You poor thing."

Humor danced across Lil's stormy eyes like lightning. "Not all of us live and breathe rodeo," she said.

AJ frowned. "I refuse to believe it."

Lil laughed. "It's true. But before I walked away, I rode in college and for the INFR."

AJ could picture it. The Indian rodeo circuit bred tough cowboys, but the PBRA resisted crossover. He'd never understand why so many people were committed to the idea that there wasn't enough pie to go around.

"So what brought you back?" he asked.

Lil said, "Oh, just the usual—saving the family ranch."

AJ's eyes widened. "Oooo. That's the juicy stuff. I hope you gave them some of that in your interview."

Lil frowned. "What do you mean?"

"For your feature. Saving the country home you love? It's a good rodeo angle."

She shook her head. "It didn't come up specifically."

"No?" he asked.

"No."

"What'd you talk about?" he asked, a sense of unease developing in his stomach—the feeling he always got before a bad ride.

Lil rolled her eyes. "Girl power and my relationship status."

It sounded like a waste of an interview, then, given the rich material she had to work with, but that was neither here nor there as her comment opened the door for more important avenues of inquiry. "Which is?"

The look she gave him was dry enough to use as a towel. "I'm single."

"And?"

She frowned, confusion all over her face. "That's all. I'm just single," she said.

"Does anyone else live on the ranch with you?" he pressed. She'd thought he was only flirting. Fortunately, he was an adept multitasker. Telling her story to him was practice for telling it to the camera.

"My grandmother."

"That it?"

"And my cousin and our ranch hand," she added.

"Are you Amish?"

"What?" she asked.

AJ grimaced. "You're boring, but it doesn't matter. You can ride. What about your parents?"

She opened her mouth, then closed it and he realized he'd touched a nerve. It was long enough before she finally responded that he had begun to think she wasn't going to. "My mom died when I was young and took the secret of my paternity to the grave with her. For most of my life it was just Gran and Granddad and me."

"How'd she die?" he asked, familiar with the pain of losing a parent young.

But instead of answering, her expression shuttered, the light in her eyes went dark, hidden behind a cold veil. "Sad and alone, but nobody wants to hear about all of that. Past is past. Besides, all it seems anyone with a mic and camera around here cares about is the kind of parts I'm equipped with and who I'm kissing."

A deep blush stole over her face as soon as the words left her mouth. She'd obviously meant the comment to be a joke to change the subject but he knew she was thinking about the kiss they'd shared—and he'd be lying if he said that being the one she'd been kissing didn't bring a sense of satisfaction with it. But she was clearly mortified by the slip of the tongue.

Giving her an uncharacteristic break, AJ asked, "You said you started young. How young was that?"

She smiled, not her move-space-and-time smile, but one that softened the lines of her face, drawing the eye to fanciful details about her, like how her eyelashes curled and that her lips, upon closer examination, were near purple-rose in duskiness, and even fuller than they appeared at first glance.

"I was a pest after my grandad, so he figured he might as well put me to work," she said, jumping onto the questions like a lifeline. "I always say five, but I couldn't have been older than preschool aged."

That gave her a head start on AJ of a good decade or so, but the detail fit the packaging.

In the distance a bell sounded, signaling the end of the event. At the end of the night the caravan would be rearranged according to the new rankings.

Lil had beat AJ in three out of five events, which meant it was going to be him and Winnie for another stretch of the road.

At least until they got to Shamrock, Texas. Then things would change. He'd make sure of it.

Lil pushed away from the barn and held out a hand.

AJ reached out and took it, still mystified that such a small hand belonged to a rodeo pro, and was startled by the electric current that passed between them on contact.

"Well fought," Lil said, grinning with a shine to her.

AJ smiled. "Well fought, though I think we both know the score…"

Like any good punk kid, she couldn't hide the gloat in her voice. "There's always next round…"

AJ snorted. "Just enjoy it while it lasts, shrimp—it never does."

This time Lil snorted. "Spoken like a true *role model*."

They walked back to the ring together, laughing all the way.

13

Who had ever heard of a world record bonus?

Lil grumbled and groused mentally as she shoved clothes into her duffel bag, altogether ignoring the voice in her head that sounded like Gran and had a lot to say about this being exactly the kind of situation that proved it was a good idea to keep her things tidy.

Being more inclined to keep things strewn about, she was now scrambling to get things packed up just as frantically as the boys in the bullpens were.

Of course, they were reshuffling because twenty-five of them were going home tonight.

She just had to switch RVs with AJ.

Because of his completely made-up, out of the blue, *world record bonus.*

Standing next to each other on the stage earlier in the evening, Lil had been agonizingly aware of the incredible nearness of him, just as she'd been agonizingly aware of every second they'd been near each other over the past four days.

Now, untangling her bra from the comforter on her un-made bed and shoving it in the bag, she was mortified by the fact that AJ was going to be sleeping in her bed tonight. Or, rather, his bed. But what had started out as her bed. And all because of some random fine print.

Even though she had won by way of competition, AJ had set a world record in one of the few events where he beat her, and the Closed Circuit, desperate for attention as they were, had a world record points bonus for any cowboys who set re-cords during the tour.

So, due to a contractual sub clause, AJ had wedged her out of the top spot and wormed his way into the first-place RV.

And her bed.

The thought refreshed her mind's crystalline image of him in that towel, which had become part of its permanent collec-tion, constantly displayed in her imagination.

He was the most beautifully built man she'd ever seen.

And they'd kissed. And, if her recent dreams were any in-dication, there apparently wasn't anything she wanted to do more than kiss him again.

Pinching herself, she said, "Abigail Lane Island."

Just as she'd intended, saying her mother's name out loud had the same effect as pouring a bucket of cold water over her head.

She shuddered in its aftereffects, but desperate times called for desperate measures. And she was desperate.

She had no business and no time to spend daydreaming about AJ Garza. She wasn't a teenage girl anymore, she was a woman on the brink of showing the PBRA just what they robbed themselves of by keeping so many out.

She had no business woolgathering, caught up in mem-ories of *fraternizing with the enemy*, as his friend had so elo-quently put it.

But it seemed that the fraternizing story between her and AJ was all that anyone wanted to woolgather about, herself included. To the media and the Closed Circuit, it was even more sensational than her being the PBRA's first female rough stock champion, or the highest-scoring transfer from the INFR to date. It was even more remarked upon than the fact that she was coming back to the spot after a near six-year hiatus.

Apparently, none of that was "the story" of Lil Sorrow—the name of which was another point of growing irritation. She wished her gran had just signed her up as Lilian Island—it would have made things a lot easier.

For all the world cared, the story of Lil Sorrow was a kiss that she couldn't seem to shake, inside or out.

But shake it or not, she still had to move.

With her clothes packed, her mind no less a battlefield, she moved on to toiletries, images of the night before replaying in her head.

AJ had whooped like a hooligan at the surprise upset of the points announcement, hollering, "Goodbye, Winnie!" before throwing his head back to laugh at Lil's unguarded expression, the movements highlighting the strong column of his neck and his disconcertingly appealing Adam's apple.

Lil's face had revealed her initial shock before quickly settling into a not-very-sportsman-like scowl, all captured for the camera, as Sierra announced that AJ would be awarded a five-point bonus for setting a new PBRA record in steer wrestling.

The worst about it all had been that he'd looked so good doing it—both the crowing over his surprise victory and the steer wrestling.

If it weren't for the fact that he was her primary competition, her inner seventeen-year-old would have reveled in the fact that she, Lilian Island from Muskogee, Oklahoma, had been chute side to see AJ Garza set a new PBRA record, not to mention the fact that she had weeks of front row seats to watch AJ Garza in action ahead of her.

That she had kissed him as well, and that that kiss had been as natural and wild and addictive as the rodeo itself, was far beyond her inner teen girl's ability to compute. That was territory even the grown woman didn't know what to do with.

In real life Lil didn't kiss anyone, let alone rodeo cowboys. Whether that was because she'd grown up trying to be one, or simply because all she knew about her father was that he'd been chasing rodeo when she'd been conceived, the type had never appealed to her. In fact, she had, until recently, had a strict no rodeo cowboys romance policy.

Of course, looking back at it now, she could almost say she'd enforced a strict no romance policy near her whole life. Romance was dangerous so she'd kept her focus on rodeo.

And like it had back then, it was a technique that could still save her from wayward thoughts.

She would focus on what was familiar: the work of the rodeo.

In that regard, AJ was even more astounding up close and personal than he had been watching from afar through her teen and college years.

And the fact that he'd come to her for advice—it was the stuff of dreams.

Literally.

In her early competitive days, she had had recurring dreams in which she talked shop with AJ Garza. She always woke up right as he leaned close to tell her how much he admired something of hers, but whether it was her rope handling, her riding, or what, she never knew. It always cut off before he could finish the sentence. Always, it ended before she could tell him she'd learned it all from her granddad.

Her every experience with the Closed Circuit had validated

what she'd always believed: her granddad, his way of training, his way of doing rodeo, was just as good—if not better—than the very best the PBRA had to offer.

When he'd been snubbed, jeered at, called a negro playing cowboys and Indians and worse, he'd held his head high and walked his own way. And he'd been right. Although he was a traditional man, his methods and approaches looked nothing like the way traditional rodeo cowboys worked, but it didn't matter—what mattered was that they were effective. They had churned out a cowboy unlike any the PBRA had ever seen—even if that was in large part due to her being a cowgirl.

But if AJ and riding for the Closed Circuit were validation for her granddad's ways, they were also proof that even a gym rat could make it if he had the try.

If AJ hadn't sought her out before they'd gone live, she would have never believed he hadn't been around wild horses before. He was what people meant when they called someone a natural.

Rodeo seemed to come as smoothly to him as smiling and breathing.

She had to work her butt off out there and he sauntered out and made it look easy.

And sexy.

Bastard.

She didn't truly begrudge him the talent, though. Her granddad had taught her that competition was the greatest motivation to improve, and her recent rides had shown that to be true. And by now, she was even beginning to accept the base interjections of her inner dialogue regarding his anatomy. She'd seen the miles of dripping muscles wrapped in a stupid white towel that was AJ and the sight had permanently damaged her brain. All of it was what was and there was no use fighting it.

Picking up her bulging duffel and the plastic bag that held her shampoos, she gave the RV one final scan. Greenies would come through and change linens and take out garbage and, fresh and clean, it wouldn't be hers anymore.

But there was no use crying over it, the only thing to do was work hard and regain her title.

Heading to the second-place RV, she put her bags in the lower storage compartment without looking back. The lights were on inside, and someone—she guessed AJ—was moving around inside.

The thought brought a smile to her lips until she realized what was happening and forcibly frowned.

She needed to take herself in hand. She had strict rules, both about rodeo cowboys and mixing work with pleasure, and all of them could be summed up in one word: *no*.

Someone tapped her on the shoulder, setting her jumping three feet in the air, much to the person's low-chuckling delight.

When she caught her breath she whipped around, asking, "You trying to kill someone?"

AJ laughed, dimples and white teeth flashing.

Did he have to smile so much?

"Just wanted to remind you to treat Winnie right," he said, patting the RV lovingly. "She's been good to me and she's a smooth ride if you take care of her."

Lil lifted an eyebrow. "Mine doesn't have a name."

AJ scoffed. "Of course she does, she just wouldn't give it up for a poser."

Lil flipped him off and turned to leave. She didn't like the effect their banter was having on her chest—hot and tight and dangerous.

"I'm really looking forward to the next event," AJ said to her back. "Especially after resting up in the lap of luxury."

Lil kept her grin to herself as she walked. Let him gloat—all of it was luxury to her.

Which wasn't to say that home wasn't nice—because it was. Granddad had made sure of that through the years, updating appliances, changing outdated fixtures, and tacking on a couple additions.

But Lil was used to traveling in a compact car and paying for her own gas.

Compared to that, even the second-place RV would be a pleasure cruise.

Plus, if she had anything to say about it, she wouldn't be in it long.

Lil left the RV circle and headed out farther into the open side of the parking field. The sun was beginning to set and she'd rather be out looking up at the sky than standing outside the second-place RV waiting for AJ and the greenies to clear it so she could get ready for one of the more horror-inducing activities of the tour.

As soon as the RV transfer was done, a Closed Circuit bus was due to pick up all the contestants and take them to a real-live local honky-tonk—on camera, of course.

Excepting a brief period she chalked up to the magic of studying abroad, Lil had never been one for either drinking in public or staying up late.

Unfortunately, all the contestants were required to go. It was supposed to build camaraderie, and more importantly, generate more content for broadcast fill and the website. The thing about reality TV was that it was never satisfied—it always wanted more. Regular reality, at least, knew when to let up.

As the sun sank below the horizon line, darker blue beginning to chase away the gorgeous canvas of purples, pinks, and orange, she pulled out her phone.

The bus was due in twenty minutes and she still had to get ready.

The whole thing was ridiculous. She didn't even go out with her friends, let alone a bunch of cowboys she barely knew.

Lil knew a recipe for disaster when she approached one, and that was even without tossing AJ and alcohol into the mix. In fact, in that mix, there was only one thing she could control, and that meant that, in addition to being miserable, it was going to be a very dry night for her.

Despite riding rough stock rodeo, in general, Lil would pick safe over sorry any day of the week. It wasn't an accident that she didn't have a past full of regrets and foolish behavior.

And now, more than ever, she had more pressing reasons to stay sober. The primary of those being the way her mind kept swinging back to the earthshaking kiss she'd shared with AJ every time she let her guard down.

She'd never had a kiss like that in her life—a connection with another human so powerful that it overwhelmed her sense of time and place.

It was the kind of kiss that complicated things. It was the kind of kiss that made things charged where they should be grounded, clouded and unstable where they should be clear and balanced. In fact, it was a lot like alcohol itself. All the more reason to be on guard, then, when they were on their way to a bar.

14

Ardmore's honky-tonk was more of a dive bar, but fill any place with over two dozen cowboys and it was more than halfway there. Toss in a few cameras and drinks—on the show's tab—and it was a regular hoedown.

AJ's elbows rested on the bar. A half-drunk beer sat on a coaster in front of him. Of-age greenies milled about, taking photos, quotes, and making suggestions to impressionable, more than half-drunk young men.

A camerawoman hollered, "Do a line dance!" and one of the boys going home from the bullpens thought either the suggestion or the suggester was delightful, so he sashayed over to the jukebox and whistled for the others from his RV to join him.

After some debate, Garth Brooks and a fiddle filled the room with his urgent need to make a long distance phone call and the crew of five cowboys cleared the floor to dance.

AJ watched it all with a half smile on his face. He'd give

them credit—the youngsters could move their hips pretty well for a bunch of white boys. As with everything else, though, he could stroll over and show them how it was really done. It just wouldn't be nice to embarrass them on TV.

The cameras were eating it up without the added drama anyway AJ was beginning to find the Closed Circuit's relentless and obvious pursuit of viewership almost endearing. Though nobody had ever tried to call it so, reality TV wasn't subtle.

AJ finished his beer as the boys finished their dance.

Across the bar, Hank DeRoy held court in a shadowed corner booth with a group of cowboys.

The man never lacked for lackeys. Year after year, the faces changed, but the personalities didn't. To a certain kind of man, Hank was a king.

Gaze sliding away from Hank and his cadre of clowns, AJ scanned the bar for Lil's long braid and undercut for the third time since sidling up to bar—which he had done for the express purpose of looking for her there. The second-place rider had disappeared as soon as they got off the bus and hadn't been seen since.

And that wasn't being a good sport to AJ's mind. He wanted to gloat.

Throughout the bar, cowboys played pool, shot darts and sat around drinking in small clusters. While it wasn't his normal nigh-out scene, all in all, it wasn't a bad way to spend an evening.

There was a distinct dearth in the way of female company, but that was the trouble with being in the middle of nowhere—the pickings were slim, tanned, and tough, or taken.

The sliver that remained were looking for husbands in the wrong place.

The bar door swung open on that depressing thought, framing a small silhouette.

The tension AJ didn't know he'd been holding dissolved.

Lil made her way to the bar, choosing a stool at the far end, half-hidden in the shadows.

AJ finished off his beer, stood up, and walked over to her, stopping short of her, a strange tightness in his throat at the sight. For the first time since their kiss at the qualifier, she'd worn her hair down and loose, her glossy black curls tumbling in a riot from beneath her hat. Adding to the gut punch of it all, she'd lined her thunderstorm eyes in black, and colored her full lips red, making them impossible to ignore.

The memory of sparking gray eyes and small callused hands wrapping around his neck to pull him deeper into a kiss pushed its way to the forefront of his mind, and fast on its heels, the memory of her scent, sweet and rich as bourbon infused with vanilla.

"Now where've you been?" he asked, only after collecting himself, unable to ignore the satiny texture of her smooth brown skin in the neon bar lighting.

Face pleasantly bland, Lil shrugged. "Just pissin' in the wind."

AJ laughed. Her brand of deadpan rudeness was becoming as welcome to him as Diablo's dry sarcasm. That she had a voice like a chain-smoking jazz singer from a different era, and delivered it all with a sweet country cadence and old-fashioned cowboy manners made it all the more intoxicating.

"Your manners are terrible," AJ observed, proud of the ease in his tone.

"Odd. No one's ever mentioned that before. You'd think in twenty-seven years…"

At the other side of the bar, the bartender picked up AJ's empty glass and looked around the bar in alarm. He waved to her from his seat next to Lil and the relief on the woman's face was almost comical. For a moment, he wondered if this was the kind of establishment that made the bartender pay when someone bailed on their tab.

Starting their way, hips swaying, the bartender sent him a slow smile and he couldn't stop the corners of his own mouth from curling.

She wasn't worried about the tab.

And although he didn't plan to encourage her—she wasn't his type, though he had nothing against her—he couldn't help but smile at her obvious appreciation.

Like rodeo, here was a game older than mankind itself that never lost its edge. And the bartender was an appropriate, seasoned opponent, far more so than the salty cowgirl that sat at his side.

In fact, tall, curvaceous, and bright blond as she was, the bartender had a lot going for her.

It just wasn't anything he was looking for. These days, his interest seemed to lean shorter, more athletic, and utterly fearless on the back of a beast—a list dangerously specific to the woman sitting by his side.

The bartender's come-hither smile said she was most definitely drawn to him, despite his lack of encouragement. The looks she was serving weren't the most sophisticated, but he gave her points for primal. He also, however, did the gentlemanly thing, angling his body and averting his gaze in a way that told her the only thing he was interested in was a beer.

She was around his age, and neither jerky nor marriage-bait. She gave the impression of competence without hardness and he knew, if he wanted, the evening could have ended happily. But his mind rejected the idea, instead choosing that moment to recall the fact that Lil's bright red lips were as soft as her rear end was full, firm, and round.

He shook the image clear with a frown.

It was one thing to get carried away in the thrill of a moment—it was another thing entirely to actively fantasize about his colleagues. He needed to remember that that was what Lil was: a colleague, a resource, and a competitor for a prize that was far bigger than the way she felt in his arms.

The bartender took their order and he said: "Two IPAs for my friend and myself, please."

"Coming right up." She punctuated her sentence with a wink and sauntered away.

When the bartender left, Lil said, "Hope you're planning on double fisting."

There was a strange note of serenity woven through Lil's gravelly rasp that set alarm bells off in AJ's head.

Side-eyeing her, AJ shook his head. "No. I'm too old for that. One of them is for you."

Lil shook her head. "Not for me. I'm not drinking tonight."

AJ raised an eyebrow. "Now is that polite of you? The standard thing to do is to offer me a drink and toast in concession to the better man."

Lil shook her head with a small smile. "You know how sensitive I am to your feelings, old-timer. I'm just racking my brains how to break it to you that that's me—even without all the required equipment."

Like the snap of a twig in the woods that gave away one's location, AJ's bark of laughter was loud enough to draw the attention of the full room, including the eyes of nearly thirty cowboys, and nearly every camera, to himself and the lone cowgirl in the room—and while she certainly wasn't the only woman in the establishment, she was certainly the only woman who'd turned dancing circles around each and every cowboy in the place into a habit. And looked pretty doing it.

AJ felt the uncharacteristic urge to curse under his breath.

He could weather anything this group might throw at him, but when it came to interacting with humans, Lil was as likely to spook and bolt as she was to go on the attack. Either could be disastrous.

That she was considering both was as clear as day on her face.

Amidst their new audience, Hank DeRoy's gaze moved slowly toward them, scanning the bar until he met AJ's with a smarmy glint. Seeing who sat beside AJ at the epicenter of the moment, Hank stood. He separated himself from his cronies to make his way toward the bar.

AJ made a small noise in the back of his throat, disgusted. Hank would come over and add fuel to the fire, throwing clumsy come-ons at Lil until she got up and left. It was as predictable as the sunrise.

Equally obvious was the fact that the other man had extended their field of competition to encompass Lil. That he was the kind of man who didn't see the problem with that, regardless of the fact that he was way off base with respect to AJ's intentions toward Lil, was enough to condemn him in AJ's mind.

He hadn't held Hank in the highest esteem before, but any man who was willing to pursue a woman for the sake of making a point wasn't worth a damn, in his opinion.

"Is this man bothering you, miss?" Hank slid up to the stool on Lil's other side, a corny smile plastered on his face.

Lil sighed, moving to excuse herself from the bar, but Hank stopped her with a hand on her elbow. Her body went still.

The hair on the back of AJ's neck stood up and he rose from the bar stool, taking a step forward without meaning to.

The energy shifted in the room, tension cast like a fishing net over every soul in the establishment. The cameras zoomed in, the background arguments of the cameramen about angles and lighting mingling with the warbling of the jukebox to make a strange buzzing backdrop for a scene that seemed like it needed someone to step in and say something but was generating an audience instead.

These were the moments reality TV lived for, a room full of mostly hotheaded testosterone-led young men on the edge of their seats. It was a new kind of spectacle for rodeo, though.

Not the hotheads, and not even the potential for a fight that everyone was aware of, bubbling under the surface—that was as commonplace at the rodeo as it was wherever there was beer and loud music—but the underlying hunger for it, the desire for sensation, no matter how tawdry.

Rodeo, after all, was family friendly. Buckle bunnies might chase cowboys, but that was a story for insiders. The official line was the bright, wholesome, rodeo queen and the cowboy married to the sport.

But here, amidst the neon and brass and wood, the crowd's desires were more salacious.

Lil's nostrils flared, her lips pressing into a thin line of irritation before she recovered enough to lift one corner of her mouth into a lopsided smirk. "In fact, he is, DeRoy, but only since he robbed me of a good night's sleep in my rightful bed. You see, the only kind of man that bothers me—really, the only kind of man I notice—is the one sitting higher than me in the standings."

A chorus of playground *oooo's* rippled through the bar, but the insult rolled right off him. His smile was as saccharine and heavy as the Kentucky gentleman in his voice. Smacking his lips, he let out a long *hmmm*. "Princess, you sound like a woman looking for a firm hand and I just happen to be famous for my grip."

A spattering of chuckles met his statement, but Lil just snorted, cringing.

AJ's reaction wasn't so casual.

Once again, he was moving before he processed his intention to do so, closing the distance between himself and DeRoy at the same time as he wedged his body between Lil and Hank, subtly blocking her from both the cameras and Hank's flirtations.

"The standings indicate that between the two of you, hers is the stronger hand, Hankey, which puts you out of the running." AJ kept his voice light, though his muscles were as taut as if he were in the arena. A handful of cowboys in the room hissed, likely Hank's pals, while the rest laughed at what they thought was a light razz.

But instead of backing down with a bunch of hot air, as AJ expected of Hank after years of push and pull and despite the obvious height and weight AJ had on him, this time DeRoy didn't back down.

They'd competed against each other for nearly all of their adult lives and never once had they progressed this far down the path of physical violence, despite having exchanged fighting words on many an occasion.

AJ shouldn't have been surprised that it was happening now, though.

Some men couldn't help acting like fools when women were involved.

But understanding that didn't mean putting up with it.

Rodeo was rodeo, and this was rodeo—even if it was a dive bar in Ardmore.

And whether Lil liked it or not, AJ was obligated to look out for her. The Closed Circuit might not be her first rodeo, but it was her first PBRA rodeo, and the difference was the same as the difference between indie film and big budget Hollywood. There was real money to be made in PBRA, even when it was the pet project of an eccentric producer, as the

Closed Circuit was. And where there was money to be made, there would always be sharks in the water.

Lil might put up a tough front, but she was sheltered and, he suspected, naive enough to fall into a trap before she knew to be wary—a trap like DeRoy.

It wouldn't happen while he was around, though, and if Hank didn't know how to quit, AJ would just make sure he was around all the time. It was as simple as that.

"Garza, you jump in so much, I might think you were jealous of this little thing going on between me and the first lady of rodeo." Hank smiled at Lil around AJ's form, and AJ wondered if the expression ever worked to pick up women, transparently sleazy as it was. There was nothing but bedpost notches and a big picture of himself hidden behind Hank's baby blues.

He looked the part of the golden son of the south, which should have been enough to send women running, but, like the cronies he collected everywhere he went, Hank never appeared to lack for female company.

With an easy chuckle, AJ shook his head, opening his mouth to say that he didn't mind at all what the first lady of rodeo was into, so long as he didn't have to deal with its breathing in his face, when a new voice broke into the conversation.

"Now, Hank DeRoy, I am wounded!" Sierra Quintanilla's words, perfectly pitched and utterly feminine, carried high over the crowd noise, laden with coquettish offense. "Lil Sorrow might be our brand-new feminist icon, but everybody knows that *I* am the first lady of rodeo!"

Hank was smooth when he turned to Sierra with a tip of his hat. "Pardon me, Miss Sierra. What I meant to say was the first lady of rough stock."

AJ almost snorted, but held back in respect for the rodeo queen's efforts.

As far as expert redirections went, hers had been well done. AJ didn't know how calling Lil a feminist icon would go down, though. He was a feminist himself—his mama would accept no less—but he also knew, just like Sierra did, that this wasn't a crowd where the label was considered a compliment.

Sierra's interruption, followed by her abandoning her position in the center of the line dance, surrounded by cowboys on either side, to cross the room and give Hank a theatrical punch in the arm, gave Lil enough time to reach over and pinch AJ's biceps.

Securing his attention, she made a quick cut motion with her hand at her neck, the universal sign for "cut the bull, I can fight my own battles." To which AJ responded with a shrug and a grin. As she'd wanted, though, he stepped back.

With more space between the two, and made into a group by the presence of Sierra, the lingering threat in the air dissipated. No longer was it a case of two rivals fighting over a single woman. It'd turned into a regular double date.

Smile growing, with lots of teeth aimed in Hank's direction, AJ shook his head and said, "So sad, a man trying to put strong women against each other." Leaning back against the bar stool, AJ crossed his arms over his chest with a sigh. "Insecure if you ask me. Now, I look at these two phenomenal women, and there's no question. Sierra Quintanilla, rodeo queen extraordinaire, is the undisputed first lady of the rodeo, and Lil Sorrow, sweeping in and embarrassing cowboys like the grim reaper of rodeo dreams, is the Empress of Arena. Both of them are blessed with crowns." He uncrossed his arms to give a little chef's kiss, to the loud delight of the less-trained men in the room.

Beside him, Lil closed her eyes and sighed, but the cowboys in the bar devoured the drama like it was candy. Hooting and hollering, whistling, and jeering, mostly at Hank, though his friends loyally jeered at AJ, the rest of them stomped and ordered more rounds, their attention on the foursome breaking apart as they separated back into smaller groups.

Sierra might be the show's hostess, but AJ was as much a master of the scene as she was, and if monikers were being thrown around for Lil, he was going to have the last word on it.

No longer the direct center of attention, and with no more blows about to be come to, the four of them stared at each other.

There was no reason to remain clumped together as they were, other than the fact that without hitting anything, and without a bull in sight, AJ was left with the fight lingering in his blood, bubbling and rolling, and nowhere for it to go.

"I propose a drinking game," he said.

Sierra spoke first. "Yes!" Immediate and a tad breathless.

Lil, as expected, shook her head. "Not for me, thanks. Not one for games."

Hank laughed, thinking she was joking. AJ laughed, knowing she wasn't.

"You play tonight. The prize I claim for ousting you from the top spot."

Lil crossed her arms in front of her chest and lifted an eyebrow. "We never made a bet."

"Now that's not very sporting, Lil," Sierra said quickly, her eyes on AJ.

At her side, Hank nodded. "Never pass a chance to make a fool of Garza."

Lil laughed, shaking her head. "No thanks. I'm not much for drinking, either, so the only fool I'd be making is of myself."

Their conversation had once again caught the attention of

greenies and the camera crew. Zeroing in on their quartet, they in turn alerted the rest of the bullpen cowboys.

Lil's face set, and AJ was impressed, knowing that no amount of peer pressure, not the whole bar nor the Closed Circuit contract she'd signed was going to make her drink now.

She began to shake her head, opening her gorgeous mouth to say as much, when Sierra broke in with a bright, artificial laugh. "Oh, I *love* games! Why don't we just play without her."

Lil's mouth snapped shut, her eyes narrowing, and AJ almost laughed. He didn't think it'd been her intent, but Sierra's words had been exactly what hypercompetitive Lil needed to hear. The woman might not like games, but she sure as hell liked to win. Almost as much as he did.

Eyebrow arched, she said, "I'll play, but just one round. We have a show tomorrow."

He grinned. For the second time in a row, he'd beat her, and the feeling just kept getting sweeter.

The game was as simple: rodeo trivia. Answer the question right, no drink—answer the question wrong, drink. Complexity wasn't his point. Snagging Lil's attention, hooking her into the fun in a way even she couldn't resist, that was his game. Fortunately, just like him, he knew she couldn't resist a chance to show off around the rodeo. And if he got to make a fool of Hank along the way, so much the better.

15

Eyes opening, Lil wasn't sure when one round had turned into six, or where her things were, but when all was said and done, one thing she was absolutely certain of: she was the undisputed champion of rodeo…trivia.

And just like in the real competition, winning had been a near thing, with AJ on her heels the whole time.

Things had started easy enough. She set off strong, peacocking her knowledge with an air of sober remove, the last player to take their first drink, lasting rounds longer than anyone else.

Sierra had bowed out of the game first, which was predictable. The Closed Circuit might be a rodeo like no other, but that didn't mean there was any room for rodeo queen's gone wild—especially not the hostess of it all.

Cowboys, on the other hand, could be as bad as they wanted to be.

Lil, Hank, and AJ remained, locked in competition, their game of trivia a fierce microcosm of their dynamic in the circuit. In a particularly heated moment, it occurred to her that when the two men weren't chest puffing and posturing, the three of them made for excellent competition, each one dedicated to rodeo, in the arena and out.

Hank had the corner on all things horse related, which made sense when Lil learned he was the son of a respected breeding legacy based in Kentucky. Lil's expertise was broad and pragmatic, anchored in the daily affairs of the ranch, her granddad's training, and a lifetime of going to the rodeo. Unsurprisingly, AJ gave her a run for her money whenever a technicality came up. It was obvious he'd studied the rules, regulations, and history of rodeo the way an artisan studies his craft.

But breadth beat depth in both of their cases. But not without a lot more than one beer.

Lil had lost track after three. She knew there hadn't been many more than that, but with her size, she knew the calculus didn't matter that much. She had had too much.

This she reflected on as she watched the ground, her upper body bobbing and bouncing against AJ's back in time to the rhythm of his step. Her lower half was draped over his shoulder, his arm an iron band tight around her thighs.

"I'm a walker, you know," she said, certain she had a problem with the situation though not entirely sure what it was.

AJ's voice carried a laugh. "And a joker and a smoker, too. But I got you for now…"

He did not sound drunk, and she suspected he was not. She had won the game, which meant he'd had more drinks than she had, but when size and tolerance were added to the mixture, it didn't much matter. Life graded on a curve, it seemed, and on a curve, she was drunk.

"I'm not a smoker," she said.

He did laugh this time. "I'm not surprised."

"What?" He was confusing her, jumping all over the place.

She decided he must be when he said, "I'm taking you back to Winnie."

"Who's Winnie?"

Again he laughed, the sound a rumbling chuckle that vibrated through Lil's body, sending warmth through her veins, as comforting as being covered with a hand-sewn quilt.

"Your RV."

Startled, she bounced up, going rigid in order to look around. "When'd we get back home?" she asked, referring to the parking lot where their tour vehicles were parked.

"After you tried to badger a local into bringing his calves out to the bar to prove, once and for all, you were the better steer wrestler, I lured you onto the bus with taunts, where you promptly fell asleep, and stayed asleep, long after everyone got off the bus, at which point I picked you up, and here we are."

Lil groaned. "And the cameras caught it all, I assume?"

AJ nodded. "Sure did."

"Wonderful."

He shrugged, bouncing her on his shoulder as he did. "You won."

Suspicion took root. "Did you throw the game?"

AJ shrugged again and she realized he was doing it on purpose. "You'll never know, will you? Now, where are your keys?"

Lil's stomach sank. "In my purse."

AJ stopped in his tracks. "Purse?"

"Put me down," she demanded with a groan. "I have to go back." She knew she shouldn't have drunk anything.

Obliging her, he made sure she was steady before taking his hands off her shoulders once he'd placed her on her feet.

When she was sure she was steady, she looked up at him to see her purse dangling in his hand, a naughty, boyish grin on his face and, for a moment, she was mesmerized.

Backlit by moonlight, he was wearing the same baseball cap he'd had on all night long—his signature look. AJ had made rodeo accept his baseball hat years ago, so much so that now it would be strange to see him in a Stetson outside of the arena or on the podium. On AJ, the cowboy hat was formal wear.

But even casual, he was breathtaking, more so in person than he had ever been in the interviews and clips she'd watched of him over the years. He'd been so far away then. Now he was up close and personal, in the flesh—and the flesh was so good.

There was nothing soft about him, but the word that floated across her mind looking at him was *beautiful*. His smooth, even skin, a rich golden brown tone, lighter than hers and underlaid with terra cotta. And he'd remembered her purse.

This late in the day, his face was all five-o'clock scruff and shadowed planes in low lighting and she fought the urge to run her fingers along his jawline.

The look in his dark gaze shifted, becoming arresting, capturing her own and holding her in place, promising that he would hold her to it, if she decided to probe the secret places her eyes were begging to explore.

For a moment she hesitated. They stood outside the second-place RV—Winnie, as he insisted on calling it—the sounds of the caravan dying down around them. Cowboys were bedding down, lights going off, blinds drawing closed all around them, but they remained where they were.

"It's late and we've got a show tomorrow. Better get to sleep," she said, wishing she'd said a million other things but that.

He nodded, but neither of them moved.

And then she was kissing him again, pulling him toward her until their lips met with the urgent need of a drowning person gasping for air.

She reached her arms around his neck, and his palms came to her hips to lift her. She wrapped her legs around his waist as the déjà vu of their lips connecting threatened to overwhelm her.

Just like at the qualifier, they became a world unto themselves, with Lil only dimly aware of the fact that in the process of lifting her he'd also carried them up the three steps to her door, opened it, and carried them inside.

How he squeezed them through the door with such ease, she'd never know, but he set her down gently once they were inside before turning to close and lock the door.

Because they'd kissed again and because she wanted to again, all she could think of to say after kicking her boots off was, "You got my purse."

With a chuckle, he nodded. "I did."

Something simultaneously melted and clicked in her chest, though she'd have been hard-pressed to explain the kind of mechanism that behaved that way in the human body.

"Thank you."

Stepping closer to run his fingertips along the edge of her cheek, he said, "Thanks for playing with me."

Shivers followed the path of his fingers, her skin tightening in response, breaths turning short. "I'm not usually one for games."

"I could take or leave them. I was more interested in playing with you." His words were suggestive and the look in his eyes said he meant them to be.

Lil's pulse leaped in her throat, a stuttering and fluttery beat gone erratic in the face of the man before her.

The appreciation in his gaze would have been enough to carry her away, her desire to reach into the unknown stronger than it had ever been before, even if he hadn't been AJ Garza, the only other man besides her granddad that she'd admired in her whole life. But he was. It was AJ Garza looking at her like that.

Unable to tolerate any distance between them, she closed the space, bringing their bodies flush against one another as she lifted onto her tiptoes, face tilted toward his.

He was happy to oblige, smoothly capturing her lips, drawing her closer, lending his strength so that she could lean more fully into their embrace, trusting he would hold both of them steady.

She didn't realize he was guiding them to the bed until gravity shifted around her as he drew her down on top of him.

Never breaking contact, for which she was grateful for, he rolled them around, so that he enveloped her with his body and his warmth, bathing her senses in him.

Even then, it wasn't enough. She wanted more of him, wanted him closer, though he had already come closer than she let anyone get.

When his hands came to the top of her jeans, she wiggled her hips impatiently. He made quick work of them, rolling the tight denim down and over her hips with practiced ease. A barrage of sensations followed: the kiss of air on skin, the caress of his calloused hand along the bare skin of her inner thigh, the sound of her long sigh rippling through the quiet of the RV.

"You ready for this?" he asked. His eyes were fixed on hers, hungry in a way that sent a tremor through her body. She nodded, ready in a way that she had never been, and the light that lit in his eyes was possessive and triumphant all at once.

He covered her again, his body radiating heat and strength as his hands came to her breasts beneath her shirt.

She moaned on contact, the sound a loud outburst that had her clamping a hand over her mouth. The RVs were remarkably soundproof, but there was only so much they could do.

Above her, AJ laughed quietly, leaning down to press a kiss behind her ear while his brilliant fingers found her nipples to the sound of her gasp.

She was breaking down into a jumble of sensations and impressions, no longer a woman, but a series of simultaneous occurring phenomena that all had to do with AJ: What AJ was doing with his hands, what AJ was doing with his mouth—was it possible to press even closer to AJ?

Finally impatient with the barrier of her shirt, in a smooth motion he pulled it open, freeing all the snaps with ease.

Feasting on the sight of her breasts, his eyes turned wolfish, and heat flooded Lil's upper body, turning her skin deep dusky rose.

"You're the most beautiful woman I've ever seen, Lil."

For the briefest moment doubt flashed across her mind, gone nearly as quickly as it had entered: Was it true? AJ was a worldwide rodeo star, it stood to reason he had had his pick of some of the most beautiful women the globe had to offer.

AJ's palm running downward along her side, the pad of his thumb brushing the side of her breast as he trailed over her ribs and lower, shook her mind free of thoughts of AJ and other women, drawing Lil immediately back into the present.

She hadn't known the side of her ribs could be such a delicious place to be touched.

Reaching between them, AJ began to unbuckle the massive silver thing that rested at the top of his jeans, just one of his many, and Lil held back a snort. She was so used to seeing his buckles that she was beginning to think of world championships as commonplace. She'd certainly come up in the world.

Buckle unfastened, he slipped his hand around to his back pocket and pulled out a flash of silver.

Confusion rippled across Lil's face for a moment and he

smiled reassuringly. "Protection. 'A cowboy is always pre-pared.'"

His words stopped her in her tracks.

Noticing, he grinned. "It's just something The Old Man used to drill into us."

It sounded like it, like some kind of rodeo guidance counselor joke to remind young men to be safe. More than that, though, like an ice bucket, it reminded her of who she was and where she came from—who she had, or rather, *not* had, for a mother. And a father.

Abby Lane had been beautiful, impulsive, and about as responsible as a box of puppies for the entirety of her twenty years on earth. The greatest example of that behavior being Lil's origin story, when, at sixteen, Abby Lane had gone to watch her father, Lil's granddad, compete in his first ever PBRA rodeo. She came home pregnant and her grandad had missed the one shot he'd had at going pro in mainstream rodeo.

Lil was born thirty-seven weeks later, a whopping six and a half pounds and eighteen inches of screaming, hollering, girl child. Her mother had labored for thirty long hours and not once during the whole ordeal did she utter the name of Lil's father—a feat all the more impressive for Abby Lane not being known for her ability to suffer in silence.

On this matter, however, she was resolute. Until the day she died, in fact, for all the world ever knew—and for all Lil knew—Abby Lane had been impregnated by the Holy Spirit. She had never been one to care about other people's opinions about her life, and was even less so with a brand-new baby.

For those first three months, Lil's mother had been changed—in love, real love, with someone outside herself for the first time in her life. She didn't begrudge her infant's mid-night cries or dirty diapers, instead reveling in the intensity of being another creature's entire whole world. The glow of motherhood wore off, however, as Lil grew. By the time she was a damage-prone toddler, her mother was over parenting.

Eighteen and looking for some space away from her toddler, Abby picked up a job at the local grange, which happened to be right next door to the local tavern. Not long after she started coming home late.

According to Gran, the first time Abby Lane didn't come home at all was the worst. After getting Lil down for bed, assuring her Mommy would be home later, her grandparents sat up all night by the phone. Abby Lane never called.

Instead, she came back after her next scheduled shift at the grange, buzzing and jumpy and full of news: she was in love. His name was Todd and he worked at the bar next door to the grange. He made her feel alive, and didn't seem to mind that she brought another man's child to the relationship. They were going to get married and buy a house and be a real family, once they got enough money, of course.

The next time, when she didn't come home for a week, earning money was the excuse. They'd landed a job with a big paycheck—so big and intense that she'd lost weight by the time she got back. She said they put in eighty hours each and hadn't had much time to eat and sleep, let alone enough time to call home to say when they'd be back.

Two days into her disappearance, though, Gran had called the grange to see if she'd shown up there. They let her know that Abby Lane hadn't been employed with them for over a month. A detail she never shared with her parents.

When Granddad stopped by the tavern, the owner, Old George, a second cousin of Gran's, said he'd fired Todd for stealing from the register.

When Abby finally came back home, Gran and Granddad

put their foot down: if she wanted to step out with Todd, she wasn't doing it under their roof.

Abby responded by saying she'd go somewhere else then, but when she angrily tried to push past Gran to collect Lil from the room where she napped, Granddad had held up an arm and uttered the words that haunted him until the day he died: "Abby Lane Island. You may be too old to take my orders, but you ain't taking my granddaughter anywhere. You touch that girl in there and I'll be laying my own hands on you."

His voice had been dead calm, his eyes hard and black, and Abby knew he meant what he said.

Gran said the color left Abby's face in that moment and that she gasped before spitting on the floor. Her whole life that detail had always stood out the most starkly to Lil. Abby Lane had spit on Gran and Granddad's floor.

The detail that stuck with Gran and Granddad was that that was the last time they saw their daughter alive. After that, she'd turned on her heel, walked out the door, and hopped into the passenger seat of an old blue Chevy. They never saw the driver.

Two years later, on a warm Tuesday in May when Lil was four, the phone rang. Gran was in the garden with Lil. Granddad was away, somewhere between Muskogee and Amarillo, running a herd for their elderly neighbors.

Wrist-deep in fresh soil, and accompanied by Lil, who'd spent their garden time whipping up a prize-worthy batch of mud pies, Gran didn't make it to the phone in time. That was another one of those details that had mattered more to Gran and Granddad than it did to Lil.

When Gran checked the call log, she said she saw it was a Tulsa number and that that was when she knew.

They didn't have anybody in Tulsa and the farmhouse number was unlisted. The call could only be Abby.

But it wasn't Abby. It was the Tulsa Police Department and

they had a body that needed identification. Gran dropped the phone. Lil remembered it falling, an old cordless thing, the kind that felt like you were making a phone call with a brick. The floor tile that cracked on impact was still broken to this day—a tiny memorial in itself.

Gran had taken the trip alone. Granddad wasn't due back for a week and there wasn't time to wait. She had dropped Lil off with their old neighbors, Mr. and Mrs. Parker, who plied her with sweets and distraction for the whole time Gran was gone. Lil couldn't eat caramel to this day because it reminded her of that visit. The Parkers had done their best to spoil the little girl who had no idea her mother was dead. Along with the sweets, they let her stay up until the sugar and unusual routine left her in an exhausted pile on their living room floor.

Gran was back the next day, changed in a way that even a four-year-old could see.

Abby Lane was gone, a drug overdose in a lonely motel. Lonely because when the owners had broken into the room with the police, the only sign of the man she'd checked in with was the second rig next to her body on the bed.

For Lil, the story wasn't merely the tragedy of their family cannon. It was a cautionary tale to avoid the same mistakes—the biggest of which being taking up with fly-by-night rodeo cowboys who dallied so casually they were always prepared.

"Stop." The command in her voice, enough to overwhelm the embarrassment and shame hidden beneath it, was assured and abrupt. AJ froze immediately.

Pulling back, he searched her face. "Everything okay?" he asked.

Lil nodded, then shook her head, then blew out a frustrated breath and a sigh. Then she tried again. This time the words poured out. "I'm sorry. I shouldn't have let this get this far. We have to stop. This is crazy." She sat up to scoot away from

him, palms up. "You're—" she broke off. "You're AJ Garza."
Even just his name was a silken temptation in her mouth, as
good to say in this intimate space as every daydream she'd
ever had had suggested. No. That wasn't true. In truth, none
of her daydreams had ever come anywhere near so good as
the real thing. But it wasn't right. "We're enemies," she said,
once again borrowing his friend's word. "We have to remember we're enemies."

The smile he'd been wearing as she spoke slid into a frown.
"We don't have to be," he said.

But Lil shook her head sadly. "We do. You need to win just
as badly as me. And I—" She gestured to her state of undress,
realizing he still had his clothes on. "I don't do this kind of
thing with rodeo cowboys."

The words were stiff and awkward; her face was ruby toned
to go along with them. Every ounce of ease that had existed
between them was sucked out of the air in an instant.

For a moment, AJ was quiet, his ragged breathing slowly
returning to normal. Then he slid off the bed.

Standing, he looked away from her while he adjusted his
clothing.

Then he turned to her, a smile planted firmly in place, and
nodded. "You're right. I was just thinking that myself at the
beginning of the night. You know what they say about the
best laid plans…" As usual, there was laughter in his voice,
but the fact that it was forced, put on like he was on camera,
curdled Lil's stomach.

"I'd better get going," he said, voice low. "We've got a
show tomorrow."

And after waiting for Lil's nod in response, he turned and
left, closing the door on his way out.

16

The caravan pulled into the OKC arena parking lot exactly on schedule at 11:00 a.m. AJ at its head, followed by Lil, Hank, and finally the remaining bullpens. Security closed a barricade around them as soon as they parked, which struck AJ as overkill until he stepped outside.

Hundreds of young girls stood behind what appeared to be a hastily set up rope line at the far end of the parking lot. The pitch and volume of their screeching reached him, lancing through his mild hangover, even at that distance.

Tapping the first greenie that walked by on the shoulder, he said, "Excuse me. Can you tell me what that's all about?"

The redheaded young man stuttered in response, "Y-yes, Mr. Garza."

AJ wondered if it was somewhere in their training manual that they had to stutter when they spoke to him. "So…?" he asked, pointing to the young women.

As if he'd asked for the first time, understanding lit up the greenie's face and he said, "Oh, that! That's because of Lil Sorrow!"

AJ's right eye twitched.

The kid didn't notice. His eagerness to talk about Lil Sorrow melted away all traces of intimidation, as well as any basic ability to read his audience. "Lil Sorrow's feature got picked up by StoryLaunch and went viral, and long story short, the Closed Circuit is trending worldwide!" The kid gushed. That was the only word for it.

AJ's head hurt, but not as much as his body ached for the woman that wouldn't leave him alone, even when she wasn't around. And now, apparently, it wasn't enough that she was the bright new star of rodeo, she had to go and become a worldwide phenomenon. She was going to be the death of him. "When'd it go out?" he asked the greenie.

"Yesterday!"

Even content about Lil wasted no time climbing to the top.

"What's it called?" he asked, recognizing he'd get more from the source than the kid in front of him at this point.

The kid blushed a little. "Rodeo's Triple Crown Princess."

AJ brought his fingers to his temples and rubbed. "Thanks."

The kid nodded and darted off, the cacophony of young women in the background creating a strange soundtrack for his run.

AJ pulled his phone out of his pocket and pulled the article up.

The headline read "Rodeo's Triple Crown Princess: rodeo's first female rough stock champion is lean, mean, and coming for her man."

The lead image was a close-up of Lil's face, her head angled toward the bottom right of the frame, a mischievous grin aimed at something outside of the shot.

A piece of wheat stuck out from between her sharp teeth,

the hungry glint in her eyes reminding him of the way she'd looked at him outside of Winnie the night before.

He ran a hand down his face, letting out a loud breath.

Things were getting complicated.

This was why it was always a better idea to save the wildness inside of him for the bulls and broncs. Anywhere else, whether it was the top of a hill in Houston or a dingy hole-in-the-wall in Ardmore, and there were consequences.

Brow furrowed, he returned to the article, forcing himself to start with the words, to read through the entire thing, before he let himself look at the rest of the pictures.

But as he finished, reading the final line with a smug grin, Lil chose the moment to throw open the door of the second-place RV and dash down her stairs, dressed in full rodeo attire as if they were due to go on within the next hour, instead of eight.

Her hair was braided and she wore no makeup or jewelry, which meant she was probably heading out to practice or ride or something else having to do with the actual work of rodeo, as opposed to the promotions work of the Closed Circuit reality rodeo.

Taking her in, he at least had the answer to his question about her practice habits. Of course she practiced, there was no way a body could show up like she did, ride like she did, and not practice—that he'd even considered the alternative was crazy. She just practiced in the wee hours, when no one was around, the little sneak.

But there were plenty of people around now. And buried in the why was a fantastic reason to grin.

Lil stopped dead in her tracks when she noticed the crowd, which had gotten only louder since her door opened.

"You're a regular idol, Lil." AJ's smugness was heavy enough to crack through the pavement.

She shot him a wary glance, her eyebrows drawn low and together as she opened her mouth.

Whatever she was going to say was cut off by the greenie from before running over to greet her. "Can I help you with anything, Lil?" he asked, confident, if overly friendly.

"No, no thanks," she sputtered.

AJ almost laughed. It looked like Lil was dealing with her own consequences this morning, and while it might sting a little that, fresh pressed and ready to go as she was, hers didn't seem to have anything to do with him, the look on her face suggested that they were her particular brand of miserable.

"Anything at all?" the kid asked again, face hopeful.

Lil repeated, "Uh. No thanks. I think I'll just go back inside."

"You're not even going to ask what all this is about?" AJ asked lazily, gesturing to the mob of estrogen, which took his motion as a signal to get louder.

She shook her head, already taking steps backward.

"Oh no, you don't," he said, grin growing to nothing short of shit eating. "I think you really might be interested in the source of all of this hullabaloo."

Cringing, Lil kept backing up. "I'm sure I can catch up in my RV."

Shaking his head slowly, AJ advanced on her, catching her delicate wrist in his hand.

Their audience erupted at the contact—as he'd known they would.

That his body would as well, his senses heightening, his attention zeroing in on the place where their skin touched, the incredibly tiny bones that went toe-to-toe with massive beasts, was a surprise. So was Lil's quiet inhalation.

At least she wasn't as unaffected as she appeared. If the article was to be believed, which he didn't for a minute, she was much more than unaffected.

But while his body was ready to pick up where they'd left off the night before, his mind had a bit more insight as to how they'd gotten here in the first place now. And had, perhaps, even identified a course with which they might once again end up in the place where it seemed both his mind and body wanted to go.

AJ nodded to the greenie. "Why don't you read Lil Sorrow the article?"

Eager to assist rodeo's brightest new star, the redheaded greenie read the article aloud.

> "Like the cowboys of old, on the surface, Lil Sorrow is a woman of few words—outwardly as cool, calm, and collected as the flint her eyes call to mind. But boiling below lurks the passionate heart of a primal fighter—and lover—as fierce and free as the wild mustangs she's here to catch. Lil Sorrow is pressing the limits of the sport as we know it—and, if she's lucky, she just might catch a dream-come-true love along the way."

The greenie paused to offer them a sly playground smile before continuing.

> "Both sides of her head are shaved, her fresh fades accented by lightning bolts on either side. Her long fishtail braid reaches down the middle of her back, and even without knowing she rides bulls better than most men, it's already clear she's cooler than I'll ever be. About a foot shorter than your average rodeo cowboy, it's more than her pretty features and

femininity that throw off the scent of rodeo around her. With her tailored clothing, often black, always at the front edge of fashion, she initially looks more like a television personality than a real cowboy—but you'd be mistaken to believe the impression. In fact, though you'd never know it, the slight figure rocking the rodeo world, utterly redefining what a champion looks like, is one of the most traditional riders the PBRA has seen in a decade. With her thick, straight eyebrows, and naturally curling lashes that perfectly frame the mystery of her storm-gray half-moon eyes. She's certainly the prettiest."

Lil's eyes bulged as the greenie continued reading.

"A born and bred rancher, Lil is the old-fashioned real deal, having learned the tricks of roping and riding working the family land—but her story goes deeper than that. She's no mere ringer, though—the girl comes from good stock, the granddaughter of INFR champion Herman 'The Horsefly' Island. A bad start early in his PBRA crossover meant Herman never fully achieved his dream of being the first major crossover from the INFR to the PBRA, but now, nearly three decades later, his granddaughter is here to get the job done. But for the first woman to reach rough stock riding heights, a PBRA buckle isn't enough—not when her one shot to show the world that girls can ride as well as the boys also happens to be the final tour for the legendary AJ Garza. 'The stars just aligned,' she says with a faint blush and a private laugh, referring to the surprise announcement that Garza would be entering the competition. 'I've followed him since he first appeared on the scene. I love him… The opportunity to be up close and personal is a dream come true. All that said, though, obviously I'm going to try to beat him,' she adds with a twinkle in her usual gaze. Her words are all the more intoxicating, delivered as they are by a voice that sounds like an old-fashioned mixed by a bartender with nothing to prove."

A sound bubbled out of Lil's mouth that AJ would've called a croak, momentarily interrupting the greenie, who picked back up with the final paragraph of the article.

"Well, this reporter, for one, couldn't be happier for her or for the world of rodeo—she's the best new thing the sport has had to offer since they added bareback broncs to the roster. Watch out, rodeo, watch out, world, and mostly, watch out, Garza. Your days on top are numbered."

The warmth he felt hearing the words read out loud could only be described as wicked.

Proudly, the greenie concluded,

"Because in the end, my money is on Lil, who winked on her way out, tossing over her shoulder as if it explained everything, 'Skill is sexy,' and even though I'm happily married and old enough to be her father, heat rushes to my face and I know she's right. Skill is sexy, and she's got it in spades. And judging from the famous kiss we all saw, Mr. Garza sees it, too."

Lil grimaced, but AJ urged the greenie on. "Keep reading." The kid took a deep breath and went on.

> "In the realm of rodeo, more famous for clinging to images of a mythologized Wild West that never quite was than for breaking new ground, she's just what the doctor ordered. A breath of fresh country air. Unsurprisingly, it has taken a woman to get the job done, reminding us every time she enters the arena what the heart and soul of rodeo is really about: man pitting himself—or, in this case, woman pitting herself—against the greatest forces that nature has to offer. Whether they be a three-thousand pound man killer, or the most dangerous beast of all: love."

AJ smiled as the greenie finished reading the article, the young man's voice going syrupy along with the author's final sentiment.

"He's not wrong, you know," AJ said through the Cheshire cat grin stretched across his face. "Even if he gets a bit sentimental toward the end."

Lil's mouth had dropped open, her skin going a shade somewhere between ashen gray and brownish green.

AJ added idly, "About you being pretty, I mean."

A squeak emerged from the back of Lil's throat, sounding as if it were coming from far away.

AJ's mood was improving by the minute.

Head shaking, in too loud a voice, Lil insisted, "That's not what I said."

It was obvious it came as an absolute surprise to her that her words might be misrepresented in print. That it did was one of the few signs of just how green she really was.

Audiences always fixated on sex—especially reporters.

The greenie piped in proudly, "You went viral!"

"Oh no." Lil's lips came together, lush and full, as distracting naked as they'd been stained red, while she brought her hand to her forehead.

"You're internet famous now," AJ said cheerfully.

Eyes closing, she moaned, the miserable sound nothing like those he'd heard the night before.

His mind's willful return to the sights and sounds of the previous evening, despite the fact that in reality they'd amounted to little more than heavy petting in the end, wasn't the kind of relived experience of youth he was looking for when he'd had the idea to ride for CityBoyz, however.

"For all the wrong reasons," she muttered to herself, under the noise of the greenie clapping beside her. "This is terrible. I didn't say that."

She was repeating herself, but he didn't hold it against her. It was a lot, all at once.

"But Lil, I had no idea…" he began.

Her now-famous gray eyes darted to him, narrowing as they went. "Don't you even think about it, Garza."

"…that you were in love with me," he finished.

The greenie squealed beside them, whipping his phone out to catch the interaction on film, the chorus of Lil's screaming girl army like a full orchestra in the background.

Lil's face turned red and she opened her mouth, undoubtedly to unload some words that might not be airable on the evening news, for which AJ was both eager and delighted, when she thought better of it, clamped her mouth shut, and made a mad dash back to her RV.

He shook his head after her, feeling lighter than he had before. The retreat would only fuel the belief that she carried a torch for him, but she'd have to learn that on her own.

Outside of the arena, Lil was like a Great Dane in a room

full of mousetraps. On the back of a beast, though, she was all calm focus and silky control. Not so much as a hint of temper or reactivity. Those who rode by temper were erratic, muscling their victories out with brute force and deep spurs.

AJ felt for the draws of those riders. Especially the horses.

Unlike the last show, which had showcased a series of timed events, the OKC stop was an homage to saddle bronc riding, rough stock at its prettiest.

If there was one place in the rodeo where temper didn't belong, it was the saddle bronc ride.

Whereas bareback riding was an exercise in taking a beating, saddle bronc riding was one in finesse. It was the only rough stock event that truly demanded style and grace alongside the ever-requisite strength, precision, and grit—it turned cowboys into dancers.

Like everything else that perfectly fused form and function, it was considered classic. By this point in his career, AJ had mastered all of the classics.

Saddle bronc riding evolved from breaking and training wild horses. To AJ, that translated into coaxing raw and untamed power to follow your lead. It was meeting wildness with the strength of your body and will and convincing it that where you wanted it to go would be good for both of you—uniting two wild spirits in a primal dance, movements complementary and synchronized, an encounter as old as humans on horses.

The event required perfect control balanced alongside the fluidity to constantly adjust and respond to the present moment. The prize was worth it if you could manage, though: man and horse temporarily one—a centaur for eight precious seconds.

It was his most treasured and strongest event.

Altering his plans in the face of the unforeseen teenyboppers, AJ followed Lil's lead, returning to the first-place RV, confident the security of his position in the top spot was under no threat.

Two hours later, when AJ came back out, there were even more young women in the crowd.

Security escorted all twenty-five contestants, protecting them from the crowd of women as they made their way from the RVs to the arena.

Like everything else they did in the Closed Circuit, they walked in order of rank. Lil followed AJ, Hank followed Lil, and so on, all the way back to the last, a phalanx of cowboys on their way to the battlefield.

Behind him, Lil was quiet, her boots hitting the ground the only real sound coming off her. She took two steps for every one of AJ's. They marched that way all the way to the arena, trudging in in single file.

As first-place rider, AJ opened the evening's competition, riding right after "The Star-Spangled Banner" and the local girls' riding club's trick riding presentation.

When a greenie signaled, he mounted his bronc in the chute. Grabbing the thick bronc rein with his right hand at just the spot he liked it, he marked up his spurs and raised his left arm in the air, elbow slightly curved.

This time, he had a fiery draw, banging them both against the sides of the chute.

There would be no repeat of the last Closed Circuit bronc he'd ridden.

He tensed his thighs and the outer muscles of his shins, using the strength in his legs to hold his mark over the dig of his spurs. The gate swung open and man and horse leaped out.

AJ's grip was uncompromising, his arm fully controlled. His lifted arm swayed in time with the horse's bucking, touching neither man nor beast.

He followed the horse's rhythm with his spurring, heels making contact each time the horse's forelegs touched ground.

The seconds stretched into long measures of the body's endurance, but AJ maintained. Eight seconds flashed the end of his ride and then the pickup men were at his side, taking control of the horse. He dismounted to the cheers of the audience and a score of 96, with a strange buzzing in his ears.

Returning to the gate, he found a good spot to watch Lil's ride. What limited free space there was in the competitors' staging area was filled with teen fans—more than he'd ever seen at a single event. They were in every space that wasn't cowboy or greenie, a highly charged colony of fangirls.

AJ shuddered. They were going to eat Lil up, but only after serving her on a silver pedestal.

Steeling himself, he wove through them to find a space near the chute.

Lil shot out, well marked, her form exceptional, as usual.

She and her bronco hit their sweet spot instantly—bucking and spurring in time like choreographed dancers.

She rode in a way that turned frenzied seconds into lazy, smooth stretches of time, more akin to hours passing on the porch than urgent struggles for survival.

The buzzer rang, the pickup men rode out, and Lil hopped free, having made the saddle bronc ride look like an evening at the ballet.

Her ride earned 98 points, a new PBRA record, and the stadium went nuts, and amidst the deafening noise, one thing was absolutely clear: she might have "loved" him as a teen, but she loved beating him as a woman even more.

17

Lil woke in the second-place RV still buzzing from her ride the night before. The entire world might think she was nothing more than a lovesick superfan chasing after AJ Garza, but she was still riding the best she ever had in her life.

Thinking about him, she wondered what he was doing before chastising herself for the direction of the thought, which proved she was exactly the lovesick superfan the world thought she was.

At seven in the morning he was probably sleeping—which was entirely beside the point since it shouldn't matter to her what AJ was doing at all, especially now that her feature piece had so grossly misrepresented her feelings toward him.

Though how she would describe her feelings, or their relationship, she didn't have an answer to. They'd kissed and more, going further and faster than she had with anyone else before, and they treated each other more like teammates than competitors, but they were by no means something more. And how did she reconcile that with the part of her that had never been casual physically?

Her actual words in the interview had been, "I love seeing him in the arena. The chance to watch him in action, the opportunity to be up close and personal to an idol, is a dream come true." She'd been expressing the sentiments of a longtime admirer rather than a desperate ring hunter. And while he might be handsome, and as amazing in the arena as she'd unfortunately gushed, and capable of magic when his hands and lips got involved, he certainly wasn't what she was looking for when it came to a relationship.

So why all the easy touching? Why kiss him like kissing didn't mean something? a counter voice protested.

None of their kisses had been meaningless, and it would take both a liar and a fool to convince anyone of that. She had watched AJ rise to the top of the sport that was her whole life, doing it his way, as her granddad had taught her to do. It was normal that the fact that he was handsome and charming and intelligent would nudge that longtime admiration in a stronger direction. What wasn't normal was the way it was impacting her. She'd never been one to budge an inch once she'd made her mind up, not even in the face of all the nudging—and cajoling and begging—in the world.

And AJ was the primary thing standing between her and protecting her home. He was the thing standing between her and victory for cowgirls and Black natives the world over.

AJ wasn't her friend, and was most certainly not her lover, and she needed to get that straight. He was her competition, even if that line had blurred once or twice.

Disgusted with herself, she decided to give up and get out of bed. They had the day off, but it wasn't like she'd be getting any more sleep and she refused to lie in bed and think about AJ.

Pulling on a pair of black sweats, she was working on getting a black tank top on when she heard a knock at the door.

AJ stood on the other side.

He wore his characteristic white baseball hat, but was missing his usual smile. That he stood on the bottom step put her face-to-face with him.

His forehead was creased, and her first urge was to reach out and soothe the worry away.

"What's wrong?" she asked, unable to stop herself from the words even as she held back the touch.

He held up a red envelope. "You get one of these yet?"

She shook her head.

He offered it to her.

Lil took out the card inside and read.

> *The Closed Circuit is no place for city slickers. You're going to prove it with an old-fashioned cattle drive. In teams of two, contestants will have twenty-four hours to round up, drive, sort, and pen twenty head of cattle. Your stock handling, horsemanship, rope skills, and teamwork will be put to the test. Late returns and missing cattle are automatic disqualifications.*

Her temperature rose as she read.

They were going to be on teams. Overnight.

She was going to have to put up with another cowboy, one-on-one, for a full twenty-four hours, on camera. She brought a hand to her face and rubbed it with a groan.

AJ raised an eyebrow, one corner of his mouth lifting. "You okay there, champ? I was worried for a 'gym rat' like myself but figured a real cowpoke like you would think this was a breeze."

Lil frowned, trying to figure out what he was talking about. Finally, she just asked, "What?"

AJ gave her a stern look that reminded her of her granddad and her mouth quirked up unintentionally.

AJ's grandpa scowl deepened. "You read the thing?" he asked. "We're doing a cattle drive. I don't know how to drive cattle."

Lil snorted. "Sure you do. You know how to rope and ride and you're not scared of cows. You know how to drive cattle."

AJ crossed his arms in front of his chest, drawing Lil's eyes to the tight expanse of navy blue fabric that stretched across his chest.

Observing her, he said, "Somehow I think there's a little more to it than that."

Lil shook her head laughing. "Not much more, really. It's easy enough that so-called 'city slickers' do it all the time."

Some of the tension left AJ's body, and Lil's cheeks warmed. Like each of his real smiles, the easing of some of his stress felt like a personal victory.

"What about the roundup?" he asked.

"Novices do that part all the time, too. Gran and I looked into turning the ranch into an experience tour after we lost Grand-dad, and drives are a big part of that. You've got more know-how than the requirements we were considering for guests."

"You didn't do it, though?"

Lil shot him a one-sided grin. "Nope."

His eyes narrowed. "Why?"

She tilted her head, grin in place. "Greenhorns are irritating."

The glint that came to his eye was laced with lazy triumph. "Sorry in advance, then."

"What do you mean by that?" she asked.

AJ stepped back from her door and said, "Flip the card over."

She did. The opposite side of the card listed the teams. She read her name and AJ's listed right next to the number one. Her stomach dropped. It looked like she and AJ were going to spend the night together after all.

18

The massive blue truck towed a beat-up white horse trailer through a grassy sea of pasture. Four people were crammed in the cab. Two greenies, Lil, and AJ. AJ sat in the passenger seat. Lil and a greenie sat in the back, the other one drove.

Behind them, a van filled with the film crew followed.

There wasn't a cow in sight, and hadn't been one for the last twenty minutes.

The back-seat greenie peppered Lil and AJ with questions.

"How are you going to go about rounding up the cattle?"

AJ wore a gray T-shirt, jeans, and his ever-present baseball hat. The only new addition to his look was a pair of reflective aviator sunglasses.

Lil hoped he'd packed a long-sleeve shirt.

Gazing silently through the front window, it was obvious AJ was not going to answer the question, but Lil could see he wore a grin through the side view mirror.

She ground her teeth but smiled at the greenie. He was a

skinny blond boy whose tight jeans and big belt buckle spoke
of pro rodeo dreams.

"There's no real trick to it," she said more tersely than she
should have. "You just look for signs of cows."

A blush brought some color to the kid's face but he braved
on. "What signs are those?"

Lil heard the real question in the kid's words, and it was
AJ's face that flashed in her mind—not mocking her from
the front seat, as he was now, but uncertain, as he'd been at
her doorstep.

The kid wasn't asking just for the sake of some social media
posts. He was asking because *he* wanted to know.

Resigned, Lil gave him a real smile, it wasn't his fault he
was irritating.

His mouth dropped open slightly.

Making an effort to project more warmth into her voice, she
said, "You start with your basic senses. The first one—better
than even sight—is smell. Sound is next as listening is better
than looking more than half the time. Then, finally, you can
turn to sight, but usually if you can see them, you don't need
to be looking for them. If they're moving fast, even your sense
of touch is better than sight. Either way, your greatest ally is
the cows themselves. It's their nature to group up, so usually
once you find one, you're not far from the lot."

The boy took notes furiously.

In the front seat, AJ sat straighter, his posture alert. He was
listening in, too.

Good.

They hadn't seen any cattle in miles, which meant they'd
have to track them down.

He needed to know as much as, if not more than, the kid
beside her.

The driver stopped the truck in a spot so similar and unremarkable to the rest of the ride that it felt like it couldn't be anything but random, but then he double-checked the location on his phone, nodded, cranked his door open, and hopped out with a grunt. Behind him, the van also parked.

The kid scrambled to follow him out of the truck, saying over his shoulder, "That's enough to get a post out. Thank you, Ms. Sorrow."

Lil sighed behind the kid's back, mentally thanking Gran once again. It would be absolutely futile to tell the kid her last name wasn't Sorrow, but Island.

Working together, the greenies unloaded and saddled the horses and packed the saddlebags. It was all Lil could do not to snort. *Real* cowboys took care of their own gear. But the Closed Circuit was the Closed Circuit: it would prove its contestants had grit its own way.

In reality, it had to respect union rules. Since the competition was being filmed, all the contestants were considered on-screen talent and had to be treated with kid gloves when it came to things like luggage handling and wet sidewalks.

In the cab of the truck, Lil asked, "You ready?"

AJ gave her a nonchalant smile through the rearview mirror and said, "Of course."

Lil raised an eyebrow and pressed, wanting to push him past his front. "Really?"

AJ took his sunglasses off to meet her eyes in the mirror, and her heart did a little flip like it always did when their gazes connected. With more seriousness, he said, "We're about to start, aren't we?"

Lil couldn't help the slight upward quirk of her lips at his response. It was a kind of logic she understood. "You're right, there, Garza," she said.

AJ opened the door and slid out of the truck. Lil followed him out, grateful to stretch her legs.

Standing by the horses, AJ pulled on a navy-colored Western-style long-sleeve over his T-shirt and started to button it while the older greenie gave them the rundown on their supplies.

The chatter faded into a quiet buzz in the back of Lil's mind as she watched the quick work of AJ's fingers moving up his chest, button by button.

It was going to be a long twenty-four hours.

Shading her eyes with her hand, she distracted herself with scanning the horizon around them. *The best way out*, she thought, *was always through*, which meant finding the cows and getting them back. Quickly.

The older greenie handed Lil her horse's reins and she thanked him. The horse was a blond buckskin that Lil immediately named Becky. Patting her neck in introduction, Lil breathed in deep and pressed her forehead against Becky's white blaze, the scent and sensation momentarily transporting her back home to Rory and the ranch and Gran, all of whom she missed more and more with each passing day of the tour.

The old-timer asked them once more, "You guys know the rules?"

Lil and AJ nodded, though she was sure there was probably a rule in there against stripping your partner with your eyes. The man checked his phone one more time before finishing up with, "Good. This is the spot. The cows aren't too far from here. Round them up, get them to the corrals, then pen 'em up before time's up." He nodded toward the saddlebags. "You've got all the supplies you need and then some. Good luck."

Both greenies hopped back into the truck. The engine turned over and then they drove off, empty horse trailer rattling as they sped away. The van stayed behind, maintaining a discrete distance from Lil and AJ, as they'd been told to expect.

Lil and AJ stood next to their horses, watching the truck and trailer disappear.

Somewhere along the way, AJ had swapped out his baseball cap for his Stetson, and standing there, he was tall and gorgeous and everything a cowboy should be.

Lil groaned internally.

With one last pat on Becky's neck, she said to him, "Well. We better get to it, then."

She checked the saddle before mounting. Her granddad had always been fond of saying, *Never let another man saddle your horse.*

She noted that AJ did the same and wondered if it was his habit as well or if he'd just noticed her doing it.

They rode for an hour before they found their first sign of the herd. Sure enough, it happened when they came downwind.

All twenty cows had stuck relatively close together—hence the pungency. Lil held up a hand, signaling they should stop, and AJ stopped, eyes on the cows.

Lil spoke low, slow, and evenly. "Remember the basics. Herd animals want a leader. Be that leader and everything else is easy. Stay calm and firm. They'll respect someone solid and dependable. You don't need to shove, yell, or make loud noises at them. That scares them and they won't follow something they're scared of. That said, don't be afraid to tell them what to do with your body—repeat yourself if you have to."

AJ gave a small nod and she continued in the same even tone, "When you want them to turn, pull wide to the opposite side. Otherwise stick closer in. Don't move fast and don't come up on them from directly behind where they can't see you."

"And if something goes wrong?"

Lil shrugged and grinned. "Depends on what goes wrong."

AJ's eyebrows came together as he scowled at the cows.

Afraid he would scare the cows if he kept glaring at them like that, Lil leaned in toward him and whispered, "They can sense your emotions—at least the predatory ones."

AJ plastered a terrifying fake smile on his face and asked through clenched teeth, "Better?"

Lil laughed and the sound whistled across the pasture, alerting the cows. A few mooed their disapproval, but none bolted. That was good—a sign the cows were well trained. Of course, she and AJ would find out for sure soon when they went in closer, but things were off to a good start.

It was just past one o'clock in the afternoon, which meant that if the cattle were amenable, as they seemed to be, and if she and AJ pushed it, which they could, there was a slim chance they could get the drive done just a few hours past nightfall. No need for any overnighting after all.

Lil nosed her horse more directly toward the cattle.

"Since you're newer at this," she said, "you take point. Usually that's a position for the experienced drivers, but I'll need to watch from the back to troubleshoot. Ride big, steady, and calm and they'll follow you. I'll catch any wanderers or stragglers and worry about turning them when the time comes. It'd be better if we had three more of us—that way we could put two up front, two on the sides, and one in back, but we'll make do…" The last lines she said more to herself than AJ, mentally calculating how fast they could move the herd with what little manpower they had.

It wouldn't be a good idea to rush—not underhanded as they were. So they wouldn't rush.

Lil looked up at the sky, trying to breathe away the urge to try. The sun was still high, but past its zenith. There was no way they'd cover the full fifteen miles before sunset—which was part of the point of starting so late in the day. It upped the drama to force them to overnight. Making the contestants show off their cowboy camping skills, as well.

All skills, though, that she and AJ were strong enough in to get away with pushing it a little.

The cows seemed docile, she was seasoned, and their route was straightforward.

She turned to AJ. "You know where we're going?"

He patted his saddlebag. "Doesn't matter. They gave us GPS devices, chargers, a map, and a compass."

Lil laughed, "Well, get yourself pointed in the right direction and get to it, then."

He gave a nod and nosed his horse toward the front of the herd while Lil followed him down the slight hill toward the dip where the cattle grazed.

Their paths split as they drew nearer to the cows, AJ ambling away confidently, clearly at ease in the saddle, a fact that Lil was relieved to see, since they had hours of riding ahead of them—he needed more than eight seconds of riding in him.

The thought brought with it a rush of heat to Lil's cheeks as well as the part of her pressed against the molded leather of her saddle. Shuddering, she gave herself a little shake and stern set down.

Her raging hormones were a strong reason to rush.

On that thought, she clicked her tongue and guided her horse to take position at the back left flank of the herd. She would act as their swing rider, flank rider, drag rider, and wrangler all wrapped up in one. There was no time for having wild thoughts in all of that.

She and her horse kept pace with the cows while she turned on her own GPS.

To her right, the cows mooed and walked, sometimes breaking out into mini trots to stay together. Everywhere else was blue sky and golden pasture. Behind them, the camera van followed at a respectable distance.

Ignoring the van, she scanned the horizon.

Ahead of her, AJ looked as good from the back as he did from the front, utterly commanding in position at the head of the herd. The distance between them was finally enough to give her some breathing room—space for her mind to be full of something other than every detail about him.

She sucked in a breath of cow-rank air and felt grounded for the first time in days. Maybe she could handle this for twenty-four hours.

For the first two, the cows cheerfully moved at a steady clip on a relatively straight route.

AJ rode point, a Western silhouette against the horizon line, his form as timeless as their activity, and she kept an eye on the herd from behind when she wasn't keeping an eye on him. Watching him from a distance, she could let her heart roll over as much as it wanted to. The landscape was large enough to take on anything she might have rolling around inside, childish and impossible as it might be.

A different voice inside, an older one, more concerned with anatomy and heat than rodeos and ranches, argued that there was nothing *more* possible. He wanted her, she wanted him. Simple.

Only the cows could see her blush, and their thinking was more in line with the second voice. Of course, they didn't know the mother she had—or that her own face in the mirror was a daily reminder that the road to ruin started with risky dalliances with rodeo cowboys.

Especially when those cowboys stood between her and saving the only home she'd ever known.

Heart and loins girded, Lil scanned for AJ's familiar form. He led with the same ease he'd shown since they'd begun the drive. She could appreciate the competency without turning it into something else.

And if she slipped up again, all she had to do was think about her mother.

The GPS said they had to turn south in another two miles, so Lil slowly circled around the back of the herd to come in close on the right flank. She'd push out far to right when it came time to turn, but eased into her new position close in.

Hints of purple hid amongst the pasture grasses, and Lil felt some of the lightness that always came with being on a drive. She'd been twelve the first time her granddad had taken her along. They never drove their own cattle—they didn't need to, and didn't have anywhere to take them to, besides. Her granddad wasn't interested in public grazing, didn't trust the government not to be out there sabotaging unwary ranchers, planting fescue and the like, as if there were a mighty conspiracy—never mind the fact that there wasn't much land in Oklahoma for public grazing to begin with.

No, she and Granddad did it for extra cash. His regular ranch hands could handle their place and look out for Gran for the two to three weeks they were gone, hired out by neighboring ranchers with larger spreads and more cattle than they'd ever have. Usually they drove herds south from Oklahoma, into Texas, where everything was meant to be bigger.

The drives gave them the money for extras, including Lil's rodeo dreams. Travel, entrance fees, gear—none of it came cheap. More hopefuls dropped out for that reason than any other. Rodeo was a money pit until you started bringing home prizes, and for youth riders, available prizes tended to be more about scholarships and acknowledgment than liquid compensation.

So when she'd gotten old enough, Granddad had started to take her along to make her work for it. With seven other men, they led herds from Muskogee to North Texas. Apart from competing in the rodeo and sitting in her gran's kitchen, there wasn't a time in Lil's childhood that she'd been happier than on those drives.

Lil had always been small, but the men didn't go easy on her because of it—her granddad wouldn't have it. There was too much work to be done. She rode drag first, the traditional dusty and smelly job set aside for greenhorns. As she got more experience, she took flank—even as new cowboys, sometimes twice her age, replaced her on drag. Back then, she floated from flank to flank, much like she did today, keeping an eye on the cows, especially looking out for signs of distress, injury, and stragglers. The country they had crossed through back then was vast and dry, a beige ocean meant for pounding hooves, flat-toothed grazers, and long sunsets. Today, tendrils of late spring clung to the landscape, the remaining flowers like little bits of purple lace left where they were thrown during that season's explosive bursts of love.

Lil snorted to herself. *Love* was a pretty strong word to use for the wild rutting most creatures got up to in the springtime, but wide-open spaces tended to have the effect of dragging her mind to poetry.

Their turn was coming up, though, so the time for poetry was done.

AJ had already begun to shift left, the lead cows following his steady direction.

Lil consulted her GPS one last time before pulling wide from the herd for the turn. The cows responded with a chorus of disgruntled moos but turned left, and she grinned. They were good cows.

AJ was good, too—cool, calm, collected, and all cowboy—like he'd done this a million times. A jolt of electricity that was becoming all too familiar traveled up Lil's spine and she blew a breath out of her mouth. She didn't have time for that. She needed to make sure the turn went off without a hitch.

The herd spread as they moved, loosening their formation as they made the wide turn.

Gray eyes narrowed, Lil scanned them. If one of them were going to bolt, this would be the time. She rode up and down each flank alongside the herd, noting that a few cows in the rear were slowing. She could speed them up when they straightened out again. For now she'd pulled in closer, gently pressuring the whole group to retighten their bunch.

A yearling calf chose that as its moment to break away at the front. The creature's panic took it an arc away from the rest of the herd at full speed to the sound of Lil cursing.

Taking off after the escapee, Lil startled the cows she'd been near into a trot.

There's that, at least, she thought, racing after the calf.

AJ twisted around in his saddle, calling out, "Alright back there?"

Lil hollered back, "Yeah, just got a breakaway. Keep 'em going."

She cut through the cow's path with a straight line, lasso shooting out to catch it around the neck.

Pulling back, body angling against her horse, Lil slowed them all into an easy curve back toward the rest of the herd, grateful it had been as simple as all of that.

The rest of the herd had mostly straightened out and nicely bunched, so there was no rush to get back to them. All the better to let the one who had spooked settle. It was obvious that something had gotten to her. Her large brown eyes were wild and wide, even still.

Lil and the calf followed the footsteps of the rest of the herd, coming back to the spot where the cow had bolted in the first place. Keeping an eye out for signs of something that might spook a cow, Lil observed a small cluster of rocks hidden amongst the tall grass, but not much else. Not that it necessarily required a lot to startle a cow.

They passed the rocks without issue and Lil let out a breath she hadn't realized she'd been holding. She rolled her shoulders and neck and settled back into the ride.

More rocks stuck out from the ground here and there, but for the most part, the way was smooth and clear.

Lil held her reins lightly, trusting her horse to navigate the terrain, while keeping a firm grip on the cow's lead. She wouldn't put it past the startled youth to bolt again. Rocky ground wasn't known for calming anxious cows.

By now, the sky had taken on a dusty film—like daytime had given up fighting the mess and instead settled in for a nice glass of rosé. Twilight and sunset were a ways away yet, but their arrival was inevitable.

Lil, Becky the horse, and the calf were about thirty feet behind the herd, nearly free of the rocky patch when the cow yanked away for the second time with a wild-eyed moo of panic. With her grip on the lead tight and her reins loose, Lil went flying off the horse.

After a full rotation in the air, she hit the ground on her stomach hard, but held fast to the rope. The cow dragged her over the jagged stones, once again racing in an arc away from the path and the herd, mooing in a frenzy and stirring up the rest of the cattle at the same time. With considerable effort, Lil finally wrestled her body around to roll up and onto her butt, grounding her boot heels into the ground to bring them to a stop.

For a moment she didn't do anything except breathe hard and hold tight to the rope. The cow continued to moo in alarm, drawing other cows to break off from the herd and head her direction.

Up ahead, AJ had turned and was making slow progress toward her, as was her Becky. She was proud of them both— Becky for keeping her cool and AJ for maintaining his slow and steady pace as he went. It would do no good for him to come harrying off after her and go scattering the herd further.

The camera van was a speck on the horizon, lacking maneuverability on the terrain and contractually obligated to film at a distance unless given the preapproved warning signal. Lil almost laughed. Reality TV was a trip.

As its brethren neared, the wayward calf lunged again, but Lil was ready. Her boots dug in and her arms strained, but the cow made it only a few more feet. Then, as suddenly as it had yanked, it gave up, the sudden lack of tension at the end of her rope sending Lil backward, her butt narrowly missing a particularly wicked rock that jutted out.

Laughing at herself because it beat crying, she noted that the prairie ground here was remarkably hard and rocky and that her derrière had come out the worse for their meeting. Gingerly, she came to her feet, calf still secure.

Cattle milled about around her, and Becky nosed at her shoulder, having beaten AJ's sedate pace with her trot.

After giving Becky's nose a quick pat, Lil untied the calf, which promptly ambled off to join its mother, and remounted.

She'd be feeling it tomorrow, and for the next few days after that, but she didn't think she was any worse for the wear after her fall—other than pride maybe. She'd have made quite the sight, flying through the air after the calf like some kind of human kite at the end of a rope. It made for good television, at least. The Closed Circuit wouldn't be disappointed with their footage.

Twisting around in her saddle, she checked behind her, and sure enough, the camera van still trailed behind them, closer now, capturing their follies for the delight of viewers around the world. She saw too that AJ had nearly reached her, his expression relieved, she assumed, to see her whole and hearty after her tumble.

Relative to the kinds of falls she'd seen cowboys take on the range, she felt lucky. Nothing was broken or even permanently damaged.

Her smile said as much, airy and full of the cowboy grace that came from walking away from a near miss with the skin still on your knees.

AJ frowned at her, surprising her by not sharing in the moment.

Her grin paused.

Both of AJ's eyebrows rose to his eyebrows, his eyes widening in panic.

Lil realized in an instant that he hadn't been looking at her at all, and that with whatever it was he had been looking at, something wasn't right.

Whipping back around in her saddle she saw exactly what had snagged his attention right as he whispered, voice dead serious, "Stampede."

19

AJ had been concerned when Lil had broken away after the calf, and more so when she'd flown off her horse, but she'd seemed to have the problem well in hand.

He'd only even planned to check on her for caution's sake, trusting that the steadiness in her stance and the smile on her face were enough evidence to suggest she hadn't sustained any serious damage.

But when the cows started to get restless again, he knew something was wrong.

As time was wont to do in the rodeo, seconds warped, truncating themselves even further than their regular momentary scale. In an instant, the cows went from milling about in mild disgruntlement to racing at full speed, every one pointed in the same wrong direction, a small, docile herd transformed into a single, enormously powerful beast.

"GO!" Lil screamed, taking off after the herd.

"How do we stop them?" AJ called, racing after her.

"We don't!" she hollered back. "We just hope they tire out soon!"

And that's what they did, racing to keep up with the cows until the herd exhausted itself, breaking up once again into clusters of cows.

Horses and riders breathing hard, sun beginning to set overhead, AJ reached into his saddlebag for his GPS device while his heartbeat slowed.

They'd veered off their course to the northwest in a large arc—almost a half circle.

At his side, Lil's tired rasp broke into his mapping. "The van's gone."

Looking up and around, he realized she was right. They must've lost them in the process of keeping up with the herd. But while the circuit would be sorry to lose the footage, he and Lil had bigger fish to fry, most pressingly, the fact that their little stampede had taken them an extra twenty miles off course.

"We've got a problem," he said.

She laughed, "Besides the fact we misplaced a camera crew?"

Snorting, he retorted, "They lost us." Sobering, he added, "But we do have a problem. We're about twenty miles off course."

Lil's curse ended in a long hiss.

"That's going to be tough to make up," she said.

He nodded, though it was an understatement. By more than doubling the distance they had to travel, their chances at placing in the challenge had all but vanished. And to think the whole drama had taken less than an hour.

He smiled. "Good thing we're the best there is."

Her smile was tired, but real, and seeing it, he felt oddly stronger, like coaxing the mirth out of her had given his own battery a charge.

Straightening in her saddle, shadowed and fierce in the twilight, she said, "We're not out of this yet. Here's what we're going to do. It's early, but we'll set up camp now. If we hit the hay early, we can wake early and get going before dawn. Current evidence to the contrary, these are well-trained cows. It'll be a stretch, but if we push them double-time, we've still got a chance at a good time."

AJ nodded. "I like it. But before all that, I'm going to check you out."

"What?" Exasperation colored the word, as if she couldn't believe he would stoop to cheap flirtation in a situation like this. Serious person that she was, she had yet to learn that there was always time for cheap flirtation.

"You took a pretty bad fall there." He held up two fingers. "How many fingers am I holding up?"

The look she gave him was dry and dusty and just like the Lil he knew and loved. Or rather, didn't really know at all but…enjoyed all the same.

"We're not doing this whole thing," she said.

His heart stuttered in his chest, his brain miscomputing her words for an instant, before he covered it all with a stretched-out drawl, languid and lazy as a cat. "We sure are."

Her mouth formed a stubborn line, but he continued on, unbothered. "We're going through the whole rigmarole and if you don't pass we're heading straight in. Forget the cows."

She raised her eyebrow. "Oh, we are, are we?"

He stared her dead in her eyes. "We sure as hell are. No competition is worth your life."

A flash of lightning streaked through her eyes, but she gave a sharp nod.

"Two fingers," she said.

AJ's smile returned. "Good. What's your birthday?"

"October 26."

"How old are you?"

"Twenty-seven." Her answers came fast and curt, which was reassuring since it was both like her and further sign that she wasn't experiencing any obvious cognitive side effects.

"What's your address?" he asked, getting a little trickier with the questions.

"1000 Bear Lane, Muskogee, Oklahoma 74447."

She rattled off the numbers without thinking, so he threw her a harder one. "What's thirty-six times seventy-two?"

"Seriously? I couldn't tell you that before I hit my head."

AJ responded with a withering look and said, "Guess we're going back in without the cows."

Lil glared at him silently for less time than it would have taken him to do the problem in his head and came back with, "Two-thousand, five-hundred and ninety-two. Happy?"

AJ shook his head and took out his phone. He opened the calculator and nodded only after he confirmed the answer, grinning at her outrage. "Good work. You pass."

She snorted. "It wasn't a bad fall."

"Better safe than sorry."

"This from a rodeo cowboy?" She lifted an eyebrow.

"A man can be complex, Lil."

She laughed out loud. "Sure they can."

That she could smile like that, coltish and free even when she'd been thrown from her horse and they'd been blown badly off course, struck him as powerfully as the beauty of it did.

"You sit," he said. "I'll set up camp."

She raised an eyebrow. "Do you even know how to set up a camp?"

AJ mirrored her expression, "Didn't know you had to own a ranch to go camping."

"Who knows what you people get up to in the city…"

Lil's words echoed between them, laced with electricity, and he decided it was a good time to set up camp. Clearing her throat, she wiped her palms on the front of her jeans, and added, "We'll set up camp together."

And that was just what they did.

20

"Who taught you how to start a fire?" Lil's voice was filled with a strange combination of respect and confusion.

The fire came to life and AJ smiled. "The Old Man. He forced us all out enough times that we learned how to camp."

"Your dad?" she asked.

AJ shook his head in a firm negative. "No. Henry Bowman—the founder of CityBoyz."

"The CityBoyz are the 'us,' then?"

AJ nodded, adding the rest of the smaller kindling to the fire. "D and I were part of the first group to go through the program. There've been eight more since."

"I've never seen anyone start a fire like that," she said, coming back to it, and he understood.

He'd only ever seen The Old Man do it like that.

Her husky voice slid over his skin like silk, which he tried to ignore while his body ignored him.

"The Old Man is one of a kind," he said, escaping the moment in business. "What sounds good for dinner? We've got beans and chili and s'mores supplies."

Lil stared at him blankly. "You're joking."

AJ held up a bag of marshmallows. "Gladly, no."

Lil closed her eyes on a sigh. "That is seriously the least cowboy thing ever."

"I don't know. Chasing a wild herd of cattle off course seems pretty cowboy to me. So, you want the chili, then?"

"Absolutely no to chili, and they're hardly wild."

AJ laughed. "What do you want, then?" he asked, even though he knew the answer.

When she mumbled her reply, AJ cupped his ear. "What was that? I couldn't hear you."

"You're an asshole."

"Hurtful, but audible. Why don't you try again with your dinner request? What does the big bad cowboy want for dinner?"

Lil muttered, "S'mores," and AJ let out a whoop.

In the darkness, the cows mooed.

Though she obviously resisted it, across the fire Lil smiled, bringing her fingers up to pinch the bridge of her nose, a chuckle escaping as she moved.

AJ forgot about the s'mores.

He forgot about the challenge.

He forgot about CityBoyz and the gaping lifetime stretching out ahead of him, and for the first time since he'd found it, he forgot about rodeo.

The only thing on his mind was figuring out the key to unlocking that easy, private, smile. Something told him it might be the kind of mystery that took years to unravel.

"Hand that stick over," Lil demanded, breaking into his swirling thoughts.

She sat close to the fire, legs crisscrossed, arm outstretched.

He looked down at the marshmallow stick he held before he handed it to her.

"Thank you. Chow time." She gave him a little salute before turning her attention to roasting her marshmallows, holding the stick well away from the flame as she rotated slowly and evenly, like a human rotisserie.

She was one of those people.

AJ sat beside her and stuck his own marshmallows directly into the flames. When they caught fire, he pulled them out, blew on them, and then squished them between two graham cracker pieces with a bit of chocolate beneath them.

Lil waited until he was finished to say, "You're a monster."

Her marshmallows had taken on a golden brown color and were evenly plump all around. She sandwiched them between graham crackers and chocolate, set her stick down, took a bite, and moaned.

AJ's jeans squeezed.

"I love s'mores," she said.

"Who doesn't?" he asked, mouth dry.

Lil smiled. "My gran hates them. Hates sweets, altogether. Prefers salty."

"The Old Man's the same way. Personally, I prefer spicy—be it sweet or salty."

"Sweet spicy?" she asked before polishing off her s'more. As she licked her fingers, AJ didn't need to ask which she preferred.

He did, however, need looser pants.

Answering her question, he said, "Rebanaditas—chili watermelon suckers—those are my favorite."

She wasn't licking her fingers to make a production of it—he knew that, logically—she did it just to get the marshmallow off. That didn't change the fact that her full lips wrapped around each digit and sucked it clean in a way that had him imagining her working on other things.

"So what's your real story?" he asked lightly, hoping the subject change would get his mind out of the gutter. "Lil Sorrow can't be your real name."

Her eyes widened in surprise, like she'd thought he would never bring it up.

When he'd just about given up on her answering, she replied, "It is, actually. Lilian Sorrow Island. I really do go by Lil, though."

Lilian. It was so…feminine. Like sunsets, lemonade on porch swings, and class. It was so far from the world of rodeo and yet, taking in her fine-boned strength, it absolutely suited her.

He didn't say that, though. Instead, he said, "Your middle name is Sorrow?"

She shrugged. "It's a family name."

"So Lil Sorrow is your real name. I thought it was a stage name. You know, because you reap sorrow, leaving a trail of cowboy dreams in your wake."

Lil groaned. "You and everybody else. It would have been simpler if Gran had signed me up with my regular name."

"It's got a nice ring to it."

Giving him a baleful look, she said, "No, it doesn't."

AJ's grin turned wicked. "Lilian. I think it's time we address the elephant in the room."

She side-eyed him dryly. "We're not in a room, Garza."

"I think we're on more intimate terms than that, Lilian."

Her name rolled off his tongue with a smoothness that demanded a second taste. Everything about her demanded a second taste.

"We kissed, and then near did more."

"Nothing to talk about," she said with a shrug. "It was just a kiss and drinking too much."

"And you're just alright at riding."

Her cheeks darkened once more and his chest warmed. He liked making her blush.

"You're truly amazing, you know," he added.

Instead of brushing him off, she surprised him by saying, "Thanks. For a long time, it was all I wanted to do."

"What changed?" He found himself holding his breath for her answer.

"I—" She seemed at a loss. Then she frowned and continued in a lowered voice, "I gave up."

He hadn't expected the answer from her and he found himself disappointed. Still, he asked, "Why would you do that? You've obviously got prize money in you."

Lil looked up at the sky, full dark now and peppered with stars.

"I gave up because I was a girl."

Her words hung heavy and ridiculous in the air until AJ said, "That's quite the statement."

Lil chuckled, "No, no. I don't mean girls give up. I gave up because I'm a girl and I couldn't ride bulls."

AJ smiled. "You're not really making your case stronger."

The joke earned a full laugh from Lil and AJ felt like he'd just earned another buckle.

"I'm a great bull rider," she said, continuing, "even better back then—more fire, less caution. But no one would let me compete in professional rough stock events outside of the INFR."

"You could have done barrel racing." He glanced at her out of the corner of his eyes. "Unless that was too girly for a tough cowpoke like you?"

She wrinkled her nose at him.

He didn't think he'd ever noticed her doing that before.

"Not at all," she said, adding, "I'm an excellent barrel racer, too, which you'll see soon enough. I just wasn't willing to settle for almost when it came to rodeo."

Her words sank into him and he understood—in his forever-aching shoulder, his long-ago healed bones that still hurt, and in the rhythm of his heart. They gave voice to the same part of him that could see himself doing rodeo, and nothing else, for the rest of time.

Though at the moment his mind wasn't having any trouble coming up with other things for him to do.

His eyes found Lil's and they both paused. Their breath synchronized and deepened until her chest's rise and fall became a gravitational pull. He fought the urge, but lost, his gaze drifting lower.

Her black Western shirt didn't offer much for the imagination to work with, but he looked nonetheless, noting her slight shivers.

"Why didn't you say you were cold?" he asked, roughly cutting into the soft sounds of fire crackling against the night.

"What?" Lil looked down, startled. "Oh. I guess I hadn't noticed."

AJ lifted an eyebrow. "Well, you're cold."

She laughed. "Just not much for complaining, I guess."

"Or asking for help," AJ said gruffly as he stood, walking to the saddlebag and rummaging through until he found the sheep's wool–lined jean jacket he'd packed for the challenge.

"Here." His fingers brushed against her skin as he handed her the jacket, sending a jolt of electricity up his arm.

Her eyes glittered in the firelight, and her skin felt like some kind of hybrid of silk and baby powder, far softer than any bull rider had a right to. Especially one as good as she was.

This close to her, the vanilla bourbon scent that was hers whispered its way to his nose and he took a deep breath.

Beneath her clothes, her body was defined and strong, he knew, like an Olympic athlete's.

She might be petite, but he'd never have to worry about breaking a woman like her.

Keeping his thoughts to himself, though, he said, "Your braid is loose."

It was true. The sleek line was messier than he'd ever seen it. Even the tightest coif wasn't a match for getting dragged off a horse.

"I can help you with it," he offered.

Eyeballing him like he'd grown horns and a pencil 'stache, she said, "You do hair now?"

He grinned and shrugged. "Pays to be diversified."

Her gray eyes narrowed to slits. "You got a lot of practice, then?"

He winked. "Probably about as much as you."

"Somehow I doubt that…"

"I'd be willing to bet I make a better girl than you," he claimed boldly, ridiculously.

Laughing, she angled her head to the side and said, "Oh really? I used to wear pink, you know."

Lips stretching he said, "Somehow, I doubt that…"

She smiled. "It's true, though. It helped me stand out in the crowd."

He'd never known a woman whose banter included rodeo strategy, but he found he loved it. He countered with, "Helps even more to actually compete."

"They've got to let you first," she shot back.

"They let women in all over the place now."

She looked away. "It's too late for me. I stopped wanting it."

"But you used to?"

"A long time ago."

He wasn't so sure about that. He asked, "So why are you here now?"

She looked away, shame clouding her expression. "My granddad took out a reverse mortgage on our ranch and we don't have the money to get it back. This was the only way we could think to come up with quick cash."

"Excuse me?" He pressed his lips into a line. It was never a good idea to use rodeo for investment purposes. That he'd made a lifetime of doing so was beside the point.

Lil's explanation was staccato and matter-of-fact. "My gran got the bright idea to sign me up for the circuit, certain I would take home the top prize and save the homestead."

The story was absurd, something worthy of a soap opera. So absurd that for a moment, AJ didn't say anything. He opened his mouth to try a few times, only to close it again and frown.

Finally, he said, "Your Gran kind of pimped you out."

Lil looked like she didn't know whether to be outraged or to laugh. She decided to laugh. A lot.

She laughed so hard, tears came to her eyes. Wiping them from the corners, she said, "She sure did, the wicked old woman."

Her reasons for riding the circuit weren't that far from his own, but the motivation for them couldn't have been more distant. She would happily walk away when the whole thing was over because she didn't really want to be there. She was a star rider who could walk away.

What that must be like…

That line of thinking brought a heavy feeling to the pit of his stomach and nothing good ever came out of that, so he changed the subject.

"So what'd you do when you quit rodeo?"

A bubble of laughter escaped her lips, and he felt his own

quirk upward. He liked that she was as quick to laugh as she was to temper.

"You make it sound like I did it cold turkey. It wasn't like that. I just decided not to pursue a professional career. I went to college on a rodeo scholarship, actually."

AJ smiled. "My best friend did that. He's a lawyer in Arizona, now. What did you study?"

"Nonprofit management," she said. "Thought I would go into addiction recovery work."

"But you didn't?"

She shook her head. "I didn't. Granddad died right after I graduated, so I stayed home and ran the ranch with Gran for a while. We were bleeding out, though, without the supplemental income from Granddad's drives."

"Drives?"

Lil nodded toward the cows. "Right up until the end we thought he was still taking two to three cattle drives every year. Turned out that wasn't the case—he'd stopped when he'd just got too old but was too ashamed of the fact to tell us."

Her words bounced around in his chest uncomfortably, echoing Diablo's and The Old Man's. "I know the type. What'd you do?"

"I tried to get a few drive commissions, but nobody wanted to send a young woman out on a drive team. Things have been tight, but we've been managing—until we got the notice that the terms of the reverse mortgage had come due."

AJ smiled. "We never expect the piper, do we? The Old Man started CityBoyz to give boys who lived in Houston a chance to learn how to cowboy. One of his old sponsors loved the idea and funded the whole project. When that sponsor died suddenly this year, the money disappeared in an instant."

"And he never got nonprofit status?" she asked. "I remember that from your bio." She added the last bit at his look of confusion.

He grinned. "You read my bio?"

Lil's cheeks turned pink. "I read everyone's bio."

His right dimple peeked out with a smile and a spark lit his eyes. "Sure you did."

"I did," she insisted.

The other side of AJ's lopsided smile lifted. "Sure you did," he repeated.

"You don't have a lot of friends, do you?" she asked irritably.

He shook his head. "Not really, no. You either, I bet."

She hit him on the shoulder, but smiled and didn't lie. "Nope."

He shrugged. "It's lonely at the top."

"You're impossible."

"I think I'm very possible. Want to try me?"

Lil made a choking sound in the back of her throat and scooted away from him. "No thank you. Not one for cowboys, myself."

"Funny, that's not been my experience," he said, returning her long ago words to her with delight.

Outrage lit her face. Eyes narrowing, she sassed, "Cowboys aren't known for their stamina…"

AJ gave her his best stern look. "Now don't go making any eight-second-ride jokes. You're better than that."

She shrugged, a mischievous light coming to her eyes. "If the shoe fits…"

AJ scooted closer. "I could show you how it fits."

Lil scooted away like she she'd touched fire, eyes wide and glittering. "No thanks. I'm good."

AJ stretched lazily and watched her eyes follow the movement. She was lying. But all he said was, "Suit yourself."

"I will," she said with too much conviction.

AJ chuckled. "Tell me more of the Lilian Sorrow Island story."

She shook her head. "Nope. It's your turn."

"I won't do it. Not until you give me more. You don't know your daddy, but what about your mom? What was she like? You talk about your grandparents. Do you have any memories of her? How did she die?" It was strange, the way the spare details of her life had stayed with him. He'd never been good with birthdays, names, or faces—for AJ, if it wasn't attached to rodeo it didn't stick. At least that's how it had been. Until Lil.

Her smile froze before she took a moment to look down and straighten his jacket, pulling it tighter around herself. When she looked back up the smile was still stuck on her face, though her eyes had gone as cold and gray as a lake he had seen during his first trip to the snow. "I was four when she died and three when she started down the path, so mostly she's fuzzy, but I remember her singing. She loved to sing and dance." What had started out terse and matter-of-fact had softened into sad before his eyes, but AJ didn't think Lil had been aware of the transition.

As honored as he was that she had opened up, even slightly, he wanted her smile back more.

"And she died in a horrible dancing accident?" He was solemn, placing a hand over his heart.

Again she punched his shoulder, this time adding, "Excuse you. That's got to be speaking ill of the dead or something."

Looking affronted, he said, "I don't see how so. People die dancing all the time. Sounds to me like you're the one being disrespectful, acting like death is some kind of absurd comedy."

Her shook her head. "Impossible."

He grinned, licking his lips as he did. "We've already gone over this, but if you want to again…"

Closing her mouth, she crossed her arms tight in front of

her chest and puffed it up. "I certainly do not, thank you very much. And no, my mother did not die dancing. She died of being wild and brokenhearted."

Her show of affront was admirable, but he sensed the truth in her words. And something else.

"And it was a cowboy that broke her heart?"

Lil sucked in a breath and gave a short nod, her posture going stiffer than he'd ever seen it—so stiff she could no sooner ride a bike than a horse or a bull. It was strange to see her like that, the body he'd spent so much time watching as closely as he had gone alien in its lack of flow.

And he realized another thing.

"That cowboy was your daddy."

Lil let out the breath she'd been holding and her shoulders sagged—but only for a moment. Then the line of her lips firmed, her spine straightened, her shoulders squared, and she gave him a smile that was real, if tired. "He was. At least that's what we've pieced together from the bit she let slip. The way I see it, the best thing to do is avoid cowboys altogether."

AJ snorted. "What is history for if not to learn from the mistakes of the past? We'll be more careful."

Lil laughed. "Said every fool ever."

"How're you ever going to find your daddy if you avoid cowboys?" he challenged.

Lil made a rude noise in the back of her throat. "Who says I'm looking for my daddy?"

AJ aimed a dry look in her direction. "Just a few things…"

"I did not come to the rodeo looking for my daddy, thank you very much."

He loved how she could simultaneously sound like a septuagenarian and a playboy bunny at the same time.

"Right…" Provoking her had become one of his favorite pastimes.

But instead of rising to the bait, she just shook her head at him, smiling all the while. "I see what you're doing, but I'll let you get away with it. Except for one thing—I came to the rodeo because of my granddad."

"How's that?" he asked, loving the way the fire cast dancing shadows and light across her skin, heating the smug ease with which she regarded him into something deeper, something real, and comfortable—into the kind of thing that lasted.

"When I was four, just before my mom died, my granddad was out in the pasture working with a wild horse. Gran had left the door open for just a second, but it was long enough for me to run outside and straight into the front pasture to him. Granddad did some fancy tricks, including a bareback mount I'll remember to the day I die. He kept me out of harm's way that day, and gave me the bug at the same time."

"So you're a horse girl, then?" he wheedled.

She bared her teeth. "Now that's not what I said, at all. That's what gave me the bug. The passion came later."

"You're welcome to tell me anything you want to about your passion."

She opened her mouth to speak and then closed it.

Grinning, he said, "Anything's possible."

Rolling her eyes, she said pointedly and with heavy sass, "Not quite anything."

He laughed. "Are we making a wager?"

"Absolutely not."

"If I win…" he continued, as if he hadn't heard her.

"You know you can't win. It's in my blood."

The most decorated rodeo champion in the world laughed. "On both sides, it sounds like."

She paused as if she really hadn't thought of it that way.

"You really don't daydream about your cowboy daddy?" he asked, the surprise in his voice genuine.

Looking away with a shrug, Lil projected forced nonchalance. "Only in the same way you think about what happens after you die. I gave up thinking I might find the answer one day. There are a lot of cowboys out there in the world. It gets exhausting searching faces and wondering." Her voice was weary but not sad when she finished, and she had turned back to him, smiling with a new determination in her expression. "Now you know more of my dirty laundry. It's time for you to do a little airin' yourself. Tell me about your people."

AJ shrugged with a grin, keeping it simple. "I grew up in Houston. Joined CityBoyz when I was twelve and have been chasing rodeo ever since. That's all there is to it."

"There's more to the story than that."

"Not really. It's been a pretty straightforward path for me." He kept his grin in place, but behind it, he fought the rising urge to actually tell her his life story, as if genuinely opening up was something he did with other people.

Some of it slipped out anyway, the words leaving his mouth without his permission. "My mom still lives in Houston, but I bought her a house in Piney Point." He heard the boast for what it was, but it was something he'd never not be proud of. Buying his mom a house was making it, as far as he was concerned.

"You've made a lot in prize money?" she asked.

"I have. Made even more through investments."

She crossed her arms in front of her chest and gave him a look that said she'd seen his kind before. "So why didn't you just fund the program, then? Sounds like you could have carried it."

"The Old Man wouldn't take my money."

She snorted. "Make it an anonymous donation."

AJ scoffed. Did she think he'd been born yesterday? Or that The Old Man had been for that matter? "He'd know."

"So instead this was your plan?"

"He can't refuse his own money."

Lil laughed and the sound skipped through his system.

In the dancing firelight, the skin of her face and neck was buttery smooth. It glowed from a light from within, as if a small personal sun powered her core. The way she was willing to take anything and everything on, he half believed one did.

She could ride and she knew her way around a nonprofit. She really would have been a great asset to CityBoyz. His instincts hadn't failed him on that point. That they aberrantly continued to egg him on, pressing him to pursue her despite the fact that their lives were going in different directions, stood out only more for its contrast.

"We should turn in," he said. "We've got an early morning and a long day ahead of us." He stood as he spoke, scanning for the most even patch of ground around the fire. Beside him, Lil nodded and came to her feet as well, but he waved her away. Surprisingly, she accepted his brush-off with ease, wandered off on her own, probably to pee, with only a faint stiffness to her step.

The Closed Circuit had packed them both three-season rectangular sleeping bags that rolled up into the size of a small pillow.

Rather than lay them side by side, though, he unrolled and unzipped them and then zipped them together to make one large sleeping bag. She wasn't going to like it, but staying toasty warm through the night was the only way her body was going to have the resources to make up for their lost time tomorrow.

21

"We're not sleeping like that." Lil was proud of how steady and no-nonsense her voice came out. It certainly didn't match anything going on inside.

The fool had gone and zipped their sleeping bags together. She stood beside him, staring down at the bags.

Without turning to her, he said, "We are. Heat is the only chance you have to recover in time for tomorrow. Our only chance at a decent score."

She raised an eyebrow. "Right…"

His head whipped around and he pinned her with a look that set off the roller coaster she'd been riding since they'd started the challenge. The man was too much.

With an all-too-sensual curve in his lips, he said, "There won't be any games when I get you in bed."

And then she was blushing again and thinking about their kiss again, and the night in her RV, and wanting more. Her throat felt thick and heavy, her nipples hard and sensitive.

And here he was trying to share a sleeping bag.

The man was insane. Honestly.

"No way," she repeated, her voice catching in her dry throat.

"We lost a lot of time today. You need to be at your best tomorrow if we're going to make it up. That means warm."

He wasn't playing fair. It was like he was inside her, as if he knew exactly what buttons to push to secure her compliance. The one-two punch of guilt and cold competition wormed into her, working its magic until her resistance crumbled. It was completely reasonable to sleep together in the name of the competition. Rational even.

"Fine. Clothes stay on."

He called her a prude and her laugh bubbled out without her permission. It was hard to hold on to stern around him.

The laughter broke the tension of the moment, or at least that was what Lil told herself as she lowered herself to the ground. One of the sponsors had provided the contestants with long johns, and AJ tossed her hers. She slipped into the now-oversized sleeping bag and wiggled out of her jeans and into the long johns.

AJ just took his jeans off where he stood, and Lil's mouth went dry as she watched, knowing her eyes should be on anything else but him. He wore boxer briefs, cotton and plain-colored, just like the T-shirts he preferred. His well-muscled thighs were golden brown and smooth and she pictured running her tongue up the length of one toward the part of him so clearly outlined by the fit of his boxers.

"My eyes are up here, Lilian."

Her cheeks flamed, and she looked away while he laughed, the damage already done.

She snuggled down into the sleeping bag and turned to lie on her side. Lying, her body took the opportunity to voice its complaints over her earlier fall. Her head felt thick and heavy, far too large a burden for her tired neck to carry all night, which would mean she'd have a crick in it for the rest of the day challenge.

Lil didn't know what was worse: the soreness or her mental moaning and groaning about it. Whining like this, even in her own head, wasn't her way.

AJ slipping into the sleeping bag, however, chased away all complaints.

She didn't move, but it didn't matter. The heat of his body reached out to caress her without an inch of their skin touching. Her breath caught, then started again, heavy and not subtle at all.

He scooted closer, and her heart stuttered. He was going to spoon her. AJ Garza, the world's greatest rodeo cowboy, was about to spoon her.

He didn't fully close the space between them, though. Simply slipped his arm between the ground and her head, underneath her neck. Lil sighed. With the simple movement, it was like the screws in her head had been loosened.

He said, "Thought that might be more comfortable."

He smelled clean, like fresh cut grass and sheets drying in the sun and his body was a solid wall of warmth behind her. It took every ounce of willpower she had not to snuggle back into him and revel in the easy security she felt lurking beneath the surface.

His breath was deep and even behind her and she wondered if he was asleep. They'd had a long day and he'd done more than his fair share for the last part of it. He'd be well within his rights to conk out.

And completely oblivious to the tension that had her own body, abused as it was, feeling about as sleepy as a live wire.

His grand warmth plan was backfiring spectacularly. There

was no way she'd ever be able to sleep like this, head cradled on the arm of a man she'd been lusting after all day long. It was too much for anyone.

He'd brought their kiss up enough that she knew he was open for more. All it'd take was a little scoot and neither one of them would be thinking about staying warm or sleeping.

Her skin flushed and the thought crossed her mind that it might just be her destiny to be a human beet around him.

But destiny didn't have anything to do with the way her stomach clenched. It wasn't the source of the electric aware-ness of her skin, or the heaviness of her breasts.

Destiny was the ranch. Leaning in to sensation was her mother's way.

"You're awfully quiet over there." His words whispered across the back of her neck, deep, slow and ready for bed.

She shivered, whispering back, "Thought you were asleep." Her own voice came out more hoarse and weighted than usual, hinting of things she wasn't inviting him to enjoy.

At least not out loud.

Out loud, she had a ranch to keep safe and a rodeo to win. But pulling her mind back to the competition wasn't having quite the same dampening effect as it had earlier.

"Do you see the stars?" he asked.

Heat filled her core. The mere timbre of his voice was enough to set her off, it seemed. His words took a bit longer to get through, but when they did, it was her out.

"I haven't," she said, carefully rolling onto her back—careful not to brush her body up against his, careful not to touch any more than they already were. He stayed where he was, lying on his side, his arm her pillow.

Overhead, the sky sparkled like a child's glitter art, the Milky Way a deep river of light slashing across the sky, roaring overhead, its current of stars thick and palpable, even from the earth.

AJ was a radiator at her side and the sky overhead was made of diamonds, and she couldn't remember ever feeling quite so soft.

She'd never been the type of girl to fantasize about romance, but if she had been, this moment would have been it.

Minus the stampede.

"Beautiful, isn't it?" he said.

Turning her head slightly, she found his gaze on her and grinned. "Ancient, but it never gets old."

He ran a finger down the side of her cheek, almost absentmindedly, his expression taking on an openness in the moonlight that she'd never seen during the day. "There aren't many things like that in the world."

His rough fingertip against her skin robbed her of breath, so Lil gave only a small shake of her head in response, pulled in by the gravity of his velvety brown eyes.

Something was pretty, but it wasn't the stars.

Closing her eyes, she dragged her mind to counting sheep since thinking about AJ and the stars did not seem to lead down the path of sleep.

Not when he was warm, right there, and willing. Not when the stars were good at keeping secrets…

But that wasn't her.

She hadn't even gone all the way with her longest boyfriend. Though in that case the timing and situation had never worked. Dorm mates coming home unexpectedly, lack of condoms, the occasion not feeling right…

And then Granddad passed and that time of her life was over.

Then it was all ranching and missing him. There hadn't been room—or energy—left for men.

"You're not sleeping." There was a smile in his voice, but Lil didn't open her eyes to see it. "Your eyes are squeezed shut too tight."

Lil still didn't open them, but said, "Might be if you weren't gabbing away."

He chuckled softly and the sound wrapped around Lil, low, genuine, and silky—sound candy made for her pleasure alone.

Her breath caught and she shivered, her breasts turning heavy and sensitive beneath the material of her shirt.

He angled his body toward hers, almost imperceptibly, his muscles taking on a taut readiness that hadn't been there moments before.

He knew.

He could tell she wanted him.

Without looking at her face, he knew.

The thought brought heat to her cheeks, but instead of hiding, she turned to face him.

She might be transparent where he was concerned, but she wasn't a coward.

His eyes were hot and deep and she felt the now-familiar pull of them.

His mouth lifted at the corners, but the smile was neither his usual mask nor the one she thought of as real.

This one was all wicked teeth and the promise to consume and be consumed—to be entirely engulfed in his flame.

He took her mouth in one smooth motion and like each kiss before, he devoured her. His body pressed tight against hers, only a thin layer of fabric separating them.

Her hypersensitive nipples delighted in the pressure of his chest even as they strained to be closer, touching more, merged... She moaned into his mouth, and he used it as an opportunity to take even more.

Her bones turned into gelatin, the air escaping her until

all she could focus on was the point where their mouths met. She was melting. She had to be.

She'd never been this warm before—bodies weren't meant to burn like this, to be so hot. She tilted her hips against him, pressing her most intimate parts against him, unable to hold back the breathless sound that slipped free. Instinctively, she wrapped her arms around his neck, pulling him close enough to run kisses down his neck.

He kissed her ear, murmuring, "Despacito, Liliana."

His voice in Spanish was its own form of foreplay. It caressed through her system, leaving tiny kisses everywhere it went. He turned her name into a lyrical delicacy whose sweetness shot straight to her core when it passed through his lips.

She sighed in his ear, whispering back, willing to be open and soft in another language, "Apurate, vaquero, he estado esperándote a toda mi vida."

He groaned before uttering, "Lil, you're killing me." And his voice *did* sound pained, but he seemed eager for it, leaning in closer, pressing his face against her neck to take a deep breath.

Lil reveled in the warmth of his skin against hers, hands eager and greedy for skin to skin contact.

Again, his voice was low in her ear. "Lil, you're going to burn me alive."

She was fine with burning alive as long as they went together. She kissed him everywhere her lips could reach, marveling at the perfection of his skin. His strength. He held her easily, even as she squirmed and arched against him.

His chest was a wall of smooth brown muscle and heat. He didn't have much body hair, just a light dusting of black curls at the top of his chest, separated from a small path of hair that started at his belly button and disappeared beneath his thermals by a gulf of impossible abs.

He reached an arm down to his waistband and Lil followed the motion, mouth watering when he stopped short of pushing them down his hips, her lips taking on the unfamiliar shape of a pout.

He smiled wickedly at her, saying, "Don't worry, querida. I'm just giving you time to catch up. You're overdressed over there."

She surprised herself by laughing, even as her fingers reached for the hemline of her shirt, pulling it over her head, followed quickly by her sports bra, until she was bare to him.

His eyes feasted on her, slowly taking in every inch there was to see and leaving trails of fire along her skin wherever they went. She shivered, drawing him closer. He obliged, closing the distance between them and taking her into his arms, their bare chests pressing against each other.

He held her there for a moment, lifting her off the ground slightly as his arms tightened around her. Sucking in a deep breath, he buried his face into her neck and sighed an exhale, and with the sound, something flipped over in her chest.

He let her go slowly, lowering her back to the ground beneath him, keeping their bodies close enough that the hard peaks of her nipples brushed his chest the whole way, sending electric shocks straight to the fire between her legs.

Her lips parted, and he took it as an invitation, bringing his hands up to gently cup the back of her skull and press his mouth to hers. The kiss started slow and soft, sweet and coaxing. And like he was the sun, and she a flower, she opened for him.

As she did, he took more, his tongue making forays into her mouth while she pressed against him for more. His fingers wound their way into the remains of her braid while he plundered her mouth. She made little noises into their kiss and he groaned in response, pulling her tighter against him.

His heat wound around the whole of her body, radiating from every place they touched—her breasts, hot and achy, pressed against his hard chest, his fingers working soothing magic on her aching head, the thrall of his lips. All of that heat, flowing through and around her like bright streams that pooled—hot, soft, and wet—at her most private center.

She moaned into his mouth and he used one arm to scoop her up and change their position so that he sat on the sleeping bag with her on his lap, her legs on either side of him. She wrapped her arms around his neck and pulled his kiss deeper and they stayed like that until she was sure they'd become a single burning flame, threatening to burn up the bedding and all of the plains around them.

His fingers left her scalp, and she mourned the loss, until those calloused hands gripped the bare tops of her hips to press her closer. Goose bumps sprang up along her skin, sensitizing her to the tiny breezes blowing around. The cool night wind did nothing to dim the heat. If anything, its silky caress only fanned the flames.

AJ ran his palms up her ribcage until his thumbs came to cup her breasts and find her nipples. He rubbed them in delicate, lazy, circles, pulling back just enough to watch her face.

Her head fell back with a moan and he lifted his hip. The hard length of him pressed against her center, hot through the thin fabric between them. Colors flashed behind her eyelids, and his name slipped out from between her lips.

"Can I take your braid out?" He rasped the question, and she nodded.

She was surprised when his fingers deftly untied and unbraided without tugging and tangling. He didn't touch her hair like it was a battle to be fought. He touched it like it was something to be coaxed and teased and chased and adored. Something female.

It sprang free around her. Messy curls bounced every which way, brushing against her shoulders and back, and sending shivers down her spine. Lil purred.

"There she is." The gravel in AJ's drawl was equal parts pleasure and possession and the combination was ethanol to her flame.

He kissed her earlobe, then her neck, trailing down to run along her collarbone before lifting to lay her back and hover over her, palms planted on either side of her head. His face was shadowed, but no less beautiful.

If anything, the dark hollows emphasized the gorgeous structure of his face: breathtaking jawline, proud cheekbones, the way his dimple turned wicked when he smiled like that...

Lil shook her head, trying to rein her wild thoughts in. It was too much. She had no reason to feel the kick of ownership over that smile, the sense that it existed for her alone. No reason she should be so sure—in him and this—so confident this was right, knowing that she'd always been waiting for this perfect here and now, as true and powerful as the desire that threatened to engulf them both.

And then he was reaching his arm down between their bodies, his calloused palm running down the bare skin between her breasts and down her belly, sending electric shocks all along the way to pull the drawstring of her thermals.

His fingertips, brushing lightly over her skin as they worked, were like branding irons, even through fabric and the lace of her underwear.

The whisper of cool air through lace called all of her attention to the juncture of her hips, and she instinctively lifted them so he could do the work of getting rid of her pants.

Beneath them, she wore a black lace thong, plain by her standards, but his eyes blazed, twin black flames, as he uncovered them.

"Mmmm. Hidden depths, Liliana linda." His voice was breathless, and she felt it in every cell.

The words were a hot freshet to the river of heat running through her, even as she told herself not to hold on to them, tried to remember he was a rodeo cowboy and there was an unspoken *for now* at the end of his every sentence.

She shivered, nothing between her and him but a thong. Eyes intent, he gripped her hips and pulled her up so they were flush with his.

Just the pressure of him against her was nearly enough to push her over the edge, and she hadn't even seen it yet.

The need to see him, all of him, filled her with greedy urgency. It wasn't enough to lie on her back while he took her in—even if his chest was glorious. She needed to touch him. Taste him. Mark him in some way.

She bucked him, but he caught her, grip holding fast, holding her hips at a slight elevation. That she hadn't shaken him off sent another wave of heat to pool at her center and she moaned.

"Te gustas, querida? What about this?" He pressed his own hips against her, grinding his length against her, nudging her open beneath the barrier of her thong, just slightly.

Another moan escaped her, and he smiled. "I thought you might."

She responded by rocking against him, pressing more of her wet heat along him.

This time he moaned, and taking advantage of his moment of weakness, she bucked again. He held fast, though, and the next time she pressed into him, it was because she needed to.

His smile was open and real when he said, "You're perfect, Lil."

Lil narrowed her eyes. "Take off your boxers, AJ." Her voice would have been dry, if it weren't thick with want of him.

He laughed before clicking his tongue at her. "Now, is that any way to ask?"

She growled and he used his hands to tilt the angle of her hips forward so the sensitive bud of her clit pressed directly against his shaft. Sounds she'd never made before slipped out of her lips and AJ groaned himself, falling victim to his own torture.

Slowly, as if he was loath to release his hold on her hips, he lowered her back down against the thick pad of the sleeping bag. He was over her once more an instant later, enveloping her in his heat and scent of fresh cotton, summer grass, leather, and something she could name. Something that made her want to rub her body all over his and purr.

Her hands were on his hips, pushing his boxers down, before her mind registered their intent. He caught her mouth with his, taking her into a deep kiss, and she took it as permission to keep going.

She pushed them over his hips and down his thighs, stopping when his heavy erection fell against her and he groaned into her mouth. The tip of it landed just shy of her belly button, leaving traces of the scalding moisture beading there.

When he released her from the kiss, she looked down between them and her breath caught. He was perfectly formed, primally beautiful, exuding raw masculine power from every pore.

Lil's mouth watered. Again, she was filled with a desperate urgency to touch him. To taste him. To have him inside of her. All of it, at once. She wiggled her hips, working to align herself with him, but he shook his head and leaned in to kiss her neck beside her ear, whispering, "Not yet, querida."

He trailed kisses down her neck, sending shivers down her spine as his lips brushed against the hypersensitive skin of her breasts. She cried out when he found one of her nipples.

Back arching, she pressed against his mouth, his wicked tongue coaxing her inner flames higher and higher, even as his rough palms caressed up and down the length of her side, thumbs sometimes brushing teasingly along the outer edges of her breasts as he went.

He switched to the other and the newly abandoned hardened further, chilled, wet, and exposed to the elements.

When his kisses trailed lower, down her belly, her breath came in mini gasps that were shallow, rapid, and desperate. He made his way slowly, deliberately. He kissed the spot just below her belly button and it was an electric jolt through her body.

Her breath stalled. On some level she'd recognized the trajectory of his path, but the reality, the gentle pressure of his mouth, coupled with the tiny flickering tastes of his tongue against her skin had all her blood pooling in the place that was his ultimate destination. A part of her thought of stopping him. Her past boyfriend had gone down on her, but it'd mostly just made her feel awkward and pressured. She brought her hands to rest at the top of his broad shoulders, unsure if she meant to push him away or hold him there. All thoughts fled with the gentle pressure of his lips pressing against her most intimate place.

The kiss wasn't salacious—just the gentle pressure of his lips pressed against her opening without exposing her, without plunder—and it almost broke her. She lifted her hips, unconsciously opening herself up to him, and he hummed against her. The sound vibrated through her core, triggering an answering sigh from her. And then, as if he'd been waiting for the cue of the sound, he devoured her.

His tongue found its way between her folds to lap at her inner heat. He savored, sucking, licking, and pressing soft kisses along her crease while she arched her back, fingers curling in to grip the sleeping bag on either side of her body.

He placed his hands on her inner thighs, igniting the delicate skin there with the brush of palms, roughened from years of ropes, before he spread her wider, opening her, exposing more of her to his plunder.

His tongue entered her and she didn't recognize the sound that came out of her mouth. She panted, hips bucking, and he held, digging in farther.

He said her name against her slick folds, and she nearly came.

Pulling back slightly, he murmured with a smile, "So impatient..." before blowing softly.

The cool air across her most sensitive area was a torturous interlude—soothing and calming, even as she craved more fire and heat. She squirmed for more, anything, and he obliged, sliding two thick fingers into her while using his thumb to rub the sensitive bud at the top of her entrance.

She cried out, startling answering moos from the cows grazing in the distance, and his laugh was full of triumphant male.

She felt herself fraying in the onslaught, threads of Self unraveling from the outside in, and she knew she wasn't long for the world. Lil, as she knew her, was dissolving, disappearing. Never to be seen again.

Whoever emerged when it was all over would be a different woman entirely—remade, she was afraid, in his image.

A part of her balked, ever the wild mustang, unwilling to bend or bow to him, but he held fast, his powerful, calloused thumb and slick fingers unyielding, demanding nothing less than her complete surrender. She'd broken enough horses in her lifetime to sense when she herself was breaking, bowing to a will stronger than hers. Trusting his lead.

Lil disappeared. In her place were a thousand fireworks. The entire spectrum of color going off in a sea of rainbow explosions accompanied by the sound of a single name: AJ.

When she coalesced, he was once again above her, tip poised at her entrance.

He caught her eyes, his near black in the intensity of their focus. "You're sure?"

Lil nodded and his answering smile was blinding. He reached between them to guide his head up and down her damp crease, stirring up the internal sea she thought had calmed.

He groaned and said, "Lil, you feel like heaven and I'm not even inside you," and she flushed.

He was hot, and so large she knew she'd have been scared if she hadn't grown up on a farm, and she wanted him inside her. He teased her, though. And kept teasing her. Until she was wetter than she'd ever been in her life and teetering on the edge again.

He didn't stop until she said please.

"Dios mío, Liliana," he growled. "I thought you'd never ask." And then he was pressing into her, slowly, giving her time to adjust with every inch. "Jesus Christ, Lil."

She moaned, his words sending electric thrills along her spine.

The pressure of making space for him inside her was intense, but not the pain she'd been told to expect. It was...good. Immense. Heavy. Hot. A new heartbeat pulsing deep inside her.

And then he started to move. Slowly.

Her body answered in a shuddering wave of pleasure. She dug her fingers into his shoulders and let it carry her over the slow, easy edge.

He leaned down to press kisses across her face, repeating her name, over and over, "Lil. Lil. Lil."

She opened her mouth to say something but her face stalled as another molten wave of pleasure crested over her. Whatever words she had were lost in a moan.

His thrusts grew deeper and harder, and with each one she grew wetter, her body delighting in his bombardment.

Her hips found his rhythm, leaping to meet his, striving to give him greater access. To take more of him in.

He groaned and the sound reverberated through her from the inside out. She gasped as her inner muscles began to clench, yet again, surprised that there was anything left of her to fall apart.

He growled, "Let go, Lil," and she did.

She ceased to exist, once and for all, fragmenting into a mere collection of sensations—tremors and moans driven by a primal pulse of grip and release—until finally it was too much for him, too. His last thrust sank deep, the deepest yet, and he roared her name as he came.

22

The sound of restless cows was the first thing Lil noticed when she woke. The second was that she had, after all was said and done, snuggled into AJ during the night. What made the situation more complicated was that he had done the same.

It was still dark outside, but she knew it was morning, probably somewhere around 5:30 or 6:00 a.m. She was on her back, her head resting in the crook of his arm, her side snug against his. Somewhere during the night, he had wrapped his arm around her, crossing her chest and stomach, his palm cupping her hip bone.

He smelled good. Really good. His scent was fresh and earthy, not like hay, but somehow tangible and right in the same way. It was the smell of steady mornings through changing seasons. It smelled like safety, and a place to turn to—and everything that AJ was not.

Dragging her mind away from its waxing rhapsodic about his body chemistry, she turned her attention instead to the arm draped across her chest. She'd have to move it if she wanted to get untangled.

He'd missed her nipples, but barely, and both of them, not to mention the places where her breasts touched the weight of his arm, were very aware of the fact, sending charged signals to her brain to let her know it'd only take a little movement in either direction to make things interesting.

Enough of that, she thought. She was an adult woman. She was just going to lift his arm and scoot away. She reached for the hand on her hip.

He responded by pulling her closer and murmuring some form of protest, his strong arm drawing her closer into his chest, pressing the length of her body against his. Close enough that suddenly all her focus was on the fact that the hot, hard length of him pressed against her thigh.

Her body flushed and, interpreting the contact as the sign that all bets were off, readied for round two, nipples hardening and skin turning needy again, demanding she roll over, lift her face, and kiss him.

Instead, she blew a breath through her mouth and shook her head clear. What she needed to do was to get away from him. Pronto.

He solved the problem for her by waking up. His eyes flew open—he looked at her, looked down at their position, then grinned.

"Well, isn't this a nice way to wake up," he drawled. His accent, like his voice, and…other parts of him, was thicker in the morning.

Lil pushed his arm off and sat up, body protesting the sudden movement.

"You're shameless," she said. "You haven't even gotten out of bed yet."

"Mmm," he said. "That's when it's the best..." His voice carried an offer to prove it, but Lil inched away.

AJ sent her a "suit yourself" shrug and sat up. The sleeping bag pooled in his lap, and if there was a force in the world with a chance of tearing her eyes away from the broad expanse of him, Lil didn't know what it was.

She had a problem. She refocused her attention on her own body, hoping the concrete sensations of discomfort would be an anchor against the sea of input that was AJ.

After being thrown from her horse, sleeping—and other things—under the stars, she certainly wasn't going to feel good when all was said and done—especially since "all said and done" was yet to be concluded with timed sorting and penning—but she wasn't so hurt they'd be out of the challenge. Which was as it should be. This was rodeo and there hadn't been a day in all its history that rodeo had ever been about feeling good when all was said and done.

Lil's voice was all business when it came out. "We're both up. Might as well get going."

Not moving, AJ laughed, "No breakfast? We've got more marshmallows." He said the last bit in the same cajoling tone that Gran had used to get Lil to try new things when she was little. Lil responded the way she always had: she gave one shake of her head, pursed her lips into a stubborn line, and drew her eyebrows down, face turning dark and serious.

She crossed her arms in front of her chest and said, "We've got to make up for lost time. Best get going."

AJ's eyes took on a competitive spark and he nodded. "You're absolutely right. Early bird and all that." He slid out of the sleeping bag and stood up as he spoke and Lil's mouth dropped open.

They might have slept out in the open under the stars, but

the man could pitch a tent. Lil's entire body flamed so fast she was sure she blended in with the red of her long johns.

He was huge.

He stretched luxuriously, long arms reaching high, his shirt lifting at the hem to reveal hints of rock-hard abs and defined hip muscles. All somehow guiding and directing the eye back to the proud centerpiece, AJ in his full glory. He sauntered over to his saddlebag, the very definition of shameless.

Lil was equally torn between laughing and meeting his dare head-on. She was a coward, though, so she laughed.

She didn't laugh at him. How could she? He was beautiful. Close to perfect. No, she laughed because he made the whole thing light and free. A power that'd always eluded her.

He pulled on his jeans slowly, and she enjoyed the view.

Today's button-up was emerald green, by far the loudest thing she'd seen him wear all circuit.

"Think they might miss you from far away?"

AJ snorted. "Nope. I just want to make it easier for them to film me coming in first place of course."

"You mean us."

AJ grinned over his shoulder. "Sure."

Lil scowled, reality intruding. He was teasing, but it was also the truth. She'd do well not to forget.

"Speaking of, do you think the camera van is looking for us? By day they can probably track our GPS."

He looked thoughtful. "Maybe? They seemed like they were having trouble with the rocks yesterday. I wouldn't be surprised if they settled in for the night and plan to catch up today."

"Them and us both."

AJ turned around, finishing up with the top buttons before tucking his shirt in his jeans and around his still rather obvious erection.

He followed her gaze and his smile turned predatory.

He said, "Don't you worry about me. I'll settle right out after a few hours in the saddle."

Lil burned red but didn't shy away. "I'd expect as much. Nothing much different about you from any other mammal."

He just laughed and pulled his boots on.

Lil headed over to get dressed herself. If her movements lacked her usual grace, they made up for it by not being unbearable.

She pulled her jeans on, followed by a simple button-up with a paisley pattern and classic Western piping. The print and accent color were both a dark peach and the buttons had an opalescent sheen.

AJ made sure he noted its fanciness with a raised eyebrow, but otherwise made no comment. Lil could hear his thoughts anyway, and they just made her puff out her chest.

Once dressed, she began to finger comb through her curls. A glance his direction told her AJ was watching, attention rapt on her fingertips.

Her hair bounding free, was riotous and thick despite her undercut. It sprang every which way, defying and escaping her hands before it ultimately submitted to her will.

They packed up camp and saddled up together in quiet, letting the sounds of the morning prairie wash over them while the cows grazed drowsily, evidently not in any rush to get moving to greener pasture. It was companionable in a way Lil hadn't ever experienced, not even with Piper—the first and only employee Granddad had let her hire on. Piper's room and board was included as part of her salary, and she didn't make much, but that Lil's grandparents had let her stay, a young woman fresh out of the penitentiary without a ranch skill to her name, that they let that young woman be the one

Lil chose to bring on and pay when resources were so scarce had been no small act of trust.

These days Piper knew the ins and outs of the ranch well enough to be trusted with working it while Lil was away and had started a fledgling horse breeding program at the ranch that she hoped would one day bring supplemental income, though it was still in its infancy. Or rather, not quite in its infancy, but in its gestation.

Piper's pride and joy mare, Reckoning, was pregnant. Piper had the touch with the horses, and Lil loved her to pieces.

There was a different peace with AJ, though, and she realized it was full trust. He might act lighthearted and carefree, but he was serious about the things he loved.

Lil turned her horse toward the back of the herd.

"Oh no. Where do you think you're going?"

Lil nodded toward the cows. "Was planning on taking flank to start out with before doing a stint as drag."

AJ shook his head. "I don't think so. You're lead today. I'll take the back."

Lil frowned. "You're a bit green to take on the whole rear."

He snickered and Lil realized too late what she'd said.

"Don't you worry, Lil." He smiled. "I can take the whole rear. I can even spank it if you want me, too."

Lil mustered the driest look she could, considering the moist heat building up in unmentionable places, and said, "Does your mother know you talk to women like that?"

"Nope. And I'd deny it if you told her. She teaches Spanish and Women's Studies at a community college in Houston. She'd have my hide."

Lil whistled. "Smart lady."

AJ nodded. "And terrifying."

"It's not attractive for a grown man to be afraid of his mother."

"You just wait until you meet my mother before you go passing judgments."

Lil wasn't entirely sure if he was serious or not and didn't press, though a laugh slipped out.

She wouldn't be meeting his mother.

A strange pang in her chest followed the thought, but she shrugged it off, instead nosing her horse toward the flank once more.

"I was serious." AJ's voice came from behind, carrying all of its usual relaxed confidence, but different somehow—like a steel rod ran through its center. It rang of finality and the hairs on the back of Lil's neck stood up.

Nobody told her what to do.

"Excuse you?" she asked, turning her horse around to face him.

He had his cowboy hat back on and it was almost too much for her with the gorgeous green of his shirt and his perfect jawline. Her stomach did a somersault.

"You're riding lead today, and if you're really so concerned about making up for lost time, I suggest you get up there quick and get us started."

They stared each other down, both mounted and stubborn on the horizon, brown eyes meeting gray.

They would have been on more equal footing if she hadn't had to look up at him. Even when she was on a horse, he towered over her.

He wasn't going to budge—she knew it, whether it was from the set of his shoulders or the look in his eye. He'd throw the competition before giving in. She felt it in her gut as if she was inside his mind as he thought it.

She broke the stare and blew air through her nose in frustration.

"Fine," she said.

She turned her horse toward the front and grumbled, "Holler if you need help."

AJ said to her back, "If you're to be believed, I've got all the skill I need."

Lil ignored him, focusing instead on catching the lead of the cows.

Like everything else with these cows, or rather, *almost everything*, the process was easy. She'd seen her granddad do it so many times that the motions were familiar, comfortable, and practiced as if she'd been doing it for decades, rather than for the first time today.

It wasn't lost on her that this moment, too, was another forgotten dream coming true. Or that she owed that fact to AJ.

The sun rose fully, a bright greeting of orange and yellow, and the cows followed close behind her. Picking up the pace as the light improved, she got them moving at a nice clip, cows, horses, and cowboys happy and content.

They rode like that for a few hours before AJ made his way toward the front.

Lil twisted around in the saddle to check the cows before turning to him. "What's up? You want to switch?"

He shook his head, not losing any of his speed. "No. Lonesome back there is all."

Lil rolled her eyes. "Get back there."

"Nah. The cows are fine."

"And that means you need to be up here because?"

"How else am I going to get to know you better?"

Lil wondered if she could blow out her blush mechanism. Was that possible? Could a human blush too much in a twenty-four-hour span? She didn't know, but she had a feeling that she'd find out before the day was over.

23

Lil's face was priceless.

She'd turned beet red and looked deeply insulted that he wanted to get to know her better. It was the cutest thing he'd seen since D's cousin had had a baby.

"What's your favorite color?" He couldn't help himself.

She sputtered, "Whatever color it takes to get you back into your position."

AJ looked back over his shoulder. The cows were contentedly following along, possibly even in a tighter bunch now that they had two strong leads to follow.

"They're fine. What do you hate?"

Lil raised an eyebrow. "Hate?"

AJ nodded. "My mom says dislikes say more about a person than anything else."

The corners of her mouth tugged up into a smile and she said, "Tomatoes."

He pulled back on his reins. "What? Nobody hates tomatoes."

Lil let out a full-throated laugh, and the sound of it partially soothed the fact that she didn't like tomatoes. *Who didn't like tomatoes?*

"Careful what you ask for…" she admonished.

"That's for sure. I had no idea I was riding with a monster."

She snorted, offering, "You could just go back and watch the rear."

"You won't get rid of me that easy."

She snapped her fingers. "Darn."

AJ laughed, "It was all a ruse, then."

"Not at all. I really don't like tomatoes."

His shoulders slumped. "Fine."

"Cheer up, buddy."

He brightened. "What about pico de gallo?" Hope beat in his chest.

She shook her head. "Not even pico."

Hope died.

She wasn't perfect. Neither was he. He could live with a tomato hater. "To each his own," he finally said.

She gave him a shrewd look. "Had to come to terms with that one, didn't you?"

He nodded solemnly. "Nobody's perfect."

She laughed again. The sound was bright in the early sunlight. Behind them, the cows mooed. She'd taken a serious beating and come back up laughing. He had to admire that.

He asked, "How do you feel today?"

She thought for a moment before she said, "Stiff. Sore." Then she grinned and leaned in to add, "Good enough to get through the rest of the day."

He hadn't been worried. He knew her well enough already to know she wouldn't quit.

She had literal smudges of dirt on her face, but the fine bones of her face, her round nose, and heavily lashed almond-shaped eyes, steadfastly declared her resilience.

As he stared, he noted that her body resisted the rhythm of the horse in a way it hadn't yesterday. She was favoring her left side and her neck was as rigid as a tree trunk. She was making up for her upper body's stiffness with the strength and flexibility of her legs, which were, fortunately, more than up to the task. They were surprisingly long for her lack of height, and perfectly formed. She held the reins with her hands, but he could see that it was her legs and seat that were guiding the horse.

Clearing his throat, he said, "We don't need first. We both have enough points that we can afford a second place. You shouldn't push it after yesterday."

She threw him a look that said exactly what she thought about that, and he couldn't say it didn't turn him on. She went all in, or not at all, just like he did.

She said, "It'll take a few more falls before I'm ready to 'take a second place,' thank you very much."

AJ laughed. She'd actually said 'thank you very much.' Because he couldn't help himself, he said, "Well, there's no need to push it," when he'd always pushed it. "We're almost done with the competition and your top spot is secure. No use killing yourself. When all is said and done you're going back to your ranch and never going to bring any of this up again." The sentence echoed back at him hollowly.

Regardless of who won, when all was said and done, they'd both return to their respective homes. She would be happier to do that than be recognized as the first world-class female bull rider, and he would end up back in Houston, his belt buckle hung up on the wall, ready to dive into coaching. It was a fitting, if anticlimactic, end for a retired champion bull rider.

"More use killing you for suggesting such a thing," she retorted, unaware of the undercurrents sweeping through him.

"Have you ever been to Houston?" he asked, changing the subject.

She shook her head. "Outside the qualifier, no."

"You should come with me sometime. The food is delicious."

"I heard it's a bit dangerous."

"No more dangerous than climbing on top of three thousand pounds of animal that doesn't want you to be there."

"Bulls don't have guns."

"Bulls don't need them. Houston gets a bad rap—it's a great place."

"Says the man who started bull riding as an at-risk youth?"

AJ snorted. "I wasn't an 'at-risk' youth. I was just angry. My parents were both college professors."

Lil looked taken aback. "Professors? I thought you were some kind of reformed troublemaker."

Her comment earned a full-blown laugh. "Not me. That's Diablo."

"Diablo?"

"You'll meet him."

"Oh, I will?"

AJ ignored her arched eyebrow, saying, "He and I were both in the first cohort. Diablo was there by order of a judge. I was by my mom."

Lil chuckled to herself. "Because you were an angry twelve-year-old? Your mom was hard-core."

"No, she—" AJ stopped with a frown. He didn't generally get this deep into how he got into bull riding.

Lil watched him expectantly and he wondered what he was going to tell her. That his dad had died and it had been AJ's fault, but that it'd happened when he still hated his dad for breaking their family apart? It was a part of his story he didn't share with people, but the words were on the tip of his tongue.

Rather than let them out, he said, "She knew I needed a big outlet. My dad had died and I had a lot of anger."

"I'm so sorry." Her low voice went even huskier with empathy and the growling thing inside of him found the effect was strangely soothing.

He smiled. "The bulls worked. I was hooked right away. Fortunately, I had a knack for it and that's all it took. Drive, knack, practice, and the rest is history." He was proud of how he muscled the story back to its normal track of general positivity, emphasizing that anyone could do what he had done.

Lil said, "I'm sorry your dad died."

He shrugged. "It was a long time ago."

"Hard for a kid." She was a terrier, even when she didn't realize it.

He looked away. "Hard for anyone."

"And Diablo?"

"He was a delinquent and the judge was a redneck."

Lil snorted. "That sounds like a country song."

"He's a lawyer now."

"Fancy."

"He thinks so."

"What did your dad teach?" she asked.

She was good, keeping him off balance by jumping around.

"He taught Chicano Literature at the University of Houston."

Lil whistled. "Really fancy."

"He thought so, too. Thought so so much that he couldn't fathom why my mom would leave her position teaching Spanish there to go take a leadership position at a community college." The words poured out from his mouth, unplanned and far too revealing.

Lil's eyebrows drew together. "Her job sounds fantastic, though."

"It is," AJ agreed. "It's perfect for her. It didn't fit his sense of pedigree, though."

"And so he divorced her?" As usual, Lil's expression and voice gave her away. She didn't approve.

He appreciated not having to play guessing games.

"No," he said. "She divorced him after he decided to soothe his bruised ego and thinning hair by having an affair with a graduate student."

They rode a few yards in silence before she spoke again. "That's so cliché."

It wasn't what AJ had been expecting and it broke the tension in his chest. "I said as much to him. At a high volume."

"I would've been angry, too."

She didn't say she was sorry for something she had nothing to do with. She didn't pat him on the head. She didn't brush him off as a temperamental kid.

He surprised himself by saying, "It got worse."

"How so?"

He looked away, eyes scanning the horizon. "One night I got mad enough to tell him what I thought."

She winced and he sensed it was empathy, rather than mere sympathy. Somehow it wasn't hard to imagine her in a similar position, shouting things she'd later regret. The thought made him feel less alone, even though he imagined she was the kind of person who came back and apologized once she'd cooled down. He'd never quite gotten that down.

He said, "I stormed out of the house at the same time as a storm rolled in. He came out after me. I stomped through the rain and blew off steam for a few hours. He got caught in a flash flood and died. So then in addition to being angry about what he'd done, I was angry about what I'd done. I carried it with me everywhere I went."

Again, Lil let the words sink in before she spoke. Yet again, when she finally said something, it wasn't what he was expecting. "Bulls make sense, then. Smart woman, your mom."

AJ shook his head and laughed, feeling somehow lighter than he had before. "You really take the whole cowboy thing to the next level."

"I don't take any 'thing' anywhere."

"That's why it works so well."

She threw her arms up. "This is what I get for helping people."

"No. This is what you get for your grandma helping people. You wouldn't even be here if she hadn't signed you up."

She looked like she wanted to shake her fist at him, but decided to smile and shrug instead. "Same thing."

"Is it?" he poked.

She frowned. "I owe that woman everything."

"I have a feeling she doesn't see it that way."

Lil looked away this time. "I'm guessing she didn't plan on burying her daughter or raising her granddaughter. People look forward to retirement."

"Not all people. If she's anything like you—" and he thought she might be "—I suspect that she didn't."

"I was a handful," she said.

One side of his mouth quirked up and his eyes dropped to her saddle. "I know."

She blushed and his grin stretched wider. Every reaction was all up-front with her.

"You're impossible," she said. It was a refrain he loved the sound of.

He grinned. "You want to do it again?"

Her blush was hot enough he feared she might spontaneously combust.

"You're a shameless man," she hissed.

He shrugged, laughter in his voice when he answered, "So long as I'm your only man, it doesn't matter."

"Very evolved of you."

"I think so." He patted his thigh and said cordially, "Care to come ride on my lap over here?"

"Excuse me?" She was incredulous, as if he were really inviting her to sit on his lap while they traveled at a steady trot, surrounded by cows.

So of course he said, "I invite you to slide your sassy ass across my lap and rest your head on my shoulder."

Laughing, she said, "You wish."

He grinned. "Sure do."

She sucked in a breath, but he saw the tension in her body relax as her exhale morphed into a laugh. If she wouldn't take the ride, he'd just have to keep her laughing as much as he could until they were done with the challenge.

"Gran always says you can wish in one hand and spit in the other and see which one fills up first."

"That a dare?"

Her eyebrows shot up. "What? No! How'd you get to that?"

Rather than answer, he commented, "Your gran's version is a lot cleaner than my grandpa's."

She ran it through a couple times in her head before it hit her—he could virtually see the wheels turning, as well as the ah-ha.

A chuckle escaped her lips and she tried to disguise it by looking back at the cattle, but it didn't work, and never would, because he somehow knew that she'd never be able to hide herself from him.

She had snagged his attention, sharpened it, intensified it in a way unlike any he could recall experiencing—more like the way he felt about rodeo than women.

"So that's a no on the ride?" he verified.

He was being ridiculous. He knew it, and would stop the second it started to make her uncomfortable. For now, though, whether she realized it or not, it made her forget how much they still had left to do.

"Are you always like this with women?" she asked, playing the part of the exasperated woman perfectly.

He paused, initially for dramatic affect, but in that brief space, he realized he couldn't remember this kind of ease with any other woman.

When he answered, his face was thoughtful, his answer devoid of facade or charm. "No."

Lil rolled her eyes. "Now you're going to tell me it's because I'm so special."

He shook his head and said, "Nope," even though it was true. She was. Perpetual grin returning, he said, "It's because the women came after me."

Tone effortlessly casual, she said, "You're ridiculous, but not lying. The way they go after you is over-the-top."

She emphasized *over-the-top* as if she were worried he was going to miss the fact that she was calling him that, but he didn't care. He was more interested in the thread of jealousy woven through her words. That she'd noticed—and been bothered by—the buckle bunnies that forever followed him made him feel all warm and fuzzy inside.

"If I really wanted to get over-the-top, I'd pull the evergreen buckle bunny move of bribing security so I could sneak into your room, take off all my clothes, slip into your sheets, and wait for you to find me. How's that sound?"

"Stalker-ish."

AJ laughed, "I thought so, too. Didn't sleep with that one."

"I should hope not. If you did, anything that happened after would be your own damn fault."

"Agreed. Any more sage advice, oh experienced one?"

She turned as bright red as the tomatoes she shunned. Recovering herself, she rolled her eyes and said, "How about you getting back into position so we can finish this thing."

"I like it when you talk dirty to me, Liliana," he said before checking on the cows over his shoulder, and adding, "Seems like we're finishing just fine with me where I am, so I'll kindly pass on your offer."

"Impossible."

"To stay mad at me, you mean?"

"Something like that," she muttered.

"So what do you do when you're not breaking the rodeo?" he asked casually.

Lil's laugh bubbled out like she couldn't help herself. "Run a ranch."

"The 'all work and no play' type, then?"

Lil's eyebrows drew together. "I know how to have a good time."

"Is that so? All it seems I've heard about is work and more work. What do you do for fun?"

Lil thought for a moment before replying, "I ride my horse."

"Alone?"

She nodded.

"Do you ever go out?"

"You mean to bars and the like?"

"And the like," he said dryly.

She shook her head. She explained, "I've lost people to drugs and alcohol. A bar's not typically my scene."

"That doesn't have to keep you from going out," he pointed out.

"Bars are the only place to go out in Muskogee."

"You don't have longtime girlfriends you drink wine with? You strike me as the kind who'd have two best friends she's known since childhood."

"How'd you come by that?" she asked with a laugh.

"You're covered in that homegrown country girl thing. Usually comes with the territory."

Lil laughed, shaking her head. "Well, I don't. A combo of not having many neighbors and not having much in common with my fellow homegrown country girls. They were more interested in winning crowns than buckles. Our paths didn't cross much."

"But you did go to school, though?"

Lil rolled her eyes. "Rather than take offense, I'll just write that question off as city-boy rudeness…"

AJ laughed. "So why no lifelong school friends?"

"I do have two friends now, you know. Good ones. I just haven't known them since back in school. Back then, I suspect my lack of friends was due to the same reason that your own best friend is from CityBoyz."

"Rodeo," he said.

He knew it even as he realized he'd known before he ever asked her the question in the first place.

Rodeo, real passion for it, didn't leave much room for friends—especially non-rodeo friends. To be close, people had to be willing to travel long dusty roads at your side, or be comfortable with your absence. Middle schoolers and high schoolers weren't particularly known for being comfortable with anything, let alone the complications of long-distance friendships.

She had people in her life now, though.

"So you work and ride your horse?"

"And sign up for harebrained rodeo contests in my spare time."

"The simple life."

She laughed, "Yeah. It's the simple life, alright. Riding bulls by night and chasing cows by day."

AJ grinned. "What more could you ask for?"

"What more, indeed. And you. Do you go out?"

AJ's grin stretched further. "Of course. I go out all the time."

"'Cause you don't have a real job?"

"I had a real job, once. The pay sucked."

Lil snorted. "And what was that?"

"I was an EMT."

Her mouth dropped open.

Dryly, he said, "Rather than take offense, I'll just write that face off as country girl rudeness."

Lil closed her mouth, but still managed to convey complete shock. "When did you have time for that?"

"Right after high school. Only way my mom would sign off on me going pro instead of going to college."

"Technically, you didn't need her permission. You were eighteen."

He laughed, "My mom's a *badass,* though, remember? My going into pro rodeo didn't fit with the gentleman scholar image she had for me."

"But that would have never worked for you. Your dad did that."

Her words slipped through his shields like small fish through a loose net, and he wondered if she saw through him as clearly as he through her.

He nodded. "He did."

Lil gave a little sigh. "But she's still a college professor, so what can you expect?"

"Exactly. EMT training was as good a compromise as I was going to get, so I took the deal."

"She suggested it?"

"She did." He looked into her eyes and grinned. "Looking back, I'm sure she chose emergency response because she wanted to scare me away from rodeo."

Lil's answering grin brought a light to her gray eyes. "Didn't work."

"It certainly did not. But it got me through those lean early years as a pro—before the prize money really started flowing in. And it turns out emergency training comes in handy at the rodeo."

"I can imagine," she laughed. Gesturing to the pasture around them, she added, "And on the range, too."

He tipped his hat to her in agreement. "And on the range." Using her segue as a way to check in, he asked, "How're you feeling after the fall, by the way?" He was worried about the possibility of concussion.

"Good."

"Good. You should take it easy after the challenge. A hot bath would be best, but a shower in the RV will have to do."

"Bossy."

"I'm a professional."

"Are you? Don't you have to keep up some kind of license for that?"

He raised an eyebrow. "And what if I do?"

Once again, she looked shocked. "Do you?"

"Your country girl rudeness is showing again."

She flipped him off and he smiled.

"I told you it comes in handy," he said. "I once saved a man's leg, resetting it after a bronc stomped him. Stopped a lot of blood flow over the years. Kept young fools from riding with concussions, that kind of thing." He said the last bit looking her over, and she stared coolly back, eyebrow lifted.

Behind them the cows mooed.

She ignored him, asking instead, "Will you go back to it when this is over?"

He hated every version of the "what are you going to do next?" question, even coming from her. It was hard to say exactly what you were going to do with the rest of your life when you'd climbed your personal Everest by thirty-six. "No. You've got to get off on the job for it to last. I was happy to say goodbye."

"Why?"

He shrugged. "There's a lot of stuff you can't save and I was already in love—with rodeo. Leaving emergency response was like coming home from a long stint away—and I never even stopped rodeo."

"Good skills to have, though," she said.

He nodded. "Good skills to have. You never know when the next emergency is going to show up."

As if his words had conjured the moment, the cows erupted in frantic mooing. A knot formed in the left flank of the herd, while several cows from the front and right flank broke into a trot, stretching and elongating the herd block like pizza dough. Looking around to see what had startled them, he saw a strange moving dust mote on the horizon. As he watched it, it grew larger, coalescing into the shape of the camera van.

"Ah shit, camera crew startled them." Lil's curse wasn't panicked, merely resigned, and it calmed AJ. She began to nose her horse toward the knot of cows, but AJ maneuvered to block her.

"Let me do it," he said.

"You don't know what to do."

"Tell me."

"Takes too long to explain," she said testily.

He didn't have to say anything for her to sense that he would not be moved.

She heaved a frustrated sigh. "Fine. Go check out the bunch.

You've got a set of skills, so assess the situation and determine which one to use: rope, tie, wrestle, or herd."

He moved as soon as she was done speaking, guiding his horse toward the bunch. Lil turned her horse the opposite direction and began to pick up speed.

What's she doing? he wondered. He figured she'd hold tight where she was, but as she surged ahead of the scattering cows, he realized she was recapturing the lead. She looked like something from a movie, her hair whipping and coming undone in the wind behind her as she rode. But as much as he wanted to, he couldn't afford to spend any more time watching her in action—he had his own mess to untangle.

24

Lil allowed herself only a moment to watch AJ ride toward the distressed cows before she took off to catch the rest of the herd. She had to recapture the lead before they built up too much steam. So far things were controllable, but even a docile herd could become dangerous if they got too riled.

Lil and Becky the Horse broke ahead of the trotting cows and then slowed their pace.

"Whoa, there. Atta girl." Lil spoke louder than she needed to—her calm, soothing command voice wasn't for the horse. It was for the cows.

Herd animals craved cool and competent leadership. Give them that and they were down to follow you wherever.

And follow they did.

It was almost comical how easily they settled down and got in line behind her. Their sea of moos beginning to fade.

Lil twisted around in her saddle to check on AJ.

As always, and even from a distance, the sight of him made

her heart do a little flip. He was gorgeous in his seat, expertly nosing his horse between cows to break up the cluster.

One by one, cows broke free from the chaos and trotted to rejoin the rest of the herd with Lil, until all that remained were a single female and a younger male.

The male's rear left foot looked to be stuck. The female mooed anxiously at his side.

Lil was relieved. The female was probably the male's mother and when he'd gotten stuck, she'd stopped in her tracks and sent off the distress call, causing a mini traffic jam.

Lil sat back and watched as AJ circled the two cows, deciding what to do next.

The rest of the herd had recoalesced behind Lil, who had them clustered and relatively still. They grazed patiently, now that they felt safe.

AJ circled his duo one more time, and Lil wondered if she should ride out and help him. She hesitated. The cows behind her would be easy to spook again, and twice spooked was twice as hard to calm back down.

But AJ looked like he needed help.

Resolved, she began turning her horse to ride his way only to see he didn't need her help after all.

His lasso floated through the air like it was weightless itself to gracefully land around the male's neck.

Lil kept her eyes glued on AJ. His roping was so smooth, you'd think he'd been born and bred on a ranch.

He tightened his end of the rope and gave it an experimental tug with his arms. The cow budged, but didn't come free.

Holding the rope still, he twisted around to face forward in the saddle and wrapped the rope around the pommel a few times, then spurred his horse forward.

The horse pressed forward only to stutter into a sidestep, not expecting the resistance of the cow's weight. Then the horse's instinct to pull kicked in and it surged forward, this time prepared for its load.

The cow came free with a distressed moo, then proceeded to try to buck and kick itself free from AJ's hold. After a handful of halfhearted attempts, the freed cow resigned himself to the rope around his neck, thereby allowing AJ close enough to release it from its bondage.

There was a metaphor there, but Lil was more interested in the way AJ's muscles bulged as he freed the cow. He coiled his rope back up with grace, his movements economical and practiced, and watching made her heart pound. Her very own private show from the world's greatest rodeo cowboy. She'd come a long way from the ranch.

In fact, they were both a long way away from everything. Just the two of them, a herd of cows, and the open range all around. Heat rushed to unmentionable places and she sucked in a deep breath.

Not again. As much as the idea burned in her gut, it could never happen again.

A magical, once-in-a-lifetime moment beneath the stars was one thing, a clandestine affair was something else entirely. Something she didn't do.

Just like you don't do cowboys, an unrepentant internal voice sneered in reminder.

But she could be harsh and ruthless too, and she shoved it down. She had broken rules around AJ, but she wouldn't continue.

He was her competition and, besides that, he was a rodeo cowboy through and through. Being the world's greatest only made him more so.

Infinitely more so.

Which meant no future, no second time around, and absolutely no to the longing pulsing in her heart.

She wrested her attention back to the cows.

Heifer and son were nearly caught up to the rest of the herd and AJ nearly back to the rear flank, where he should have been the whole time and where she knew he wouldn't stop now.

Sure enough, he didn't.

Returning to his place at her side, he exuded everything that was male, exhilarated, and satisfied.

She cut off his nonsense before it could start: "Pretty bold to come right back to the place you got in trouble."

"That was amazing. You were right. I knew how to do everything."

His grin flashed and her stomach flipped.

The man was too much.

"You're just going to ride here the whole day, aren't you?"

He nodded and started to whistle a tune.

"And what happens if I take rear?" she asked.

"I'll be there," he said.

And so she did the smart thing and let it go.

The adrenaline of the their mini scatter was fading,

Lil stole a glance at AJ.

He was strong and firm outside, and good and upright inside, and it showed all over.

His square jaw was clean-shaven and golden brown, a perfect warm canvas for the works of art that were his mouth and dimples. His body was honed and tough, not the mere product of a gym, as she'd initially pegged, but from doggedly perfecting the same skills that she used every day on the ranch—that *anyone* used on a ranch on any day.

So maybe it didn't matter that the circuit had set them up with tame cows and fully packed sacks. Maybe the challenge proved something after all.

AJ was a cowboy, even if he didn't believe it deep down. He was a tall, dark, and gorgeous cowboy who kissed like the devil that lived inside him.

And she needed to think about something else. *Anything* else.

The task at hand was generally the most responsible, so she dragged her mind away from AJ and back to the challenge.

They would have to sort and pen the cows at the end of challenge, so she might as well start getting a sense of their numbers and marks. Pushing AJ's strong hands out of her mind, she scanned the cows, matching each number with a distinctive feature of the cow it was attached to. When she had that down, she memorized which numbers were marked. Things wouldn't be near so calm when it came time to actually sort them, but she'd have an easier time finding them once she knew where they were to go.

She would share the trick with AJ.

He broke into her thoughts, putting an end to the worry. "What're you brooding about over there?"

She snorted, breath shallow. "We've got a lot of ground to cover, and not a lot of time."

The grin he flashed her could be described as nothing short of boyish. "Well, let's get to it, then!"

And they did. A respectable distance behind them, the film crew followed.

When the pens were in sight they picked up speed, moving in sync with one another.

After the intensity of the overnight portion of the challenge, sorting and penning flew by in a strange dazed blur, their motions a smooth duet.

Afterward, a few claps on the back and cheering amongst the greenies and filming crew simply added to her sense of the surreal.

She and AJ were the first team back, returning a full hour before any teams were expected, their top positions now iron-clad after a challenge whose job it was to eliminate all but the top three cowboys. She heard the news dimly, mind bouncing from one thing to another, and always, back to AJ.

25

The hot water of the shower when she'd finally made it back to the RV had been both a miracle and sin: A miracle to a full body's worth of muscles chastising her for doing more than she should have on less than a full tank. A sin because the hot water rushing over her skin set off memories of other things…

She shook the momentary fog off and reached over to flip the lever that held the RV bathroom door closed. The door popped open. She walked out and rummaged carelessly through her duffel for something to wear.

Clean, fully clothed, and comfortable for the first time in twenty-four hours, she took a bag of popcorn out of the box and tossed it in the microwave. It was too late for a real dinner, but after the whirlwind of the overnight challenge, she needed sustenance.

Moments later, the sounds and smells of popcorn filled the camper and she took a deep breath.

She hummed as she waited for the microwave, not particularly concerned with following an established tune, hum turning into a squeak at the knock on her door.

She called, "Just a minute."

A muffled voice came through the door. "Let me in."

Recognizing AJ, Lil hurried over. She opened the door and pulled him inside.

"Are you crazy? You can't just come over here at this time of night. Someone will see."

AJ laughed, shaking his head. "So, competitors can be friends too, Lil."

Lil put her hands on her hips and said, "You know what I mean."

AJ closed the space between them and cupped her chin, tilting her face up for a kiss. "I do. I missed you."

She smiled into his kiss despite herself. Nuzzling into him was as natural as breathing—and that was a problem.

She grumbled, "You've only been away from me for about six of the last forty-eight hours."

His palms came to her hips to slide up her rib cage. "Six hours too many. You don't have a bra on."

Her words came out breathy, but she managed: "You have a one-track mind, Garza."

He grinned. "You don't need more than one track when it's a good one."

Lil rolled her eyes. "Right…"

The microwave dinged, and Lil reluctantly pulled out of his arms to take the bag out and vent it, carefully keeping her fingers away from the outpouring of hot steam.

AJ sniffed the air. "Popcorn. Perfect. Glad we're on the same page."

Lil raised an eyebrow at him. "The same page?"

He looked like he'd had a shower. Like her, he'd opted for sweatpants after. His were light gray and he'd paired them with one of his endlessly touchable white T-shirts. In the crook of his arm, he held a pillow, which he pointed to with his free hand.

"Slumber party."

Lil snorted. "Cowboys don't have slumber parties."

AJ rolled his eyes this time. "Don't be sexist, Lil. Grab the popcorn. We've still got to pick out a movie."

Lil laughed, "You can't stay here."

He grinned at her, one dimple peeking out. "Why not?"

"You've got sweats on."

He raised an eyebrow. "Yeah? It's a slumber party. You expect a suit?"

"Cowboys don't have slumber parties with each other. In suits or sweatpants," Lil insisted.

AJ shook his head thoughtfully. "You know, you're right, and that's really a shame. They should. We're breaking real barriers tonight. You might want to put in another bag of popcorn. I love popcorn."

Instead of kicking him out, Lil pulled a second bag of popcorn out of the box. They couldn't sleep together again, no matter how simple and easy it would be to slide into his arms. There was too much on the line and their bubble of privacy was long gone, but that didn't mean they couldn't enjoy each other's company. She had to be careful with him, she knew it. It would be all too easy to tumble right into friendship with AJ Garza, but a human needed companionship every now and then. Even at the ranch she knew how to wind down. Cowboys were allowed to eat popcorn together, for a little while at least.

She told herself that as she joined him on the padded bench that served as a sofa in the camper, setting the popcorn down as she went. Opening her computer, she wished her mind would only stop cackling in disbelief.

He reached for a handful of popcorn and asked, "So what're we watching?"

Lil's eyes took on a wicked gleam. "*The North*. It's an Irish period drama about a Catholic girl and a Protestant boy who fall in love during The Troubles..."

He grinned cheerfully back at her and tossed a piece of popcorn in his mouth. "Sounds great. Of course, we'd be more comfortable if we watched on the bed."

She punched his shoulder. "You'd dare take popcorn into my bed?"

He shrugged. "Whatever it takes to get you there."

She tried her best to look stern. "You're shameless, you know."

"Is it working?" he asked hopefully.

She frowned, unanchored at the same time as she knew exactly what she was supposed to be doing. "I don't know."

"That means yes. Popcorn?" He offered her a piece.

She opened her mouth, not intending to.

He pressed the popcorn into her mouth softly, fingertips pressing against her bottom lip along the way. She closed her mouth and the popcorn dissolved on her tongue as she stared into his eyes, losing herself almost immediately, just like she did every time he caught her in his gaze.

She leaned toward him, suddenly understanding irresistibility. Whoever he was, wherever he was, if her father had been anything like AJ in this moment, Lil realized her mother, so young and dreamy, wouldn't have stood a chance.

The trick of comparing herself to her mother should have cooled the intense need she felt to eliminate the space between them and press her lips to AJ's, but it didn't.

Her levees were cracking.

She was letting them.

Something in his smile told her he knew it—and knowing

that he knew only made the sensation more compelling and molten. She liked that he liked that she wanted him, that she was powerless to do anything but to lean toward him. Whatever it was inside of her that drew her to him was older and deeper than she could control and he knew it. He knew it, and like the champion he was, he played it to his advantage.

That she could read all of that in him astounded her. To know anything about another human so certainly, without words—let alone to trust it—was nothing short of miraculous.

He hooked his arm around her waist and pulled her close. On a deep inhale, he said, "You smell good. How're you feeling?"

She smiled at his divergent thoughts. "Thank you, and good. Amazing what a hot shower can accomplish."

"Agreed. You did great out there."

A wicked light lit Lil's eye. "In the challenge, or before?"

He kissed the tip of her nose. "Don't be a pervert."

She hit him. "I'm the pervert?"

He nuzzled his face into her neck and pressed his lips against her skin. "You were phenomenal. Your body is as out of this world as your talent and I've never done anything in my life remotely worthy of deserving either."

Her breath caught, her body heated, and her skin tightened and she didn't know if it was because of the way his words drilled into her heart, or his lips moved against her skin, or the low timbre of his voice slipping deep inside and lighting little fires everywhere.

She opened her mouth to say something clever, but was saved from revealing the fact that she'd lost her wits by the ding of the microwave.

The second bag of popcorn was done.

Heart beating like a sprinter, Lil took the coward's way

out and eased away from AJ, saying, "Popcorn's done. Better grab it."

She didn't have to look at his face to know he was smiling. She heard it in the note of triumph in his voice when he drawled, "Wouldn't want it to get cold, now would we?"

She pulled the second popcorn out of the microwave.

He'd been right. They needed two. The first one was nearly gone and they hadn't even started the show.

She carried it back over to the table, snuggled in next to him, and decisively pressed Play. He watched her do it all with a little satisfied smirk, so she ignored him, pointedly staring at the screen as the sweeping classical music of the intro began.

Normally, she was hooked by the third bar, but this time she was finding it somewhat harder to focus. It was difficult to pay attention to the screen with AJ's eyes running silky caresses up and down her face and neck.

Finally, she turned and looked at him, where she found even more of a distraction.

He grinned at her, his teeth bright white and chipped in the front, dimples showing.

Her heart skipped a beat—all that shine was aimed at her.

"You're not watching the show," she observed.

He shook his head, completely unrepentant. "Nope."

"You're going to miss important information."

"Right now the most important information I can think of is what color is today's thong?"

Heat flushed her body. "That is not slumber party talk."

"Sure it is. Slumber parties are all about hanging out in undies and revealing secrets, desires, and dreams. How else do you become BFFs?"

Lil laughed, "Is that so? You're a slumber party expert now?"

He nodded sagely. "I am. Dreams, desires, and pillow fights."

"Pillow fights? Everybody knows no one really has pillow fights—unless they want to end up in real fights."

AJ brought a hand to his chest. "Blasphemy. Every young man knows that slumber parties always end in lingerie-clad pillow fights."

"Ridiculous. Now you're just describing the porn you watch."

"You're probably right. It's easy to confuse porn and real life when I'm around you."

She choked on popcorn. He patted her back laughing.

When she could finally speak, she said, "You're a dog. You know that right?"

"Only for you, Liliana mía."

"Is that supposed to be romantic?" she asked, throwing a piece of popcorn at him, slightly surprised she did—she wasn't the type to throw food. Why make more work for herself for no reason?

"Por supuesto. What woman doesn't want a big faithful dog at her side?"

She laughed, shaking her head even as she scooted closer to him. "Stop being ridiculous. Tell me something about yourself."

"I thought we were watching *The North*?" he said.

"I was, but you were watching me."

"I can do that all night."

"No, you can't. You won't distract me. Besides, you have to leave sometime tonight."

"Sometime."

"So?"

"Sew buttons."

She chuckled. "Ridiculous. Tell me something."

"You know all the important things."

"How many buckles have you won?"

He made a purring sound in the back of his throat that rumbled through his body and into hers. "Mmmm. I see you want to discuss my prowess. I could just show you…"

"Nothing but a hound dog."

"Nah, darlin'. That's Elvis and he's from Mississippi. I'm Texas all the way through."

Lil gave a dramatic sigh. "Something you won't let any of us forget, just like everything else from Texas."

He shrugged. "You know what they say about Texas…"

Lil rolled her eyes. "Shameless."

"But now you know it's true." He grinned, something silly and boyish in his smile, even while his eyes twinkled with what she knew were naughty ideas.

Her heart hitched again. More to herself than him, she said softly, "Now I know."

His gaze turned searching and he snagged her chin to draw her face closer to his own. After looking into her eyes for a moment he gave her a soft kiss on the lips and pulled back. "I'm glad the cows stampeded."

She laughed, unable to stop. She laughed so long that tears came out of her eyes and she had to catch her breath.

A cautionary wind chose that moment to blow cold through her heart. She had to be careful not to get too used to any of this. He was married to the rodeo and she had a ranch to get back to—theirs was a temporary romance, and also likely the only one she'd ever have.

Holding back the small sigh that wanted to escape, she smiled instead. "Me, too," she said, and because she couldn't help it—and because saying it in Spanish made it feel somehow less painfully true and earnest—she repeated herself, "Yo también."

He pulled her into a hug and she let the sigh out as an exhale in his arms. She'd never experienced sadness and joy at the same time like this before.

Thankfully, he saved her from having to sit with the feeling with his question, "Where'd you learn to speak Spanish?"

This time, her smile was easy. This was safe territory.

"Ranching. High school. Spain."

He laughed, "One of those things is not like the others..."

She snorted. "I learned my first words and phrases working the ranch after school and in the summers—a bunch of the other workers and their kids spoke Spanish. Because I already had some conversation skills, it made sense to take it as my language requirement for high school." She paused and grinned. "Spain is where I got really good, though."

He raised an eyebrow. "At what exactly?"

Her eyes flicked to the side and she shrugged one shoulder. "Spanish...mostly."

"Explains the classy accent."

"You think my accent's classy?" she teased.

He shook his head. "No. I think it's sexy."

Warmth blossomed in the center of her chest. Her language skills were just like everything else about her: practical. That they could be a turn-on was something new.

He watched her face, waiting for her response, and she was filled with a powerful urge to tilt her chin, lean up, and press her lips to his.

So she did.

She couldn't tell him any of the things he was stirring up inside—that was too personal. Not when she knew he'd only end up leaving. But she could kiss him.

He responded by maneuvering their bodies so that she rested on his chest on top of the sofa bench.

"The bed would be more comfortable," he said.

She smiled down at his face. "I'm comfortable right here."

Then she pressed another kiss to his lips, lingering there before pulling back to look at him. He was the perfect blend of pretty and real and she wanted him again.

She said, "I'm glad you came over."

He smiled and ran his fingers along the side of her face, pushing a curl behind her ear along the way. "Me, too. Can we move to the bed now?"

She laughed, nodding. "Add relentless to shameless."

He scooped her up as he sat, so she was cradled in his lap. "Sure thing. Ready?"

She frowned. "Ready?"

He picked her up, grinning like a kid, and carried her to the bed where he set her down and then sat down beside her. It was all of four steps, but Lil was willing to be impressed.

"Isn't this better?" he asked.

Lil snorted. His head was about an inch shy of the overbed cabinets and he looked far too large for the full bed, let alone the alcove it fit in. "Depends on what you're intending."

"Why might a bed be better than a couch, Lilian?" His voice caressed her name and a shiver ran down her spine hearing him say it in English for the first time.

She still managed, "Sleep. If you want to go to sleep, a bed is better." And if her voice was breathy, it still delivered the words.

His dimple peeked out. "Smartass."

"I went to college."

He chuckled and said, "Well, I want to get you naked. That makes it better than the couch."

Lil choked on spit, which set off a fit of coughing. When she could finally speak, she said, "I thought you were here for a slumber party."

"Yeah. This is the slumber part."

"Naked?"

"I always sleep naked. Don't you?"

He was ridiculous, but her lips curled up just the same.

"I don't. I sleep in underwear and a T-shirt."

He nodded, sagely. "Yes. Classic. So do you typically sleep in a thong, as well?"

"I don't think you're supposed to ask a lady things like that."

"You're right. I'm supposed to already know when it gets as intimate as panties. I've seen them, after all," he continued, "which means I'm close enough to be allowed to take them off—"

Lil crossed her arms in front of her chest. "I see right through you."

AJ's eyes lit like she'd issued a challenge. He sighed, "You're right. It's too much to ask how the meal I'm planning to devour is usually dressed…"

"Not working."

It was absolutely working. Her body was going haywire with every word, filling her mind with images not only of his mouth trailing kisses down her stomach and lower, but of her doing the same to him.

Her mouth watered. She swallowed. He watched her throat move.

Their eyes met.

He reached an arm around to cup the back of her skull and draw her into a kiss. She leaned in and opened for him immediately, even as images of taking him in her mouth flickered through her mind. The combination swirled inside of her, heating at the same time, until her system was one humming mass, a tropical storm brewing.

They were both breathing heavily when he finally broke the kiss, chests rising and falling in time. As if the movement drew his eye, AJ's attention dropped to her chest. Her breath caught when his hands replaced his eyes. A moan escaped her as he cupped her and began rubbing her nipples with his thumbs.

His name slipped out on a sigh. "AJ…"

He groaned. "Mmmm. Yes, Lil?"

She didn't know. She wanted him to hurry up and to never stop at the same time as she wanted him standing naked while she kneeled in front of him and worshipped him with her mouth.

He moaned in her ear like he could not only see everything she thought, but that he wanted it all just as bad as she did, and a wave of pleasure rolled through her, nearly breaking her apart in the process.

"Take your clothes off," she urged.

He didn't say anything, just obeyed. His shirt flew off first. She didn't notice where. She was busy pressing kisses across his newly bare chest as he pushed his pants down his hips.

Naked, he was otherworldly. Her heart stuttered and she wondered if she would ever be able to get used to him. Of course she wouldn't, though. Perfection never ceased to amaze, and she wouldn't have him long enough to even test the theory. But she wouldn't let thoughts like that dampen the moment. Not when she had him hot and hard and at her command.

"Lie down," she said.

He obeyed.

She took him in her hand and wrapped her fingers around him, squeezing firmly and evenly as she slowly began to move her fist up and down.

He moaned her name: "Lil."

Then she replaced her hands with her mouth. His body jerked and the noise he made didn't sound like any single word.

He shuddered, one hand coming to grip her loose braid. He wound it around in his palm, twice, gently increasing the pressure of the pull as she took more of him in with each bob of her head.

She continued until the pressure neared boiling for both of them, stopping only when he reached his hands down, grabbed her shoulders, and pulled her up to capture her mouth with his own. She shivered, her nipples tightening against his chest, setting off even more electric charges along her skin.

There was a slight growl to his voice as he said, "That was wonderful, darlin', but I don't want the party to be over before I get to any of the things I had in mind."

She shuddered, desperate for him to do each and every thing that he might be thinking, but unwilling to admit it.

His grin stretched fully across his face and the chipped tooth that looked so charming when he smiled for the cameras suddenly took on a more predatory look.

He trailed his palms down her sides to her hips, each finger slowly caressing the outer edge of her breasts along the way. When each hand arrived, he gripped and lifted her hips and adjusted his own so that he was positioned just outside of her entrance.

She shuddered, her entire being now focused on the juncture where their bodies nearly merged. She tried to wiggle closer only to have him stop the movement of her hips with his hands.

Digging her fingers into his shoulders, she moaned his name: "AJ."

"Lilian. Lilian. Lilian. It's too late. I must have you now." He repeated her name like a prayer before pressing a soft kiss against her temple. "You're perfect."

He shifted her body slightly and slid inside of her, threatening to send her hurtling over the edge.

Her inner muscles squeezed around him, pulsing around

him. She cried out his name, fearing there wasn't anything left of her to fall apart. He shook his head.

"Hold on, Lil. Ride's not done yet." His words ripped out between clenched teeth and rough exhales, but he didn't slow and she didn't, either.

Instead, her hips lifted to meet his, her rhythm driven not by his demand, but hers. The storm brewing inside promised to tear apart even the memory of who she was. No one would be able to put her together again.

"That's it," AJ gritted out.

The pressure built, strangely emanating from her chest, and the sound that came out of her was somewhere between a cry and a moan.

Heat flooded her, so much she knew she was on the verge of melting, and as it rose, AJ's rhythm skipped a beat.

He shuddered but held, his fingers digging into her hips as he pulsated, ready to explode. The knowledge that he was near climax, teetering as she was on the brink of something far larger than a simple orgasm, pushed her over the edge.

Lil bucked and the world went black. AJ's growl of triumph surrounded her and his hands came to grip her hips as he slammed into her with three monstrous thrusts before landing deep and shattering with a roar.

26

AJ came back to himself to Lil's cheek resting on his chest, her breathing long and slow and in time with his. He brought a hand to the side of her head and hugged her to him, pressing her close against his heart.

She sighed and snuggled against him, and he felt anchored for the first time since he'd announced his retirement.

"Why'd you go to Spain?" he asked.

Lil snorted. "That's what's on your mind right now?"

AJ smiled, eyes closed. "Yeah."

Her answering smile was in her voice when she said, "Why do you think it was anything more than a familiar language and Mediterranean climate?"

"You're not the beach type."

Spinning a finger in lazy circles on his chest, she said mildly, "You've figured me out so quickly?"

He grinned, recognizing a trap when he saw one. "No, ma'am."

Her voice went soft. "Guess why."

He was quiet for a moment, reviewing everything he'd learned about her. Raised by grandparents. Ranch girl. Stubborn. Rodeo lifer...

He guessed: "The running of the bulls?"

She pushed up to her forearms to stare down at him smiling. "Close, actually. And I did go to that, too. But, no, that's not why I went." Above him, faintly blue and backlit from the flickering laptop screen on the table and the camper's low wattage lights, she looked soft and open and everything he'd ever wanted.

Her braid, nearly all out now, fell to the right side of her head, with random curls escaping every which way, highlighting and framing the elegant bare lines of her skull and neck. The corner of his mouth lifted in a dazed little smile.

"Why'd you go?" he asked.

Lightning flashed in her gray eyes. "Bull dancing."

"Bull dancing?" He'd been through Spain on his tour, but had made only a few stops so there were likely local events he'd missed. This was one he'd never heard of.

"You versus the bull—on foot."

"Like a clown?" he asked.

Lil frowned. "It's more elegant than that..."

"I've seen some elegant moves from the clowns..."

She laughed, "You know what I mean. You try to move as smoothly as you can—'dancing'—to avoid getting gored in close range. It's lovely." Her eyes glowed.

He reached up to tuck a curl behind her ear. It bounced free almost as soon as he released his hand.

"And they do it in Spain?"

She nodded. "It wasn't officially part of the program but I got permission to participate."

He laughed, "You signed a waiver."

She grinned. "Pretty much."

"Sounds risky," he said.

She said nothing in response, merely raised an eyebrow.

"That's why it's fun," he conceded. "Where's it from? I didn't see it at any of my rodeos in Spain."

She shook her head. "It's not rodeo. It's a modern revival of ancient Minoan bull leaping."

This time AJ raised an eyebrow.

"Have you ever seen pottery with figures flipping over bulls? It's that. But modern."

"Ancient cow tipping with bulls?"

Lil laughed. "No. No. No. There are stories of athletes who leaped at the heads of bulls, used their horns and foreheads as springboards and flipped their bodies in the air over the animals."

AJ looked incredulous. "You went to Spain to do that?"

Again, Lil shook her head. "No. I just did the dancing. That's all you can do anymore." Her eyebrows came together, face turning thoughtful. "Although, I suppose you could always just try on private property. People are probably doing it everywhere…"

AJ's tone was dry enough to rival Diablo's. "Somehow I doubt that…"

Lil chuckled. "You're right. People are more interested in staying alive than ancient bull leaping, I guess."

AJ smiled at the longing that was still obvious in her voice. "Not all people. Did you enjoy it?"

She said, quietly, "It was wonderful."

AJ gave her a squeeze, happy for her for the experience. It was a hell of a lot more unique than traveling all the way around the world only to do the same damn thing over and over again.

She laid her head back down on his chest and nuzzled close and for a few moments, neither of them spoke.

She finally asked: "What are you most proud of about your career?"

He grinned. "That's easy—the kids I've mentored."

She smiled.

"That's sweet of you to say."

"It's true. CityBoyz changed my life, gave me passion and drive during a dark time. I was a loose cannon for a long time—like Hank. When I started, I was angry and couldn't control my temper."

"But after control, you were still angry?" she asked, picking up on what he hadn't voiced.

"I was. I brought it to the bull." He felt her grimace against his chest and laughed. "Landed on my ass a lot."

"Granddad said it's the surest way to get beat," she said.

"Your granddad was a smart man."

Lil smiled.

"It took me a little longer to learn that one," he said.

"Yeah?"

He nodded, a faint smile on his face at remembering. "But the hard way had its benefits. I learned how to muscle through everything first. By the time I figured out how to keep my cool, I'd bulked up. Strength and control are a deadly combo."

Lil laughed softly. "That sounds like an interview line."

"It's true, though. That's what drove me so crazy about you when we met. It was so obvious you had strength and skill—I hated to see that wasted by lack of control."

"I have control." Lil's body had gone as stiff as her words.

AJ smiled. "You started a brawl at the registration table."

"Not my lack of control in that case," she pointed out. "I am stone-cold."

He snorted. "Really? Can't say it's been my experience of Lil Sorrow…"

"On the bull," she ground out. "I learned to be stone-cold up there a long time ago."

He heard her glare rather than felt it, and grinned. "That's lucky. It took me a while to catch up. Of course, once I did, I realized it was one of those rodeo lessons that applies outside of the arena, too…"

She pinched him, and his smile widened. He said, "You lose when they get to you. When I stopped letting them get to me, it drove them crazy—didn't matter if it was the other competitors, broncs, bulls…women."

This time she punched him and he laughed out loud and kissed the top of her head, breathing her in deep at the same time. Squeezed her close again. "Bulls, rodeo, and more bulls. Not your typical pillow talk."

She chuckled, "I don't imagine so. Wouldn't know myself."

"For shame, Lil. I didn't peg you as the love 'em and leave 'em type."

He'd been joking, but he felt her go faintly rigid.

Her words were bright but brittle when she responded: "Oh, you know, more of the never love 'em in the first place type…"

Sensing a fragile point, he rubbed his palms up and down her back and spoke softly, keeping his tone easy and light. "You got something against emotional attachment?"

She exhaled and relaxed into him once more. "No," she said after her breathing evened out. "I just didn't want my body calling the shots."

AJ chuckled. "And here I thought I had control issues."

"When your story sounds like an after-school special, it makes you cautious."

"About falling for someone?" he asked.

She snorted. "Having sex."

He frowned. "What are we talking about?"

She answered, "Having sex?"

That she'd responded with a question, and one delivered with a slight thread of uncertainty woven through it, didn't immediately register in his mind.

Instead, he was stuck on a catch-up loop that kept coming back to the same thing: Lil had been a virgin.

Had been.

Until him.

The knowledge gave him a strange sense of vertigo even as it made him hard again. Her weight still rested comfortably on him; they still breathed in unison; he still ran his hand up and down her back—but suddenly he had become a permanent feature of her story. Vertigo spun him around as it sank in that unlike his typical encounters, they were both forever changed. He had never been a part of someone's life story in that way, and with the powerful shift it brought, he realized he liked it. He wanted to be a milestone in her life. For the first time, he wanted to be more.

Like rodeo, she would be a demanding and tempestuous mistress, one who would never go easy on him, as likely to break him as she was to save him. Like the sport he'd given everything to, her mere existence called his best forth and refused to accept anything less. But, unlike the other great passion of his life, Lil was an experience entirely his own. One he realized he wanted to keep. Maybe forever.

In fact, for the first time since he'd decided to retire, the future didn't look like a long stretch of watching from the sidelines, a slow decline the only thing left to him after reaching his pinnacle.

Instead, it looked like Lil. Lil in the morning, Lil at the dinner table, Lil at night. It looked like holding her hand through hard times, and watching her grow even more cantankerous with each passing year.

The squeezing sensation that was becoming familiar whenever Lil was around returned to his chest as his erection throbbed. He wanted her again, now more than ever, but knowing she was new to it all—making love as well as being the subject of complete focus—he worried she'd need a break. He wasn't small. She was.

His mental groan was half desire and half guilt. She would be the death of him. A part of him, the part concerned with mortality and survival, resisted, even as his body knew it was the death he'd been running toward his whole life. He pressed against her, and she made a little noise of approval that shot straight to his rigid heat.

And then he remembered her first time had been on a sleeping bag in the middle of a field.

He was a grown-ass man and the first time he'd given her had been worse than most high schoolers. He winced.

"AJ?"

He kissed the top of her head.

She tilted her face up, gaze questioning, and he caught her mouth with his own. She opened for him immediately and he almost growled. She was his, alright, and he would hold on—but first he needed to make up for her first experience being more akin to a pioneer diary rather than a fairy tale.

She settled against him, and he gave her shoulders a squeeze. Her breath soon took on the even rhythm of sleep, while he continued to stare at the overhead storage compartments.

Hours later, leaving her just before dawn broke, it was still on his mind.

She made a mumbled protest as he pulled away from her.

"Just a little longer," she murmured, still more than half asleep.

He smiled. "I'm not supposed to be here, remember?"

She grumbled and he almost caved. Instead, he gave her

another kiss and whispered, "I'm sorry. I'll make it up to you. Go back to sleep."

She smile-sighed and said sleepily, "Bye, AJ. I'm glad you came over."

He smiled and ran his finger along her cheek before forcing himself to leave.

The morning light was really more of a dusky hint of brightness in the sky as he opened the door, but he still looked around. Seeing no one, he stepped outside and quietly closed Lil's door behind him.

Together, they'd blown away the competition in the overnight challenge. Alone, she'd blown him away.

The arena show scheduled for later in the evening, hours and hours from this crack of dawn, would be the first bull ride of the tour—Lil's first bull ride for the PBRA—and then, at the end of the night, every cowboy except for the final three would be sent home.

27

Lil remained in bed for only a short while longer after AJ left before getting up herself. Between the high of spending two nights in a row with him and tonight being her first bull ride for the PBRA, she had energy to burn.

It was just too bad her granddad wasn't around to see it. Not the AJ part, of course, but her performance on the tour. In the face of all this joy, the space he'd cut out in her heart felt bigger, more hollow than usual, a more insistent reminder of everything that was absent in her life.

He'd been there the first time she'd climbed on a bull and picked her up afterward. He'd been there the first time she'd ridden a bull for prize money, too, and comforted her when she hadn't won. The ache that he wouldn't be there tonight was as persistent as it was illogical. She wouldn't be here if he were still around, and yet she wanted him with her more than ever.

But if she couldn't have him, she could at least wear his vest, and through it, he would ride with her as if he could be there in person. Her grandmother, who was saving the trip money for the finale, was unable to come to this ride, but was there in it too, through her beadwork.

Once again she wore a fish braid. Something about the style's fine lines always reminded her to keep her spine fluid. Her jeans were tight, thick, and stiff—just the way she liked them for a ride. Her chaps were sturdy and tough, but molded to her, like a catcher's mitt to her hand. She was as ready as she'd ever be, and she looked good, too.

In all black, the vest was what caught the eye.

Despite wearing it for multiple rides now, not a single bead was missing, no strands of ribbon torn, loose, or out of place. Her gran didn't mess around with anything she did, and her beadwork held strong. The woman didn't believe in doing anything halfway and refused to accept it from anyone around her—especially those she raised. It was a hard standard to live up to, but all the more rewarding for it. Maybe that was why Lil's mother had gone so wild.

A person could drive themselves crazy with maybes.

Maybe if Lil had been a bit more well behaved and agreeable as a child, her mother wouldn't have dreaded coming home so much. Maybe if they'd known who her father was, her granddad could have run him down and forced him to do the right thing and they could have been a family, with folks in their proper roles—not grandparents raising children, parents in the grave.

But then she wouldn't be here, with so many girlhood dreams coming true she wasn't sure if she was even awake. For now, she'd take the waking dream.

In full gear, she was all crisp lines and presentation, fresh pressed and tucked, her boots polished. All of it was too much, and obvious, but she couldn't help herself. She'd literally prayed for this night since she was a little girl.

She would die before admitting it, but she'd ironed and starched her jeans, luxuriating in every element of preparation.

For tonight's show, she wanted to look cowboy to the core. The Closed Circuit wanted their marketing photos and recorded interviews to convey the full pageantry and magic of the rodeo, but in truth, reality rodeo was about as far away from real cowboying as it could get, but that didn't mean she wouldn't do her part. They were all there to ride bulls and win money, after all, and there wasn't much more cowboy than that.

Twelve hours and thirty-five minutes later, long after the photos and publicity sessions, tears threatened to spill out Lil's eyes in front of fifty thousand people.

Her bull, Terror Nuevo, a new-to-the-arena baby bull, had spun exactly twice, bucked halfheartedly a half-dozen times, and then otherwise done its well best to sabotage her ride. Well over halfway through her eight seconds, her form perfect, she knew there was no saving it. When you weren't AJ Garza, the only thing to do about a sluggish and reluctant draw was to accept it.

After all her big words about women riding bulls for the PBRA and when she'd finally come to back up her words, the matter had been taken out of her hands.

She'd shown up battered and bruised, like a cowboy should be. Standing by sheer will after the first month of the tour, the shows, the challenges, the promos, all of it nonstop, she'd gotten on the back of this bull ready to end the debate once and for all.

The crowd cheered her, her bevy of girl fans ensuring the noise was right.

The lights were right—bright, hot, beaming down unforgiving truth on her ride—everything was right, except for the result.

Lil Sorrow, the PBRA's first female rough stock champion was proving a fact long known in rodeo and just about every other arena of life: a cowboy could have all the skill in the world, could do it all right, but if that spark—that urgent wildness—wasn't there, then nobody would be truly satisfied. Not the judges, not the people who paid money to feel their hearts race, and not Lil, with what was sure to be a lackluster score for her debut bull ride.

But the alignment of the stars wasn't something that could be manufactured or forced, and the union of rider and draw was as much a matter of the stars aligning as love or any other kind of magic.

Her granddad had told her that countless times during her years in youth and college rodeo. Back then, however, there had been far less at stake. Back then she hadn't been the barrier-busting, first-ever female rough stock rodeo champion. She didn't have the weight of a thousand little girls watching her every move, praying for her to prove what the old-timers were so reluctant to believe: girls had try.

Well, it hadn't happened tonight.

The buzzer had rung and she'd dismounted in a blur. Her score, in the seventies, rang out, and the audience made it sound like they didn't mind the dull performance, but there was no cheering from her.

In the end, it had been a good thing her granddad hadn't been there to watch. If he had been, he would have taken one look at her face and seen right to her railing heart, stiff and angry with the pain of having let them all down. And if he had been there and seen all of that in just a glance, understanding and compassion would have creased his face—with its square jaw, round nose, wide mouth, dark skin, and deep brown half-moon eyes—and she wouldn't have been able to hold back the hot angry tears that chased all of her disappointments.

It was a struggle as it was, even with the threat of the mortification of being witnessed looming large.

Keeping her head down she tried to make her way through the gauntlet and straight back to the green room without being waylaid, but Sierra stepped into her path, high-beam smile cemented in place and aimed blindingly in Lil's face. Blinking, both in the glare of Sierra's shine and to ward off the evidence of her inner turmoil, Lil took a moment to focus on the other woman's face, bracing for the usual undercurrent of aggression inevitably headed her way.

But Sierra surprised her. A quick flick of her big doe eyes was the only indicator that she'd scanned Lil and quickly summed up the situation. Without a change to her smile and as smooth as if it had always been her intent, she angled her body, brought an arm up to wrap around Lil's shoulders and gave an imperceptibly light squeeze with her manicured hand as she did, saying to the camera, "Let's hear it for Lil Sorrow, out here doing it for us girls!"

Knowing it was her cue, Lil forced the smile, only to realize with a start that the other woman had walked her the length of the gauntlet. With another comforting squeeze, Sierra set her free, ensuring that no one had the chance to pepper her with questions about her ride.

Lil didn't waste the other woman's gift, making her way quickly down the hall to the green room like there was fire behind her.

She was still there, pacing back and forth in front of the refrigerator, when AJ found her.

The door had hardly closed behind him before she burst

out with, "He might as well have been goddamn Ferdinand the Bull!"

AJ raised his hands, palms up, his expression a mixture of smile and fear, and asked, "Who's Ferdinand?"

She didn't blame him. She was being ridiculous. How many times had her granddad reminded her that the luck of the draw was always her invisible partner in the arena? It couldn't be everywhere all the time, and tonight it hadn't been with her.

"Ferdinand is a bull who likes to smell flowers," she said, to which AJ looked even more confused.

"Terror Nuevo didn't seem particularly interested in flowers," he said.

Lil exhaled and counted to ten. Another surge of anger that was really disappointment bubbled up in her gorge. She breathed that one out, too.

She understood the Closed Circuit's logic behind using young, untried bulls for the first round of bull riding. Every now and then an untried bull, overwhelmed by the situation, went crazy, giving a cowboy the ride of their life. For the show tonight, it had worked that way for about half the contestants—golden child AJ included. But the other half of the contestants, the group Lil ended the night in, got scared baby bulls that were more interested in freezing than bucking or turning.

Her granddad's voice repeated in her head, with growing sternness: *luck of the draw.*

And finally they penetrated her anger, dissolving it of its steam, leaving her with shame. She stopped pacing and sighed, going to sit beside AJ. He wrapped an arm around her shoulders and she leaned her head against his.

After a moment, he said quietly, "I'm sorry, Lil."

A hot tear escaped the corner of her eye, but she didn't wipe at it. Voice thickening, she said, "It's okay."

He kissed the top of her head. "It sucks."

An airless laugh escaped and she nodded, but the corners of her mouth lifted. "It does."

He gave her shoulders a squeeze. "You rode well."

She looked down at her boots and gave a small snort. "Not much to ride."

"Sometimes it's like that," he said. No explanation for it. It just was. Another important life lesson from rodeo.

Somehow it was softer coming from AJ, though. Maybe because, like her granddad, he understood.

Lil took a deep breath and pulled her shoulders back. "There's always next time."

Watching her, AJ's smile heated, eyes dancing. "You're incredible," he said.

Lil's entire body flushed. In just a few words he touched her everywhere, and she had no idea what to do about it.

Blushing, she looked at the door and did the sensible thing—changed the subject. "They're going to be looking for us."

AJ shrugged. "We're fine. There're a lot of riders left and it's their last hurrah. I'd think you'd let them have the spotlight before they go, Lil."

With the end of tonight's show, the Closed Circuit would be officially halfway over. The final three contestants would be announced, and tomorrow, those going on and those going home would all say goodbye to their RVs.

They would get to the remaining stops on the tour via airplane, flying to the locations of the to-be-announced final three challenges, and then on to the grand finale in Vegas.

Even without the announcement, they knew where they stood. Lil's success with AJ in the overnight challenge had nearly been enough to push her over the edge, but after tonight's dud, she would remain in second place, just two points behind AJ. Trailing behind them by fifteen points but a good fifty points ahead of the rest of the pack, Hank would likely maintain his stranglehold on third place, which meant everyone else was going home.

Both she and AJ knew that as cocky as she was in the arena, though, there wasn't an ounce of spotlight hog in her.

A chuckle worked its way past her hurt and disappointment as she shook her head at him. "You're a ridiculous man, you know."

And though she wished it weren't true, his responding grin snagged at the ragged edges of her mood, soothing, smoothing, and sewing them back up until they were as good as new.

28

They landed at the Blue Grass Airport in Lexington, Kentucky, just before 6:00 a.m. local time. The flight from Santa Fe, first-class and uneventful, had provided ample napping time, though, so while it was still dark and he'd ridden a bull the night before, AJ felt rested and energized for the first of the final challenges, which wasn't too bad for an old man.

Maintaining his first-place position, and knowing Lil's bunk would be just down the hall from his at the thoroughbred farm where the weeklong challenge would take place, didn't hurt his mood, either.

This far into the competition what had already felt like constant filming had kicked up a notch, with cameras constantly trained on the final three cowboys, hungry and hoping for drama, which meant there'd be no more sneaking into her bunk late at night, but he felt a strange sense of comfort just knowing she was close, a kind of steady reassurance he normally associated with family. It was new, wanting to spend time with a woman, to simply be near her, as opposed to pursuing and delighting, and after the dull horizon of the future with active rodeo, it was a novelty he could appreciate.

Their challenge, inspired by DeRoy's coming from Kentucky horse breeding stock, was to finish up fitting thoroughbred yearlings for sale. Each cowboy would be assigned their own, field-wild, blue-blooded yearling, which they were responsible for cleaning up and preparing for auction. Points would be based on a combination of readiness, appearance, and price earned. The Closed Circuit had promised to make up the difference to the operation that volunteered the space and yearlings—and to pocket anything that came in above their preestablished appraisal value.

Business was business, even when business was reality rodeo.

Hank would have the advantage going into the challenge, but if the Closed Circuit showed true to form, their stock would be pretty yearlings, just this side of plump, that really just needed a good brushing.

In reality, the yearlings turned out to be a bit more complicated.

On Sunday, Hank, AJ, and Lil had their pick of yearlings from a pasture full of bright young things.

In third place, Hank was allowed to choose first, and, true to type, he chose the obvious standout amongst the bunch. Clean lines, muscular and large without teetering near chubby, the blood bay colt looked like money on legs, just a few buckets oats away from being ready for the downs. There was no doubt the man knew his horseflesh, and he flashed a snide grin at AJ as he passed by him, leading the colt away.

Walking by Lil, he offered, "Go for the one that looks the best now because there ain't much getting better than that in a week's time."

AJ almost laughed. That Hank'd intended to snub him, leaving him out of the advice, was clear as day, but did nothing to offset the fact that AJ still had ears.

"I'll be sure to keep that in mind." Lil's brush-off was as classic as it was obvious, and, chuckling under his breath, AJ loved her all the more for it.

Hank didn't sputter in offense the way he would have if AJ had delivered the line, though. Instead, he just smiled wider, speaking slow and suggestively as he said, "Now don't get mad, sugar. I just know how you women go gaga over a runt. But don't worry, a quick little thing like you won't take too long to identify the real quality."

He sauntered off with his colt before Lil or AJ could respond, which was just as well because the cameras had been filming the whole thing like salivating jackals.

Tempers bubbled close to the surface this close to the end of the competition, and even the greenies had started getting tense and mean.

Once Hank was gone, Lil was up next. Unlike Hank, Lil took her time in choosing.

Climbing up to perch on top a thick white wooden fence post, she sat silently for a long time, just watching the field of yearlings.

AJ wondered what was going through her mind, wondering which of her inner voices led the conversation—the part of her that was practical and helpful, offering sage advice without beating around the bush; the part of her that loved the flash of the arena, cocky and full of high spirits; or the part of her that had something prove.

Whatever was going through her mind, she was in no rush about it.

Crews filmed anxiously, likely dreading the editing that would be required by all of this extended footage of her brooding, but AJ didn't mind the show. She looked right, sitting like she was, staring out at the gangly fillies and colts playing in the pasture. She wore blue jeans and a black-and-white-checkered button-up, formfitting and tucked into her jeans, over which her qualifier champion buckle shined. Her hair was braided, the elegant lines her neck and undercut obscured only where her hat rested.

Lil would always look right wherever you pictured a cowboy: on the range, in the arena, on a fence in a pasture. The only place he couldn't picture her was in a dusty gym in Houston. The realization brought an unfamiliar twisting sensation to his gut.

They were from different worlds, and soon they would both return to them.

Finally, Lil made her selection: a spirited blue roan filly, not quite grown into her prettiness but just bursting with potential. She led the young horse away, speaking low and quiet in her ear the whole time.

AJ chose in far less time than Lil, but not quite as quickly as Hank, picking out a chestnut colt that looked near seasoned already and played well with others in the field. He led him back to their paddock and bunk, adjoined like the two of them would be for the next week until it came time to say goodbye at the auction.

For this challenge, the Closed Circuit had made regular 4-H kids out of the final three, which, while making sense on one level—the audience for rodeo was often the same pond from which 4-H drew—was a novel experience in the sport.

Three days later, however, the novelty was wearing off.

Acting as a nonstop nursemaid to an untrained colt was proving to be more challenging than the previous real-cowboy-life simulation challenges had been, and by a long shot. While on the surface this task was easier, in truth it was an endurance form of torture.

To pass for readiness, each animal was required to be paddock ready, trained on lead, walking, trotting, and cantering, as well as shoed and shined. For appearance, the yearlings would be judged on their muscular conditioning and coat.

It sounded easy, a simple recipe of good diet, exercise, and training, even if he was a bit new with the animals—but it turned out to be far more than that.

He was monitoring his colt's diet, but anytime he took the animal out for a bit of free time, the foolish thing tried to taste anything that looked vaguely plant-ish and came back covered in burs and mud, with the occasional tuft of fur missing.

Then there was training, which he'd learned could only occur in fifteen- to twenty-minute intervals, in order to lessen the risk of lameness. Depending upon how intense the activity was—because God forbid the delicate creatures walk uphill for too long—the colt might need to be rested for the whole rest of the day. AJ had learned that the hard way, losing an entire day of training and having to reorganize the whole week's schedule to accommodate.

And now, on day five of seven, for reasons completely unknown to him, his shiny, shoed, toned, and honed little boy, ready for the ring in nearly every way, was off his feed.

He didn't know what to do.

The day before, he'd tried to tempt the little guy, whom he'd temporarily named Bullet, with all his favorite treats, heedless of the risk the extra calories might have to his sale if it encouraged him to eat.

It hadn't worked.

After that, he'd tried to trick him, distracting him with training and silly sounds in order that he might eat absent-mindedly.

It didn't work.

Today, he was knocking on Lil's door, the cameras rolling.

Lil answered, fresh faced, smiling, her eyes unguarded, posture easier and more open than he'd ever seen before.

While he'd been up all night with a picky eater, she was glowing, pretty hair pulled back into a curly ponytail, having clearly had a long, sweet night of beauty sleep.

Horse sitting agreed with her. He shouldn't be surprised. Hadn't she said her horse was her favorite person to hang out with?

"AJ."

He liked the way her tone warmed when she said his name, transforming the raspy kick into the sweet comfort of a hot toddy, particularly soothing in the face of her aggressive and obvious wellness.

"My horse won't eat." Normally, he wouldn't be so blunt, easing into the thing with a little conversation before running her down with his needs, but a night with no sleep, following multiple nights with poor sleep, coupled with a hungry yearling, and he didn't have time for niceties. His horse needed help and he knew she was honorable enough to give it, no matter how close they were in the competition.

Lil frowned, her familiar seriousness returning to her visage. "Where's he at now?"

That she'd remembered he'd chosen a colt said something about her attention to horses.

Noting the signs of horse madness on her, he smiled, tucking the detail away as he led her through his bunk, the bed obviously unslept in, and into the connecting stall.

Inside, Bullet stood against the far wall of the stall, half-hidden in shadows.

Immediately, Lil started making babbling soothing noises and the horse's ears began to twitch.

Not long after, the colt had made its way to Lil and was sniffing at the oat mix she held in her hand.

Soon, the horse was eating, albeit right next to Lil, chestnut flank pressed against her thigh, while AJ watched in amazement as she accomplished in minutes what he hadn't been able to do all night.

"How'd you do it?" he asked.

"I didn't do anything," she replied. "He's just lonely." She said it matter-of-factly, like she'd heard it directly from the horse's mouth, when there'd been not a real word exchanged.

"Oh," he said lamely. What she said made sense, though.

They'd been instructed to keep the colts separate, scheduling the round pens individually and using the pastures, treadmills, and lead machines on a rotating basis. AJ'd been good about following the rule but hadn't otherwise thought about the colt's company.

Reading his thoughts, Lil said, "It's a big adjustment to go from being wild and free, playing with your friends and nuzzling your mother, to settling down and getting to the work of life. A horse can get lonely."

If she weren't talking about his charge, and the situation hadn't had genuine consequences, he might have laughed at her complete earnestness. She was unselfconscious in her methods, whether they were the little twist she added to steer wrestling, or her consideration for a horse's emotional life, and he admired that about her.

"I guess I'll be spending more time with him, then."

Bullet headbutted her in the thigh, and she laughed at him before patting his neck, her smile entirely for him, the lucky little bastard.

She wore a thin old T-shirt with her jeans and boots, the faded words *I* and *rodeo* separated by a big red heart. The

T-shirt, combined with the ponytail, made her look about ten years younger, far too young for a man his age.

Yet, despite the fact that she was nearly eight years younger than he was, she was an adult woman, well old enough to decide if she wanted the same thing he did.

The bigger question, then, was was he sure about what he wanted?

From the ages of twelve to thirty, there had been no question: the only thing he wanted was rodeo. For the last six years, though, and particularly since he'd retired, things had become more complicated. What did he want to do with the rest of his time? He'd exhausted himself running from the answer for so long, but looking at Lil, her attention back on the horse, snuggling and breathing deep, to its coltish delight, he was reminded once again that now those questions had an answer, at least a part of it, and she was right in front of him.

Now he just needed to figure out if she would bolt if he told her, or stick around.

Sensing his stare, she looked up, her cheeks heating, going dark with their blush. Straightening, she separated herself from the horse and brushed her palms off on her thighs.

"I'd better get back. Little Beauty will be missing me by now."

"Little Beauty?" he asked, eyebrow lifting. They'd all been instructed not to name their horses. Clearly, he wasn't the only renegade.

Lil shrugged. "I had to call her something. It's more of an adjective than a name, anyway."

He laughed, the sound of Bullet munching in the background bringing him a greater level of relief than he would have expected.

"Thank you. I was worried about the little guy."

Looking away, she mumbled, "Didn't do much, ultimately."

He shook his head. "You cured him and more." And if there hadn't been cameras trained on them, he would have drawn her into a kiss to show her how much he really appreciated it.

Hell, even with the cameras, he was tempted, but he knew she wouldn't appreciate the audience.

And it was a shame, really, because as he watched her leave, he reflected that she was a bottled ray of sunshine, and he was thirst starved for light.

He didn't see her again until the auction, and then only in passing, as the contestants were responsible for showing their charges for sale.

The event passed in a blur, far more emotional than AJ had anticipated. For every other event of the Closed Circuit, he'd been able to maintain his normal level of rodeo professionalism, but this time he'd gone and gotten attached. The breeder who bought Bullet promised that AJ would be welcome to come visit the little colt whenever he wanted.

And in a surprise upset, Lil had come in first place.

While much of the evening hadn't gone quite as predicted, with AJ's colt going into a bidding war that seemed to have more to do with its trainer's name than the colt itself, the fact that Lil beat out Hank, a legacy horseman, and by a long shot, was the most unexpected.

In the end, it was Hank's expertise that bit him in the butt, though.

Thinking he'd score a little higher on appearance and raise his price, Hank had tried to sweat his colt before the sale, a cheap little trick to enhance muscle definition before a sale. It backfired for Hank when his horse came down with a cold, sinking his score.

Lil, on the other hand, as she told Sierra from the top spot on the stage, just "looked for the yearling that looked most ready for the next stage of life. Bold and brave enough to venture far from mama with the curiosity to explore." Playing with words and a wink, she added, "That's a yearling that's fit for sale."

The audience loved it, the pretty cowgirl who could ride like the best of the boys as well as she could nurture a filly out of the nest. None of them, though, he realized with a certainty he hadn't felt about anything outside of rodeo, loved her more than he did.

Now he just needed to figure out what to do about it.

29

Getting to Muskogee was a bit more complicated than traveling to Lexington.

Fortunately, as the field was narrowed down to three, it'd taken only one rented bus to transport Lil, AJ, Hank, and Sierra, plus the full camera crew and greenies, from the Tulsa airport to Golden Acres, the massive ranch spread where the challenge inspired by Lil would take place.

Just thinking about it made her groan.

For Lil's challenge, the true cowgirl of the bunch, the competitors were going to take on one of the most important aspects of ranch management: stock breeding.

"Explain it to me again." Sierra's face did not look like she wanted Lil to explain it to her again, no matter what her words said.

Lil sighed.

Behind them, AJ laughed.

Behind him, Hank continued to snore.

He'd fallen asleep ten minutes into the hour-and-a-half drive to Golden Acres, his snores providing an orchestral soundtrack to their drive.

Fifteen minutes in, Sierra had begun asking questions.

"One of us will hold the steer, one of us will handle the bull, and one of us will collect the sample."

"But why?" She was aghast. Aghast, on Sierra, looked like a royal blue Western shirt, blue jeans, her embroidered white chaps and hat, and a cherry-red mouth opened in a wide O.

Lil didn't buy it for a second.

They were down to the last two weeks of the circuit and Sierra spent more time with the producers than anyone else in the van. Lil was willing to bet that there wasn't a thing about the whole production that Sierra didn't know the why of.

But calling her out wasn't the way to win the game, so Lil put on her best exasperated cowboy impression, calling to mind every time her gran had brought another barn cat indoors, and said, "Where else do you think little bulls and broncs come from? The stork?"

AJ laughed out loud, and Sierra's eyes flashed, but her silly smile held.

When the moment was right, she let out a tinkle of laughter and flipped her hair over her shoulders. There were cameras on the bus.

"I guess I never really thought about where they come from! Unlike you, I steer clear of bulls. Imagine what they would do to my nails." She punctuated the sentence by bringing her hand to her mouth, the nails in question painted red, white, and blue and glossy.

"You've been missing out, Sierra, I hear there's big money—plenty for nail repair—in bull sperm," AJ added from the back seat, the cadence of his voice doing things to Lil's stomach that didn't seem reasonable given that it'd been over a week since they'd truly had a moment alone and likely wouldn't again for the remainder of the competition. She'd have thought her system would have settled down and accepted the inevitable by now.

The Closed Circuit tour was nearly complete, now. Soon they would go back to their regular lives, Lil back to the ranch—which was closer now distance-wise than it had been in over a month—and AJ back to where it had all begun, Houston.

The thought brought a heaviness to her chest that she couldn't afford, not at this stage in the game and not with the scores so close. She and AJ had remained neck and neck throughout the competition, trading the number one spot back and forth like kids on a playground, but they couldn't keep doing that much longer. Sooner rather than later, one of them would emerge the champion. One of them would walk away with enough money to save the thing they loved most in the world, and the other wouldn't.

She tried to comfort herself that, at $500,000, far larger than any INFR prize she'd ever gone for, the second-place prize wasn't anything to sniff at—that it was plenty to make a huge dent toward either one of their goals.

It just wasn't enough.

Not enough to keep a youth-based, high-risk, nonprofit in an expensive city up and running, and not enough to ensure she and Gran didn't lose the ranch to a series of snowballing debts.

And that didn't even begin to touch the rest of it, all of the parts she would never be able to forget and didn't know how in the world she would ever walk away from. Nothing could bring Houston closer to Muskogee.

But none of that mattered at the moment, because if she didn't get every ounce of it off her heart and out of mind, her gran was going to know the second she laid eyes on her when they reunited at Golden Acres. They hadn't seen each other in over a month and it was the longest they'd spent apart outside of her trip abroad. But it wasn't long enough to evade her grandmother's sharp perceptions.

Golden Acres was a stud operation, making their money, and very good money at that, in livestock insemination, and particularly that of Black Angus beef. And because stock was a rancher's gold, and Lil was their resident rancher, the Closed Circuit had devised a challenge around stock and its insemination, one of the most important tasks on the ranch.

And one of the most uncomfortable, because no matter how you sliced it, whether you used a portable stall and an electro-ejaculator, or a team and an artificial vagina, when it came right down to it, it was a bunch of humans getting involved in the private business of bulls.

But for the next three days, and for three times a day, Lil, AJ, and Hank would be the ones to do it. Working as a team, each contestant would fill each role three times: managing the teaser, managing the bull, and catching the sperm. They'd be judged on how successful they encouraged mounting with the teaser, animal distress, and how much seminal fluid they collected. Their scores for each day would be added together and averaged, the same amount of points awarded to each cowboy as the base score. The following three days, they would work alone, with an electro-ejaculator and a stall. Once again, they would be judged on the amount of fluid collected, the additional points added to their score and totaled.

The final rankings, determining bulls and ride order for the grand finale, would be decided only after AJ's back-home challenge was completed and all possible points totaled, but because this was her challenge, it represented her last best chance to amass real points. AJ would have the advantage on his home turf.

"Never thought I'd say it's cleaner making money at the rodeo!"

Even Lil cracked a smile at Sierra's joke, corny as it was. Rodeo had never been accused of cleanliness.

"Don't be so quick to write it off, Sierra. There's drama and intrigue, as well," AJ said.

She lifted a brow, expression game, overbright and genuinely interested, likely because it was AJ who was speaking. "Oh really," she purred, eyes alight.

Lil had observed that Sierra's… Sierraness…took on a layer of genuine feeling it lacked with everyone else when it came to AJ.

But there was no more time to dwell on Sierra's crush, or the mild sour taste it left in her mouth, because they had arrived at Golden Acres.

The insemination orgy was about to begin.

But before that, a reunion that was long overdue.

Outside of the entrance at the ranch's main office, Gran stood in her Sunday best, her arms stretched wide.

Seeing her as she stepped off the bus, Lil let out a whoop and dashed across the asphalt to catch the older woman, smaller even than Lil, up in her arms and swing her around in a circle.

The cameras ate it up.

"Now, put me down, Lilian. You know I'm too old for all of that."

Lil obliged, too excited to see her gran to mind the fact she'd used her full name in front of her colleagues.

"And just who might this ravishing woman be?" AJ asked, joining them, Texas heavy in his voice, his charm on full blast.

Lil's stomach did a one-eighty. She'd been so worried about keeping her feelings for AJ off her face when her grandma was around she'd completely forgotten about their inevitable meeting.

Gran turned to him slowly, deliberate no doubt, gave him an excruciatingly obvious once-over, and then said, "So this is the handsy cowboy that thinks he can kiss my granddaughter on national television."

Lil's stomach, and her lungs, and all the rest of her guts fell right out of her.

Hank guffawed and Sierra's laughter tinkled overhead like wind chimes.

Even a few of the greenies chuckled.

Gran simply stared, face absolutely straight, waiting for her answer.

AJ didn't bat an eye. "Why yes, it is, ma'am."

Gran cracked a smile, the mischievous, naughty, up-to-something expression Lil knew so well it hurt. Lil let out the breath she'd been holding and did the proper thing.

"Gran, AJ Garza. AJ, Seneca Grace Island, known to most as Gran." Lil couldn't keep the pride out of her voice, introducing the woman who raised her, nor would she ever want to. If Granddad had been her guiding star, Gran was her lodestone and her heart, strong and ageless outside, pure putty within.

AJ took off his hat, inclining his head in a respectful nod.

Gran gave him another once-over, this time even more thorough, and when she was through, Lil saw a spark approval in Gran's eyes—as if he was just what she'd ordered.

Seeing it, a shiver shimmered down Lil's arms, lifting the tiny hairs to stand.

Gran turned to Lil, abruptly changing the subject. "I talked to the producers and I'll tell you, I'm not happy. They said you couldn't sleep at home since you were contracted to be on film—and I sure as hell won't let men with cameras in rooms where my granddaughter sleeps, that's just not right—

so you have to stay here even though the ranch is just twenty minutes away…" She looked in the direction Lil knew their home lay, before waving the thought away to continue with, "You're all having dinner at the ranch tonight."

Lil's mouth dropped open, her gaze shooting to AJ. He hadn't signed up for meeting the family. But AJ just looked as smug as a cat in the cream, pleased as punch to tag along on this ride.

Sierra and Hank joined them, and Gran turned to them. "Well, Lil. Are you going to introduce the rest of your friends?" Again, the word struck.

Piper and Tommy were her friends. The circuit members were not. But she showed her manners.

"Sierra Quintanilla, multicrown rodeo queen and the Closed Circuit hostess." Lil pointed her palm toward Sierra who gave a darling curtsy, before she gestured to Hank, voice losing some of its warmth. "And this is Hank DeRoy, the cowboy rounding out the top three."

Gran snorted. "I know all of that. I have been watching, you know."

Lil's cheeks heated, but she didn't say anything. Gran was feeling fiery and Lil knew better than to try and test her. Gran would win every time.

Gran smiled and said, "As my granddaughter was saying, I am Seneca Grace Island. You may all call me Gran."

Charmed, and probably intimidated, the group paid their respects before greenies called them over to be debriefed.

"I'll see you for dinner, Gran," Lil called, heading to join the rest of the group.

Unexpected as it was, and uncertain she wanted her home on display, Lil realized she was nonetheless truly happy to see Gran. And maybe even more so to eat her home cooking.

30

Lil's palms were sweating when the van turned into the long dirt driveway.

The farmhouse, two stories painted yellow with white trim, as sweet as a freshly frosted cake, looked pretty and well kept, but she fretted over its vulnerability in front of the camera. It was her home and it hadn't signed up for the scrutiny of the wide world. Especially a world that knew its story, and her family's story.

That she was riding to preserve it only increased the pressure. Now it would have to prove its worth.

Would the hundreds of thousands who tuned in to each episode and extra see the value in her gran's impeccable housekeeping and that one-of-a-kind tile floor? Would her fans continue to root for her after seeing this compared to the charm of Hank's yearlings and the heartstring pull of AJ's CityBoyz?

Regardless, it was too late to do anything about it now. They would either see it, see how one family holding on to their legacy when the whole world seemed determined to stamp it out might be important on a grander scale, or they wouldn't.

Either way, she was glad she'd carved out the time to repaint when the weather had turned nice enough the past spring. It was amazing what a fresh coat of paint could do to a house.

The whole crew accompanied her, literally: AJ and Hank, Sierra, the greenies, and the film crew. All in all there would be fifteen at Gran's table tonight, counting Piper and Tommy. Lil hoped she'd enlisted the two of them to bring in the rectangular holiday table. It was the only one that was large enough for a group of that size.

Arriving with the largest party she could ever remember gathering in her house, she felt like she was bringing a boy home for the first time.

As soon as she crossed the threshold, however, her time to fret came to an abrupt end. Unlike her companions, she wasn't a guest in town for a night. This was her home, absent though she'd been, which meant she had work to do.

Gran set her first to the task of washing the cooking dishes—Gran believed the more dishes done before dinner, the better.

When AJ tried to follow her, Gran intercepted him, engaging him in conversation so that it would be rude to continue on his path toward Lil, and once again Lil suspected the move was deliberate. No one was wily like her gran.

Instead of AJ, however, Piper, whom she hadn't seen enter the kitchen, joined her at the sink, sliding an arm around her waist and squeezing.

If the house hadn't been full of strangers, Lil would have squealed in delight. As it was, she leaned into the other woman's embrace and let out a long, slow breath.

"Tell me everything," Piper whispered, reaching into the sink to wash with her.

Lil laughed. "Absolutely not. There're people everywhere. You have to wait until it's all done."

"Escape with me into the barn."

This time Lil snorted, leaning close to keep their conversation between the two of them. "I'm expected back after dinner, and they're filming everything."

Piper blew out a frustrated breath, tinged with a whine. "Fine. Whatever. But when you get back, you're telling me everything. And I mean EVERYTHING, because it's written all over you."

Lil blanched. "It's not."

Piper cackled her witchy cackle and the conversation in the room stopped for a moment while everyone looked at them.

Lil's temperature climbed a million degrees, while she was certain Piper grew horns.

Only after everyone had returned to their own conversations did Lil whisper, "Of course it's not, when there's nothing to be written."

Piper laughed again, but quieter this time. "Oh, it's written all over you. And if it wasn't before, now you've confirmed it..."

Lil groaned. "What am I going to tell Gran?"

Piper side-eyed her. "Why would you tell her anything?"

"She'll know. If you knew, she'll know."

"Lil. You are a grown woman."

"I know, but my mom..."

Piper stopped washing dishes to look Lil in the eye, green meeting gray. "Lil, Gran knows you're not your mom. You're the only one unsure about it."

Lil opened her mouth to deny it, but Gran chose the moment to announce dinner, and everyone sat down, Lil, in her usual spot beside Gran, but instead of Piper at her side, Gran had placed AJ there, and, for better or worse, Lil knew that Gran knew.

They were wrapping up dessert a leisurely two and half hours later, stomachs full of divine food—her gran having pulled out all of the stops to impress the Closed Circuit—faces hurting from smiling too much, and bellies sore from laughing. Lil couldn't remember a more successful gathering at the house, and the thought was tinged with a hint of sadness because it was true and because her granddad wasn't a part of it.

"I don't see why they have to have y'all collecting materials on national television. Seems indecent to air the bulls' business like that."

Lil agreed, but wouldn't be caught on camera saying as much.

Piper answered Gran instead, pitching her voice to mimic an arena announcer. "You know why, Gran. They say it enough during every show! *'These aren't your average arena cowboys, the Closed Circuit cowboys are the real deal.'*"

Sierra laughed, the sound as musical as ever, and Piper sent her a small glare, making Lil laugh, grateful she wasn't the only one.

"You've got a skill there," Sierra bubbled. "Ever think of making money off that voice?"

Piper stilled, but Lil was the only one who noticed. Recovering quickly, faster than she used to, Piper shook her head with a forced smile. "No. I'm not one for making money with my body."

She didn't add *these days*, like she might have in the past and Lil was proud of her. Piper used to throw her history in people's faces, using her own wound as a weapon. That it hadn't worked on Lil was one of the reasons they were friends. Over the years, and over the healing, though, Piper had learned to respect her past, bringing it to the surface on her terms, a message of hope and strength, rather than a weapon.

"Well, you're missing out, honey." Sierra winked at her. "With those cat eyes and a voice like gold, you could go far."

Lil reflected that despite Sierra's cattiness, it was impossible to stay mad at her, especially when she brought you in on the joke that was always playing in her laughing brown eyes, which happened to be as big as Bambi's and twice as pretty. That there wasn't actually any of that subtle cattiness in the statement only served to pop the lingering bubble of tension around Piper.

Shoulders relaxing, Piper offered Sierra one of her real smiles, the one that promised fun, saying, "I'll leave being professionally beautiful to you," which immediately and comically endeared her to Sierra, a fact obvious to everyone.

Lil looked around the room as familiar as the back of her hand and it felt brand-new, filled with people as it was. Despite the cameras and the looming conclusion of the tour, the unavoidable moment when someone had to win and someone had to lose, Gran had worked her magic. Everyone was relaxed and easy, laughing and smiling, cracking jokes and antics entertaining enough for television, but without the tawdry drama that usually sold so well. But it was still good TV, even if it was just joyful. Enough so that, for the moment, Lil didn't even mind the cameras.

For the first time she could remember in the two years since her granddad had passed, her home was filled with people and laughter. She hadn't realized she'd missed that so badly.

One of the greenies announced it was time to go, and Gran insisted on serving everyone coffee, which meant no one actually left for another hour. Making their way out the door, Gran sent everyone, greenies included, home with Ziploc bag care packages filled with homemade baked goods, and Lil had the surreal experience of suddenly becoming the most popular kid in the group.

She might be an adult, but she wasn't too old to deny the fact that it felt good.

Bringing up the rear, she was the last to lean in to the warm embrace of Gran's hug.

Mouth close to Lil's ear, Gran whispered, "I'm proud of you," before pulling back to look at her.

Lil smiled, her gran's words going down warm and spreading, like the first sip of whiskey after a long day in the cold. She knew her gran was proud of her every day, but there was something special about hearing it after she'd really earned it. It was the kind of warmth found only at home, and being home, being in the kitchen that'd seen her highest highs and lowest lows in the embrace of the woman who'd been there for each and every one of them, only jackhammered how important it was for her to keep up her streak, to let nothing distract her from her purpose. "I can't make any promises," she said, her voice full of promise, "but it's like you said, Gran. I actually have a shot at winning. I have what it takes to beat AJ."

Gran brushed a curl that had shaken loose over the night from her face with a soft smile. "I certainly did not mean I was proud of you for winning a bunch of money, you silly girl—though I told you so, and lord knows we need it. I'm proud of you for taking a big scary chance and putting your heart out there."

"You mean going for all or nothing, like granddad and I always talked about?"

Gran shook her head and held up a palm, signaling for her granddaughter to stop guessing. "It's been lonely here, Lil."

Lil opened her mouth to say how much she missed her,

too, but another firm shake of the head from her grandmother stopped her.

"It's been so lonely since your granddad passed, Lil. I can't tell you how much it hurts. How dearly I wish I could see him again. I'll tell you, Lil. There isn't a lot I wouldn't offer up for the chance to spend just one instant with him—I know, because I've offered near all of it. And do you know what I have wished all this time, through all this pain?"

Lil shook her head.

"That you would find someone you loved even half as much. That you might someday love someone so hard that it'd hurt just as bad as all of this if you lost them."

Certain she was sinking into the floor though her body remained perfectly still, all Lil could do was stare as her grandmother spoke to her in a way that she never had before. Like a woman.

"But you've never let yourself," she continued. "You fooled yourself into thinking you could substitute that kind of love with loving us and loving this ranch and nothing I could do, or you were willing to do, could change your mind. But I think you might be reconsidering now, and for that, I'm proud of you."

Outside, the van honked. It was well past one in the morning and their cattle breeding work-study was due to start at 9:00 a.m.

Glancing at the van and then back to her grandmother without any words, all she could do was hug her one more time and then dash off the porch and back to the van to rejoin the tour.

She was quiet on the way home, sitting as far away from AJ as she could get, trying to figure out what her grandmother meant and what she was going to do about it.

Seven days and way too much bull semen later, Lil wasn't any wiser on either subject.

She was, however, in first place.

There hadn't been time again, or permission, to return back home once the challenge started, only enough for a quick goodbye at the end before the van was honking out front once more, this time eager to get them back to Tulsa and on their way back to Houston for the final challenge of the Closed Circuit.

She wouldn't see her family again until the finale in Las Vegas. Whoever walked out on top in Houston would get first draw in Vegas. First draw, best luck. Her granddad had never said that, and would have more than likely disagreed, as he didn't keep with talk of luck, but she'd kept it on repeat in her mind since she'd begun competing in elementary school.

She'd been second in OKC and it had been a flop. Whether luck was real or not, she wanted to make sure she was first in Las Vegas. That meant she had to win in Houston. The only problem was that this was the challenge based on AJ, the city-based challenge that would be most likely to throw her for a complete loop.

A suspicion supported only by the note she held in her hand, slipped into her boot while she'd been passed out on the plane.

Recognizing the scrawl for AJ's handwriting, Lil read it for the three thousandth time.

You're on my turf next time. Meet me outside Tito's tomorrow at 7. Wear something nice.

She had no idea what Tito's was, and she had no idea how she was going to get away to find a dress in a city she didn't know, but the mere act of looking at the note lit her up like a torch and she knew she was going to be there at 6:45.

31

AJ resisted the urge to check his outfit in the large mirror that decorated the restaurant's lobby. That kind of move was supposed to have been long behind him. These days, he generally left the looking at himself to his date, but he wanted to look good for Lil.

He wanted a lot of unusual things when it came to Lil.

Now that he knew what she was fighting for, he wanted to fight for it alongside her. No matter what the outcome of the competition, he wouldn't let her lose her home. Swallowtail Ranch was a place like none he'd known. He was used to big skies and flat vistas, but he was brand-new to old farmhouses and porch views and tidy well-kept barns that said humbly, *Love lives here and you're welcome to stay.*

Though they'd been out of sight and bedded down for the night while he'd been there, he'd known that somewhere on the property were stock, and horses, and all the other picturesque creatures that belonged on a farm. He'd sensed them, in the faint scent of warm large mammals on the breeze and the tangible hush in the air of being surrounded by sleeping animals.

But while the scents were familiar, reminiscent of the rodeos at which he'd first encountered them, they were also different—less frantic and chaotic, less edgy and looking for a good time, less desperate and willing to lay it on the line.

Swallowtail was peace, carved out of the chaos of nature but made of the same blood and dirt that he'd been chasing his whole life. It was easy to see why she loved it. Just like it was easy to see so many things with Lil, things like sending CityBoyz participants to a real ranch, things like working together to save both of the things they loved, for the long haul.

And because he could see those things, he was waiting at Tito's, a top-rated restaurant in Houston, at 6:40, trying not to check out his outfit in the mirror like a jerk.

He looked at his watch instead. A minute had passed.

Waiting on a woman was a novel experience.

It was a relief when she arrived five minutes early, particularly as it took another five minutes thereafter to reorient the world upon seeing her walk through the door.

Her dress was white and off the shoulder, decorated with colorful Mexican embroidery. Her hair was unbraided and curly, falling to one side, leaving the bare side of her head exposed, the other hidden in an explosion of riotous glossy black curls. The smooth bare brown skin of her shoulders looked as silky and soft as he knew it to be, and in the restaurant lighting, her eyes swirled and flashed like a summer storm.

He fought the urge to stand and stride over to her and trace the fine-boned architecture of her shoulders and collarbone with his fingertips—not because he didn't know she'd welcome him, but because he wasn't sure he'd be able to stop himself from sliding his hand up her thigh, and her dress along with it, at the same time.

The dress ended midthigh, leaving plenty of gorgeous muscled leg on display and causing AJ to send a thanks up to the lord for bulls and this reckless woman who rode them.

Everything about her glowed, including the sweet, shy smile she wore.

She was stunning, her legs looking even longer than usual in the platform sandals she wore, and he wondered what it'd be like to kiss her with the extra height. He closed the remaining distance between them to find out.

As he'd suspected, the additional inches made it that much easier to capture her full lips with his own and make her forget they stood in a restaurant lobby. To remind her how well they fit.

When their kiss ended, her cheeks were dark from blushing and her eyes dazed. Taking the sight in, his heart flipped over in his chest.

"Hi," she said when she finally found words. Her voice was a breathy rasp that went straight to his groin. He loved how responsive she was—that he could distract her from the entire world while he made her dizzy with his kisses.

"Hi." He smiled. "Glad you could make it."

"I had a cab take me into town earlier. Finding a dress in time was harder…"

His grin flashed, wicked and satisfied. "Worth it. You look phenomenal."

Her dusky blush darkened even more. "Thank you," she said, before looking away, around the restaurant, taking in her surroundings for the first time. "Where are we?"

"Spanish steak house. Felt somehow appropriate…"

She laughed. "How do you know I'm not a vegetarian?"

He raised an eyebrow. "You're a rancher. And I've seen you inseminate a cow."

Her laughter was like a wind chime. She nodded. "You're right. And I happen to love steak." Her grin showed her canines and he considered skipping the date and dragging her back to the hotel.

But that wasn't the point of tonight. Tonight he was taking her out. And there were cameras all over the hotel. Escaping them had required creativity.

"Somehow, I got that impression," he said, his voice only faintly hinting at the heat rising in his body.

Her pulse picked up in her neck and he knew she caught it anyway. She reached out her hand to him palm up, an electric nervousness to the movement, and said, "So are we on a date, then?"

He took her arm into the crook of his and walked her toward the secluded corner where their table was. "We are."

She looked up at him through her eyelashes as she took a seat in the chair he'd pulled up for her, a slight lift to one corner of her mouth.

She said, "You didn't ask," as he pushed her chair in and he laughed.

"I didn't," he agreed, moving to take his own seat. "You didn't have to come."

He didn't expect her to counter with just as much suggestion in her voice when she said, "That's debatable..."

He chuckled, flames leaping in his eyes, "Glad you remember."

She snorted. "You're impossible."

He grinned. "You started it."

Laughing, she picked up a menu. The laughter stopped abruptly when she opened it up, closed it, and set it down. "I can't eat here. It's robbery."

This time AJ laughed. "Yes, you can. It's a date, Lil."

"I can't. A meal here could run the ranch for a day."

"You sound like The Old Man, so I'm going to tell you what I tell him."

Lil raised an eyebrow, head faintly cocked. "And what's that?"

AJ grinned. "Order whatever you want."

She couldn't stop the smile from spreading across her face—he watched her try and lose the battle, and he loved it.

A waiter came to take their drink order and he watched her discuss the wines with a strange tightness in his chest.

Her brightness and spirit shone through, whether she discussed Tempranillo or rodeo. Parts of her were as raw and wild as the animals they rode. Other parts as refined and focused as the sharpest professional. She was fire, but she'd been right when she'd said she knew how to be ice when she needed to be. A whole set of contradictions and the perfect balance was Lil. He could spend the rest of his life diving into her and never get bored.

When the waiter left, she placed her elbows on the table and leaned toward him, resting her chin in her hands, eyes bright and mischievous in the flickering tabletop candlelight. "So, what's the occasion?"

AJ raised his eyebrow. "It can't be just wanting to have a nice meal with the beautiful woman I'm sleeping with?"

Another blush colored Lil's cheeks at his words but she didn't give up. "Slept with, past tense. There hasn't been any time for that lately. And if that were all, we could have done that with room service at the hotel and it would have been a whole lot easier. This took effort." She gestured around the full restaurant.

Theirs was the best table.

He shrugged. "Most things don't take much effort when you're AJ Garza…"

She snorted. "There's not room at this table for your ego and the rest of us."

He brought a hand to his chest. "Words hurt more when they come from gorgeous women, you know…"

She laughed. "You're outrageous."

"I've heard."

Talking with Lil was like playing with an electrical outlet, every time he got buzzed, he wanted to come back for more.

"I'm not surprised. Your poor mother." She sighed, doing an excellent job of looking serious and regretful for his mom.

"My mom adores me."

Lil patted his hand on the table. "Of course she does."

He was chuckling when the waiter arrived with their drinks—a glass of wine for Lil and a sipping tequila for AJ. When they were alone again, he raised his glass.

"To the Closed Circuit."

She lifted her glass to clink it against his. "The Closed Circuit?"

"Without it, we wouldn't have met and you'd still be a virgin."

Lil made a choking noise in her throat, quickly looking around the room and AJ kept his face carefully neutral.

When she could breathe again, she said, "Don't say things like that in public."

He looked around the room innocently. "Oh, I hadn't noticed there were so many people around…" When she made another pinched sound, he gestured to her glass. "Here, have some water."

They had to ask for more time when the waiter returned for their food order. When he came back, Lil ordered a flank steak, AJ a T-bone.

"You're a Texas stereotype, you know," she said.

He sat back in his chair and took a sip of his tequila. "I'd better be. My people've been in Texas longer than it's been in the US."

"You talk about your dad's side a lot," she observed. "Where's your mom's family?"

He shrugged. "She was an only child and her parents were

estranged from the rest of her family. We know who they are, but aren't connected."

"That's too bad. Must be hard for her, not having anybody outside of you."

He shook his head. "Not too hard. She's got my dad's family."

Lil raised an eyebrow and he continued. "I'd be lying if I said my grandmother didn't care about a paper marriage, but to her, once you bring a Garza into the world, you're a Garza for life."

Lil smiled. "She sounds fierce."

AJ nodded. "She is. Kicked my dad's ass with a spoon when he left my mom. For the whole first year after the divorce she wouldn't invite him to holidays—just my mom and me."

"She liked your mom?"

He chuckled, shaking his head. "Not at first. When my dad introduced my mom to her, the first words out of her mouth were, *You couldn't find a woman who speaks Spanish?*"

Lil frowned. "I thought your mom *taught* Spanish."

"She did! And my grandma knew it, too. She only warmed up to my mom after I was born."

Lil's eyebrows lifted. "Clearly—if she picked your mom's side after the divorce."

Still smiling, AJ shook his head. "She picked family. Nothing is more important to her, certainly not her third son's midlife crisis."

"So you're mom's not alone?"

He shook his head. "Nope. She lives alone in Houston, but we spend Christmas in Oaxaca every year with my cousins, and Thanksgiving at my grandma's."

Lil's eyes sparkled. "I've always wanted to go there."

"Oaxaca?" AJ leaned toward her without meaning to.

She nodded. "I've wanted to go ever since high school. I bet Christmastime is wonderful."

"It is." The combination of the tequila and the company lent additional warmth to the memories, softening the edges of images in his mind enough that he realized he missed it. That a part of him missed it all—his home and family—more than he ever let himself acknowledge. Not when there'd always been another shiny buckle on the horizon. "When I'm not traveling," he added, "we go for Día de los Muertos, as well. It's just not quite the same anywhere else."

"I bet!" Lil's eyes were bright. Her head was tilted to the side, a wide, dreamy smile on her face as she pictured it, and he knew she'd hate how revealing of her heart the gesture and expression were.

"Do you like to travel?" he asked, already knowing the answer.

She nodded. "I do. Haven't made it far, though. Spain, and most of the southwest, is all. My choir went to Canada once. The ranch keeps me pretty close to home these days."

His interest piqued. "You were in choir?"

She cocked her head toward him, eyebrow lifting. "Yes."

"Will you sing for me?"

"Absolutely not."

"Pretty please," he begged, grinning the whole time. "You sing for me now and I'll make your body sing later."

"No. And all your Spanish and travel and dirty talk won't change my mind."

Judging from the flush in her cheeks and the way she shifted in her seat, they were already working their magic, but he wasn't going to rub it in. Yet.

Smile knowing, he reached for his tequila, letting his shirt stretch tight against the muscles of his arm as he did so, before taking it back for a slow sip. She watched the whole thing as if her eyes were magnetized to him. He licked his lips, and she swallowed and he felt the sound in his soul. And the growing bulge in his pants.

"How's the wine?" he drawled heavy at her, and her eyes darted back up to his.

"Hmm? Oh. It's nice," she said.

"Nice?" he asked with a smile.

"Nice," she repeated and their eyes locked. She said softly, "I've had the best."

A jolt of possessiveness shot through him so strongly that his whole body tensed. Again, he strongly considered abandoning the rest of his plan for the night and taking her somewhere with a bed.

But beyond having a great night out with a fascinating woman, this was about *not* throwing her on whatever flat surface he could find. He wanted to show her a different side of himself and his hometown. Tailoring that to Lil had taken planning and it'd be a shame for all the effort to go to waste.

The waiter arrived with their dinner, putting an end to the debate for the time being.

Lil took a bite first, vegetables, and made an *mmmm* of approval. "Delicious."

"You start with the vegetables at a steakhouse?"

"I always start with the vegetables." She said it like it was a perfectly normal adult thing to do.

"Why?" he asked.

She shrugged. "They're good for you."

"I feel like that says something about you," AJ said, taking a bite of his T-bone. It was a perfect medium rare and served with a chimichurri sauce that tasted like it'd been made fresh for his plate. Perfectly cooked steak and dinner with the most fascinating woman he'd ever met—life didn't get better.

An image of Lil's face as she came apart beneath the stars

flashed across his mind and he amended the thought: life *could* get better, but Lil was the common denominator.

He had a feeling he'd only scratched the surface as to just how good life could get with Lil.

And at this rate, he'd be swooning over the simple act of her breathing by the end of the night.

Breaking into his thoughts, thankfully, she asked, "How do you select the mentees for CityBoyz?"

"Applications. It's a fairly straightforward form with a few essay questions. We're not bringing them into our homes or anything like that."

"How many kids do you have at a time?"

"Up to seven. Beyond that can get dangerous."

"I can imagine." She shuddered. "Seven teenage boys anywhere is a recipe for trouble, let alone around bulls."

He laughed, "It can be. But they're good kids. Rodeo makes them better."

Lil raised her glass to that, a half smile on her face and a twinkle in her eye. "Hear! Hear!"

AJ drank her in, though he'd gotten drunk on her long ago and lifted his glass in return. "I didn't come to woo you with shop talk all night, though."

She chuckled, "Why not? It's working."

He didn't resist the thrill her words set off. "You want to know I'm well-rounded, don't you?"

"I know you're well-rounded."

AJ caught her with a mock stern look, laughter in his eyes. "Lilian Sorrow Island. What would your grandmother say?"

Lil snorted. "Something outrageous."

"I like her more and more all the time."

"You two are peas in a pod, alright."

"Says the woman dirty talking at the dinner table."

Lil laughed and he realized the sound had become one of

his most favorite—its own form of music. He marveled again at the astounding rightness of her. Her mind, her heart, her body—there was no other way to say it—the girl had a try. And try as he might, he knew he'd never find another that fit him quite so well. The hard part, he sensed, would be convincing her of that.

"Do you want dessert?" he asked.

She shook her head. "Too full."

He smiled. "Perfect. There should be more food where we're going next."

She laughed. "As long as you're comfortable being the father of my food baby."

Her words teased at a primal urge in him, as ridiculous as they were, and his smile went feral. His next words were a risk, but he'd never been known for his caution. "I'm comfortable being the father of any of your babies…"

For an instant her shoulders stiffened, but then she let out a soft chuckle that sounded only faintly forced. "There won't be any cowboy babies coming out of me, thank you very much."

He snorted. "Any baby that comes out of you is arriving with a Stetson and a lasso."

Entirely relaxed again, she laughed and countered, engaging rather than avoiding, "With my luck, they'll love banking."

He shrugged, smile wicked. "Then we'd just have to try again."

Her eyes widened to two bright gray half-moons in her face, a strange vulnerability clear in them, one that urged him to make the words true right then and there, to prove to her that cowboys could keep promises and stick around and love every minute of it.

Instead, he laughed at her and signalled for the waiter as she took a gulp of her wine.

The place they were going next wasn't exactly private, but there, at least, he'd be able to satisfy his need to touch her.

Pulling her chair out for her after he'd paid, he slid his hands along her shoulders and down her arms, loving it when she shivered.

Offering her his arm, he led her out to the rental hybrid parked in the lot.

She raised an eyebrow. "Electric?"

He cocked his head to the side. "You got a problem with protecting the earth?"

She lifted her arms, laughing. "I'm all for it. Just didn't expect it of you."

"Assumptions hurt, Lil," he said, mock wounded, before he shrugged. "Of course, this is just a rental. I drive a truck at home."

She snorted. "See?"

He made his voice serious. "It's also a hybrid, though."

Laughter burst out of her. "I give up!"

He insisted, shaking his head. "It is. Love it, or hate it, Lil, everybody's got to do their part."

"You sound like a wartime advertisement."

He shrugged again. "It fits."

She shook her head with a smile while she buckled her seat belt. When that was done, she looked up, caught his eyes in her stormy gray ones, and smiled.

He would have given her anything she wanted right then.

But she didn't want anything from him beyond a good time.

"So," she said. "Where are we going?"

Grinning, though the thought had brought a hollow sensation to his throat, he said, "It's a secret."

32

"This is the part where you murder me, isn't it?" Lil asked, eyeing the abandoned warehouse in the shuttered and darkened Houston industrial district. From the outside, the large square building at the outer edges of the city looked closed. The lights were out and a few of the windows were broken. The doors were chained shut.

If it weren't for the full parking lot she wouldn't have believed there was anyone else around.

Shaking his head, he said, "This is the part where I sweep you off your feet."

Lil was still skeptical. "Not literally, though, right? My feet like being on the ground…attached to my legs."

AJ laughed, "As far as I know, all your limbs will remain attached."

"As far as you know?"

He shrugged, adding, "Nothing is certain in this life." He offered her his arm and she took it.

If this was where he turned out to be a secret serial killer, this was probably about as good as the night was going to get. She said, "I usually like better odds for my nights out, but fair point."

He countered with, "I thought you didn't have 'nights out.'"

"Ouch," she said, reaching for her purse and quickly realizing she didn't have it with her. She stopped.

"I need to go back to the car—left my purse."

"You won't need it."

She frowned at him and he grinned, completely unrepentant and charming.

"I need my ID at least," she insisted.

His smile turned indulgent. "You're adorable, but it's not that kind of place."

She shrugged, releasing the idea of another drink. She wasn't sure what kind of place it was, but anyplace she knew that served drinks tended to require IDs.

They walked up to a door that looked as locked as the rest of the building and he knocked three times. Up close, Lil could hear and feel the muffled rumble of bass vibrating the thick door. There was music inside. That was a good sign.

After a moment, three responding knocks came from the other side of the door. AJ replied with two more raps and the door opened.

Sound blasted them in deafening waves. The cacophony was a mishmash of traditional Mexican music and hip-hop and it took Lil's senses a moment to sort out that the sound was the combined noise of two separate dance rooms—one playing traditional Mexican dances, the other blasting reggaeton.

AJ handed the doorman cash and they were ushered inside, their hands stamped.

Like the rest of the building, the foyer was crowded. People milled through the area switching back and forth between the dance floors fluidly. Lil held on to AJ's hand.

He led her first to the traditional room. There, the absence of such heavy bass meant they could hear each other's shouts if they really tried.

Her heart steadied to the beat of the music as her ears adjusted to the volume and the crush. Taking more in, she noticed the room was filled with people of all ages. Children darted in and out of people's legs, creating their own level of activity in the tiered canopy of the room.

On the dance floor, old and young couples showed off their skills with varying levels of effort—young men spun young women in bandage dresses and impossibly high heels exuberantly while old-timers put hyper focus on precise movements and serving looks that gave the youngins a run for their money. Everyone moved together, though, all in time to the common rhythm.

Along the back wall, long folding tables bowed under the weight of Crock-Pots, cakes, and aluminum baking trays. The air was filled with the aromas of those various delights, as well as a war of women's perfume and knock-you-on-your-ass clouds of cologne. Almost every word she heard spoken was in Spanish.

She'd never been anywhere like it, and it was wonderful.

Eyes wide as she continued to scan the scene, she accidentally connected with a tall young man in a cream-colored cowboy hat and freshly shined boots. He flashed her a blindingly white smile and began making his way in her direction.

AJ watched him approach quietly, sliding an arm around Lil's bare shoulders as the younger man reached his palm out to Lil.

"Está conmigo," AJ said.

The young man looked him up and down with a frown before he shrugged and shot Lil a little wink before turning and fading back into the crowd.

AJ glowered at him as he drifted away, but Lil laughed. "What is this place?" she asked, raising her voice.

He turned back to her with a smile. "Pop-up dance."

She drew her eyebrows together, and he explained, "Somebody gets the idea, finds a space, and spreads the word. If it works, people bring food and booze and everybody dances. Totally illegal."

She looked up at him, a little awed. "How'd you even find out about it?"

His grin flashed, chipped tooth and dimple coming along for the ride. "I know people."

"Why go to the trouble?" Lil asked, touched.

He pulled her into his arms and kissed the top of her head, murmuring into her hair. "I wanted to take you dancing."

Her stomach did a flip even as she blanched at the thought of dancing. She was a good dancer, but she'd never done anything with actual steps. Certainly not like the dancers out on the floor now. All of them seemed to know both the steps, and how to make them their own.

He offered her a hand. Butterflies loop-di-looped in her stomach.

"Listo?" he asked.

She shook her head. "What are they dancing?" she asked.

"Cumbia," he said, his body beginning to sway in time with the music.

"I don't know how," she said.

He grinned. "Doesn't matter. I do." And then he swept her out onto the dance floor.

She went, helpless to resist him, and tried to watch the other dancers and figure out the moves on the way. It seemed to be comprised of a shuffling step and some half twirls.

She could handle that.

He took her arm and spun her to face him. Their eyes locked, gray and brown, the intensity there even amidst the crowd and noise. He gestured for her to watch his feet with two fingers and quickly showed her the basic step, which was just a back step and return on both sides of the body. She picked it up quickly, realizing abruptly that they were already halfway to doing what everyone else on the floor was.

He kept things basic for a few bars, letting the rhythm get into her body, before he added more.

"Keep up the same step," he whispered in her ear after pulling her close, before she stepped back away from him. She nodded and while she focused on holding the same step pattern, he made the dance come alive.

He spun her under his arm partially, then back, before lifting her arm and dipping under it himself, the bounce in his knees and movement adding a little hip-hop flare to the dance.

Before she knew it, she'd completely stopped focusing on steps, her body memorizing the movements and rhythm so her mind could be free to elaborate and add her own flair. His eyes burned the first time she put her own signature on a spin, twisting her hips away from his at the last minute, avoiding the palm that wanted to land on her hip, making him work that much harder for the contact.

Her heart raced in her chest and her whole body was flushed, but she couldn't remember having more fun outside an arena in her whole life.

They danced like that for three more songs until he led her off the floor sweating and unsure if it was possible for one's hips to get *too* loose. Even still, her heart protested their leaving the dance floor.

He wove them through the crowd that had only thickened since their arrival, drawing her along with him to the food table.

Various beers lined the table and he grabbed two Modelos, dropping a five in the money jar on the table. He opened them and handed her one, nodding toward the jar.

"Part of how they make up the effort."

He toasted her, smiling into her eyes, and she didn't look away as she took a sip of the beer, letting the carbonated cold fool her into thinking she was rehydrating.

She knew her hair had to have gained a couple inches in volume, but didn't worry too much about it. One of the pluses of wearing her hair natural was that more volume meant sexier rather than a frizzed edges mess. Straightening and perms meant always being worried about losing your style to moisture and, as a full-time rancher, she'd never had the time to worry about trying to keep her hair dry. Still, it'd taken her a while to make the big chop.

He scanned the table for a moment before zeroing in on the cakes. She stayed put while he cut a piece, put it on a plate, and brought it back to her.

"Have you ever had tres leches?" he asked.

She shook her head and he said, "Get ready to have your mind blown."

She raised an eyebrow, eyes dancing, and opened her mouth. He obliged by forking a bite for her and feeding her, and once again he was responsible for her world changing.

The cake was the definition of delectable, with gorgeous whipped cream frosting and fresh strawberry filling. It was the best cake she'd ever had. "Mmmmmm. You're right. Delicious. A little sweet for the beer maybe," she said, raising her bottle, "but I'll take it." She opened her mouth for another bite and he gave it to her.

He replied, "You're sweeter," the heat in his eyes telling her he had a lot more than cake on his mind.

Blushing, she changed the subject. "You're a great dancer."

His grin turned cocky. "I am. You're a natural."

"I bet you say that to all the girls."

He shook his head. "Not a single one."

Her breath caught in her throat, and she took a sip of her

beer to distract from her loss of words. He was doing something to her. She didn't know what it was, but she was afraid it might be permanent.

As if he sensed her unease, he said: "Want to check out the other dance floor?"

She nodded, grasping at something safe, and he offered her his arm once again. Taking it, she followed him out of the room leaving the Western and brass sounds of the cumbia, crossed the foyer, and followed him into the thunderous bass of the reggaeton room.

The music was loud and fast and stampeded her heartbeat into its rhythm. Tension she didn't know she'd been holding eased out of her shoulders. Here was something she was familiar with.

She didn't get out often, but it had been the tradition for her college rodeo team to go out dancing in Tulsa at the end of every quarter. She was no phenom, but she knew she could hold her own on this dance floor.

She was wearing a dress, and a bit of a sundress at that, so there would be nothing really risqué with him tonight, but that didn't mean they couldn't have fun.

She moved her shoulders and head in time to the music almost automatically, unwilling to wait until he found them a space in the crowd. Her hips had joined in on the action by the time he'd picked a spot and twirled her around to draw her up against him, her rear pressing against his groin. His hand was firm on one hip, lending her balance and stamping possession at the same time. She leaned back into him and their bodies seemed to move together in perfect sync with the sound of their own accord.

She hadn't danced close like this since Spain—in the States, drinking safety rules kept her from letting anyone so far into her bubble.

In Spain, the night hadn't ever started until after 11:00

p.m. and never ended before six in the morning. At twenty-one, living in a foreign country, she'd been sure that, next to rodeo, there was no better way to tap into the part of herself that was forever wild and free than to dance into the morning. She was wrong, though. Dancing with AJ was more thrilling than both.

Having him in her bed even more than that.

While she swirled in thoughts of him, their dance transitioned into a smooth two-step, bodies fused, both of them taken over by the heat and pace of the beat.

She threw him a curve, stuttering the beat so that her behind bounced against him and he caught on immediately, adjusting his own movement to pull his hips away and thrust back to meet her bounce. They were both fully clothed, but she felt the thrill of each thrust as if they were naked and alone.

Her dress prevented things from getting acrobatic, but the sense that their bodies could take it there thrummed between them like a power line. He had the flow to go with her paired with the strength to lure her to come close. Whether she pushed or pulled, his body promised he'd meet her with exactly what she needed. She closed her eyes and shivered despite the heat of the dance floor.

The song transitioned into a popular dance song with a smooth, heavy beat. Lil wasn't sure who led the change, but their movement slowed, becoming more fluid and sensual. He wrapped his arms around her, drawing her closer at the same time as he leaned in to press a kiss to her neck, just below her ear, all without losing the beat. It was so tender, even in the middle of the throng of grinding bodies that her breath caught in her throat.

Then he spun her away and back so they were face-to-face and chest to chest. Eyes locked, both of them were breathing hard, their feet moving together in a quick-paced two-step.

Lil couldn't think of another time she'd ever been so in tune with another human in her life.

His eyes lit with pleasure as if he could read her mind and he grinned, lifting his arm and twirling her around to spin again. It was all she could do to spot and hold on, and she laughed, feeling carefree in a way she hadn't since she'd outgrown the merry-go-round.

Pulling her out of the spin with a mini dip and a kiss, AJ gave her a small twirl in the opposite direction to counter dizziness. As he had before, he spun her first in and then away from him. This time, though, instead of flicking his wrist to spiral her body back toward his, a pair of hands grabbed her waist from behind, used her momentum against her, and spun her around to take her into their own dip and kiss.

The stranger's lips were hard and cold against hers, his hands like frozen solid ice packs on her back. She balled her fists and slammed them against his chest, but he just laughed before righting them both. She leaped away from him as soon as they were balanced and her mouth dropped open.

It was Hank.

She experienced a moment of strange double vision, images of Hank in the arena running simultaneously to the picture of him standing in front of her. Her skin felt strangely numb.

How did Hank end up at the same spot as the two of them? The place had a secret knock, for crying out loud.

The music that had only moments ago pounded in her blood now just pounded in her head. She refused to rub her temples, even as they begged for the gentle pressure of her fingertips to ease the throbbing.

What was Hank doing there?

She didn't have time to answer the question, though. Instead, AJ's fist came flying out of her peripheral vision to land in the center of Hank's face.

33

Unlike the outbursts of his youth, no storm raged inside as AJ swung his fist into the face of a twenty-year-long annoyance.

He wasn't hitting Hank because he was annoying, though.

He wasn't even hitting him because he'd cut in on his dance with Lil, though that was rude.

AJ was hitting Hank, and with deadly calm, because of the way Lil's body had stiffened when the other man had touched her.

Her freezing, all that joyful fluid grace going rigid, struck him as an injustice that needed immediate righting.

She had been happy and safe and Hank had taken that away from her. So even though AJ might've been the one to throw the first punch, Hank had been the one to start it. And once started, neither man was about to back down. Hank swung back and AJ dodged, dimly noting the rising tide of phones in the background, all aimed toward the fight.

This is going to be a scandal… The thought floated through his mind like a leaf on a river, lazy and unmolested, while he caught Hank in the gut with an uppercut.

Doubled over, it was easy to knock him to the ground, but the guy didn't stay down long. Rebounding with surprising agility, Hank jumped up swinging into AJ's side, catching him in the center of his left-side ribs.

The air escaped AJ's lungs with the force of a car wreck and he nearly doubled over himself. Hank had a helluva swing. Probably cracked a rib.

Now wasn't the time to dwell on it, though. AJ stepped to the right to avoid another one of Hank's hammer punches and tripped the bastard, this time ready to use the guy's rapid leap to his feet against him. Hank popped up right into AJ's outstretched forearm, clotheslining himself with his own force.

Landing on his ass, Hank lost his spring and couldn't hop up so quick, and AJ got a moment to recapture his breath. The guy hit like a bear.

When he did come back, it looked like he was going for a sucker punch and AJ blocked, but at the last minute he switched swinging arms and hit AJ dead in the eye. AJ's head snapped back, but he got his block up before it even had time to whip back, so Hank's number two hit didn't make its mark. They danced around each other—an odd pair of bare-knuckle boxers both dressed in their go-to-towns.

By this point, they'd captured the attention of folks from both sides of the warehouse. The crowd that encircled them was a thick sea of people and dollar bills and bets were starting to swim through it. There were more phones out recording the scene than he could count.

In the corner of his eye, Lil was a figure in white, separate from both the sea of people and the brawl, but still within the circle.

A feint to the left and a quick jab with the right and he

clipped Hank in the side of the head. The other man's eyes momentarily pointed in two different directions and AJ ignored the twinge of conscience he blamed on his EMT training in order to finish it with a hook from the left. Hank fell backward, landing flat on the floor. AJ knelt quickly and checked for a pulse—it was the least he could do to satisfy the part of him that cared about helping people—before standing up to find Lil. At his feet, Hank groaned, though his figure remained prone. It didn't matter to AJ, he'd met his professional obligation as far as Hank was concerned and no longer had time for him.

He only had time for Lil.

His blood was a rushing river in his veins, his breath still coming fast and hard as he strode over to Lil. She stood her ground as he closed the distance between them, lifting her face to his when he stood in front of her. Her eyes were hurricane dark, her thick eyebrows drawn together in a frown as she scanned his face. He'd never seen a woman more stunning. All that compressed beauty around a core of steel… She was the sexiest thing he'd ever encountered.

She lifted a hand up to cup his cheek softly. "You okay?" she asked.

He nodded, the thunderous beat of his heart beginning to slow. "You?"

She nodded. "We should probably get out of here."

Aware of the phones still pointed their direction, he wrapped an arm around her, hiding her in the shadow of his body. If they were going to get in trouble over this, he wanted to spare her as much as possible.

His body calmed as he led them out, the crowd parting to allow them through. As they went, the consequences of getting in a fight when you were too old for that kind of thing started to let themselves be known.

His ribs were the worst, but his left eye ached where Hank'd landed a solid one, as well. His shoulders, never particularly pleased with him, throbbed their displeasure at those full-armed punches while his back went rigid in disapproval.

Outside of the rental, he opened Lil's door. She got in with a quick thank-you and he walked around to take the driver's seat.

They left Hank behind. He'd figured out how to get to the spot on his own. He could get home that way, too.

Lil was quiet as they left downtown Houston, heading back to their hotel.

After they'd driven for a while he said: "Sorry about that. I shouldn't have caused a scene."

Lil's voice was quiet when she replied, but there was laughter in it. "He started it."

AJ chuckled. "I finished it. Sorry he grabbed you like that."

"Wasn't your fault."

"You're right. But it was probably because of me."

She raised an eyebrow, tone dry. "It certainly couldn't be because I look like such a snack in this dress…"

He let out a barking laugh that made his ribs ache. "That you do, darlin'. You can dance, too."

She smiled. "You're not so bad yourself. Thanks for taking me out tonight. I had a good time."

Warmth spread through AJ's chest. "Even with the brawl?"

She laughed and the sound wrapped around him like a warm blanket. "You know about me and brawls…"

The night of the qualifier came back to him, her in her black vest in the middle of the melee. Even then she'd somehow stood apart, a body in her own glow, as if she walked the earth under her own personal spotlight.

"I'm in love with you, Lil."

She sucked in a breath and held it, and a thickness settled in the air between them that hadn't been there before.

Her face was a study in surprise, mouth open slightly, eyebrows lifted, eyes swirling. She'd paled, her brown skin taking on an ashen hue, except for the two pops of red on her cheeks, and her nostrils were faintly flared.

When it was clear she wasn't going to say anything he added, "I know you can't leave the ranch. I'm willing to come to you."

Her voice came out as a croak: "No."

He looked at her. "No?" His body ached with a dull throb, bruised areas making themselves heard more and more with each passing moment.

"No," she repeated.

"No what?" He didn't try to keep the irritation out of his voice. He'd waited thirty-six years to tell a woman he loved her only to have her tell him no like he'd asked for her spare change.

"You're not in love with me." Her voice was high and thin.

This time he put effort into keeping his tone even. "Yes, I am."

"You're in love with rodeo."

It took him a moment to process her words, but as soon as he did sparks of temper flickered that he'd thought had been long ago doused.

"I am a grown man, Lilian."

She shook her head, and he could swear he saw her digging phantom heels in. "You think you love me. But you don't. You can't. You can't settle down. You can't even retire." She picked up both volume and speed as she spoke, the taut lines of her neck lending a note of panic to the whole delivery. She was freaking out.

And even though he'd heard them before, the words took

on a new sting when it was Lil throwing them back in his face after he'd trusted her with them.

But she was acting like he'd backed her into a corner, so he kept his voice even when he repeated: "I'm a grown man, Lil."

She either didn't hear or didn't heed the warning his words carried. Still pitchy and strange, she said, "No, AJ. You're a rodeo cowboy and I'm not. You're not going to be able to stay and I'm not willing to get hurt when you leave."

He heard what she said like it was coming from far away and through a tunnel. Blood rushed in his ears as she went on, deciding for both of them.

"We don't suit. You want to travel and ride and dance. There's no dancing like that in Muskogee…"

The strain and tension she radiated were like knives against the thin skin of his temper.

There was danger in the flatness of his voice when he said, "You're afraid."

She didn't hear it. She was spiraling too much off on her own. "Afraid?" she scoffed, young and foolish and completely unaware of the fire she stoked. "I'm not afraid of anything. You're just mad that I'm right."

He swatted away her ridiculous attempts at baiting with his next words: "You already said it. You're afraid to get hurt."

Her voice rasped out. "I'm practical. I'm the one who gets left with a broken heart—and maybe more—when you get bored."

"That's your cowboy bullshit, Lil. Not mine."

She glared and he turned right, pulling into the hotel parking lot.

"You've been retired for three years, yet here you are. You can't quit rodeo any more than I can leave the ranch."

Instead of answering, he parked, got out of the car, and walked around to open her door. He unbuckled her seat belt and she sat there, staring up at him. He could feel the heat from her body and smell the smoky vanilla that was her scent. She was beautiful—her dress smooth over her lap, her hair thick and curly, falling around her back and shoulders, and he wasn't willing to accept anything less than all of her. He couldn't. It wasn't in his nature.

So when he spoke, his voice was raw and abrasive, stripping them both bare: "I'm not playing the role of passing-through cowboy here, Lil. You are. If you walk away from this, you're a coward. Just like every other cowboy who rode off into the sunset rather than stick around and take a risk." *Just like my dad*, he thought. *Just like your dad.*

He held out a hand to her, and she took it, even though her eyes were angry and glistening. After helping her out of the car, he closed the door behind her and walked her in silence to the hotel's rear entrance.

"Good night, Lil. See you tomorrow," he said.

But he didn't kiss her.

34

If Lil's eyes were puffy when she woke up at least there was no one in her room to see it. And if she'd cried angry, hot tears alone in her bed, well, there was no one in the world she'd ever share it with.

He'd called her a coward. Her? A coward? A woman who'd never backed down from a challenge in her whole damn life. She wasn't a coward. She was a realist. AJ was used to women with stars in their eyes and he just didn't like the fact that she called it like it was.

She was no coward. Through the night, she'd thought about it all. She'd pictured AJ riding fences with her, using his greater strength to break through the tough, hard dirt of high summer when a fence post had to be replaced. She'd imagined him walking through the front door over and over, at every time of day, in every season, taking his hat off and smiling at her, fresh and happy from tending the things they grew together and her stomach had clenched with a stabbing sensation that stole her breath and brought tears to her eyes.

He'd better be grateful, she ground out in her mind, because while she was saving him, it was killing her along the way.

This is good, though, she said to herself over again. She needed to focus on the competition.

He wasn't the stick-around type. He was bored and trying to run away from the fact that he couldn't quit rodeo. A few months of tedious ranch life and he'd get the itch, but after a few months more of AJ, Lil didn't think she'd be able to watch him leave.

This was for the best.

She repeated it to herself in the shower, in front of the mirror, and as she slipped on her vest as she prepared for the first day of the last challenge of the competition. She needed her head in the game—especially if she wanted first draw in Vegas.

She just had to keep her endgame in mind and she'd be fine.

Getting fresh with the enemy was a luxury the ranch, and she, couldn't afford.

And he would've gotten bored, anyway.

He needed the pace of the circuit and the nightclubs of Houston to feel alive, things that might as well be as far away from Muskogee as the moon.

Showered and dressed, she headed down to the lobby for the van that would take them to CityBoyz. She didn't know what it was yet, but she knew the challenge was based out of the place that had shaped AJ. She wondered if she'd recognize the ways it had once she got there, her mind always circling back to him. She stopped the train of thought harshly.

That was done. AJ was just another cowboy to beat. He had to be.

The ride to the gym was lost in thought, Lil no company for any of the others on the bus. Hank approached her and said a few words, apologizing, knowing his type, but she was too preoccupied with the loop in her mind to bother making sense of what he said.

AJ wasn't there.

No one else tried to talk to her.

By the time they pulled into CityBoyz, Lil was certain she was strung out, never mind the fact she'd never so much as seen a drug in her entire life.

The building wasn't much to look at, just a big warehouse-y box, not unlike the one they'd danced in the night before.

Her heart twisted at the memory, and she scrambled to switch tracks. The sooner she walked through the doors, the sooner she could win the challenge and walk out, and the sooner the whole thing was over and she could go home.

Lil went in, followed by Hank and Sierra, her swollen eyes taking longer to adjust to the change in the lighting than they might have otherwise.

They stood in a smaller sectioned entryway, next to which a tiny cube office was positioned, its one sliding glass window the only effort to pretend like it was anything more than a closet.

Outside of the entryway, the space opened up into a cavernous box. Light poured in from high windows, illuminating floating dust motes and high rafters. Drafty and echoing, it would never be called cozy, or even comfortable, for that matter, but it was AJ's home. She could feel it.

She stepped in, awash in the sacred of hush despite the fact that there was a steady jumble of noise ricocheting throughout the space, including the group of people gathered beside the mechanical bull ring and gym equipment, the giant fans overhead circulating air, and the constant and yet unique Closed Circuit sound of greenies debating camera angles and shots.

Somewhere in there was AJ. She'd heard his voice, her heart

picking out its threads the second she'd walked through the door, but her will had resisted the urge to locate him.

The thought of seeing him hurt as much as she wanted it. So she looked for someone else instead.

Finding a likely looking greenie, she tapped the woman on the shoulder and asked, "Pardon me, do you know where I might find out more about our challenge today?"

The woman smiled, her curly blond haircut close to her head giving Lil the impression of the sheep back home, and said, "Not me! But you can go talk to that gentleman, right over there. He runs the place and set up the challenge with the producers."

Lil tracked the line of the woman's finger to land on the straight spine of a black-clad cowboy a couple yards away. Tipping her hat to the greenie, Lil began to walk in his direction, her long strides closing the distance easily while he remained engaged in conversation with another one of the greenies.

Sensing her behind him as she neared, however, he finished his conversation with the young man and turned around to face her, his lined gray eyes warm with welcome, an easy smile at the ready.

Lil started, her world completely flipping on its axis because of a man for the second time in less than twenty-four hours.

His skin was rich black, darker than hers and looser, his aura older, though, than the mild aging his face belied. He was slender and not particularly tall, though he was commanding like a tall man, with a neat salt-and-pepper beard a good half-inch thick. His shirt was a black Western with gray piping and obsidian snaps; his jeans, black Wranglers; and his boots black ostrich. His hands were wide, gnarled, and scarred and there was a rope at his hip. He was missing a chunk of one of his eyebrows and his cheeks showed a light dusting of age spots.

That he was a rodeo old-timer was as obvious as it was that

this was The Old Man that AJ had referred to so often and so lovingly.

Standing before him, she could see herself in him. In so many ways. In ways that made the parts of herself that had been so mysterious, the features that so clearly didn't come from her mother's people, suddenly make sense.

But really, it was the eyes that did it. In all the world, she'd never met another person with eyes like hers. Until her father.

She opened her mouth to speak, then closed it, then opened it again, only to close it again.

She had imagined this moment an infinite number of times throughout her life, mentally playing out every emotion and then looping back around to cycle through the ones she felt the most—anger, fear, sorrow, joy—and none of it had been any preparation at all for the reality.

And though she'd thought out the first thing she would say to him so many times that she was known for whispering words in her sleep—*why didn't you look for me?*—the words that actually came out of her mouth, the first words she had ever spoken to her father, weren't her own, but AJ's:

"*'A cowboy is always prepared,'* my ass."

She didn't think she'd yelled them, but apparently she had.

Every sound in the room ground to a screeching halt, even the fans.

Every eye and camera trained on Lil and the man in front of her.

Familiar gray eyes, narrower and closer set but the same in surprise as her own, widened into horrified shock in slow motion, though his body was as frozen as if he'd been carved from stone.

The expression was more than Lil's lacerated heart could take.

All this time, and he had had no idea she'd even existed.

That much was clear in his expression. She'd pined and wondered and pushed it all so deep she could barely register it
anymore, and he'd never even known. All of that she could
forgive, but not the fact that in finding out, he wasn't happy.
There was no rejoicing in the face that stared back at her.

A strange, high-pitched twisting sound escaped him, and Lil
realized it was air, seeping out from between his petrified lips.

From far away AJ's voice carried. "What's going on? Where's
The Old Man? I need to ask him something."

The sound was yet another sword through her heart, his
nearness when she couldn't have him somehow more painful
in this moment than it had been the night before.

Probably for the first time since winning his first world
championship, no one in the gym moved a muscle or spoke
at AJ's command.

But it didn't matter because a moment later he was there,
positioned between her and her father, looking back and forth
between them, a true scowl on his face.

The reality of him was even more potent than the sound,
and the fact that she was right about everything did absolutely
nothing to lessen the sting of no longer having the freedom to
reach out and take his hand. Especially not when she needed
to so badly.

Beside AJ stood the friend who'd called her the enemy at the
qualifier. He too scowled, his expression aimed entirely at her.

Finally, nearing three decades too late, The Old Man spoke.
"It can't be."

Lil's blood turned to ice in her veins, a part of her reflect-
ing that his first words had been just as abysmal as hers had,
the rest of her sinking in the affirmation of her worst childhood fears, long buried but no less potent.

Piper had once asked if she'd ever thought of looking for
him, the fly-by-night cowboy she was supposed to call a fa-

ther, and Lil had laughed as she shook her head no. She never had. She'd told Piper it was because she didn't need another man in her life trying to tell her what to do. In reality, it was because she was petrified he wouldn't want her.

Like he didn't right now.

"Will somebody explain to me what is going on? We've got a truckload of boys here that are ready for us to get this challenge rolling," AJ said, no easy smile in his voice this time to soften the words.

Cracking back to life, The Old Man recovered first. He answered without taking his steel eyes off Lil, his voice resonant and deep with a bit of rasp to it, not unlike her own, his rigid spine straightening further. "This young woman is my daughter."

Beside him AJ paled, his brown skin losing all its light, but neither Lil nor The Old Man saw. They had eyes only for each other.

Horrifyingly, hers filled with moisture. More horrifyingly, his did, too.

Shaking his head, he whispered, the sound carrying in his rich voice but meant for her, "I didn't know. I'm sorry."

She'd waited a lifetime to hear those words, and they'd been perfect, exactly what she'd wanted him to say and never even known. He somehow had. The thought flickered across her mind and heart that the knowing was what they meant when they talked about inheritance—the bond that connected them explained all the strange quirks of her personality and existence.

But after AJ she was already bleeding out. She couldn't lose any more of herself and still survive.

Shaking her head, she shuttered her gaze, slamming an invisible wall down between them as if holding him at a distance could undo the revelation that had already occurred.

"It's too late." She didn't mean to say the words out loud, but they were true. It was too late. It was all too little, too late. AJ was too old to learn new tricks and she was too old to discover a father she'd never known.

It wasn't worth it. She couldn't do it.

She knew it with the same cool clarity with which she spoke. "I'm sorry. I must've been mistaken. That can't be right. I just wanted to ask you about this week's challenge." Her words were brittle, but she was proud of them. She was holding it together remarkably well.

Body rigid as if stung, The Old Man caught his breath, but simply nodded.

Still pale, AJ took a step toward her, but she shook her head.

If he touched her, she'd fall apart, and that was something she couldn't afford, not with all of the cameras in the room trained on her, not surrounded by people.

She needed air. That was what she needed. The camera was going to love this, the ratings too, she thought, strangely removed from the fact that her most private moment had been the stuff of good TV. She'd given them enough. Her hopes, her dreams, her heart—all of it for the world to see and she needed some freaking air. They could give her that.

And if they couldn't, she was going to take it anyway. She strode from the gym, posture daring anyone to try and follow her, the sound of her boots hitting the concrete floor echoing in the heavy silence she left in her wake.

They'd start talking again as soon as she was gone, she knew. Talking and generating copy and web content and editing the video for teaser trailers. The Closed Circuit couldn't have done better if they'd scripted it.

Outside, she put her hands on her hips and paced. No one approached, and for that she was grateful. She wouldn't have put it past the greenies to sidle up for video exclusives.

She was going to have to go back in there, back in there where it was too much with AJ and too late with her father. And she was going to, because the ranch was on the line, and because she was the first female rough stock champion of the PBRA, and because she was her gran and granddad's grand-daughter.

With a breath, she squared her shoulders and walked back inside.

Whatever else was going on, she had a challenge to win.

AJ's challenge was a week of serving as a mentor and coach for a select group of interested CityBoyz candidates, all of whom eagerly awaited the return of the program after AJ's sure win—never mind that Lil had been giving him a run for his money.

Each of the final three contestants had been assigned two mentees, and the goal was simple: get the greenhorn from never having ridden a horse, to lasting eight seconds on the mechanical bull known as Shirley.

"Shirley," The Old Man explained, every word he spoke a painful and yearning dart in Lil's flesh, "is old and slow, but don't think that means she doesn't still have tricks up her sleeve. Believe me, our old girl can still throw a pro." He'd smiled as he said the last, his eyes lighting warmly on AJ and AJ returned the expression with open affection.

The fact that AJ had had him in his life, a volunteer father figure, while she and gran and granddad had mourned the absence of her mother alone all those years was bitter salt in an old wound.

As an experienced coach and mentor, and having gone through the program himself, AJ already had the advantage in the challenge, not to mention the fact that all the candidates hero-worshipped him and had a vested interest in his winning—it wasn't fair that he got her father, too.

But of course he had her father, because CityBoyz was her father's creation, his heart and soul offered to the world. Swirling between emotions too big to name and the vertigo of that, of knowing that now she wasn't just trying to beat AJ, but her father as well, was threatening to unravel her.

That it was a father she'd never known somehow made it only worse. As did the fact that she'd met her father as an "enemy," just as he, and his emissary in AJ, were a threat to everything she held dear.

Torn in two directions was a terrible place to start a challenge and it didn't get easier.

Lil's mentees, a fifteen-year-old named Carlos Jones and a seventeen-year-old by the name of George Barnes, both towered over Lil and, to their minds, that meant she couldn't possibly know more than them about rodeo.

It'd taken three days of both of them getting thrown by Shirley multiple times to prove to them without a doubt that Lil, who had not been thrown once, had it—and, more importantly, that they did not—before they finally settled into listening to her. Even then, their attention was dicey, forever snagging on whatever it was that the great AJ Garza happened to be doing at any given moment—a fact she had little tolerance for no matter how much she could relate. They had two days left when they finally found their groove as a group, after Lil realized that teen boys weren't all that different from goats, which was recalcitrant, wayward, overenergized, and far too clever for their own good.

But even then, loathe to admit that she wasn't, Lil couldn't really get her head in the game. She'd be working with Carlos on balance and hear AJ and then Carlos would be on the ground. She'd catch herself midsentence, trailing off in answering George's questions about grip and positioning because her father had snagged her eye and she was as helpless as a little girl to do anything but watch him in fascination.

It was all just too much, and being so far from home, so far from the wide-open spaces where she could usually leave it, she just couldn't seem to set any of it down and get the job done. It didn't help that for the first time in her rodeo life, she also couldn't channel it into the ride. Pouring her emotional turmoil into two struggling teen boys was a recipe for disaster of monumental proportions. They'd deserved better than that from her, and she'd been determined to give it to them—even if sometimes staving that catastrophe off was about all she could muster.

Of course, it hadn't been enough—not for the boys and not to earn first draw.

Yes, both boys had made it, each one lasting the full eight seconds without being thrown or technically disqualified, but neither boy looked any good doing it. And that, and the fact that they'd tried to hide the embarrassment they felt even amongst all their triumph, felt worse than coming in third—especially after AJ's mentees looked like young pros and Hank's even seemed to have a decent grip on things. She'd let the boys down, maybe even turned them off rodeo. She certainly hadn't proven the strength of her granddad's training methods. She hadn't really shown anything at all, and because of it, she'd lost out on her draw and she was going into the finale down valuable points. And through it all, she still hadn't spoken to either AJ or Mr. Henry Bowman.

35

AJ hadn't seen her since they'd arrived in Vegas. The greenies had informed him that Lil had gone immediately to her hotel room and not been seen since, and his stomach clenched. She'd kept herself removed from everyone ever since her scene with The Old Man.

The moment never lost its intensity, no matter how many times he recalled it. That The Old Man, the man he loved like a father, was Lil's father, and he hadn't known was mind-blowing.

It was so obvious now—the way she rode, the preternatural balance, her eyes. God, her eyes. How had he not guessed? How many people had gray eyes in the world? How many Black people? It was so obvious and it hadn't even occurred to him because he'd been so lost in everything else that she was. Everything that she'd pulled back and locked up.

He was worried about her. He wanted to go to her, rattle her out of her self-imposed exile and rustle a laugh out of her, shake her loose enough to make her realize what he was offering—what The Old Man was.

The ball was in her court now, though, and they'd both just have to wait.

He'd laid his cards on the table and he wasn't about to beg after her like a sad puppy. She had to make the next move.

But he hadn't seen her now in days, so he had no idea what progress was happening. So while it might be her turn to make a move, it didn't hurt to check in and see how she was coming along.

That was why he stood outside of her hotel door, knocking.

She opened the door a crack and peeked out of it.

"What do you want?"

Her eyes were puffy again, the inside of her room dim.

"Open the door, Lil," he ordered.

When she did as he said without pushback, he worried.

She stood aside to let him come in and closed the door after him.

Her duffel bag was on the entry bench and there was a water bottle by her seat. Otherwise everything was undisturbed inside.

"We could fix this before we go on, you know." He spoke softly, like she might spook. He had a feeling that was a distinct possibility.

She eyed him, a line of alert tension visible through her body. "Nothing needs to be fixed, as far as I know."

AJ let out a laugh that was arid for joy. "I was right and you know it, Lil. Stop being stubborn and give us both what we need."

"What I need is to win and get back where I belong."

AJ made a sweeping gesture around the space. "You're going to need to do more than just show up if you want to win."

"Thanks for the advice." Her face was stony and uncompromising.

He said, "You're better with me."

Her eyes narrowed. "I'm as good as I am on my own. You've got nothing to do with it."

He took a step closer, and she tilted her chin up to keep eye contact. "Stop this foolishness," he said. "Take me home with you."

Something sharp and scared flashed through her eyes, but was gone in an instant. "You won't stay."

He leaned in, bringing his lips closer to hers, and she strained up toward him, even if she wasn't aware of it.

"I will." He spoke softly, his mouth only inches from hers.

"Cowboys always leave," she whispered before he closed the gap between their lips with a growl.

She opened for him immediately, her body going fluid as she sighed into it, relief virtually seeping from her every pore. She hadn't just been wanting him, she'd needed him. He could feel the truth of it in her body's urge to merge with his. But she needed to be the one to see it now.

He ended the kiss slowly, lingering on the first taste he'd had of her in ages, savoring even as his hunger grew for more.

He said, "You're the cowboy, Lil," and then he left.

Her taste lingered in his mouth, but he wouldn't try again. The play was doomed if he followed her around like a fool. She had to come to him, but it was more of a challenge to hold his line with the whisper of her still on his tongue than it had been before.

Fortunately, he had a room to himself and a free afternoon ahead of him. It wouldn't be glamorous, but there was relief in his future.

He'd planted the last seed with Lil. Now to wait and see if it sprouted.

36

While a woman dressed in all black rubbed Vaseline on her teeth, Lil wondered how she'd come to this place in her life.

She'd slept like garbage the night before but was dressed in her finest—the clothes she would wear for the finale. She'd braided her hair with immaculate precision that morning and it showed. A single thick braid began at her hairline and trailed along the central line of her skull and down her neck and back like an exposed spine. She'd freshened her undercut, shaving in a double lightning bolt on either side, in the process.

There were dark circles under her eyes, but they weren't puffy anymore. She hadn't cried last night, awake or in her sleep. AJ's kiss had had her tossing and turning for other reasons, but she'd taken that gratefully over the alternative—especially the night before press day.

The Vaseline forced her smile wider and she turned on cue as the team shot her from multiple angles.

"Such delicate bones!" a woman with a white-blond pixie cut exclaimed.

"You'd never guess she was a rodeo star," a bombshell redhead with shoulder-length hair said.

Everyone in the room wore black. The production team sported various combinations of boatneck tops, ballet flats, plain T-shirts, and jeans—all in black. Lil did too, but made it look Western, wearing black boots, Wranglers, and a button-up beneath her granddad's vest.

They'd lost their minds when they'd seen it.

"This is definitely going to be the theme!"

"The whole thing! All around this!"

"Grab my blue pallet, Kelly!"

"Seriously, fabulous!"

Lil'd stammered thank-yous in reply, tried to get it out there that it was her gran's work, and then followed the instructions they began shouting out at her.

"What fascinating eyes you have," a woman with a sharp short black bob said as she powdered her face.

Lil grimaced, knowing now they were her father's eyes, but mumbled, "Thank you," by reflex.

Another woman shouted, "Keep your mouth open, please!" though, so she stopped trying to respond at all.

Which left her alone in her mind to dwell on AJ. The same thing she'd had far too much time to do recently.

She'd arrived in Vegas a sweating mess, questioning her instincts in ways she never had.

Her entire life was evidence of the truth: cowboys disappeared. Even if they said they loved you. Both things could be true.

Her body told a different story. One she knew better than to pay any attention to. His kiss sure knew how to linger. It was the thought that her mind most wanted to jump to whenever she stopped being vigilant.

Her body was tricky. It would sneak into it, creating brand-new pathways with each guerrilla attack. It might start as a phantom tingle across her lips and the memory of the pressure of his against hers. The next time it would be her breath catching, nipples hardening while her chest went heavy and sensitive at the memory of the way he'd stepped into her space. Once she'd wrangled it again, it'd return as something different yet again, a flavor on her tongue, a memory of the times before the kiss, times they'd gone further and he'd set her on fire from the inside out.

But she knew what happened to women who listened to their bodies. They died, abandoned in roadside motels, with only their mothers to identify them. And those men raised other children.

So she wouldn't bend. Not when everything was at stake.

Following makeup, the day passed in a blur of videos, photo shoots, and the sponsor's dinner.

Lil avoided both AJ and Hank wherever possible, allowing herself to be corralled with the two of them only for obligatory *top three* photos. She smiled until her face hurt, sad the Vaseline was no longer there to force a smile for her.

At the end of the day, she hung her clothes up to wear again for the real deal the next day, and crawled into bed feeling painted on and sucked dry.

She woke up once, blamed it on AJ and forced herself back into a fitful sleep for the rest of the night.

In the morning, the hollows under her eyes were deeper, but her expression one of grim purpose.

One way or another, after tonight, it was all over. Tomorrow she'd be going home.

She splashed water on her face and repeated her braid from

the day before. Later, she would put on the same vest and jeans she'd worn the day before, she'd don her chaps and hat, and she'd walk out to compete in the final event of the closed circuit reality rodeo.

They would draw their bulls just before go time, AJ first, Hank second, her with what was left, but every draw was a proven beast—Cortes, Shadow Haint, and Sweet Suzy—each one undefeated. Each one a certified man killer.

Once a bull got a taste for blood, it wanted more. Just like everything else.

Her mind hopped back to AJ before she dragged it back to the day ahead. She needed a plan. Breakfast, then…what? The afternoon stretched out ahead of her, the free time before the big event really more a tyranny than a boon. She could call AJ. Spend the day distracted by his body. Her heartbeat raced at the thought. But it wasn't real. She couldn't. Not if he loved her. She would feel it, and feeling it, she wouldn't be able to deny him.

The body wouldn't win.

But she needed something good for the mind. She settled on room service and binge-watching a costume drama. She'd have to keep it light with the snacking and even the most complicated plot wouldn't be able to keep her mind fully off AJ and the event, but it was her best shot.

It was more effective than she'd imagined. Ten hours later, after her alarm had gone off, she came out of her TV stupor. She'd ordered cheese, charcuterie, and hummus platters and stuck to drinking water throughout the day and felt…good. Even when she'd changed into full gear and checked herself in the mirror one last time, the sense of peace lasted. Something good was going to happen—even if she lost, tonight was the night her stress would come to an end.

The feeling lasted about as long as it took to get to the casino arena.

Three separate groups of young men approached just to mess with her, as she was an obvious target for torment in her full riding gear.

"You're kinda small for a bull rider."

"Maybe they're all tiny, like jockeys!"

While this was met with uproarious laughter, the first group let her step around them and continue on her way without further hassle. The second bunch wasn't so magnanimous.

"Not so fast, shorty!" A stumbling man with a half-full yardstick daiquiri shouted. "You look like a woman to us. We're not letting you leave til we see your dick!" He reached out to grab Lil by the shoulder at the same time as he spoke.

She tilted her body to give him a small karate chop in the elbow, forcing him to bend his arm and let go of her shoulder.

"I am. Cut it out and use your manners when you're talking to a lady."

His buddy whispered loudly, "She's a ninja, Bret. Let's go."

Bret's eyes widened and he took a step back, then turned all the way around to walk away from the big scary ninja.

Lil offered a mental thanks to the dumb drunk who thought small and black equaled *ninja*. He'd saved her some trouble.

Like her life was a fairy tale, the third group was the worst: a bachelorette party.

"Oh my god! Female cross-dressing, I love it. So empowering! Tell me where your show is. I absolutely *have* to know." The woman's eyes were a bit glassy, but the fervor in her voice and the badge on her purple spaghetti strap midi dress that read CERTIFIED MAID OF HONOR told Lil she was the organizer behind the madness.

Lil raised her hands, palms up. "Sorry, ma'am. That isn't my performance."

A redhead in a bright green dress of the same style narrowed her emerald eyes and said, "Then tell her what your performance is." She wore a white sash diagonally across her chest that read BRIDE—not that Lil needed the label. The few weddings they'd hosted at the ranch before abandoning that idea were enough for Lil to recognize the particular tone a woman got when a day was *all about her.*

The rest of the group watched, a complete rainbow of dresses, sharing the same intensity in their same glassy glares, an intensity that had nothing to do with interest and everything to do with immense hunger—for drama, for a perfect moment to capture, for a memory to talk about for ever after, every time this night came up.

Just what I need, Lil thought. She spoke slowly and clearly, "I'm with the rodeo."

Yellow, a gorgeously tan brunette, squealed, "Oh my god! She has an accent!"

"A female rodeo cowboy? Oh my god!" Blue, a sunny blonde, also tan, covered the O of her mouth with her hand to emphasize her point.

"Oh my god, you're so brave!" This came from Red, who was milky pale, black haired, and blue eyed.

Orange, a hazel-eyed girl next-door type, asked, "Is it scary?" in a sweet, trembly, voice.

Purple silenced the rest with a hand. "Can you get us tickets?"

"Uh. I don't know. I'd have to ask."

"Will you ask?" This from the bride. Her pout had an edge to it, like a shank carved out of a bar of soap.

"I'd love to ask for you—" Lil started, but stopped as each of the women's mouths dropped open into perfect little circles. They looked like a nest of baby birds, but vacant instead of hungry.

Lil turned slowly, knowing what she'd find.

AJ stood behind her, enormously tall and muscled, turned out to a T in his navy button-up, cream cowboy hat, and crisp blue jeans. His boots were brown, soft and supple, and his freshly shaved face looked like smooth silk in the flashing lights of the casino floor.

"My friend and I can certainly assist you lovely ladies. Why don't you come along with me?" He laid the drawl on heavy at the end and the women melted in front of him.

The bride squealed and the whole crew joined in with whistles and heys, and Lil tried to steady her heart. Each and every one of these women wanted him. Hell, the bride even let out a tiny sigh following behind him while she twirled her engagement ring.

Not a single one looked back at Lil. She hadn't moved. He'd saved her, but the price was watching him walk away surrounded by a sea of adoring women. She would have rather saved herself.

With that certainty dragging through what was left of her peace, she made it the rest of the way to the draw platform unmolested.

AJ was already there. A quick glance around the gates revealed that AJ had installed the rainbow crew where buckle bunnies typically parked, which, honestly, seemed fitting. They'd certainly have something to talk about for years to come. A few of them might even walk away with cowboy memories of a more personal nature.

Hank jogged up the four stairs to the platform last, a bit out of breath, after she'd selected one of the positions around the draw bowl—a big silver thing that was way too large for the three note cards folded and tossed in its center.

The arena was packed, but hushed, and it was a strange sensation, being surrounded by thousands of people holding their breath. Everyone's attention was on the bowl, the jumbotron cameras zoomed in on its future-changing contents.

Everything was about the bulls tonight.

Shadow Haint was the lightweight of the bunch. He'd killed just once, and never otherwise maimed. Cortes came in second: he'd killed once, and broken many a cowboy's legs, collarbones, and arms. Sweet Suzy had killed twice and been responsible for paralyzing four additional men. His stompings were legendary.

The announcer built the drama until the audience was gasping and it was time to draw a card. AJ went first, then Hank, and Lil took what was left.

Her hand shook slightly as she unfolded her card. She nearly jumped as she first saw the large black *C* of *Cortes*. The sweet spot. No draw turned out to be just a fine draw after all.

She looked over to AJ to see what he'd drawn and couldn't read his face. Then he smiled and raised his card high in the air.

"Sweet Suzy!"

Lil's stomach sank. AJ got the most dangerous bull.

The bulls determined the order for the event. She was up first on the mighty Cortes, AJ up next on Sweet Suzy, and then Hank would take on Shadow Haint. But Sweet Suzy was one of the deadliest bulls in PBRA history.

She couldn't focus on that. Not when she was about to take on a man killer herself. AJ was the best of the three of them. He was the best suited to take on Sweet Suzy.

An announcer gave a five-minute-start warning over the PA system and Lil's heart thundered, her mind spinning images of bad falls and gaggles of women in rainbow dresses hanging all over AJ.

The arena seated forty thousand and was supposedly sold out. That many people were watching her.

A large warm hand clamped down on her shoulder. He stayed behind her, but leaned down to whisper in her ear: "You've got this."

She tried to turn and face him, but his firm grip on her shoulder wouldn't let her, and then he was passing her, down the stairs in a few steps, and enveloped by a rainbow sea.

She vowed to wear black for the rest of her life.

Just as soon as she found her calm place.

Gran's last words to her back at the ranch sprang into her mind unbidden.

Gran was always working some long-range plan, meddling in people's lives. Granddad said they would've been rich if she'd spent half that energy on making money.

Lil had laughed. She wasn't laughing now. Then it was her granddad's voice she heard in her head, less a memory than a transmission: *Pour it into the ride.*

A calm settled over her. The fear, the confusion, AJ, her father—it was all going into the ride. The resolution settled in her chest like an anchor and she stepped onto the platform sure.

The arena erupted, thousands of girls pinning their hopes on her.

The knowledge was a burden, but she welcomed the pressure, she bore it repeating her mantra, even as she lowered her body on the back of an angry man killer.

Pour it into the ride.

37

Clinging to a rock in a river of lava. That was what Cortes felt like. He was tall and broad and creamy, and so full of rage that the whites of his eyes were tinged pink. His was a focused and controlled emotion, so primal and timeless that the small braided bull rope seemed about as useful as a wad of floss in the face of it.

But that couldn't matter, because it was time to go.

She wrapped the rope around her right hand, weaving it through her finger to shore up her grip. She'd sacrifice the hand to keep her grip.

She lifted her arm, fear rising in her gorge along with it, but she poured it into the ride.

Whatever she had, this bull could handle it, and when it was all poured out, all she would be left with would be her calm center. There'd never been a bull that could beat that yet.

She took a final breath, deep and slow, then nodded. The gate sprang open and she and Cortes exploded into the arena.

He was the biggest thing she'd ever ridden. She gave her body over to his power, releasing resistance wherever it arose. His bucks and turns were hard enough to break her neck. Her hand screamed, but she held.

Cortes leaped, thrashing his head and tail in opposite directions as he did it, violently whipping her from side to side, but he couldn't shake her. Not when she'd found it.

Her center. The thing that let her stand on the ball.

The ball had been Granddad's idea, and just like then, he was there with her now, lending his weight to her seat through his beaded vest. The faint weight was his hand, holding her to the bull, every single bead a piece of training and advice and love, tiny reminders of his gifts to her, assuring her that like each and every one of those who'd come before her, she'd been given everything she'd ever need.

Cortes spun like the devil but Lil held her center. Spotting was useless, impossible on a spinning bull in a sea of people. You had to ground in something deeper than that. Something inside that wasn't twirling around like a windmill.

When spinning didn't work, the bull began a punishing seesaw of kicks and jumps. Lil willed her body to be as fluid as possible, to flow in time with the bull's harsh switchbacks like a river through a canyon.

And then the buzzer sounded. Catchers and clowns rushed out and soon after she cracked open her fist and slid onto a horse in front of a cowboy in a green button-up.

Her score lit up the jumbotron: 98. The highest score possible on Cortes.

The arena erupted in enormous sound.

Lil Sorrow had beaten an unbeaten man killer and gotten a perfect score doing it.

Not only that, but for the moment, she held first place. AJ was up next, though, and like the producers had somehow rigged the draw, AJ had picked the one bull with the power to beat her.

If he beat Sweet Suzy, he'd gain enough points to trump Lil, perfect score or not.

She felt a strange sense of peace at the thought. Either way, the whole thing would be settled, once and for all, in about eight seconds. AJ was already on top of Sweet Suzy when she returned to the platform. He didn't look in her direction, but she sensed he knew she was watching him.

He was beautiful. His eyebrows were thick and dark and drawn together in concentration. His five-o'clock shadow suited him, highlighting the hard lined architecture of his face that was so often obscured by his wicked dimple.

His hat was cream and looked like it'd been made specifically for him. It probably had.

He was a rich cowboy and he looked it.

Sweet Suzy was tawny and even more massive than Cortes. AJ didn't look small in comparison, though. He looked powerful and controlled, like he had it in him to beat the bull with muscle alone. She didn't doubt that he did.

And then he nodded.

The gate opened. He and Sweet Suzy were through it not a breath later. Lil'd never seen a bull so fast in her life.

But Sweet Suzy wasn't just fast. He was monstrously strong—the kind of bull they used as a model for posters about the ills of overbreeding. And he was wild.

Whereas Cortes had slowed as he transitioned from one move to another, Sweet Suzy moved fluidly from bucking to kicking, to spinning, and back around to bucking.

Lil held her breath. AJ held on.

Until he didn't.

Time slowed as Sweet Suzy's spinning flung AJ off his back.

AJ landed in the soft dirt of the arena floor with a thud that echoed in an arena that'd gone quiet in its collective gasp.

Clowns ran out, but Sweet Suzy spared them no attention. Instead, he faced AJ, who still lay in the dirt about a hundred yards away.

Sweet Suzy stomped, bowed his huge head, and snorted.

He was going to charge.

He was going to charge and stomp.

And after that, nothing would matter.

Lil leaped over the platform. Landing was a painful shock to her knees, but she ignored it. She brought her thumb and forefinger to her mouth to let out a shrill whistle, infusing the sound with every nasty thought she'd ever had about a bull.

Whether or not the thoughts had anything to do with it, the combination worked. Sweet Suzy turned his giant skull in her direction and flared his nostrils, scenting her.

The bull roared and charged. The whole thing happening faster than Lil would have ever thought possible.

She held her ground, conquering every instinct that screamed at her to run. It was too late for that. To run was to get trampled. The bull neared and she held still and someone in the audience screamed.

When Sweet Suzy was nearly upon her, she jumped back, spinning her upper body out of the way of his horns along the way, but either her timing was off, or Sweet Suzy was even faster than she'd given him credit for. The sharp tip of one of his horns caught in the flesh of her shoulder, ripping through the leather of her granddad's vest to her skin like butter. Seed beads flew everywhere, but she didn't pay attention to them, maintaining the spinning motion through the pain, and through her granddad's vest being pulled off her body, the leather of it still caught on the bull's horn.

She was free, and the bull was momentarily distracted by the vest on his head and the crowd was cheering.

She looked over at AJ just as the crowd went silent again. AJ was unharmed, so that didn't explain the crowd's reaction.

Then she noticed the mounted catchers pressing themselves against the outer edges of the arena, staring wide-eyed and open-mouthed behind her. She motioned for them to ride to AJ, but they didn't move. Then she realized why.

AJ shouted her name. "Lilian!"

Sweet Suzy wasn't distracted anymore. He was charging her. And this time she wasn't going to be able to just dance away. His charge was too close and direct, and Lil's weight was on the wrong foot. There was only one option.

She leaped.

Weightlessness was the primary sensation she noted. She felt as if the air had simply accepted that she was sailing through it. Sweet Suzy did his part, lowering his horns as he sensed the threat from above, giving Lil's palms the perfect flat surface to land on and spring forth from again, twirling her body and twisting to land on her feet, behind the bull.

The arena erupted like Krakatoa.

Lil was frozen. Stuck, knees bent, boots buried in soft dirt, heart stopped. She knew she needed to move, that Sweet Suzy would turn around and she'd be in the exact same spot and she'd probably die, but she didn't have any more in her.

But she didn't need any more because AJ snatched her up, leaning over the side of a horse to hook an arm around her waist as he rode by like an ancient warrior snatching a maiden. Lil didn't think to wonder where he'd gotten the horse from until after the clowns had ushered them through the gate and closed it behind them.

They were immediately encircled by a mass of people.

Greenies, medical staff, and reporters were the most persistent, but AJ handled them by simply refusing to dismount.

The horse, high on adrenaline from being in the same pen as Sweet Suzy, was more than happy to oblige him, stomping out a perimeter of space around them.

"Back off," AJ said. "She's hurt. Medics first!"

A man and a woman hurried forward, both wearing crisp white shirts and black slacks, and helped Lil dismount.

She thanked them and a reporter took it as a go sign, asking, "What did you think when AJ was thrown?"

AJ held up a hand. "Quiet." The man went silent.

The medics cleaned Lil's wound where she stood, putting a wide bandage over it.

Despite the commotion, the unforgettable drama, and the upset—Sierra said over the loudspeaker—the show wasn't over yet. Hank was up next on Shadow Haint.

Lil stayed where she was, beginning to shiver as the adrenaline wore off and the fact that she was standing around in full gear with a ripped-up shirt sans vest started to make itself known.

She didn't need to watch Hank. Whether or not he had a good ride didn't matter. It didn't matter if she won the Closed Circuit or if AJ did or Sierra did. It didn't matter that she had indisputably shown the world that girls had try, or proven that her granddad's way was a good way. In the end, it didn't even really matter if they kept the ranch.

Gran mattered. Piper and Tommy mattered. AJ mattered.

The people she loved mattered, those who were still alive and real and present—far more than anything else she could prove or preserve.

A sea of people swirling around her, she looked at AJ and she knew what her grandmother had meant.

In just two months, her entire world had transformed, and

now, towering at the center of it was a man whom she was willing to offer up her very life for—someone whose potential loss would bring a pain so sharp she wasn't sure she could survive it.

That was what it was all about. All for.

Her granddad had always said everything in life was reflected in rodeo, that there wasn't a lesson from it that couldn't be applied to the everyday dilemmas and tribulations of existence.

If life was the ride, she realized with a start, a lone point in a swarm of people, then like her grandfather had always told her, she had to pour her whole self into it—the fear, the anger, the hurt, the need—all of it, and trust that life, like the bulls and the broncs and the timers and the judges, were still no match for the stillness at the center.

A center that had grown bigger, so that it could hold a man who it would someday be impossible to say goodbye to.

But that day wasn't today. She reached out to grab his hand and hold, and he held her in return.

Today was a day for holding on.

And she just happened to be a woman with an iron grip.

The thought brought a blinding smile to her face as a group of men in suits cut a beeline through the crowd. At her back, AJ squeezed her hand.

One of the suits opened his mouth to speak. "Young lady." The crowd leaned in, straining to catch every word. The man cleared his throat.

Lil's stomach sank. The man looked like he'd been born for an era when people still respected rules. Until he smiled.

Instantly, his stern countenance transformed into that of a wily old codger, complete with a missing tooth front and center, and Lil realized he was a retired cowboy.

"Congratulations on becoming the first ever PBRA Closed

Circuit Champion!" And in front of the gathered cameras, including one projecting on the jumbotron, he handed her a trophy, and a shiny new buckle. And as if the moment couldn't get more surreal, AJ swept her up into a kiss, projected for the whole arena on the jumbotron, to the delight and roars of a sold-out show and a thousand screaming girls.

38

The green room was cramped and celebratory when AJ held the door open for Lil. Swimming in his navy shirt, which he'd given her as they'd walked hand in hand together to meet their people, she stole glances at him, struck each time by the wonder that he was hers.

He wore a soft white T-shirt, stretched deliciously across his chest, blue jeans, and a Stetson, looking for all the world like a cowboy coming in off the range rather than a man who'd been near stomped to death within the last hour.

That easy and carefree were as natural to him as breathing was exactly the medicine she needed to balance her own tendency to auger the omens and predict the worst.

Stepping inside, her eyes immediately searched for Gran and Piper and Tommy, landing on them where they sat grouped together in a corner.

AJ was already looking toward the place where Diablo stood, tall and dark in his cowboy hat, which should have been at odds with his three-piece suit, but somehow looked as fluid together as water.

Squeezing AJ's hand, Lil said, "You go on. I'll catch up with Gran and them and meet back with you later."

Smiling, he brought her hand to his lips and kissed her knuckles before releasing it. Wickedness came to his eyes and he said, loud enough for everyone to hear, "I love you Lılıan Island."

Lil's blush was immediate, but she hadn't risked her life to save him just to turn coward now. Stern and serious and red hued, she said, making less of a production about it than he had but no less public for any of it, "I love you, AJ Garza."

Across the room, without any of the competitive edge she typically aimed Lil's way, Sierra let out a big "Awwwww."

Diablo's head snapped up as if the rodeo queen's voice were a sound aimed at him and began making his way in her direction.

Lil glared and AJ grinned, and the world felt right.

AJ went to where Diablo now stood engaged in murmured conversation with the rodeo queen, who, for the first time Lil had ever seen, looked irritated—the real and revealed emotion a disdainful sneer on her face. Shaking her head, Lil hoped Diablo knew what he was walking into with that one but turned to make her way to her own family—only to smash into a solid wall of man.

The wall was her father, and, judging from the storms raging in the gray eyes that had given it all away, he was pissed.

"Are you some kind of damn fool?" he lashed. "I've never seen such a stupid stunt in all my years of rodeo!"

Lil's own temper rose to the surface, two storm fronts crashing into each other. She didn't know him from Adam and he had no right to comment on her behavior.

"Interesting," she replied. "I don't seem to recall asking you. In fact, I don't recall ever needing your help ever over all these years you've been playing at rodeo with other people's kids."

The room went quiet, the hush right before an explosion.

AJ and Diablo and Sierra looked up. AJ's eyes darting between his woman and his mentor, Diablo's firmly set to glaring at Lil.

She didn't mind. She felt bad for AJ, didn't want him caught in the middle, but she could take Diablo's glares, as well as the glares of the man who thought he could just waltz into her life and start telling her what to do.

Behind him, though, Gran was another matter.

Making a sound of outrage in the back of her throat, Gran's voice pitched across the room, modulated to perfectly replicate the experience of pinching Lil's ear to drag her to account. "Lilian Sorrow Island. I don't care if you are the greatest bull rider in the world, I raised you better than that kind of rudeness."

The swirling energy of tension in the room burst.

Suddenly sweaty and embarrassed, Lil looked away from her father, scuffing the toe of her boot on the floor absently as she glared at the cabinetry. "Sorry," she mumbled, unwilling to go any further than that, even with her gran watching.

The Old Man cracked a smile as he took a step back. "I'm sorry, too. That wasn't my place." When he spoke, his voice wrapped around her like a hug she'd been waiting for her whole life. She tried not to resent it.

Coming to stand at Lil's side, Gran crossed her arms over her chest and stared at Lil's father.

"And just who might you be?" she demanded, glaring up at the man as if she were staring down at him.

The old man shifted his weight, belatedly taking off his hat. Lil took the opportunity to take him in, his rich dark skin tone, the lines beginning to crease his face, the eyes that were like looking into a mirror. His head was clean-shaven, bald beneath the hat. "I'm Lil's father—" he began.

"Oh, I know who you are." Gran cut him off. "What I'm more interested in is what your name is, where you've been all these years, and why you thought you could get my daughter pregnant and abandon her."

The Old Man sputtered. AJ and Diablo let out choking noises as the entire room once again zeroed in on the unfolding family drama.

Feeling bad for him, Lil opened her mouth. "Maybe this isn't the place, Gran…"

But her gran wasn't having that, either. "Oh, I'll get to you, missy. Nearly getting yourself killed then coming in and acting up with your father. What were you thinking? You might have died. There's not a prize or a piece of land on earth worth your life!"

But instead of shaming her, Gran's words took root and blossomed.

There *was* a prize worth risking her life for, and he was crossing the room to her, Diablo at his side.

"She's right, you know," AJ said, joining them, smiling insufferably in Gran's direction.

Gran snorted. "I see your tricks."

Looping his arm around Lil's shoulders, he said breezily, "From the woman who raised the love of my life, I would expect no less."

Obvious as it was, AJ's move worked. Gran's feathers settled, and Lil and The Old Man each took long breaths, letting them out slow, mirroring each other in ways that were as natural as they'd been unexplained until now.

Gesturing to the older man, AJ said to Gran, "Gran. This is Henry Bowman, founder of CityBoyz riding program and the man who made me all that I am today."

Gran nodded, approval in her gaze. She reached out a hand to Henry, who reached his hand to her. Lil watched it happen, pinned between a thousand feelings she didn't have names for.

When their hands connected, she felt it as a physical thing.

"Thank you," Gran said to Henry, "for one of the greatest gifts of my life."

Sierra, who had joined them, stood beside Diablo, faintly

leaning toward him even as she seemed apart, and let out a long, sweet sigh and said, "That's the most beautiful thing I've ever heard."

Even Lil allowed herself to be moved, giving herself over to the flood of warmth that brought tears to her eyes and finally answered the question she'd carried her whole life: she was wanted, and cherished, and, above all, loved.

All around them, the Closed Circuit cameras rolled. The rodeo might be over, the buckles all handed out, but for the producers, the drama was the real prize, and it was solid gold.

And as if the moment needed more excitement, the old-timer from earlier, the producer with a slick suit and a missing tooth, let out a loud "Yeehaw!" and slapped his thigh, hollering out to the room, "The ratings are in, folks, and we blew them out of the water! The Closed Circuit is coming back for a second season, and it's going to be better than ever!" Another round of cheers followed the news.

Ever the professional, Sierra recaptured control of the room with her bright and well-timed announcement. "All this celebration has got me hungry! What do y'all say we close this out the right way, on the producer's dime?"

Her question was met by a resounding roar of approval, the friends and family gathered in the room and Lil and AJ—Hank was nowhere to be seen—and even the producers caught in the wave of excitement, though the idea hadn't been on the scheduled plan of events and likely wasn't in the budget.

None of that mattered. Pennies would be pinched and more cowboys would come along to take the top prize. AJ would come home with her, and together, they would figure out how to save both the ranch and CityBoyz. But more than that, they'd spend their days together, living, loving, and sometimes, riding off into the sunset.

★ ★ ★ ★ ★

AUTHOR NOTE

Thank you for picking up *The Wildest Ride*. Writing this story was its own wild ride, and I am very proud of it. In particular, I am proud to have brought Lilian Sorrow Island to life. In addition to bearing the names of my forefathers and mothers, Lil is a character who shares my family's little-known ancestry—that of the Creek Freedmen. The Creek, or Muscogee (Mvskoke), Freedmen story is one that, due to the unique interweaving of racism, Native genocide, and the imperative of cultural survival in the United States, has been swept under the rug of history. It is a fascinating and powerful story of allyship and betrayal, one that spans generations, homelands, and the formation of the United States as we know it now. Like many long-lived and ongoing stories, the way it's told changes over time and depending on the teller. *The Wildest Ride* reflects how it was told to me and how my knowledge of it has evolved as I've grown older and sought out more tellers.

My first teacher of this story, however, was the most important: my paternal grandfather. He was born Xenophon Island (last name later changed to Barnes after being legally adopted by his stepfather as a boy) in Muskogee, Oklahoma, in November of 1926. By the time I showed up on this blue planet sixty years later, he had grown old but no less proud of his roots. As an adult, I interviewed him about our heritage and his childhood, and he told me he identified as an "Indian" man first, and second as a Black man. To me, a young woman born and raised in the Pacific Northwest and therefore irrevocably stamped as "Black and nothing else" by my surrounding community despite my rich multicultural ancestry, this statement was world-shaking. I'd known of our Mvskoke Freedmen heritage through the incredibly close relationship I shared with my grandfather, as well as my mother's dedication to the idea that part of a mother's role is to impart culture to her children. To that end, she exposed and connected me with our local Native community (which are notably *not* Mvskoke). I had even begun and abandoned an application for tribal enrollment through the Portland State University Native American Student and Community Center. At that point, I was advised not to apply because my ancestors are listed as "Creek Freedmen" on the Dawes Rolls instead of "Creek by blood," which the enrollment counselor relayed to me after speaking with the Muscogee Nation enrollment office. It was mortifying for both of us to encounter an expression of racism like that in modern times. Still, tribal sovereignty is tantamount. There is nothing closer to the heart of sovereignty than the ability to determine citizenship, so I resolved to accept the news and move forward while continuing to pray for a more inclusive future. I am still praying for that future today.

However, after the fateful conversation with my grandfather, my need to own my heritage took on new strength. I knew we were Mvskoke, but to have my grandfather, a man born before the Civil Rights era in Indian Country, a man who was the quintessence of strength and dignity, share that his own cultural identity was Indian first and Black second was transformative. My grandfather used the word *Indian*, and with his cadence and accent, the word always sounded like something important. In my own speech, I use the words *Native* or *Indigenous*. In the book, however, you will have seen both. In my opinion, due to the history, *Indian* is a word reserved for the use of the elders and established institutions (for example, Indian National Finals Rodeo). Others have different opinions.

Extending the conversation of language further, the word *Creek*, as in Creek Freedmen, is an English moniker for the Muscogee (Mvskoke) Nation. Originally from the southeast, the Muscogee people were called Creek because of towns being located near waterways. Muscogee, or the less English spelling Mvskoke, is the name the people have for themselves. Like *Indian*, the term *Creek* is one I reserve for elders and official organizations. For myself, I prefer the word and spelling Mvskoke. Most of my teachers and elders have used the name *Creek*, but an important message was given to me to use *Mvskoke* rather than *Creek*. As a student of linguistics, I prefer the spelling *Mvskoke* to *Muscogee* because of its visual/auditory transmission. Mvskoke history and heritage are rich and well-documented. I encourage the curious to engage and learn more about the Mvskoke Nation and Indigenous peoples worldwide. There are wonderful resources available online and in print. Native country is alive and thriving, modern, and powerful. At the time of this writing, there are 574 federally recognized sovereign nations in the United States. The number continues to grow as more and more Native peoples reclaim their distinct histories and heritages. If you are inspired, you can become involved in supporting Native activism through campaigns like Land Back (landback.org) and Missing and

Murdered Indigenous Women (MMIW, mmiwusa.org), as well as through organizations such as the National Congress of American Indians (NCAI) and movements that oppose the use of Native peoples and iconography as mascots and aesthetics. Additionally, research and support the Freedmen. In 2017, following legal action, the Cherokee Nation granted citizenship rights to their Freedmen. The Mvskoke Freedmen continue to fight for recognition within our Nation. Never stop learning and never stop reclaiming. Mvto (Thank you).

ACKNOWLEDGMENTS

The much-beloved Fred Rogers encouraged people to take time to think of and thank the special people who have "loved us into being." Given my unique heritage and the lineages I study and practice, I have a particularly strong love for this idea. When I had the honor of writing my very own acknowledgments page, I knew this was the model I wanted to follow. This story, and all of my work as an author, would not be possible were it not for the people who loved me into being. I am guarded and insecure and struggle with a massive inferiority complex. It took A LOT of love to develop the courage and bravery to be myself and go after my dreams, including creating this book. So, chronologically (because the concept of time is a useful boundary and guideline!), here are the people who have loved me into being and, therefore, without whom this project would not have existed: my mother, whose survival and tenacity, and more importantly, whose faith and hope gave me life and the ability to take a hit and always get back up. My father, whose unshakeability, intelligence, and constant, quiet, and steady love, let me know the ground was strong enough to leap off from. My grandpa, my lodestar, the man who was not just in my corner, but fiercely guarded and held that corner long before I even knew what it was. My grandma Sharon, my Rosetta stone for white culture and musical theater, and the one who gave me a pair of rose-colored contact lenses, permanently affixing and affirming my optimistic view of life. My grandpa John, our family Buddha, who loved and understood his eldest granddaughter's discomfort with her appearance and deep love of the written word and made room for both, as well as dragons. My auntie Carol, my Tía Tía, whose kitchen was always full of my favorite kinds of foods, whose freedom and love were boundless, and whose witchy magic planted the seeds of becoming the spirulina and tea- and bee-pollen-loving yogi I am today. Kaleen, my soul sister, in the form of a cousin, my partner in crime till the end of time, my best friend since before we were born. There's more to say, and she knows it all. My cousin Jarid, for seeing beauty and strength in me long before I ever did. My fourth-grade teacher, Mrs. Moellenar, who went the extra mile for a hybrid-latchkey kid. My first stepmom, Sandy, who gave me most of my brothers and taught me what elbow grease was. My brothers, Nicholas, Conar, Tyrone, and Steven, who forced me to grapple with siblings and to discover how genuine that bond is. My second stepmom, April, who finally got it through to me that Black is beautiful and taught me how to take care of it. My great aunt Barbara, who took us to New York and loves theater and travel as much as I do, and who introduced me to my WASPy heritage. Alec Wilson, my first boyfriend, whose sweet goodness showed me it was worth it to take a shot on this whole romance idea. My University of Southern California friends, Brynn, Selkie, and

Kim, who helped me leap into the great big pond of the world. My first yoga instructor, Paul, who planted and sprouted the seed of yoga in me and taught me to practice yoga instead of ego. Sarah and Dan and Sarah, who will forever number among the small list of people I go to in hard times. Ethan Lau, whose love and example led me to be comfortable in my body. My dear friend Zoe French, whose care and nourishment are unparalleled in this chaotic world. Philly Boyle, my cousin/brother-in-law, whose presence has seasoned life and shown me what it means to grow your definition of family. My Barnes & Noble family—Trisha, Dennis, Misty, Robyn, Andrea, Aaron, Anne, Erika, Vanessa, Liam, Ed, Rebecca, Addie, and Joshua—the period when our lives were intertwined, the ways we loved each other, and the lessons I learned are stamped on my soul for all of time. Each of you helped me become a grownup. My husband, Josh, I've said it once, and I'll say it again, you are the seed of everything wonderful in my life. My mother-in-law, Sally, who welcomed me and mothered me despite my resistance, and I am still unpacking the treasure of lessons and love you gave me. My Gold, et al. family—Randy, Rebecca, Dan, Patty, Sarah, James, Louis, Rosalie, Sam, Ariella, Becca, Graham, Jeremy, Dilek, Grafton, Argyle, Paisley, Jon, Jen, Bill, James, and Allison—you all showed me a new model and mode of family. My heart has grown way more than three sizes because of it. My children, Emerson Rose and Xenophon Gold—nothing, and I mean NOTHING, inspires and teaches and rebirths me the way you do. The Ropps, who gave me the kick in the ass I needed to have a little pride in myself and remember that I know how to make new friends. Eileen M. K. Bobek, I bulldozed into your life and dreams, and you changed and reshaped mine. Everything I do is stitched with your color (and it's black). Megan Crane and Maisey Yates, look what you made me do.

I will never be the same—there's probably a Taylor Swift lyric that captures it better ★_^. Krista Holland, my sweet teacher, I won't call you what you are because of circles and honey-bees and Old Mother Dark, but we both know it's the truth. My yoga sisters and drum women spread around the world. Our lights connect like the knots of Indra's net. Flo Nicoll, for meeting with me at the very last minute after recognizing my work and lighting a spark of hope after a long journey in the dark. Nic Caws, for seeing my potential in a sea of bad grammar and my endless attempts to bury the emotion with jokes and outrageousness—the patience and fortitude are as deep as the musical theater knowledge in this one. Helen Breitwieser, who is exactly the professional champion I needed and who inspires me in every interaction to become a little stronger, a little more direct and honest, and, ultimately, a lot more comfortable stepping into my power. Mvto to all of these people, living and not, who have loved me into being. It took so much work to get here, and even though there are "miles to go before I sleep," I know that, because of you all, I will get there. And I won't go alone.